A

Death

Interrupted

A Novel

by

Eli P. Bernzweig

Llumina Press

Requests for permission to make copies of any part of this work should be mailed to Permissions Department, Llumina Press, PO Box 772246, Coral Springs, FL 33077-2246

ISBN: 1-59526-163-X

Printed in the United States of America by Llumina Press

Library of Congress Cataloging-in-Publication Data

Bernzweig, Eli P.
  A death interrupted : a novel / by Eli P. Bernzweig.
    p. cm.
  ISBN 1-59526-163-X (pbk. : alk. paper)
  1. Death--Fiction. 2. Widowers--Fiction. 3. Spiritualism--Fiction. 4. Washington (D.C.)--Fiction. I. Title.
PS3602.E7636D43 2005
813'.6--dc22   2004030772

To Lorraine

Acknowledgments

I am indebted to Sandra E. Haven, my editor at Bristol Services International, for her inspiration, her excellent advice and her profound analytical abilities in critiquing the entire manuscript. Thanks also to Barbara Egbert, editorial writer at the *San Jose Mercury News* for her invaluable advice about newspaper organization and editorial writing procedures.

Thanks are due the following, whose library research assistance or inputs regarding various aspects of this work helped me to fashion the final product: Richard Andresen; Joanne Dalton; Carlotta Green; and Kimberly Hirsch.

I owe special thanks to my wife, Lorraine, who reviewed and commented on the entire manuscript. I am also thankful to my daughters, Sara and Linda, who supplied love, support and encouragement throughout the entire writing process. Finally, I am indebted to all in the Theosophical Movement, from Helena P. Blavatsky and William Q. Judge down to the present, whose writings have inspired this fictional view of the postmortem world.

Chapter 1

I noticed the "New Message" icon blinking on my computer, but it was nearly six p.m. on Saturday evening, the place was practically deserted, and I was just about to leave my desk at the *Washington Tribune* and head for home. Who would be sending me an e-mail at this hour? At first I considered leaving it for Monday morning, but then, there was nothing pressing at home—only the cold loneliness of my apartment where lately I ate in the semidarkness, very much alone since my beloved Senta's death. The only thing these last three months that kept me from becoming even more despondent was to drown myself in my work, including working nights and weekends. You can bet that if Senta were still alive, I wouldn't be spending this Saturday evening re-working a routine editorial on prescription drug costs for Tuesday's paper.

I half-heartedly clicked "Open," fully expecting some more administrative dictums about ordering supplies or keeping better records on expenses—the sort of junk we had been receiving from management all week long. But when I saw that the sender of the e-mail was "Your Herzele," and the subject was "Happy 62nd Birthday," a shock went through my body like a jolt of electricity. My already-weakened heart started pounding like it was in atrial fibrillation—a not-uncommon experience for me—and I began feeling lightheaded and dizzy, which nearly caused me to black out. I grabbed the edge of the desk for support and eased myself slowly into my chair.

What's going on? No one at the paper knew that November 17th, 2001, was my sixty-second birthday, and there was only one person in the whole world whom I referred to as *herzele*— a German term of endearment ('little heart') we called each other—and that was Senta Trondson, the woman I had loved with all my heart and soul the past thirty-three years. But Senta died three months ago at the age of seventy, and just thinking about those last pathetic days—her gaunt body weakening by the moment, her wan smile bravely trying to mask the pain of her stomach cancer—was enough to revive the anguish of her death for me all over again. The biggest hurt of all was not being able to really get through to her because of the morphine fog that clouded her mind. And then there were the sorrowful funeral arrangements I had to make, including her cremation and the interment of her ashes at Oak Hill Cemetery, which revived still more unhappy memories.

I again stared at the screen, trying to make sense of what I was supposedly looking at: an e-mail from Senta, someone who neither owned nor knew how to use a computer. The whole thing fell into the category of the ridiculous, but it sent a cold shiver through me, nevertheless. Had I become so stressed out as a result of her death that my mind was playing tricks on me? Or, was this someone's idea of a sick practical joke? The thought made me bristle as I considered that sadistic possibility.

I don't know exactly what I expected to see, but I rose slowly to look over the half-partition separating my writing cubbyhole from the main newsroom. All I could see were a couple of young reporters down at the far end of the room, apparently arguing over the Redskins' latest in a string of losses, each trying to override the other's shouting as money changed hands. They didn't even glance my way.

I clicked the mouse to open the message and as I began reading the words on the screen, it was as though I had entered a time warp. My eyes were telling me one thing, but my brain was telling me it just wasn't possible. The net result was a mixture of wonderment, confusion and utter disbelief. The message read:

> "Darling, first, let me wish you a happy 62nd birthday. You see, I didn't forget. And let me assure you this is not a joke. It really is me, and I am here *in kama loka,* just where you would expect me to be this soon after my death, but I know it's going to be hard to believe, so let me explain.
>
> "Not long after I left my physical body and regained consciousness, I was contacted by Damodar, yes, Damodar himself, in his astral body of course, and he told me why he had come. He said that the Masters were aware not only of my lifelong devotion to the study of Theosophy but also that, at the time of my death, I had been helping you with research on your planned book about the after-death states, and those coincidental circumstances interested them greatly. And it is with this in mind that Damodar came to me here in *kama loka* and it is he who has made it possible for me to contact you by means of this e-mail process that everyone makes such a fuss about.

A Death Interrupted

"The Masters believe that my physical death and your interest in writing a work about the afterlife present a unique opportunity, one they haven't had since the late 1800s when they helped Helena Blavatsky write *The Secret Doctrine*. So, here is what Damodar has proposed, *herzele*: If you are willing to tell the world that you are in touch with me . . ."

I was suddenly startled by the sound of approaching footsteps and, before even turning around to see who was there, I quickly exited the message and closed the e-mail site, fearing being caught by prying eyes. I started shuffling papers around to make it appear as though I were working on a routine editorial assignment. But the frightened look on my face and my nervous movements apparently gave me away, because as I looked up to see who was there, I heard Ray Tuohy say, in a mock pretense of concern, "Gosh, David, I didn't mean to frighten you. Are you all right? I mean, is there anything I can do to help?"

Ray was the paper's Religion & Family Section editor and the last person in the world I would turn to for help. The small, slightly-built man in his late fifties with prematurely-receded blond hair and narrow, colorless lips was a former seminarian with a Master of Divinity degree who had abandoned the clergy to pursue a career in journalism ten years ago. I never really liked the man because he always struck me as an obsequious ass-kisser with an unctuous way about him. I never understood why the editor in chief hired him in the first place, but apparently it was done on the say-so of the *Tribune*'s owner, Adrienne Thayer, based on a personal recommendation by a friend who praised Ray's virtues.

I not only doubted his virtues, but his intellect and his ability to write. A year ago, he wrote a review that savaged my first book, *Psychic Witness*, a novel with some theosophical content about a twelve-year-old psychic who was instrumental in solving a Northern Virginia double homicide. His review, written in a rambling and pretentious manner, ridiculed me as well as Theosophy, and I was still smarting from that.

We never socialized and rarely had any professional contact, just the occasional memo or phone conversation on some pending article, so his offer of help as though he were a friend—or even a concerned ex-clergyman—was as out-of-character and phony as he was. For a moment, I even considered the possibility it might be Ray who pulled off this e-mail stunt, but then I realized that he knew little or nothing about my personal life, least of all that today was my birthday. I did my best to act as if nothing had happened.

"No, Ray, thanks. I'm all right;" I said, matter-of-factly. "Just thought the place was deserted and you startled me. What brings you around at this hour?"

"Came to pick up my briefcase. Forgot it when I left work yesterday. Now you're sure everything's okay?"

His condescending tone of voice and pretense at being concerned really irked me. On the other hand, I had to take into consideration that he, along with others at the paper, knew that I was deeply disturbed by Senta's passing. I had shown definite signs of depression and lately I seemed to be unusually distracted, taking hours to do what normally took me far less time. I again reassured him that everything was fine and said I was closing up shop and going home in a few minutes. He raised his eyebrows and shrugged his shoulders in a 'suit yourself' gesture, then gave me a perfunctory 'goodnight' before turning towards the elevators.

Ray's unexpected appearance and annoying questioning made me all the more nervous. *Was it that obvious I was acting strangely?* Despite my curiosity about the e-mail, I didn't want to chance hanging around the office any longer, so I turned off my computer and left, stopping briefly at the men's room to freshen up. While splashing cold water on my face, I paused momentarily to take stock of the face in the mirror. I saw a depressed editorial writer, hair graying and thinning, who had lost the love of his life barely three months ago, with the wound to his heart still too fresh not to show. I saw a man who had a reputation for being a superior writer by his colleagues, with a passion for fairness and accuracy in the twenty-eight years he had worked at the *Tribune*. And finally, I saw a man who, even though a serious student of the subject, had kept his theosophical beliefs a private matter between himself and the woman he loved, only rarely discussing the subject with anyone else.

I splashed some more water on my face as I wondered, *Is all this really happening, or is it a hallucination? Is it possible I'm having a nervous breakdown?* With my head still reeling from the strange e-mail I had just received, but not completely read, I left the building and started walking toward the parking garage on the other side of 15th Street. My intention was to drive back to my apartment on Kalorama Road and pick up a pizza on the way home. Though I was anxious to read the rest of the strange e-mail, I knew I could read it on my computer at home. Right now, I needed time to get a better grip on myself.

As the sharp, cold November air hit my face, I suddenly felt appetite pangs that told me my body wanted something more substantial than pizza. I quickly justified my change of heart. It *is* my birthday, after all, so why not eat out? I turned from the parking garage and walked the block and a half to *The Newsroom*, the small, American-style restaurant just around the corner on K Street that many *Tribune* reporters frequented, where the food was good but inexpensive.

As I entered the restaurant, my head was dizzy with all my conflicting thoughts and emotions. My primary concern was the authenticity of the message, at least the part I had read so far. But, just supposing it *was* authentic, how would I, an editorial writer approaching retirement age on one of the nation's top newspapers explain that I received an e-mail from a woman who is no longer alive? And how would all this affect my job, to say nothing of my personal privacy? As I weighed these questions, a perky blonde hostess with menus in her hand greeted me and began directing me to a table near the far end of the restaurant. That's when I spotted Miriam Green sitting by herself at a table near the window, her head buried in some reading material. I was pleasantly surprised and immediately veered over in her direction, with the hostess following me to the table.

Miriam was the Travel Section editor of the *Tribune*, an attractive, stylish brunette in her late fifties whose facial features, mannerisms and sultry voice often reminded me of film actress Suzanne Pleshette. As a divorcée with a reputation of being outspoken, witty and sharp, Miriam was the only person at the paper I had ever talked with openly about my personal connection with Senta, and only then because she pointedly drew me out on the subject.

When we first met, shortly after she came on board eight years ago, she undoubtedly saw me as possible husband material, which was flattering coming from someone as attractive as Miriam, and under other circumstances might have led to something serious. But once I explained the exclusive nature of my long-term commitment to Senta, she respected my feelings and never overstepped the bounds of social propriety. We've remained friends ever since.

The fact that she was eating dinner alone this Saturday evening presented an opportunity I hadn't counted on. Miriam looked up as she saw me approaching, greeted me with a genuinely surprised look and a welcoming smile and, with a dramatic wave of her hand, pointed to the chair opposite her. So, I was going to have company on my birthday after all. I felt better already.

"Hi, Miriam. What brings you here at this hour? Were you working, or did you just happen to be in the downtown area?"

"I just finished an article on the sights, sounds and tastes of the beautiful California wine country for next Saturday's paper, and it was getting too late to rustle up dinner at home. Have you been at the office, too?"

"Yeah, just left. Say, how about having a drink with me? It's my sixty-second birthday and (shaking my head) . . . boy, I sure miss Senta, especially at times like this."

The obvious change in tone of my voice made it only too plain how I was feeling. "Oh, David," she purred sympathetically, "I'm so sorry about Senta. I know how much she meant to you. Of course I'll join you in a drink. No one should be alone on their birthday." As she spoke, she fluttered her expressive brown eyes.

As I raised my hand to summon the waiter, I was trying to decide how much of what I had just been through I should tell Miriam. She was pleasant and certainly intelligent but I had no way of knowing how she'd react to the unusual event that just happened to me at the office. Would she think I'd gone off the deep end? Apart from some vague theosophical references in *Psychic Witness*, she knew nothing about my serious interest in or ties to Theosophy, or Senta's either, for that matter.

Then, too, although nothing was said openly on the subject, I sensed she might be hoping to fill the empty place in my life left by Senta's death, and I didn't need any more complications in my life at the moment, so I paused to consider whether to say anything about the e-mail. Miriam obviously noticed my hesitation to continue talking because she asked in a concerned voice, "Is something wrong, David? You look a little distracted, I mean . . . not like your usual self."

Oh, what the hell! Keeping it all bottled up in me was beginning to drive me batty. I decided I'd tell her what little I knew. "Nothing wrong, exactly, Miriam, but something did happen that I'd like to discuss with you. But, why don't we wait 'til we've had our drink? I'll get us a bottle of wine—in fact, we'll make it a California wine. That way you can add some authentic California flavor to your article."

She liked that little twist and so, after checking the wine list, I had the waiter bring a bottle of a twelve-year-old Mondavi Napa Cabernet and we clinked our glasses as she wished me a happy birthday, giving me another big, heartwarming smile. Her large brown eyes seemed to smile, also. After placing my dinner order, I edged a bit closer to the table and began my review of what had just happened at the office.

"First, let me say, Miriam, that what I'm about to tell you will be a little difficult to believe at first, but you know I'm a pretty serious person and not one to make up stories, so please try to keep an open mind. Hear me out and then I want to get your reaction to this whole thing. Will you do that for me?"

Her eyes widened as she again whispered softly, "Of course, David. Goodness, this certainly sounds mysterious." I loved the sound of her voice.

"I'll get right to the point. Just as I was preparing to leave the office, I saw I had an incoming e-mail, and when I opened it, I got the shock of my life. There on the screen was a message, or at least a purported message, from Senta, which she said was being sent to me through the technical mastery of an initiated Master of Wisdom, a Hindu sage known as Damodar." I took a deep breath, opting to skip explaining more about Damodar at the moment. Miriam would have enough to handle just hearing about the e-mail. I continued, "Senta said that Damodar made it possible for her thoughts to appear as words in e-mail messages on my computer screen."

Miriam always was a good listener, and as I paused to see how she was reacting thus far to the strange happening I had described, I saw her raise her eyebrows once or twice, but there were no overt signs of rejecting what I had said so far. She appeared to remain quietly noncommittal.

"Now, obviously," I continued, "Senta is dead, and she explained in the e-mail—at least the part I read so far—that she was given this privilege to communicate with me for a specific reason. She said the Masters— they're called Masters of Wisdom or Mahatmas by theosophists—were aware that she has been a devoted student of Theosophy. I'd known Senta was a theosophist for more than thirty years, and she'd been assisting me in gathering materials for my next book. That was to explain the theosophical view of what happens to us after the death of our physical bodies. Are you with me so far?"

Miriam's eyes blinked a few times, and I could see a frown forming on her brow, but otherwise she was attentive and seemed quite absorbed in what I was saying. "You bet," she said. "Keep going."

I continued. "In other words, Senta's spiritual life and her interest in helping me write my next book on certain theosophical doctrines gave them an incentive to do something they've never done before. Specifically, they want to make it possible for a human being who has died and entered the first state of consciousness after death—meaning Senta—to communicate directly with a living person—meaning me—in order to better explain what follows the death of the physical body. In effect, they've arranged for Senta's death process to be interrupted before her Soul moves on to higher realms, both as a demonstration and in order to better explain the theosophical teachings about the afterlife."

Hearing that, Miriam couldn't contain herself any longer and started shaking her head vigorously from side to side. "I hear what you're saying, David, but are you absolutely sure it was her? I mean, couldn't it be that this is just a computer hoax cooked up by someone, perhaps someone at the office who knew about you and Senta?"

I smiled appreciatively at my quick-witted dinner partner. "Well, that's the problem, Miriam. Except for you, no one else at the office really knew anything about my relationship with Senta. And why would anyone want to perpetrate such a sick hoax in the first place?" I, of course, never mentioned to her that it had already crossed my mind that someone like Ray Tuohy might stoop to such a trick, but that I had abandoned the thought for the very reason I had just given: he knew nothing about our relationship.

Miriam's brow wrinkled again, as she answered, "It's not that I don't believe what you're telling me, David, but you know that we live in a crazy computer age. Perhaps some weirdo who had it in for you because of something you wrote in your first book decided to get even through this e-mail stunt."

"I doubt it," I said, "but I didn't even finish reading it, so I can't be a hundred percent sure."

"Why didn't you finish reading it?" she asked, genuinely surprised.

I was ashamed to tell her about Ray's unexpected appearance at my desk and our awkward conversation, so I came up with a phony answer. "Well, I wasn't sure this whole thing might be a concoction of my imagination . . . you know, perhaps because of my lack of sleep and depressed state of mind since Senta's death. So, I decided to postpone looking at it for the moment."

I'm not sure that she bought it, but she countered immediately, "Well, then, if I were you, when I got home I'd go to the computer and take another look at it, and you know what? I'd ask this e-mail person some specific questions that only Senta would have the answers to. That way you'll know once and for all whether this thing is someone's idea of a practical joke, a sadistic hoax, or whatever."

I don't know why I hadn't thought of that myself, and it was a little embarrassing that such a logical suggestion had to come from Miriam. Still, it gave me the first ray of hope and suddenly I felt as if a weight had been lifted from my shoulders. At last I could see a possible way out of the dilemma I was facing. "That's a great idea, Miriam," I responded enthusiastically. "That's exactly what I'll do as soon as I get home." I gave her a big smile and said, "Now, let's enjoy our food and wine."

We spent the rest of the meal in pleasant, innocuous conversation, during which Miriam's solicitude for my well-being, especially her concern for my rundown physical condition and lack of sleep, came across as both genuine and touching.

We finished our respective entrées, and while we were having our desserts, Miriam asked me a question I hadn't been expecting. In a soft, serious voice, she said, "Forgive me for asking, David, but why didn't you and Senta ever get married? I know she was a widow and you've never been married—so far as I know—so how come the two of you never tied the knot?"

I smiled broadly at her question, which was not all that surprising, coming from someone like Miriam, who always showed more than a passing interest in my marital status. And since I had just burdened her with my problem, I felt it only fair to respond to her question. "Well, there are several reasons, Miriam. First, Senta's marriage wasn't an altogether happy one. Her husband, Jon, was a scholarly and industrious man, but cold and emotionless in many important ways, important to Senta, that is. In the nine years they were together before his death, he rarely gave her a birthday or anniversary card on any of those days, or a bouquet of flowers, a present at Christmas, or any other symbol of love, even though he professed to love her. To put it mildly, Miriam, he was a cold fish, and that included his behavior in the bedroom. So, marriage per se wasn't such a desirable commodity from Senta's point of view at that point in her life."

"Then, too, Jon's death came at a time when the women's liberation movement was just getting underway, and Senta began to reevaluate her

9

role as an individual, rather than merely as someone else's spouse. She was fiercely independent, you know; something that she got from her orphanage upbringing. Getting a job was one way of expressing that sense of independence, while she saw marriage to me—or anyone else, for that matter—as an interference with that newfound independence, and something that would complicate her life just when she was trying to uncomplicate it. Going to work at H.E.W. gave her a chance to meet people and spread her wings, while earning enough money to make ends meet."

Miriam nodded as she dipped into her ice cream, and was all ears as I continued, "Of course, there was also the eight years' age difference between us, something I made light of, but Senta felt quite strongly about. She pointed out that men and women age differently, and that a woman loses her looks a lot sooner than a man does. Senta frankly admitted she was vain about her appearance, so even though she was a stunning beauty when we met, I understood what she was trying to tell me."

"Well, I guess you answered *that* question," Miriam said, smiling broadly. She finished her dessert and I did likewise, then I had the waiter put everything on one bill. "Birthdays are special occasions," I announced, cheerfully, "and you've been a wonderful listener to my bizarre tale, so the check's on me." She fought me briefly, then relented, and we left the restaurant together.

I walked her to the parking garage and just before we parted, I promised to give her an update on the results of my challenge to the sender of the strange e-mail. "Oh, please do, David," she implored. "I'm intrigued by this whole thing. Please call me tomorrow."

A little while later, as I was driving my silver Lexus north on Connecticut Avenue, I reflected on several coincidences involving November 17th. This date not only was *my* birthday, but also the formal "birth" day of the Theosophical Movement in 1875. In addition, I remember Senta telling me that November 17th was one of the three "birth" days of the Dhyân Chohans, the hosts of intelligent powers and forces that theosophists say watch over the spiritual progress of mankind, and I wondered if all those natal-day circumstances were purely coincidental.

Well, whatever the connection might be, today was certainly a fateful one for me. As I pondered the type of questions I would ask my e-mail correspondent, the thought suddenly crossed my mind that I might have deleted the entire e-mail in my haste to keep it from the prying eyes of Ray Tuohy. I became panicky. Beads of perspiration started forming on my forehead and my heart again began its thunderous pounding. With my adrenaline pumping wildly, I stepped on the gas pedal to get home faster and barely missed hitting a cat scampering across Kalorama Road just as I pulled into the parking space behind my apartment building.

Once inside, I turned on the lights and charged into my study to turn on the computer and bring up my e-mail site. I heaved a sigh of relief when I could see that I hadn't deleted the e-mail after all, and, after catching my breath, continued reading where I had left off.

> "So, here is what Damodar has proposed, *herzele*. If you are willing to announce to the world that you are in touch with me, an honest-to-goodness disembodied being here in *kama loka*, and are prepared to put up with the skepticism, abuse and vilification which that is likely to provoke, Damodar will provide materials you can use in your new book to explain what *really* happens after we die, and he'll do it through this e-mail method of communication . . ."

As I got to this part, I couldn't help thinking about how I had lost nearly all interest in writing about theosophical subjects after Senta died. She had been my inspiration and number one cheerleader over the years. Although she tried to make Theosophy a part of her life, she would tell me that she didn't have the know-how of a trained teacher and was able to impart that valuable spiritual information to relatively few persons. "You, on the other hand," she would say, "not only have studied the literature but have the skills of a writer, and can explain the philosophy to a far wider audience."

After the poor reception of *Psychic Witness*, however, I wasn't sure I wanted to try again. On the other hand, I'd do anything to be able to communicate with my beloved Senta again—if it really *was* Senta. I continued reading, trying to contain my nervous excitement as my brain attempted to absorb what I was reading:

> "The Masters decided to utilize this unique method of attracting the attention of Westerners because so many of them already own computers and understand the e-mail process. And while all this is going on, you and I will be able to communicate with each other as often as we like, which I think is wonderful as well as amazing."

"You know, of course, that I never owned a computer and know nothing about how computers work. Damodar explained that all I had to do was to mentally concentrate and project the thoughts I want to transmit to you, as I am doing now, and he would receive my thoughts telepathically and reconstitute them in the proper electronic form to appear as words in e-mails on your computer. Since thoughts can be sent and received instantaneously, the process is done with lightning speed. My telepathic communication with Damodar over the past eight years while I was in my body has created a strong magnetic thread between us, making the communication process quite easy."

Now, here was something that no one except Senta and I knew about. It was our secret that for the past eight years she had been receiving theosophical information directly from Damodar by means of thought transference during her morning meditation periods at home. I continued reading:

"Damodar explained that you, and only you, David, can communicate with the two of us by e-mails sent to the address shown on this e-mail, and when you do so, he will receive the mental images of your words in the astral and will transmit them to me telepathically or respond to your inquiries directly, as the case may be. Pretty clever, don't you think?"

Assuming the e-mail was in fact from my beloved Senta, I had to admit that everything she said so far was true or at least made sense to me. Today *is* my sixty-second birthday, I *am* (or at least *was*) planning to write a book describing the postmortem states of consciousness, and Senta indeed should be in *kama loka*, according to the theosophical teachings. And, of course, we both knew that Damodar was the young Hindu who became the devoted pupil and disciple of Helena P. Blavatsky—or simply H.P.B., as she is known to theosophists—in the late 1800s and subsequently was summoned by the Masters to study further with them in Tibet.

Acting upon Miriam's suggestion, I decided it was time to put the matter to rest once and for all. I quickly came up with a series of personal questions that only the real Senta could answer. I replied to the incoming message:

"I know this doesn't seem quite fair, but just so I can verify that you really are Senta Trondson, would you please answer the following personal questions:

1. When and where did we first meet?
2. Who was your closest girlfriend as an adult, in what activity did she excel, and what medical condition did she have?
3. What was the name of the teacher at the orphanage who gave you a special present for Christmas, and what was that present?
4. In what year and where did you give a private dance performance for an important personage in the field of modern dance; who was that person; and what was the name of the musical composition that you danced to?
5. What was the name of the person who introduced you to Theosophy?

"If you can answer these questions, I most assuredly will know you are the woman I have loved so deeply all these years. And, if that is the case, I will look forward to working with you, and of course with Damodar, to make my forthcoming book the best possible product. I eagerly await your reply."

Since those questions could only be answered by Senta Trondson, I would know soon enough if someone was playing games with me. To relieve my nervousness while waiting for the answers—if, indeed, there were going to be answers—I walked quickly to the bathroom. My stomach was in knots and my heart was still thumping away furiously in my chest as I tried to comprehend the enormity of what was happening and all the ramifications of actually communicating by e-mail with my dead love. When I returned to the study a few minutes later, I could see that a new message had already been received. I took a couple of deep breaths to calm myself, sat down and opened it.

"My darling David, here are the answers to your five questions: (1) We met in the cafeteria of the Department of Health, Education & Welfare, where the Department was holding its Christmas party on December 18, 1968. (2) Isabelle McKeown was my closest and dearest friend.

She loved writing poetry, and she had agoraphobia. (3) The special Christmas present given to me was a pair of ice skates and the teacher at the orphanage who gave them to me was Pastor Von Bussey. (4) I danced for Louis Horst at my home studio in 1958, and the musical composition I danced to was *Uirapuru*, by Heitor Villa-Lobos, and (5) Margaret James was the person who introduced me to Theosophy.

"Now that you see I really am the person I claim to be, doesn't the prospect of our communicating in this manner make you ecstatic, darling? I'm sure it does. Damodar says that you can ask either or both of us any questions you like and we will do our best to answer them. He intends to send you his materials at least once a week, all by e-mail. At the same time, dearest, you and I will be able to communicate with each other as often as we like throughout this process, and I can answer any personal questions you may have. Of course, while all this is taking place my own passage through *kama loka* and the normal processes associated with my transit through the afterlife temporarily will be halted.

"The Masters have never done this sort of thing before; on the other hand, they never had the perfect opportunity to do so until now. But, as Damodar has explained to me, the very novelty of our being able to communicate with each other by e-mail will undoubtedly attract widespread public attention to the important spiritual information that can be conveyed in this manner.

"When the task is completed, these e-mail messages between us will come to an end. I have no idea when that will be, but after that our only contact will be when your earth life ends and you come this way yourself.

"That's it, *herzele*. I know all this will be mind-boggling at first, so I want to give you some time to digest everything I have said. Since you've kept your interest in Theosophy pretty much a secret up to now, neither Damodar nor I believe that it will be easy for you to convince others that these e-mail messages really have come from someone who has cast off her physical body and entered the world beyond. Nor will it be easy to show that they have been made possible by a living Adept who has acquired powers that transcend the normal frontiers of spiritual and scientific knowledge, but that is our hope.

"I will end this message by sending you my eternal love and reminding you as always, Satyât Nâsti Paro Dharmah."

The speed and complete accuracy of the responses electrified me, and I now knew that something truly momentous was occurring. My beloved Senta was really communicating with me from beyond the grave! I recognized the final four Sanskrit words, meaning, "There is no religion higher than truth," as the motto of the Theosophical Society. No one but a dedicated theosophist would be familiar with those words. What was happening was beyond belief. The thought that I would be in direct personal contact with my recently deceased Senta made my spirits soar. I ran into the kitchen, grabbed a can of Coke from the fridge and, as I tried opening it, my hands were shaking, but this time I knew the shaking was because of nervous excitement. I laughed out loud and pumped my fist in the air a couple of times, shouting "Yes" in a jubilant voice.

I replied to the e-mail immediately.

"Dearest *herzele*. Yes, I now know it really is you, and I am overwhelmed by the fact that we are able to communicate in this manner. I fully understand the nature of the process you outlined, so I will separate my questions or comments to you from those intended for Damodar. That will make your respective responses easier to comprehend and to deal with. I assume from what you have said that Damodar has no objection to my telling others not only what is happening, but also who he is. Am I right?"

The response came from Damodar himself almost immediately.

"Mr. Elliott, the whole point of using this rather odd method of communicating with you is to draw the attention of your technology-obsessed world to some very important spiritual concepts that can lead to better lives and a better world for all humanity. I could have chosen to precipitate information to you in written form, as was done with Madame Blavatsky, but my brother Adepts, as well as our revered leader, the Mahâ Chohan, believe this method will prove more impressive and believable in the present era.

"In short, we *expect* you to tell others how, and from what source, you are receiving the information being communicated. Rest assured, in so doing you will be tested severely in the crucible of public opinion and so-called scientific inquiry. We hope you will be up to the challenge."

So, there was my answer, and at lightning speed. No one could type those words as quickly as Damodar's reply had appeared, and as I reflected on the response, it dawned on me that I had just received an e-mail message from an initiated Master of Wisdom. I knew that Damodar had been Senta's theosophical guru, but I had had no prior contact with him. Now, he would be someone from whom I would be obtaining authoritative firsthand information about the Eastern occult philosophy.

Even though I knew my life would change dramatically from this point on, the prospect of communicating with my beloved Senta, as well as with Damodar, was truly exciting. I finished the e-mail correspondence with a short acknowledgment of Damodar's answer and said I'd be in touch with them soon, most likely within the next twenty-four hours.

The overwhelming mood of sadness that had dogged me throughout the day—in fact, for the last three months—had now changed to a feeling of utter joy and happiness. My heartbeat returned to normal and my hands stopped shaking. After staring at some local news on television (and absorbing none of it), I turned the set off and sat in silence for several minutes, contemplating what I would do next, but by ten I felt a sudden wave of tiredness overcome me and decided I'd better try to get some sleep.

As I buried myself under the heavy comforter, my mind returned to my chance meeting of Miriam at the restaurant, and the odd realization that she was the only woman I had socialized with in any manner—apart from Senta—in many years. The thought produced strangely mixed feelings of pleasure and guilt. Dining and speaking with the attractive, sultry-voiced Miriam had stirred emotions in me I was almost ashamed to admit; especially at the very moment that Senta had reentered my life again so unexpectedly. But I was too tired to analyze the reason for those strange, ambivalent feelings and determined to get some sleep.

Chapter 2

S enta marveled at the ease of the transition from life to death. One minute she felt her life slipping away; the next, she found herself in the strangely silent world of *kama loka*. She had no idea how much time had elapsed since she died—she recalled that she was nearing the end in August—but she was certain she was in *kama loka*. That was obvious because she no longer felt the searing pain in her stomach or weakness in her limbs because she had no physical body. And she no longer felt sad or depressed as she frequently had in the final stages of her illness.

Instead, she felt a sense of calmness and peace, a feeling that all earthly problems had been transcended. She realized that she could move about mentally, like floating from cloud to cloud, and while doing so she could see around her only the vague, etherealized faces of other inhabitants of this realm, like luminous globes of light. Besides, all her theosophical training told her to *expect* the first stage after dying to be the temporary postmortem locale of *kama loka*, which she knew from that training to be a different state of consciousness than that of earth life.

The one thought that kept running through her head was her undying love for David and her concern for his welfare now that she was no longer alive. She wondered, *Who will take care of him, now*? She recalled that he had been holding her hand for those last few hours, and she had desperately wanted to speak to him but couldn't because of the numbing effect of the morphine. She wished she could talk to him about that. God, how she loved and missed him!

One of the nice things about *kama loka*, as Senta soon learned, was that it is a state of consciousness comprised entirely of thought forms. Merely by thinking about them she could go back to some of her favorite moments in life and relive them. Likewise, by simply concentrating, she found she could transport herself at will to various places where she and David had gone together, like Bermuda, Hilton Head, Annapolis and Rehoboth, and in each instance the scene was as vivid as in real life and evoked memories of the occasion that were exceedingly pleasant.

And because she was a lifelong devotee of impressionism in orchestral and piano music, she found it easy to surround herself with the familiar sounds of Chopin, Ravel, Debussy, Satie, and other impressionistic composers simply by thinking of their works. She found this ability a pure delight, and very soothing and comforting. And she joyfully discovered it worked with colors, perfumes and flowers as well.

Senta wondered about other dead persons in *kama loka*. Would their thought forms be visible to her, too, or possibly even interfere with hers? So far, nothing like that had happened, but she was vaguely aware that other thought form activity was occurring around her because she could sense the comings and goings of others in the astral. In time she came to realize that the types of lives people lived on earth had a great deal to do with the particular *kama lokic* atmosphere and surroundings in which they found themselves. As an essentially serious, spiritually inclined aesthete, Senta found her surroundings to be extremely compatible with her earth life character and outlook.

Mahatma Damodar's appearance was an unexpected pleasure. His voice calling out her name was like a wave of thought that became spoken words in her mind. This was the way she had been communicating with him for the last eight years, after that fateful day in 1993 when she met him in the flesh at New York's JFK airport.

She recalled with pleasure the way it happened. She was there to see young Morya Bennett off on his return flight to India. Morya was the twelve-year-old Hindu spiritual prodigy who had boarded with her for a few months in the winter of 1992-1993 while attending a private school in D.C. She had been communicating with Damodar every day since that auspicious event via thought transmission, so their minds and psyches had been closely attuned for quite some time. Now, he was back again, only this time in his astral body, but with even more exciting prospects.

Damodar told her that the date was November 17th—which she knew was not only David's birthday but also a date of great occult significance—and then Damodar explained in some detail what he had in mind. She was impressed with the experiment that he had suggested. It was not only a way to get valuable spiritual information to David for his new book, but it would give her a chance to maintain continued personal contact with the man she had loved dearly for so many years. Oh, yes, this was something she approved of the minute Damodar mentioned it to her! The fact that her passage through the after-death states would be put on hold temporarily was of no great importance.

Senta voiced her primary concern to Damodar telepathically. "I know that you will be able to communicate with David, but how will I be able to communicate with him?"

"It will be very easy," he responded, "not unlike how we have been keeping in touch all these years. All you have to do is convey your word thoughts to me as though you were writing or typing them, and I will immediately convert them into words that I can make appear on your David's computer. That's all there is to it."

In what seemed like only minutes later, she had just sent David her first thought-generated e-mail, using Damodar as the vehicle for trans-mission. Senta couldn't get over the speed with which thoughts could be transmitted from one person to another, and she liked the process very much. And she soon came to appreciate that, when thoughts and feelings are conveyed from one person to another in the astral, they reveal exactly what is on one's mind. Thus, there can be no lying, insincerity, or other ways of concealing the truth as there can be with spoken words.

As she reflected on the five questions David had put to her in his first e-mail, Senta was transported back in time. She smiled inwardly thinking about how they first met at the H.E.W. Christmas party in December of 1968, especially his corny introduction as he sidled up to her, saying, "Hi, I'm David Elliott. What's a nice girl like you doing in a place like this?" She had laughed out loud and began chatting with him immediately. He seemed so unaffected and ingenuous as the two of them engaged in pleasant banter while pretending to listen to the Secretary of H.E.W. and other H.E.W. officials conveying their Christmas wishes to the assembled Department employees.

She couldn't explain it at first, but she felt comfortable with David the minute he began talking to her. She liked his good looks, his rangy ath-letic physique, his shy, disarming smile and his obvious intelligence. And then, suddenly it came to her: he was the man she had seen in her vision when she was twenty-five years old!

Little wonder that she got along so well with him, despite the eight years' difference in their ages. She knew intuitively that they had been soul mates in an earlier life and were renewing their relationship in this lifetime. And, six months later, she told him so.

David's question about Senta's closest girlfriend was a poignant re-minder of the many wonderful conversations she had had with Isabelle McKeown over the years. Issy's views of life, people and things were al-ways hilarious and she and Senta laughed continually when talking on the phone. Issy once described Senta's belly laugh as a cross between a squeal and a howl. But Senta remembered Issy best for her sublime poetry, a talent the agoraphobic Isabelle developed and nurtured as a result of her self-imposed confinement in her Bronx apartment. Issy's death in 1998 was a severe blow to Senta, and she looked forward to contacting her again now that they both had died and left their physical bodies.

Of all the questions David asked Senta, the one that brought back the saddest memories was the one about her private dance recital for Louis Horst. In her *kama lokic* reverie, she recalled only too well the comments made by the renowned dance educator and composer after she danced for him to the music of *Uirapuru* by Brazilian composer Heitor Villa-Lobos in her Washington studio. "I think you're on to something special, Senta," he said, afterward. "I like your mystical style of dancing. Keep working on it, refine it, and I have no doubt you'll be an important force in modern dance before long. I may even compose something special for you." Oh, how she valued that praise and encouragement!

Unfortunately, when Louis' praise of Senta got back to the other dancers in Martha Graham's five o'clock dance class, the professional jealousy of several dancers caused them to treat Senta like a pariah. A few began openly ridiculing her dancing technique, but most simply ignored or shunned her. This shameful mistreatment by her fellow dancers went on for several months and finally became too much for Senta. She pulled out of the class, opting to do her practicing and choreographing in her studio at home thereafter.

David knew the real reason Senta stopped her formal class work, but others were given various explanations: Jon's death and her consequent need to make a living, her advancing age, her move from New York to Washington, and so forth. Still, if there was one major regret in her life, it was having left the world of modern dance so precipitously. Senta would have loved to dance on the stage again, and she knew that she would have been good. Perhaps, the next time around, she mused ruefully.

From his past description of his boss, Senta knew David would not have an easy time trying to convince Chet Walker or anyone else that he was really in touch with her by e-mail, but she maintained an optimistic outlook. At least for the time being, she could revel in the prospect of sharing her thoughts and feelings with her beloved David, just like in the past.

Oh, this was going to be such a wonderful sojourn here in *kama loka*!

Chapter 3

After waking from a fitful, sleepless night, I began worrying all over again how I would handle the extraordinary news about receiving the e-mails from Senta and Damodar. Being in the newspaper business, I knew that no one in authority at the *Washington Tribune*, least of all the executive editor, would want to touch a story like this. Receiving direct communications from the dead was the sort of thing you read about in supermarket tabloids, not in one of the nation's major metropolitan dailies. I had to find a way to make the whole idea more palatable before I became a laughingstock, or worse. And it was pretty clear that I'd have to forget about keeping my theosophical beliefs and inclinations private. But, how to do it?

It was Sunday morning and there would be no need to tell anyone at the newspaper what had happened, not yet, at least. Then I remembered my promise to let Miriam know the result of the test I devised to challenge the identity and authenticity of my e-mail correspondent, so that would be my first order of business. I gave her a call around nine and told her I had gotten my answers, but preferred telling her about the whole situation in person. I knew that she lived in a condo in the Maclean Gardens section of the District just off Wisconsin Avenue, so I suggested that we meet at eleven for a late breakfast at a small family restaurant in Friendship Heights that we both were familiar with.

"Of course I'll come, David. But can't you at least tell me how it went—good or bad—before I get there? I'm dying of curiosity."

"No, Miriam, it's much too complicated. I'll tell you everything when I see you."

When I arrived at the restaurant, Miriam was already there, seated at a booth easily visible from the main entrance, chicly dressed, as always. I joined her and ordered my favorite bacon-and-scrambled-eggs breakfast, along with coffee and toast, and she ordered a stack of buttermilk pancakes and coffee.

No sooner had the waitress taken our orders than Miriam, barely able to contain her curiosity, began hammering away at me. "Please tell me what happened, David. Don't keep me in suspense. Did you come up with some really tough questions? What did she say? Tell me, tell me." In her delightful, husky voice, she sounded like a child begging to know what present she was getting for Christmas.

"When I got home, Miriam, taking your suggestion, I came up with a series of questions that were as far off the wall as I could devise, questions that only the real Senta Trondson could answer correctly."

"And . . .?"

"She answered them all absolutely correctly. Not only that, but she answered them in less than five minutes. Even if someone theoretically could have researched the answers, it couldn't have been done in five minutes. So the e-mail really was from Senta, without any question."

Miriam's facial expression changed ever so slightly, as though that was not exactly what she wanted to hear. After a momentary pause, she asked, "What kind of questions were they?" with considerably less enthusiasm than she had shown a few moments earlier.

"Well . . . like who was her closest girlfriend, what activity did she excel in, and what medical condition did she have? Now, you have to admit those are pretty specific questions that no casual hoaxer would know how to answer."

"And the answers?"

"Isabelle McKeown, poetry and agoraphobia."

"What's agoraphobia?" Miriam asked.

"Oh, that's a severe form of anxiety that causes a person to avoid situations or places that are likely to cause even more anxiety, like social gatherings, crowded buses, theaters, and things like that. Isabelle had it so bad she didn't venture out of her Bronx apartment for the last ten years of her life. From what Senta told me, Isabelle spent most of her time reading, watching television, and writing some pretty sublime poetry, which she shared with Senta through frequent letters. Senta was not only her best friend, but her primary lifeline to the outside world."

Miriam nodded in acknowledgment. Her eyes had a distant look as she digested what I told her. "Well, that certainly is pretty specific.

"What were the other questions like?" she asked.

I gave her another example. "This was one of the harder questions: In what year and where did you give a private dance performance for an important person in the field of modern dance? Who was that person, and what was the name of the musical composition that you danced to?"

"Well, you can't get more specific than *that*," Miriam chortled. "What was the answer that came back?"

"I guess a little background would help here. You see, Senta was a modern dancer who had trained under Martha Graham in New York. But after she left Martha, she continued choreographing in her home studio in Washington. Martha's closest associate at that time was Louis Horst, the internationally famous composer and dance educator who composed the music for most of Martha's masterpiece dances. Louis had seen Senta dancing in Martha's practice class and was so intrigued by her dancing that he wanted to see more of it. So, he made a special trip down to Washington in 1958 to watch her dance to Villa-Lobos's ballet music, *Uirapuru*.

"That was the exact answer that came back, and no one besides Senta and myself could have known all those details. Incidentally, to dance for Louis Horst privately was the equivalent of giving a command performance for the Queen. And that's exactly how Senta regarded it. It was a significant event in her life."

Miriam nodded thoughtfully. She knew nothing about Senta's interest in modern dance and seemed surprised as I was telling her about it. She changed the subject slightly. "I've heard of Villa-Lobos, but I've never heard of that particular composition of his. Does Uirapuru have any particular significance?"

"Yes, it does, Miriam. Villa-Lobos was Brazilian and his *Uirapuru* ballet music was based on the story of an actual Amazonian rain forest bird of that name. According to legend, the Uirapuru was the king of birds and sang in the rain forest only once a year—when it was building its nest. Legend has it that its song was so rare and melodious that, when it began its annual singing, all the other birds in the rain forest stopped their singing to listen to it."

Miriam broke out in a wide smile, saying, "What a beautiful legend!"

Although she appeared to accept the fact that it really was Senta Trondson who had sent the e-mail from the world beyond, Miriam had a troubled look on her face and I could tell that something was bothering her.

"So what does all this mean, David?" she asked. "It's pretty clear you're convinced that you're really communicating with someone whom we both know is dead. Now, I know that psychics and mediums on TV shows supposedly bring messages from departed loved ones and all that, but I've never heard of any honest-to-goodness two-way communication between the living and the dead like you're talking about. If that's what you're supposed to tell the world, you're going to be in one hell of a pickle. The press will make fun of you, if not cut you to shreds, and as if that's not bad enough, you can bet that the traditional religions as well as the scientific community won't let you get away with it. They'll make your life miserable."

I nodded in agreement. "I couldn't agree more, Miriam, but it's really happening and I'm stymied about how to proceed. I know this is an unfair question, but do you have any ideas? What would you do if you were in my situation?"

From the intense look in her eyes, I could see that Miriam was anxious to help, possibly because she wanted to get closer to me, but I think more because she genuinely sympathized with my plight. She replied with a question of her own. "First, tell me about this Damodar person whom both you and Senta seem to know a lot about. How does he figure into all of this?"

The waitress arrived with our coffees at that moment and I stopped to savor my first cup of the day enthusiastically before continuing. "Well, when H.P.B.—oh, that's what theosophists call Helena P. Blavatsky—when H.P.B. started her theosophical work in India in late 1879, an eighteen-year-old Hindu Brahman by the name of Damodar Mavalankar volunteered to work with her in the cause and soon became her spiritual pupil and disciple, her *chela*. He hoped eventually to become an initiate in the Eastern philosophy, and his efforts ultimately bore fruit because a few years later he was summoned by the Masters to join them in Tibet for further studies and his eventual initiation into what is known as the Great White Lodge or Brotherhood of Adepts."

"So you're saying that this Damodar is a still-living person, even though he's well over a hundred years old? Come on, David, that's a little hard to accept."

I could see that I had a lot more explaining to do, but at least Miriam seemed to be listening attentively and hadn't rejected outright anything I had said so far.

"Yes, he's a living person, Miriam, but he's more than that. An initiated Adept like Damodar—who's commonly referred to as a 'Mahatma,' which means 'great soul' in Sanskrit—is someone who has developed and perfected his physical, mental, psychic and higher spiritual faculties to the utmost possible degree after passing through many incarnations. Once an Ego has reached that exalted stage of development, he has acquired power over space, time, mind and matter. Exercising his will, he can perform many marvelous feats, including the ability to exit his physical body and transport himself to wherever he desires, merely by using what's called his 'astral body.' And age is no consideration at that stage of development. So, Mahatmas like Damodar theoretically can live for well over a hundred years, and most do."

"And you're saying that Damodar communicated with *you* personally via e-mail, as well as Senta?"

"Uh-huh, he's the one who made it all possible, and he offered the help of the entire Brotherhood of Masters of Wisdom, including the Mahâ Chohan, who's the revered leader of that hierarchy of holy mortals. That's what's so mind-boggling about all of this, Miriam, that I'm being given the opportunity to communicate not only with Senta, but with a spiritual being of the highest order."

She gave a slight nod in acknowledgment, then made a suggestion for dealing with the issue that, although unhelpful, was at least logical.

"Why tell anyone about this, David? If you really can communicate with Senta and this Damodar in the way you have described why not just send your e-mails back and forth and put your book together without anyone knowing how you got the information? At least that way you won't be the object of ridicule and you won't have to worry about losing your job."

"No good," I said, shaking my head. "Damodar said the Masters *want* me to tell how I got the information, to impress upon Western society that spiritual beings like themselves not only exist, but have achieved mastery of scientific as well as spiritual knowledge. You've got to admit that converting mental thoughts into electronically transmitted signals that appear as words on a computer screen is quite a feat. As they see it, a book merely reiterating theosophical doctrines of the sort H.P.B. set forth over a century ago would be just one more literary effort likely to be ignored by the public. You may remember my first book met that dismal fate."

"Well, then, David," my sympathetic breakfast companion intoned, with a sense of resignation in her voice, "it looks like you've got yourself a first class dilemma. On the one hand, I know you want to communicate with Senta, and on the other, the only way that that's going to be possible is to let the cat out of the bag, and once you do that, the floodgates will be opened.

"I don't have to tell you that millions of people all over the world want to know if there is life after death, and if so, what it's like. My God, dozens of motion pictures have employed that theme, and I read in a magazine article recently that more books have been written on death and the afterlife than on any other single subject . . . ."

Miriam interrupted her response with a pronounced widening of her large brown eyes. "Say, wait a minute. Since this is all about communicating with the dead and getting spiritual information from some really high sources, wouldn't it be a good idea to bounce this whole thing off Ray Tuohy? You know it does sort of fall within his general bailiwick."

"God, no, not Ray!" was my knee-jerk reaction to her suggestion, making a face like I had just sucked a lemon. "Anything out of mainline religion just isn't his bag. He's got too small a mind, Miriam. And this is far too important an issue to dump on someone like Ray."

I was reluctant to tell her about Ray's unexpected appearance and our awkward conversation at the office last night. Still, I knew that my choices were limited. If not Ray, then someone in authority would have to be informed, because what was about to happen was a major news story in itself. Given my reaction to her suggestion about Ray, Miriam offered the only plausible solution.

"Well, if not Ray, then I think you better tell Chet before this goes any further."

She was right, of course. If anyone should be informed of this bizarre turn of events, it was Chet Walker, the executive editor of the *Tribune*. He'd find out about it soon enough, so why not hear it from me directly? If this matter wasn't handled properly, my job definitely could be in jeopardy. Certainly, if Chet caught wind of it before I had a chance to tell him what really happened, it could be bad news for me.

I thanked Miriam for the advice and told her that's what I probably would do. After we finished breakfast, she said she wanted to do some shopping at Nieman Marcus in the nearby Mazza Galleria, so we parted and I drove back to my apartment. While I was at it, I stopped at a Giant supermarket on Wisconsin Avenue to get some necessary groceries for the week ahead.

As I lounged on my living room sofa later in the day, contemplating all the potential pitfalls I would soon have to face, I suddenly remembered I hadn't even told Miriam to keep the matter to herself, simply taking it for granted she would respect the confidentiality of our conversations. *But, would she?*

Chapter 4

M iriam walked the two short blocks to the Mazza Galleria shopping center with a heavy heart. Things just weren't going as planned. As she casually browsed the windows in Nieman Marcus before the Sunday noontime opening, her mind was not on the cruise wear on the store manikins but on her disappointing discussion with David. *Why did Senta have to come back into his life now, just when I've started to make some progress?*

Ever since Senta's death, she had been hoping to draw closer to David, the one person at the *Tribune* she really admired. She had always liked his tall, rangy looks, and she definitely admired and respected his intellect, which came through clearly in his editorial writings on health and environmental issues. Above all, she found his morally straight character a definite plus—evidenced by his loyalty to one woman for so many years—something she didn't see in other men, certainly hadn't seen in her own unhappy marriage.

Miriam browsed the cosmetics counter, a familiar haunt. She'd known from the time she was a little girl that she possessed the same good looks as her free-spirited, pretty Irish-Catholic mother. She glanced in a counter mirror. Yes, she still had her good looks, but time—and disappointments—had left their marks too. She made her rounds past the jewelry counter.

Her father, a Jewish transplant from Brooklyn, had managed a chain jewelry store. As an only child growing up in Mainline Philly's upscale Bryn Mawr community in the 1950s, she had been doted on as long as she could remember. Miriam could have stayed in that area to attend college, but had chosen Vassar College in New York, excelling in English literature and the humanities. After college, she moved to New York City, working first as a copy specialist in an advertising agency, then as a model, and eventually as an American Express travel representative. She'd loved that work—traveling worldwide in the process of inspecting and rating hotels, airlines, cruise lines, resorts and other facilities desired by the growing breed of worldwide travelers.

But by 1981, at the age of thirty-two, she wanted to settle down and raise a family. She met and married a divorced man who was several years older. He was handsome, athletic, intelligent and financially well fixed in his job as a securities broker.

Miriam quit her American Express job, decorated their Manhattan condo tastefully and desperately tried to get pregnant before her biological clock ran out. Eventually—and too late—her husband admitted he had contracted mumps at the age of thirty and had been rendered permanently sterile. To make matters worse, she caught him having sex with her nineteen-year-old cousin who had been visiting with them.

Miriam divorced him, packed up and headed for the nation's capitol, eventually becoming the editor of the *Washington Tribune*'s new Travel Section. Of all the potential marriage partners she considered in Washington, David Elliott was the only one who came up to her standards—until he told her he was already committed to Senta. After eight years actively searching for a mate in Washington, however, she still was without a decent prospect for a husband. All that changed after Senta died, and Miriam once again focused her sights on David.

Their fortuitous dinner meeting at *The Newsroom* stirred up all her old romantic feelings for him. Despite his tired, depressed state of mind following Senta's death, she still found him physically appealing. But the news he brought about the e-mail from Senta complicated things all over again. As though it wasn't bad enough that she had to compete with David's lifetime of memories about Senta, now she had to contend with the mysteriously revivified Senta herself, or her not-quite-dead ghost. That was more than she could bear, and Miriam decided right then and there to do something about it.

After purchasing a black shell top and some pantyhose at Nieman Marcus, she taxied home and a short while later phoned Ray Tuohy at his home in Fairfax. She didn't particularly like Ray, because he was so insipid and always seemed preoccupied with externals, how things *looked* rather than their fundamental merits. But that fit nicely into her plans at the moment.

Predictably, when she told the Religion & Family Section editor about her two conversations with David, he blew a fuse. "He's flipped his lid, Miriam. None of it makes any sense. I'm afraid the death of his lady friend has pushed him over the edge. Have you noticed the way he's been acting lately?"

"Yes I have, Ray, but that's why I called. I thought maybe you could talk to him, perhaps give him a little pastoral counseling, something to get him off this e-mail kick." She knew David loathed Ray and surmised that the feelings were probably reciprocal, but she felt she had to offer some rationale for calling the former clergyman for help.

"No, Miriam, it's too late for that. Besides, I tried talking to him a little at the office last night, but he refused my offer of help and virtually kicked me out.

Miriam was surprised. "Funny, he never mentioned that he saw you at the office when we were at dinner. I don't know what's going on, Ray, but I'm worried about him—and the paper."

She knew full well what he'd say next, and she was right. "You're right about that. I think I should bring this matter to Chet's attention right away, before the whole thing gets out of hand. If David is that far gone, maybe he ought to be put on extended sick leave or something. Chet will know how to handle it."

She felt guilty doing it, but Miriam didn't see any other way out of her dilemma. Unless David was stopped now, who knew how long he might be tied up with this e-mail nonsense? Her hope was that Ray would be able to persuade Chet to see the terrible adverse publicity the *Tribune* would garner as a result of David's actions, and that Chet would force him to abandon the course of action he was pursuing.

"Well, do whatever you think is best, Ray," she replied.

"I will, and by the way," he asked almost as an afterthought, "did you give him a promise of confidentiality."

"No, he didn't say anything about keeping it quiet, so you can tell Chet whatever you want."

"I'll do it first thing tomorrow morning. Thanks, Miriam. I'm glad you called me on something as important as this."

Miriam knew the die was cast, but still felt guilty and had serious doubts that everything would work out exactly as she hoped it would. She figured that David probably would be angry, but felt reasonably sure she could assuage his feelings—if not right away, perhaps in two or three weeks.

Well, at least that was her fond hope.

Chapter 5

After Ray thanked Miriam for bringing the matter to his attention he returned the kitchen phone to its wall cradle. As he did so, he couldn't help shaking his head and snickering. His wife, Carole, browsing the Sunday edition of the *Tribune* on the kitchen table, noticed and was curious. "What was that all about?" she asked.

"That was Miriam Green. She was calling about David Elliott. You remember, that Jewish editorial writer I told you about. Can you believe this, Carole, he told Miriam he received an e-mail from his dead girlfriend and insists he's telling the truth? I think he's gone around the bend since she passed away a few months ago. I tried speaking to him when I saw him at the office last night, but he wouldn't talk about anything, let alone e-mails from outer space."

"What's Miriam got to do with it?"

"Nothing, except he met her at *The Newsroom* restaurant last night, so he gave her the whole story, and spoke with her about it again this morning. You know, if something like this ever got out to the public, the paper would look utterly foolish. I don't want that to happen."

"So what are you going to do about it?" his wife of twenty years asked, as she lazily perused the newspaper. "I'm not sure. I've got to think about it before I decide what to do." Ray walked out of the kitchen of their modest, three-bedroom rambler in suburban Fairfax, Virginia, and went to his book-lined study, ostensibly to map out his plan of action. In point of fact, he already knew what he was going to do. He saw David's aberrant behavior as the basis for his possible firing by Chet Walker, and nothing would make him happier.

Ray didn't like David Elliott from the very beginning. First, he knew David was Jewish and he didn't like Jews—period. As a former Methodist minister, he gave lip service to the concept of ecumenism. Yet, the Religion & Family Section editor of the *Tribune* was in fact a bigot and an anti-Semite, a family prejudice he acquired during his early upbringing in the small coal mining community of Logan, West Virginia. His father had been an active member of the local Ku Klux Klan and in the vernacular of the Klan his rants against "niggers, spics and Jews" were commonplace in the household.

Ray was the only boy in his family who refused to become a miner, despite his father's persistent attempts to persuade him to do so. He chose instead to enter the ministry, and after graduating West Virginia Wesleyan College in 1986, he applied for and was accepted at the United Methodist Wesleyan Theological Seminary in Washington, D.C.

Once he completed his studies at Wesleyan, and obtained his Masters in Divinity degree, he tried pastoral work in the Northern Virginia suburbs, but after two years he found he didn't like it, and began looking for something else. That's when a friend introduced him to Adrienne Thayer at a charity event in D.C. in 1994.

For some unknown reason, Adrienne took to Ray quickly, and when he let her know he was anxious to make a change in his occupation, she suggested that he might try his hand at writing some articles on family and religious matters for the *Tribune*. He jumped at the opportunity and with Adrienne's recommendation, he was hired. After several years, he was elevated to the position of editor of the new Religion & Family Section of the paper.

But Ray didn't like David Elliott for another reason besides the man's religious background: David's avowed belief in Theosophy. This came across quite clearly in Ray's review of David's book, *Psychic Witness*, which appeared in the Sunday Supplement section in May of 2000. Ray had no personal knowledge of the Eastern philosophy upon which Theosophy supposedly was founded, but he saw it as just another New Age attempt to undermine mainstream Christianity.

Receiving e-mails from a dead person! Indeed! He took out his fountain pen and jotted on a note pad a few points he would make in talking to Chet about David's behavior. This would be the first opportunity he'd had in years to make real trouble for the writer he so detested. Yes, it just might do the trick!

The first thing on Monday morning, Ray hurried in to speak with Chet Walker about the purported e-mail incident. He caught the boss at a particularly bad time. Chet was trying to read three draft articles at once and it wasn't coming off well, so Ray's sudden appearance was an unwelcome interruption. That didn't bode well for Ray who always seemed to be on the outs with Chet and regarded the curmudgeon executive editor with fear as well as loathing. Chet looked up with a half scowl and uttered an impatient, "What is it, Ray?" as he shifted his dark Honduran cheroot from one side of his mouth to the other, still mentally trying to focus on the drafts on his desk.

"Chet, Miriam Green called me yesterday afternoon to ask for my help. It seems David Elliott met her at *The Newsroom* on Saturday night and told her that he had just received an e-mail from Senta Trondson—that's his lady friend of many years. The only problem is, Senta died last August. I tell you, Chet, ever since her death the man has been acting strangely, and frankly, I think he's gone overboard. From what Miriam told me, he's preparing to announce to the whole world that he's in direct contact with this dead woman."

Chet raised his eyebrows and gave an 'Is that so?' look, but let Ray continue.

"Now, you and I both know that if he decides to go that route, the *Tribune* will have to put up with untold embarrassment and ridicule. I think you should put a stop to this ridiculous thing before it gets out of hand."

Chet raised his hand and motioned for Ray to stop talking. He didn't like Ray much to begin with, but the man's pretentious concern for the *Trib* was more than he could bear at the moment. This was not the sort of news the executive editor wanted to hear so early on a busy Monday, and in any event he was too experienced a newspaperman to take Ray's report of the situation at face value. Then, too, he was aware of the fact that Ray and David were not exactly on the best of terms, especially after Ray's scathing review of David's book last year. So, he figured, there just might be an overlay of personal animosity involved in Ray's reporting of what Miriam had told him. He decided to proceed with caution.

"Well, if what you say is true, Ray, then I'd agree he's acting pretty strangely. But Dave is no fool, and I'll have to get his side of the story. Thanks for bringing this to my attention. I'll keep you informed. But don't go blabbing this to anyone else. You hear?"

"No, Chet. Not a word. I promise."

When he left, Chet shook his head, thinking, *Just what I need, first thing on a Monday morning!* Then, he told his secretary, "Leave a note on Dave Elliott's desk telling him to see me as soon as he gets into the office."

Chapter 6

I knew something was wrong the minute I arrived in the newsroom. The receptionist gave me a disturbed look, not her usual smile. The reporters working closest to my desk avoided looking directly at me and the usual buzzing in the main newsroom toned down noticeably as I approached my editorial department cubbyhole. Whatever was up was important enough for Walker to have had his secretary leave a note on my desk to see him as soon as I came to work. My heart sank as I tried to recollect what I might have written recently that would prompt such a summons to the front office, but nothing came to mind. I decided to bite the bullet and get it over with.

As I entered Walker's office, the sour look on his face told me he was in his usual foul mood. He was a man with a wide reputation as being ill tempered and impatient, and I could tell that whatever it was he wanted to talk to me about wasn't going to be pleasant.

With his balding head tilted down so he could look at me over his reading glasses, and nursing an unlit seven-inch Honduran cigar between his lips, he muttered softly, "Sit down, Dave, sit down." Most of the people who knew me called me David, but not Chet Walker. We were on pretty good terms in general, but over the years he had found me to be more of a maverick—difficult is more like it—than my fellow editorial writers, and calling me Dave was his cute way of cutting me down to size.

As I sat, he began, "Up to now, Dave, I've always considered you one of our more responsible writers, but what's all this crap about you communicating with your dead lady friend by e-mail? From what Ray Tuohy tells me, it almost sounds like you're coming unglued."

The minute he mentioned Ray's name, I had a pretty good idea what must have happened. Miriam obviously told Ray everything I had said to her about the e-mail from Senta, and knowing Ray, he probably convinced her that it was either a ridiculous figment of my imagination, attributable to my exhausted physical condition, or the result of my misguided preoccupation with Theosophy. "I'm really sorry that Ray got to you before I arrived this morning, Chet, because I had planned on speaking to you myself."

Eli P. Bernzweig

"About what?"

"About the same thing, only it's not crap. Let me begin at the beginning, so you'll get the whole picture, not some cockamamie third-hand version from someone who doesn't even know what he's talking about."

My words and tone of voice made it abundantly clear how I felt about Ray and Walker smiled while stifling a laugh, aware of those personal feelings—which he shared to some extent—and then eased back in his chair as I began my recital of events.

"Do you remember when I introduced you to my friend, Senta Trondson, at the Christmas party last December?"

"Yeah, I think so. A good-looking gal, as I recall; blonde, blue eyes. Was that the one?" With a finesse that came from years of practice, his tongue deftly shifted the huge cigar to the other side of his mouth without interfering with his words.

"Yes, that was Senta. Well, she was diagnosed with stomach cancer a couple of months later and died this last August after a relatively short final illness. She was seventy years old when she died, and because she felt that she had lived a sufficiently long and fruitful life, she rejected the usual heroic measures of treatment and chose to go the hospice route. Dying wasn't a big deal to Senta, especially since she was a theosophist and a firm believer in reincarnation."

"Yes, Ray mentioned that your lady friend had died, and I'm sorry about that, Dave, but what's all this about getting an e-mail from her? You're not serious, are you?"

"Well, I'll let you judge for yourself. Just as I was about to leave the office Saturday night, I saw that I had an incoming e-mail from someone called 'Your *Herzele*' with the subject labeled 'Happy Birthday, darling.' Saturday *was* my birthday, and only Senta and I called each other *herzele*—it's a German term of endearment; means 'little heart.' She picked up the expression at the orphanage where she was raised."

"All right, all right, and then what?" asked the ever-impatient executive editor.

"I opened the e-mail and, just as I told Miriam when I met her at *The Newsroom* restaurant a short while later, there was a message from Senta, or at least someone who purported to be Senta, wishing me a happy birthday and a lot more. I can show you the whole message. In fact, I'll make copies of all the e-mails so you can see what I'm talking about."

Walker's demeanor changed ever so slightly from one of confrontation to one of growing curiosity. "Yeah, I'd like to see these mysterious e-

34

mails. So, what's the upshot of the thing, Dave? How do you know it's not a hoax, or somebody hacking your computer? I mean, we're talking about a dead person here, with all due respect."

I took a deep breath to calm my nerves and then patiently explained what Senta had said, how I challenged her with the five questions, and how she explained Damodar's role in all of this. "Chet, you have to believe me, I'm as astounded as anyone would be to receive a message from a dead person, but I didn't make this up. I know it's hard to believe, but it's real."

Walker raised his bushy eyebrows and chomped on his cigar a few times before replying, "Whether it's real or not, Dave, is the big question, don't you think? Before I make my mind up on how to handle this, see that I get a copy of those e-mails right away. And don't talk about this to anyone, either here at the paper . . . or anywhere elsewhere. Do I make myself clear?"

I said I'd get him the e-mails right away, and also promised not to talk to anyone, which was fine with me since, frankly, I had no way of knowing how all of this would shake out. Ten minutes later, Walker had copies of the e-mails on his desk. After reading them, he had his secretary call me back in. My two special visits to the office of the executive editor, one after the other, quickly prompted speculation among the reporters in the newsroom that I must have really screwed up on something I wrote. It showed on their faces as I entered Walker's office the second time in less than fifteen minutes.

"Well, Dave, I've read all the e-mails, and on the surface I have to admit it sure looks like your lady friend has communicated with you. Now, I know how all of this must generate ambivalent feelings in you, but in my position at the *Trib* I just can't let this sort of thing get out of hand. Ray was right when he said that a thing like this could make not only you, but me and the paper look ridiculous, to say the least."

Anger welled inside me as I pictured Ray pretending to show his concern for the paper while slyly concealing his personal antagonism to me. I was about to protest, but Chet, after removing his cigar, raised his hand, saying, "Now, hold your horses, before you get yourself all worked up." There was something about the slightly conciliatory tone of his voice that lessened my anxiety somewhat. He continued, "This Damodar character seems to be the focal point of the mystery here. You and Senta apparently know all about him. Who is he, and how can he possibly arrange to send and receive e-mails from the world beyond . . . this *kama loka* place that she mentioned?"

"Damodar is a Mahatma, Chet, an initiated Master of Wisdom. He's part of a group of living persons who are highly developed spiritually and whose sole aim is to promote the spiritual welfare of the human race. Every now and then they make an effort to present spiritual truths to mankind through a special messenger or agent. That's apparently why Damodar has come at this time. By the time a Master of Wisdom reaches the stage of spiritual perfection that Damodar has attained, he has acquired unusual powers, wisdom and compassion."

"Powers? What kind of powers?"

"All kinds. For example, the power to take on any form, physical or astral; the power to communicate with others telepathically; the power to transport his body great distances at the speed of thought; the power to see into the astral light and predict the future; the power to precipitate written materials or images out of thin air; and the extraordinary power to control the forces of nature."

"What in hell is the astral light?" the executive editor barked, irritably, again moving his cigar to the other side of his mouth.

"The easiest way to describe it, Chet, is it's the basic etheric matter of the universe, an invisible spiritual substance . . ."

Walker broke in, shaking his head wildly, "Oh, Jesus, Dave, you're beginning to sound like a science-fiction nut. You talk like you really believe in this nonsense. I'm surprised at you, a person with your educational background."

His know-it-all attitude pissed me off. "Yes, I do believe in it, Chet, and so do many others. The ability to take someone's mental thoughts and convert them into e-mail messages using the astral light may be a new wrinkle but it should prove to you how accomplished Damodar is in dealing with such supernormal matters."

Walker clearly was reaching the limits of his indulgence. He put his feet up on the desk and, peering through his reading glasses, took a few moments to peruse the e-mails again, turning the pages slowly, one by one. Then he gave me his verdict. "This Damodar insists that you tell the world you're in touch with your dead girlfriend so he can convey to you—and, presumably, the readers of some forthcoming book—what the afterlife is really like. Now, I needn't remind you that this is not the *Globe* or the *National Enquirer*, and I can't allow a staff writer for this paper to become a media freak, Dave. And that's just what will happen, you can bet on it."

A Death Interrupted

Chet twirled his cigar around in his mouth a couple of times while pondering how to resolve the matter, and then issued his verdict in a deliberate tone of voice. "So, my friend, unless you can convince me that these e-mails are genuine and that you're really in touch with your deceased sweetheart, which I seriously doubt, you're gonna have to keep this whole thing a deep, dark secret . . . or else take an early retirement. Do I make myself clear?"

I held my breath as he announced his decision and I knew he wasn't kidding. We had crossed swords on several occasions over the years on editorial policy matters, and I knew I wasn't exactly the boss' favorite editorial staff writer. "Yes, clear enough," I answered gravely. And then, out of nowhere a thought suddenly popped into my head: "But, suppose I *can* convince you, Chet? What then? Would you consider making a deal with me?"

Walker, looking genuinely surprised, took his feet off the desk and again removed the well-chewed cigar from his mouth. Hunching forward with eyebrows raised and the look of a poker player holding a royal flush, he inquired in a soft, almost-mocking voice, "A deal? What kind of deal?"

"Just suppose I *can* convince you that Senta really is communicating with me via e-mail and that Damodar is the person making all this possible. How about letting Damodar's e-mails to me about what happens after we die appear as original articles in the paper, in the Religion & Family Section, perhaps? He intends to send them to me more or less weekly. Now, that's something that certainly would be newsworthy in itself, and I'll bet it would even increase circulation, provided it's handled in a serious, dignified manner. What do you think?"

He paused a second before asking, "I thought you were going to write a book yourself. Have you given up on that idea already?"

He was right. I *had* planned on writing another book, but it seemed to make so much more sense to have Damodar—a being with far more spiritual knowledge than I have—pen the material on the postmortem states himself. And I had to admit it would save me the trouble of organizing all the material, writing another book and then trying to find an agent and a publisher for that sort of work.

"No," was my hesitant reply, "But I would if you agreed to publish Damodar's articles under his byline."

Walker reinserted the cigar and, with a smirk on his face, remarked, "But surely you know that once something's in the *Trib* it's copyrighted, and you can't touch any part of it. No copyright, no royalties. Have you thought about that?"

"Don't want any royalties, and in fact that's the way I'd prefer it." The words tumbled out of my mouth almost before I realized what I was saying.

I could tell that he didn't like hearing this. Maneuvering his cigar to the other side of his mouth for the umpteenth time, Walker sneered, "You never give up, do you?" He appeared to be reaching the limits of his patience. "And suppose you can't convince me? Will you agree to drop the whole matter once and for all? I mean, no articles, no publicity, no more talk about this to anyone—ever again?"

It was too late to turn back. "Yes, I agree," I replied glumly, suddenly fearful that I might be making a big mistake. If I couldn't somehow convince Chet that Damodar is an honest-to-goodness living being with profound knowledge of spiritual matters and the possessor of unusual occult powers, I knew that my chances of being able to communicate with Senta would be reduced to zero. And that thought really bothered me.

Walker seemed surprised by my quick, unconditional answer, obviously believing I wouldn't cave in so readily. "Good enough," he said. "The ball's in your court. Now, how do you propose to go about convincing me?"

I needed more time. "Let me think about it, Chet. I'll get back to you as soon as I can, but no later than tomorrow." And, with a further promise that I wouldn't discuss the matter with anyone, our discussion ended. As I returned to my desk to begin my day's work, I was feeling a strange mixture of fear and nervous excitement, knowing that whatever idea I came up with would be crucial to my future ability to communicate with Senta. Equally important, we would have the rare opportunity to present authoritative information on life after the death of the physical body, information that the Masters earnestly wanted to disseminate to the public. And then it dawned on me: who could better help me than Damodar himself?

I sat down at my computer, gingerly typed damodar@kamaloka.com, and started my e-mail:

> "Master Damodar, I have to convince my executive editor that you are a real person, that you are an initiated Mahatma with extraordinary powers, and that I am really able to communicate with you and Senta via e-mail. How can I do this in a way that will be unassailable?"

In less than a minute, I had my answer.

> "Mr. Elliott, I was aware of your difficulties with Mr. Walker, so I have come up with an idea. Tell your superior that I will provide all the proof necessary to convince him that our Great White Lodge of Initiates does in fact exist and that the members of our occult Brotherhood not only can control the forces of nature, but we also have the ability to see into the future."

He then outlined the nature of the proof in detail and suggested that I consider who else at the newspaper should be involved, simply for verification purposes. I said I would think about that, and then asked if I could communicate with Senta. In an instant, she was online:

> "David, *herzele*, I am very happy that Damodar has suggested how to convince your Mr. Walker that all this is real and that you and I are in fact able to communicate with each other through this unique process even though I have cast off my physical body. I'm sure it will all work out. How are you feeling, darling? Is all this excitement going to put too much of a strain on your heart?"

I replied:

> "I don't think so, precious. If anything, I feel stronger than ever. But I wanted to let you know how much I miss you. I still feel your love all around me and talk to you constantly when I am alone in the car, just as though you were still here. I'm ashamed to admit that, once you died, I had all but given up the thought of writing on theosophical subjects anymore, but now that I am able to keep in touch with you via these e-mails, my interest in writing definitely has been rekindled.
>
> "I guess I'll have a whole series of questions for you eventually, about what it's like there in *kama loka* and other related matters, but all that can wait until Walker can see that what is happening is real and not some joke or hoax. So, the sooner we get this proof thing over with, the better I'll feel. I'll tell Chet that the proof will be shown to him tomorrow. Goodbye for the moment, darling. I love you."

In accordance with Walker's instructions, I told no one at the paper what was going on, and neither Miriam nor Ray made any attempt to speak to me, which was good in a way because both would be intimately involved in what was to happen tomorrow. I spent the rest of the day in my normal editorial pursuits. We had our usual ten o'clock editorial staff meeting, and the department editor gave me an environmental article for Friday's edition of the paper. To all outward appearances, my two mysterious meetings with the executive editor had no significance, but all that would change after tomorrow.

Early Tuesday morning, I found Chet in an uncharacteristically happy mood. He welcomed me with a big smile on his face, again chomping on an unlit cigar—which everyone knew he used as a mood pacifier—and got right to the point. "Well, Dave, have you figured out how you're going to convince me that the e-mails are for real?"

"I think so, Chet," I replied, trying my best to sound confident. "But we'll have to have independent witnesses to make sure the type of proof I have in mind is fair and convincing."

The smile on Walker's face turned to a disturbed, almost angry look. He removed the cigar from his mouth to emphasize his annoyance. "Why do you need witnesses? Don't you think I'm capable of judging for myself?" Obviously, he still didn't want too many others at the paper to know about my situation.

"Well, Chet, when I describe what's going to happen, by yourself you might find it a little hard to believe, but if there are others here to corroborate what occurs, then I think you'll be less inclined to say I didn't convince you." Chet shrugged his shoulders, still unhappy but unwilling to waste any more time arguing the point.

"Okay, okay. Let's get on with it. I'll call in a couple of reporters."

"No, I've thought about this. I would like Miriam and Ray to be the two witnesses. Unless I'm mistaken, aside from yourself, they're the only people in the building who have any inkling as to what's going on, so if the proof doesn't convince you, no one else need know and the matter can end right here with the minimum amount of publicity."

Walker bought that idea immediately, so he had his secretary summon Miriam and Ray to the front office. They arrived a few seconds apart and when they saw me already waiting in Chet's office, both knew that the reason they were summoned had something to do with the purported e-mails from Senta. I pointedly smiled and tried to make eye contact with them as they entered, but neither would look directly at me. Their somber faces and nervous, darting glances at each other showed their obvious concern with the uncomfortable situation. And the blank, noncommittal look they saw on Chet's face didn't help matters.

Chet briefly explained why they were called in. "Dave here is pretty sure he can convince me that a person called Damodar is responsible for the e-mail that he received from his deceased lady friend, Senta Trondson. Now, I have my doubts about that, but I'm giving him a chance to prove I'm wrong, and I've called you two in to be witnesses to whatever's going to take place."

In accordance with the plan Damodar had outlined to me the previous day, I suggested that we all go into the big, inside conference room where, once the blinds were drawn and everyone was seated, I explained in as confident a voice as I could muster what would happen.

"The purpose of this test," I began, which is really more like a demonstration, is to convince all three of you that the Master of Wisdom, Mahatma Damodar, is in fact the person who has made it possible for my recently-deceased Senta to communicate with me via e-mail. He and his fellow Mahatmas knew that I was planning to write a book presenting the theosophical view of what follows death of the physical body, so they came up with the idea to have Senta communicate with me in this unique manner, by having Damodar convert her thoughts into electronic signals appearing as words on my computer."

As I spoke these opening words, I could see Ray shaking his head and rolling his hazel eyes, not even attempting to conceal his contempt for what I was saying. Chet and Miriam noticed, too. I ignored him and continued.

"After thinking it over, instead of my writing a book on the afterlife, I suggested to Chet that it might be better if Damodar were to prepare several articles on the subject, and Chet has agreed to publish those articles in the *Trib* under Damodar's byline, provided he's convinced that the source is as I have indicated. And if not, then I've agreed to cease all further discussion of this matter, and there will be no publicity about any of this. Is that a fair enough statement of the issue, Chet?"

"Yes, yes, that's it. Now, let's get going. I don't have all day."

I continued, "The demonstration you are about to witness is to prove that Mahatma Damodar has reached such a high stage of spiritual perfection that he can control and apply the forces of nature in whatever manner he chooses. In this instance, merely by exercising his will power—his *itchasakti*, as it's called in Sanskrit—and his knowledge of occult laws, he can control the electrons in the ether surrounding us. And doing so, he can make it possible for words and pictures to appear on a computer screen. He can also reverse the process, making it possible for him and for Senta to receive my computer-generated words, as reflected in the astral light."

"What do you mean by the astral light?" Miriam asked, in her soft, deep voice.

"Yeah, what's that all about?" Walker chimed in. "You started to tell me about that yesterday."

"The astral light is an invisible electro-spiritual substance surrounding the earth that contains the images of every occurrence in nature, as well as every action, thought, sound and color. It's like a huge video camera of the cosmos, containing pictures not only of everything that has been and is, but also of what is to be. It's the medium that makes possible all kinds of occult phenomena, including thought transference, mediumship, clairvoyance, precipitation of documents and pictures out of thin air, and many other occult phenomena."

I could have gone on, but I was trying to limit the facts to what I thought they could handle. And it occurred to me that this was the first time I had mentioned in mixed company anything about the astral light or how Adepts can control the forces of nature, though Senta and I had discussed these subjects on many occasions.

Ray Tuohy couldn't contain himself any longer, and in his typical overbearing manner, interjected, "Do you know how foolish you sound, David, with all that metaphysical claptrap? You haven't a shred of scientific proof that there's such a thing as this astral light. And you actually want us to believe an invisible entity, a so-called 'Mahatma,' is going to prove to us that a dead person can send e-mails to someone who is alive?"

"Well, Ray, rather than debate the point," I said, condescendingly, "why don't we just let the demonstration speak for itself?"

"Yeah, Ray," Chet Walker said, in a further display of impatience, "let the man get on with his demonstration, or we'll be here all day."

I, too, was glad to move ahead because I knew that showing Damodar's powers would be vastly better than any explanations I might give. "Now that you know the medium that he will utilize," I began, "Damodar will give all three of you the opportunity to test his ability to manipulate the electrons in the astral that control words, pictures and symbols, and he will demonstrate it in a unique fashion for each of you.

"To do this, we will, of course, require a computer, and that's why I asked that we convene here in the big conference room, where we not only have privacy, but a computer that's operational, as well." I turned on the computer and positioned it so everyone could see the screen. The venetian blinds were already closed, so no one outside could see what was taking place in the conference room.

"Now, there will be three separate demonstrations to prove what Damodar can do: one pertaining to the past, one to the present, and one to the future. To begin, I want one of you to make a request of Damodar to have something that has happened in the past appear on the computer screen, but it must be known to you alone and it must be something that can be confirmed. The second person's request should relate to something in writing of interest in the immediate present time frame, but which that person can also confirm. And finally, one of you should request something to appear on the screen that relates to a future event, but one that can be independently confirmed or reasonably quickly ascertained. I will leave the room for three or four minutes to let you discuss the nature of your three choices among yourselves."

As I prepared to leave, I could see that Chet looked disgusted as well as impatient. Ray began shaking his head and muttered half aloud, "What a waste of time!" Miriam's face was expressionless. Although I felt reasonably confident that the test of Damodar's powers would be successful, I really had no way of knowing for sure, which gave me a twinge of doubt. But the fat was now in the fire and only time would tell.

When I returned, the smug, self-satisfied looks on all three faces indicated their confidence that they had devised tests that would disprove all my assertions about Damodar and the authenticity of the e-mails from my deceased Senta once and for all.

I began at once. "Who has a request for Damodar to make something appear that existed in the recent or distant past, but something that is readily verifiable?" I asked.

"I do," Ray Tuohy immediately replied, not even trying to conceal the smirk on his face as he spoke.

"Tell us what it is, Ray," I said.

"If I heard you correctly, you said that this Damodar person could make pictures as well as words appear by a process you referred to as 'precipitation.' Does that include photographs?"

"Yes, photographs, too. What do you have in mind?"

"Well, just before our eight-year-old daughter, Robin, died of spinal meningitis, my wife and I had a snapshot taken of the three of us by a neighbor, and we liked it so much we had an eight by ten color enlargement made up. Unfortunately, that photo, along with all our family photos, was destroyed when our house in Fairfax burned to the ground in 1988. Carol and I were devastated over the loss of those pictures, especially the one showing the three of us a few months before Robin died. Now, *that's* a picture I'd like to see again! What can your invisible Adept do about that?" he asked smugly.

Following Damodar's instructions the day before, I directed Tuohy to close his eyes and try to visualize the photo in his mind. "Take your time, so that you can recall as many of the details as possible, like the colors, the background, your relative positions and so forth. And tell me when you are done."

Ray heaved a sigh of exasperation, but did as instructed. The computer was on and the screen was black. The room remained deathly quiet, with everyone's eyes riveted on the screen. After thirty seconds, Ray opened his eyes, and as he did so, there slowly appeared on the screen, pixel by pixel and line by line, an exact replica of the photo Ray had requested. It showed his wife, his daughter and himself standing in the backyard of their home in Fairfax. Though not quite as vivid as the Kodak original, it was perfect in every other respect.

Tuohy scrutinized the screen in paralyzed silence for a full half minute as though he were looking at a sacred religious relic, and then tears slowly started rolling down his face. Miriam and Chet also watched in awe as the photo appeared on the screen and were, for the moment, speechless. Ray asked in a respectful tone of voice, "Is it possible to get a copy, or is this it?"

Ignoring his question for the moment, I asked Ray, "Can you tell us if this is the photo you had in mind, the exact photo you said was lost in the fire?" I wanted it clearly established that Damodar had come through with flying colors.

"Oh, yes, yes. But can I get a copy?" he pleaded, unashamedly, like a child begging for more candy.

Damodar had prepared me for just such an eventuality. I replied, "We can try to print out what's on the screen, but I've got a better idea, Ray. See if you can locate a large, empty envelope and put it in the center of the conference table." He raced out of the room and returned in a few seconds with an empty ten by thirteen envelope.

"Now, let's leave it there for a minute," I said, noting the stunned look on all three faces as they continued to marvel at the picture on the screen. While waiting, Chet let out a soft, "Well I'll be damned," while Miriam shook her head and muttered, "Oh, my God." After another thirty or forty seconds, I told Ray to open the previously empty envelope and look inside. He slowly withdrew from the envelope a full 8" x 10" glossy photo, heavier and clearer than the one on the screen, but containing on the back in a large script the words 'SATYÂT NÂSTI PARO DHARMAH.'

"What does that mean?" Chet asked, obviously impressed by what he had just seen.

"That's Sanskrit for 'There is no religion higher than truth.' It's the motto of the Theosophical Society," I replied.

Wanting to take advantage of the awesome impact of the first demonstration, I quickly asked, "Who has chosen something in the present time frame?"

"I have," said Miriam, still visibly shaken by what she had just seen.

"Tell us what it is," I asked.

"Well, when I got to work this morning, I wrote a note to myself, which I haven't shown to anyone. Is that the sort of thing you have in mind?"

"Exactly," I replied. "Only, since you say this is something you wrote, it's already out there in the astral, so you don't have to concentrate on it."

Within seconds the darkened computer monitor again started to light up, this time with several lines in Miriam's own handwriting: 'Make dr. apptmt. next wk. Chest pains coming more often.' "Is that what you wrote, Miriam?" I asked, surprised to learn that she, too, had a heart problem.

"My God!" she exclaimed. "Those are my exact words." She fumbled around in her jacket pocket for the original of the note and, when she found it, placed it on the table for all to see. "They're identical!" she all but screamed. And indeed they were, but as we all compared the writings, something else appeared on the computer screen, a message that was even more surprising: 'To the lady with chest pains, there is nearly total blockage of your left anterior descending artery. It is good that you plan to seek medical treatment promptly.' As Miriam, Ray and Chet exchanged looks, I could see they were not at all comfortable. It was as though they knew they were being watched by some invisible, omniscient presence and I could see that it was beginning to make them all very nervous.

I finally broke the silence by asking Walker about his request, the one pertaining to a future event that somehow could be independently substantiated.

"This really isn't fair," the executive editor intoned, condescendingly, "but what the hell, let's see what happens. I'd be interested in knowing what the *New York Times* lead editorial will look like for the Thanksgiving edition." And before I could even say a word, Walker gave me a 'take-it-easy' motion with his arms, remarking sarcastically, "Now, don't ask me to close my eyes and visualize something that I've never seen and which probably hasn't even been written yet."

"No, I won't do that, Chet," I said, "but tell me, who do you think would write the lead editorial for Thursday's paper?"

Walker thought for a moment, before replying, "More than likely Rainey Howell. He's the executive editor at the *Times*, an old pal of mine. Since this will be the first Thanksgiving since September 11th, he might say something that's tied in with the tragic events of that day. Then again, he may not have written anything at all, or maybe someone else will get the editorial assignment."

He shrugged, unable to help more. I said, "Fair enough. Let's see what comes up." The room was again deathly silent as all four of us stared at the darkened computer screen. Then, in thirty seconds or so there appeared on the monitor, line by line, a double-spaced typewritten draft of an article with the heading, 'The Thanksgiving Impulse':

> "It's pretty hard to explain just how shocking it is to hear Bing Crosby singing 'Jingle Bells' in the drugstores and malls or to see tins of Christmas crackers and boxes of wrapping paper stacked where the sandbags full of bite-size Halloween candy were just two weeks ago. But here we are, and there's no going back, which is exactly how it feels to Thanksgiving travelers, who are on the move today. Many Americans who have been innocent of air travel since Sept. 11 are hurling themselves back into the system as if it were yesteryear."

This was followed by three more paragraphs noting the changes facing travelers at airport security checkpoints and relating all the inconveniences to the real meaning of Thanksgiving this year to those anxious to be home with family and friends.

Walker easily recognized the writing style of his good friend of many years, but his grudging nature still refused to believe the words were Rainey's or that they would appear in that form in the Thursday edition of the *Times*. He simply needed more proof.

"I've got to call Rainey and see if this is something he wrote," he announced, though his subdued demeanor clearly reflected his profound shock and amazement at what all of us had just seen.

From the telephone in the corner of the conference room, Chet asked the *Tribune's* switchboard operator to try to put him through to Rainey Howell at the *New York Times*, and turned on the speakerphone so we could all hear the results. The operator was able to reach Howell almost immediately.

"Rainey, Chet Walker here. Forgive me for bothering you, my friend, but we're trying to check on something that's come up and I need your help."

"Sure, Chet. What is it?"

"Have you drafted your lead editorial yet for Wednesday's Late City Edition?"

"Still working on it, Chet, but it's almost done. Just trying to iron out some of the wrinkles. Nothing too profound, just about the mood and feelings of travelers this first Thanksgiving since September 11th. Why do you ask?"

As his words came over the speakerphone, all three participants exchanged looks of unabashed wonderment and the nervous tension in the room became palpable.

Walker continued, "Well, this is going to sound a little strange, pal, but would you mind reading just the first paragraph? This is *very* important, else I wouldn't ask you to do this."

"Hell, I don't mind, Chet. Nothing secret here." The *Times* executive editor then read the first paragraph of his draft. It matched the text that appeared on the monitor word for word. I could feel the hair on the back of my head standing on end. The others looked shocked and stunned.

"What about the caption, Rainey?" Walker asked, quietly.

"Don't have one yet, Chet. I've been diddling with a few, but the one I like best is 'The Thanksgiving Impulse.'"

That did it! The blood drained from Walker's face and both Miriam and Ray gasped openly as they heard Howell's words. The draft on the screen already contained the caption that was in the *Times* executive editor's mind! Walker thanked his colleague, wished him a Happy Thanksgiving and abruptly rang off. As he turned to the others, his face was ashen and he just kept shaking his head in disbelief.

When he finally pulled himself together, he looked me in the eye and said in a quiet, serious voice, "Well, Dave, I'm at a loss for words. But I made a promise and I'm going to keep it. This man you call Damodar was able to do everything he was asked to do, and if he's that accomplished, then I see no reason why we shouldn't let his forthcoming articles appear in the *Trib* under his own byline. I do have one more question, though. If he's able to do all the things he's shown us today, why can't he do it in person? Why all the mystery?"

Before I could even reply, the answer came from Damodar himself, in words that appeared on the computer monitor in the conference room:

> "I appreciate your desire to see me in person, Mr. Walker, but I would make an in-the-flesh appearance only under the most compelling of circumstances. Let me explain. It is difficult for members of our occult fraternity to function well in the mephitic, spiritually tainted atmosphere of the part of the world in which you live. Our abode is high up in the Himalayas where such negative magnetic emanations cannot reach or affect us. I hope this adequately explains the reason for my reluctance to appear in the flesh."

"It does for me," Walker remarked pensively, half aloud. "And considering the degree of moral stench we have to contend with every day right here in the District of Columbia, I can't really disagree with him." He then reiterated his earlier statement that the series of articles would proceed, as he promised me.

"Are you absolutely sure about that, Chet?" Ray Tuohy interjected, still trying his best to dissuade the executive editor. "This could put the paper in an indefensible position, you know, especially with the established religions."

Chet responded testily, "I'm aware of that, Ray, but merely allowing a point of view to be expressed doesn't necessarily mean we endorse it. Of course, I'll have to bounce this off the boss-lady for her approval, but otherwise I'm not too concerned."

A Death Interrupted

My heart sank when Chet mentioned the boss-lady. He was referring to Adrienne Thayer, the newspaper's seventy-year-old owner and a woman with a reputation for having ultra-conservative leanings. She did not become actively involved in the paper's management until after the death of her husband, Walter, in an airplane accident in 1998. She let Chet run the day-to-day affairs of the *Tribune*, but insisted upon his consulting her on key policy issues, and I had serious doubts about his getting her approval for something as unorthodox as publishing articles on the afterlife by an invisible Master of Wisdom.

Chet made us all promise to keep quiet about what we had witnessed and said he'd contact Adrienne right away. As we all left the conference room, I felt tightness in the well of my stomach and some new tension in my neck and shoulders, but I could only wait and wonder how things would turn out.

Chapter 7

"Does it have to be now?" Adrienne asked, peevishly. "I'm desperately trying to pull a lot of loose ends together for my Christmas party, and it's not going well, Chester. Can't it wait a day or two?"

"I'm afraid not, Adrienne. We've got a major policy issue here, and I need your input and approval right away." Chet knew this was a bad time; Adrienne would be in the midst of planning a soirée at her mansion in Georgetown for the week before Christmas, and her tone proved she was irked at having to interrupt her phone calling and other party arrangements.

"All right. Come on up," she said, in an exasperated voice. "But let's make it fast."

"I'll be right up," he said.

As a Washington socialite, Adrienne was known more for the lavish parties she threw than her acumen in the newspaper business. A tall, imposing woman in her mid-seventies, with a pretty face and silver-gray hair, she had an aristocratic look about her that fit the image of a society matron to the tee. After her husband's death in 1998, she assumed the title of publisher but gave Chet authority to handle all the day-to-day problems of running the newspaper, insisting only that he consult her on all major policy issues.

The first time he brought a policy issue to her they had argued at length and she finally vetoed his recommendation. Although it could have gone either way, Chet knew she did it to clearly establish that she was the ultimate authority on such matters, and once that was settled they got along fine. Adrienne had an innate sense of propriety with regard to the type of material that should or should not appear in Washington's number one newspaper, and Walker respected her judgment on most policy issues that came up. She, in turn, gave him considerable leeway with respect to the day-to-day management of the *Tribune* and personnel matters.

Chet exited the elevator and nodded at Adrienne's secretary as he walked into the boss-lady's private office and again marveled at the quiet elegance of the room. Adrienne used it as her private office a few hours each day when not otherwise occupied with more pressing personal matters. The office was decorated like a comfortable home library, with bookcases covering one entire wall and tasteful paintings and mirrors on the others. Her ornate, Spanish-style oak desk and matching Spanish-style oak-and-leather executive swivel chair were the focal point of the room. An ornate bronze lamp with a sandstone and brown parchment shade lighted the desk. A beautiful Persian rug with a predominantly red motif anchored the heavy furniture and added to the look of simple elegance that she, as a woman of patrician upbringing, hoped to achieve.

Chet knew, of course, that the decision to print Damodar's articles about the afterlife was a significant policy issue that Adrienne would feel strongly about, especially since she was a fairly devout High Episcopalian. He quickly came to the point, outlining everything that had happened, beginning with David's receipt of the first e-mail from Senta and then the dramatic demonstration of Damodar's prowess conducted by David in the conference room with himself, Ray and Miriam as witnesses. He also mentioned the promise he made to David about publishing Damodar's articles.

Adrienne was not at all convinced that a series on postmortem states of consciousness was a proper subject for the *Tribune*, and in a steadily rising voice she scolded the executive editor in a veritable tirade. "I don't understand you, Chester. Something like this will make utter fools of us, and that's not something I look forward to, especially with my annual Christmas party coming up in a couple of weeks. How could a savvy editor like you, with all your years of experience, fall for something as far out and unorthodox as this? I'm not even sure we wouldn't be perpetrating a fraud on our readers, and that's certainly not the kind of reputation I want the *Tribune* to have. And you had no right to make a promise you couldn't keep. E-mails from a dead woman. Indeed!"

Chet had anticipated that she would probably find objections, but never dreamt that she would be as vituperative as this. Somehow or other he hoped his detailed explanation of the demonstration by Damodar would make her change her mind. "If you had been there, Adrienne," he insisted, "you wouldn't doubt for one minute that this Damodar is all that he claims to be."

She scoffed, "Why, you've never even seen the man. I'm sorry, Chester, but I'm not impressed, nor am I convinced. I'm sure there's some plausible explanation for the things that happened in the conference room, but I don't see how you can credit this invisible entity with bringing it all about."

Chet was completely nonplussed by Adrienne's outburst, but then recalled the way David had forced the issue with him under nearly identical circumstances. He decided to try something similar with the boss-lady. "Adrienne," he said in a soft, conciliatory tone of voice, "Suppose, just suppose I'm right, and that this is not a wild-eyed scheme fostered by some invisible prankster. What would it take to convince you I'm not losing my mind and that everything I told you about Damodar is absolutely true—that he's a highly developed spiritual being who can converse with people who are dead as well as those who are alive?"

Adrienne was about to resume her tirade, but paused momentarily as a random thought seemed to cross her mind. "Hmmn," she muttered, as she cupped her chin and repeated the question half aloud, "What would it take to convince me . . . it sure would have to be something good, not some simple parlor trick." And then, with eyebrows raised her face lit up with a sudden inspiration. "I'll tell you what, Chester. I don't believe in mediumship and things like that, but if this Damodar can actually contact my son, Eric . . . well, there's something I would like to find out."

"What do you have in mind?" Chet asked, relieved at this sudden change of heart. He knew, of course, that she had taken it very hard when her twenty-year-old son committed suicide by a drug overdose in 1992, at a point in time when her husband was still publisher of the paper.

Just mentioning Eric's name had apparently rekindled in Adrienne the horror of his tragic end and the untold grief it had caused her. He had only rarely heard her talk about it. She absently brushed a tear from her eye as she explained, "When Eric died, he left me a note that I never told the police about because of the very personal nature of the contents. But, one thing he said in it has always been a mystery to me."

"What was that? Walker inquired, softly.

She paused with a distant look in her eyes, before explaining, "He said he was taking my secret to his grave. Now, if this Damodar person is all that you say he is, and can actually contact Eric, I would like to know what my dear son meant by that remark. If he can do that for me, I would consider that pretty good proof there's something to all of this business and I'd reconsider my position on the articles."

Chet felt better already. "Let me see what I can work out, Adrienne. I'll check with Dave and see if he can get Damodar to comply with your request in some manner." And with that, he left.

Once downstairs, Chet relayed to David the gist of his conversation with Adrienne and asked David to contact Damodar via e-mail immediately to see if he could help in any way. In less than ten minutes, Damodar's e-mail reply to David indicated he would prefer to deal with Mrs. Thayer directly, considering the sensitivity of the information she requested. He asked that she be prepared to receive an e-mail from him shortly.

After Chet conveyed Damodar's message to Adrienne, she didn't know what to expect. Her heart jumped a little and she nervously picked at her fingernails before settling in to her swivel chair and facing the computer behind her desk. A soft, pained look drifted across her face as she anxiously waited for something to happen. Her computer had been on all morning, but at the moment all she could see were the screensaver's shooting stars rushing to and fro.

And then it happened. The screensaver disappeared and on the screen came a message:

> "Mrs. Thayer, my name is Damodar. As Mr. Walker has already informed you, I am an Adept in the Eastern occult philosophy and, like my fellow-Adepts in our Brotherhood, am able to employ and control the forces of nature in ways that your modern scientists cannot begin to understand, let alone appreciate. But, with regard to your son's premature demise, I have already contacted him in the realm known as *kama loka* and asked him to respond to your question in his own words, which I have received telepathically and am about to make them appear on your computer screen."

Adrienne's eyes were riveted to the screen and her adrenaline began pumping wildly. *Was this really happening? An actual message from my dear Eric?* Before her brain could process the enormity of the situation, words appeared on the screen.

> "Mother, dear. A man who calls himself Damodar contacted me and said I could communicate with you by sending my thoughts to you through him, and he said you wanted to know what I meant in my note about taking your secret with me to my grave. The secret, Mother,

is that I know you had an affair with another man while Dad was still alive, and that I am the product of that liaison. I don't know who the man was, but I never held it against you. As both of us know, Dad was a cruel man in many respects and I know that his philandering hurt you terribly over the years, which angered me greatly, though there was nothing I could do about it.

"You didn't ask the reason for my taking my own life, but I want you to know that it had nothing to do with who sired me. As a result of my gay lifestyle, which you knew nothing about, I had contracted AIDS and these facts, had they become known to you and your social acquaintances, would have caused you untold worry and embarrassment. I wanted to spare you that, while sparing myself the prospect of a painful death.

"But now that I've taken my life, I terribly regret having committed that rash act. I am forced to stay here in a hellish, depressing atmosphere, where I and others who have taken their lives must remain until our normal life spans are attained. All I do is review in my mind over and over again the chain of events that caused me to do what I did. And no matter how hard I try, I can't erase the memory of what I did. It's like being sentenced to a life term in prison.

"I'm truly sorry for all the grief that I have caused you, but perhaps you'll understand I only meant to help. At least now you know what prompted such a drastic act on my part. Forgive me, Mother dear. I love you and miss you very much."

Teardrops trickled down her face as Adrienne read the words on the screen over and over again. Eric was right about her secret. She had met and fallen in love with Arthur Lowenthal, a married lawyer whose firm represented some of Washington's wealthiest corporate clients, including the *Washington Tribune*. They had had a clandestine relationship that led to her pregnancy and Eric's subsequent birth. How her son found out, she didn't know, nor did she care at this stage of her life, now that neither her husband nor her only child was still alive. But, the fact that she had received a direct communication from her dead son was a phenomenon she simply couldn't get over.

Adrienne thought of the years of agony that she went through after Eric took his life. Why? Why did he do it? That was the question that had haunted her and her then-living husband over the years. And now she had her answer, but although she was delighted to hear from Eric personally—and about this she no longer had any doubt—it was an answer that left her with mixed feelings of guilt as well as renewed sorrow.

She pondered the fact that Eric loved her so much that he wanted to protect her from embarrassment about his homosexuality. Oh, there were times that she suspected—his all-male coterie of friends, his occasional effete mannerisms—but even if he had come out of the closet, she believes that she would have stood by him, notwithstanding her concerns about appearances among her social friends. It saddened her to think her son had so little confidence in her that he would rather kill himself than admit to his homosexuality and his contraction of AIDS.

But at least now she had the answer to several key questions, and her years of anguish over Eric's death would cease being the longstanding emotional obsession in her life. Despite the sadness Eric's message produced, it clearly brought about the resolution of several previously unresolved mysteries, and for that she was truly grateful. Bless that Damodar, whoever he was.

After pulling herself together, Adrienne summoned Chet to her office, and with face aglow burst out exuberantly, "Chester, you were right. This Damodar is real and he knows *exactly* what he's talking about when he says he can contact the dead. I know, because he did it for me, and if he can do that, he certainly should be able to inform our readers about what happens in the afterlife."

"Just exactly what did he do for you?" the happily surprised executive editor asked.

"He contacted my son Eric and then had Eric communicate his thoughts to me, which came by e-mail. I don't know how he did it, and I'm not at liberty to tell you what my son said, but it was definitely my Eric, and now a ten-year-old mystery has been solved."

"So, it's happened to you, too?" Walker muttered softly, scratching his head absent-mindedly. He was still trying to assimilate the far-ranging powers Damodar had demonstrated in the conference room.

"Yes!" she replied excitedly, "and now there's absolutely no reason why we shouldn't proceed with the articles. I can see that this person is truly gifted and I would be proud to have his spiritual information on the afterlife appear in the *Tribune*. And what about Mr. Elliott's e-mail communication with his deceased lady friend? I assume you intend to carry that story, too?"

"You bet, that's all part of the package. I'll assign one of our better reporters to interview Dave and we'll give the story the type of coverage it deserves. It may be a little off the beaten path for us, but it's still one hell of a news story."

Adrienne got up and walked to the window, where she gazed absent-mindedly at the White House in the distance while mentally reviewing the financial pros and cons of what she was getting into. *What a story! What a potential moneymaker!* She clasped her hands together, turned towards Chet, and with a happy expression on her face enthusiastically began barking a series of orders to the executive editor, something she had never done before. "Chester, I'd like you to write the introduction to the series, and perhaps you ought to have Ray Tuohy handle whatever editing may be required. I'm not sure he has the necessary background in the Eastern philosophy that Damodar intends to write about, but at least we ought to give him a chance.

"I'm sure we'll take a lot of flak for this. It's certainly not our customary style." She paused for a fraction of a second before adding, "but then again, it might just attract a whole raft of new readers," as her eyes lit up she gave him a knowing wink and cheerful smile.

Chapter 8

When Chet conveyed the news to me a few minutes later, I was re-lieved, but also a little nervous, knowing that my life now would be laid bare before the public in the process of explaining my relationship with Senta. Equally disturbing was the news that Ray would have editing responsibilities over the series of articles, not only because of his personal dislike of me, but because of his unfamiliarity with the Eastern philoso-phy that Damodar espoused. But the matter was out of my hands, so that was that.

I sent a brief e-mail to Damodar about Adrienne's positive response, and he said he was already aware of it, having read her thoughts in the astral. So, at last we were about to participate in an event of monumental, if not historical, significance.

The rest of the day moved along smoothly enough. We had our usual ten o'clock editorial staff meeting, and the editorial page editor gave me a new assignment involving health care legislation, which I began working on by making a few calls to various government agencies. Around three in the af-ternoon, I received a phone call from a chagrined Miriam, who wanted to explain why she repeated our conversations to Ray the other day.

"I'm terribly sorry for what I did, David. I knew that Ray used to be a minister and I thought he might be able to help you cope with the loss of Senta. You looked like you could use some help. Believe me, I had no way of knowing he'd discuss the matter with Chet before you did."

I knew it was a partial truth at best, but I just couldn't figure out why she'd do a thing like that. I smoothed things over with a half-truth of my own. "Never mind, Miriam, I'm glad you told him, because this way eve-rything is out in the open—no sneaky infighting or anything like that. But now, both of you have to accept the fact that Damodar is real and has powers that are prodigious."

She was relieved at my comment. "There's no question about that," she said, "Any idea when the articles will begin?"

"No, not yet, but soon, I'm sure. Possibly in this Friday's Religion & Family Section."

After she hung up, I reflected on what lay ahead. A whole new phase of my life was about to begin and I couldn't help thinking back to the way this all got started. The more I thought about it, the more everything fell into place and it all made perfect sense.

Damodar's meeting with Senta in *kama loka* and his performance to-day was a logical consequence of his eight years of instructing Senta in the Eastern theosophical philosophy by thought transmission. But that, in turn, was directly related to his earlier instruction of young Morya Bennett in the Eastern philosophy—also by thought transmission—while the twelve-year-old Indian spiritual prodigy was a boarder in Senta's home during the winter of 1992.

Damodar was the key to the entire series of happenings. More than that, I now saw that everything that happened did not happen merely by chance, but was actually predestined, including—now that I thought about it—my fateful meeting of Senta in 1968, when the whole concatenation of events involving Damodar began.

Nineteen sixty-eight was a banner year in my life. Not only was it the year that I landed my first job in Washington, but more significantly it was the year I first met Senta Trondson, then thirty-seven and a secretary in the former Department of Health, Education and Welfare (H.E.W.) I was just twenty-nine and had come to Washington seeking employment after graduating from the Columbia School of Journalism and working at a newspaper in upstate New York for several years.

As an only child in a middle-class, orthodox Jewish family, my parents doted on me and hoped I would attend medical or law school when I came of college age, but my interest in writing far overshadowed everything else, so off to journalism school I went. After graduating from Columbia, a fortuitous opening at a small newspaper in a town sixty miles north of New York City landed me my first job as a professional writer. I learned a lot on that job, but after several years I felt stifled by the provinciality and the absence of a social life in that part of the Hudson Valley. An older writer at the newspaper suggested Washington, D.C. as a more appropriate setting for boosting the career of a budding writer like me, and in June of 1968 I took his advice and headed for the nation's capitol.

A Death Interrupted

I was lucky enough to land a job almost immediately as an Assistant Public Information Officer at H.E.W. but it wasn't until the Department's Christmas party in December of 1968 that I chanced to meet Senta. I thought she was the most beautiful woman I had ever seen and I couldn't take my eyes off her. Senta had the demure look and facial features of actress Vivien Leigh. Her clear alabaster skin was so delicate it was almost translucent, with no blemishes of any kind. She had a spontaneous, infectious smile, and her bright blue eyes sparkled when she beamed one of those delightful smiles. I found her natural ash blonde hair particularly appealing, with soft curls perfectly framing her lovely oval face, and a chignon on top that gave her the stately appearance of a queen. And because she was a modern dancer who had worked out daily for years, she had the shapely legs and trained body of a dancer, which explained her elegant poise and manner of walking.

I was smitten by this Scandinavian beauty and after I got to know her, learned that her husband, Jon, had died of leukemia in 1965, and that occurrence had necessitated her seeking gainful employment, which led to her job at H.E.W. I fell madly in love with her and courted her ardently for the next six months.

During that period, I saw her frequently—not only during working hours but practically every evening. Our lunch hours usually were spent on short drives to Hains Point in nearby East Potomac Park, which overlooks the Potomac River and National Airport. It was a beautiful oasis in the middle of the nation's capitol where the quiet was interrupted periodically by the sound of jets taking off from nearby National Airport. During those lunch breaks, we would talk about every conceivable subject while enjoying the peaceful and relaxing atmosphere of the park and observing the yachts and sailboats slowly gliding by on the calm waters of the Potomac.

Though I didn't know it when I first met her, Senta had several other ardent suitors, all men of substance who were her age or older, but while I courted her she managed to keep them pretty much at bay. Why she settled on me, a much younger man, was not clear at first, but one day, after we had known each other about six months, she clarified it for me.

"I knew the minute I met you, *herzele*, that we were fated to be together in this lifetime because I saw your face in a vision when I was a young woman, and I knew we had been soul mates in a prior lifetime." Senta was the first person who ever spoke to me about reincarnation and things like that, but I didn't doubt the veracity or sincerity of her statement for one moment. So long as she loved me, whatever the reason, I was in seventh heaven.

Our initial friendship gradually developed into a more intimate relationship that steadily increased in intensity and passion. This was not only to my liking, but apparently satisfied some unfulfilled sexual need in Senta as well. "You're a tiger when it comes to lovemaking," she said laughingly one night while we were locked in a passionate sexual embrace, "and that's what I love about you." Senta didn't like bland, wishy-washy people, least of all men, especially where matters of sex were concerned.

By June of 1969, barely six months after we met, I asked her to marry me, but she turned me down on the spot. "I love you, David," she said, "but I'm afraid marriage is out of the question."

"Is it because of the age difference?" I asked. The suddenness of her rejection—showing that she had already given it considerable thought—was dismaying as well as surprising.

"No, darling, that's not the reason, at least not the main reason." She pointed out how the aging process differs for men and women and how women lose their looks faster than men do. More importantly, however, she brought up the subject of independence and self-sufficiency. The Women's Liberation Movement was picking up steam at the time and Senta enjoyed the thought of being on her own and doing things for herself once her husband died. As she put it, "I don't relish the idea of being married just for the sake of being married, especially since I never wanted children, and I've gotten used to the privacy and independence I've learned to enjoy since Jon's death.

"And last but not least, I want to have more time to devote to the study of Theosophy, which has become a paramount interest of mine over the past several years. I'm too serious a person to take marriage responsibilities lightly, and I know that I couldn't give my all to a marriage while devoting so much of my time to my theosophical studies. So, those are the reasons why I must decline your flattering proposal, darling. However, I would love to—and hope to—share my life with you as much as I can."

I was understandably disheartened by her abrupt rejection of my marriage proposal, but I understood and respected the reasons for her decision. At least she hadn't rejected me entirely, and I was happy to hear her say that she wanted to share the rest of her life with me, even if we weren't married. We also discussed the possibility of marriage at a later date if her feelings changed, and that made me feel better.

Senta's interest in Theosophy had begun some years earlier and, by the time I met her, had become the philosophical cornerstone of her life, growing in importance after the death of her husband. Her sincerity about her beliefs was deeply instilled. She had told me she had been raised, from the age of eight to the age of sixteen, in a Lutheran orphanage in Westchester County, New York, where the schooling by her German-speaking teachers stressed the importance of spiritual values, moral character, discipline and personal responsibility. She approached her acceptance of Theosophy with that same sense of discipline and responsibility.

Senta and I grew closer with each passing year. Even though we did not live together—she remained in her duplex on Tunlaw Road, while I kept my Kalorama Road apartment—we shared our lives in most other respects essentially as husband and wife. We saw each other almost daily, ate dinner together, either at her home or at various area restaurants, went to the movies, attended events at the Kennedy Center, and took occasional weekend automobile jaunts to nearby places, like Rehoboth, Annapolis and Virginia Beach. We always arranged to take our annual vacations together, and especially enjoyed our vacations in Hilton Head, Bermuda and the Virgin Islands.

In 1973, as a result of professional contacts I had made through my government job at H.E.W., I was hired as a junior reporter on the Metro beat for the *Washington Tribune*. After that, Senta and I saw each other a little less during working hours, but by then we were so deeply in love that it really didn't matter.

Apart from her exquisite beauty, it was Senta's deep interest in Theosophy that intrigued me the most. As a not-too-observant Jew, after I was bar mitzvahed I had paid little attention to formal religion as I was growing up, attending religious services only on the obligatory Jewish High Holy Days. But, once she introduced me to Theosophy, I couldn't absorb it fast enough, and after I acquired the fundamental literature and began studying on my own, the two of us would talk about theosophical concepts endlessly.

The study of Theosophy seemed to me to be simply the continuation of learning I had begun in an earlier life, but it caused nothing but heartache when I tried to discuss it with my parents. And because of their negative receptivity, I not only stopped talking about Theosophy with them, but also avoided talking about the subject with my friends and my associates at the newspaper. As far as everyone there knew, I was simply a not-too-observant Jew. On the other hand, while I was an avid student of Theosophy, I never became an advocate or outspoken proponent of the philosophy. This didn't please Senta, who felt this was a character flaw in me, which disappointed her.

She chastised me, saying, "I know that because of your position at the *Tribune* you don't want to be considered a religious fanatic, or someone caught up in the latest fad of New Age spirituality. But certainly, others at the paper must express their personal beliefs at times, so why be so hesitant to mention Theosophy when the occasion arises? Don't you realize that by not speaking out you are retarding your own growth spiritually?"

She was absolutely right. I could have been more open and forthright with my colleagues and friends, but I was always afraid of opening a Pandora's Box. My parents were a totally different story. They held it against Senta for steering me away from Judaism, although I frankly never felt I was drawn away *from* anything. I did feel being drawn *to* the ancient wisdom of the East, as expressed in the theosophical literature.

Senta and I both thought it was quite a coincidence, and a good omen, that she had the same birthday as H.P.B., August 11th. While my birthday, November 17th, coincided with the founding of the Theosophical Movement and was one of the three "birth" days of the Dhyân Chohans, the host of living intelligences and powers that theosophists believe keep watch over mankind's spiritual growth.

"The other two important dates are February 19th and March 7th," she told me, "and in *The Secret Doctrine*, H.P.B. said that the trained occultist with knowledge of the astrological aspects of the constellations is able to perform extraordinary magical feats and phenomena on those four special days."

An event of major significance in both of our lives came in late 1992, when Senta, who by then had retired from her government job, was asked to become the custodian and caretaker of twelve-year-old Morya Bennett. Morya was a young Hindu spiritual prodigy whose parents had died in a tragic airplane disaster while the family was en route from India to America. Following that tragedy, his great-uncle, New Jersey lawyer Arthur Bennett, became the boy's legal guardian.

A Death Interrupted

Before leaving India, Morya had been accepted as an exchange student at the private Hopewell Friends School in Washington. Thus, Bennett undertook to search for a suitable place for the boy to live and someone to care for him while attending school. A lawyer friend of his from Washington, whose wife was a friend of Senta, suggested her as an ideal choice for the job, knowing Senta's spiritual interests and inclinations. After Bennett met with the two of us, the custodial arrangement was made, with my full blessing.

Neither Senta nor I knew at the time that Mahatma Damodar had been Morya's teacher on spiritual and philosophical subjects in India from the time the boy was seven, nor did we appreciate just how spiritually advanced Morya was until it was brought to our attention quite coincidentally some months later. That happened as a result of a chance meeting and conversation Morya had with the Dalai Lama in a hallway of the White House, a conversation that impressed His Holiness enormously and had later life-changing consequences for Morya. That chance White House meeting occurred while Morya was at the presidential mansion attending an informal dinner at the invitation of President Charles Eastman and his wife, Andrea—an invitation extended at the instigation of the Eastman's twelve-year-old son, Zachary, who was Morya's closest friend at Hopewell.

Senta learned about Damodar's role as Morya's guru shortly prior to the boy's return to India in the spring of 1993 for the purpose of renewing his spiritually significant connection with the Dalai Lama and Mahayana Buddhism. It had been arranged that he would live with his maternal grandparents while in India. On the day of Morya's departure, accompanied by his great-uncle Arthur—a day Senta told me she would never forget—Damodar appeared in person to her at New York's Kennedy International Airport, just after she had waved goodbye to Morya and Arthur. With heavy heart and eyes full of tears, she had started walking toward the terminal exit.

As she described the scene to me, suddenly she heard a cheerful, resonant baritone voice ring out, "Come, come, my child, no need to be depressed. We have important work to do." When she turned to see who spoke, she said she knew instantly it must be Damodar, even though she had never met him before. She said he was there in the flesh, tall, with a clean-shaven, swarthy face and wearing a western-style suit and a royal blue turban as he came alongside her smiling broadly. Seeing his majestic figure and hearing his strong, clear voice immediately snapped her out of her sadness and changed her mood to one of utter joy.

During their brief meeting at Kennedy, Damodar explained to her how she should set aside half an hour each morning for meditation, during which time he promised to answer any questions on Theosophy or other spiritual matters she might relay to him by thought transmission. Then, he presented her with the silver talisman that he had given to Morya years earlier and which had remained in Morya's possession up to that day. After rubbing it briefly between his palms and handing it to Senta, he told her that the talisman contained a mysterious magnetic power that would not only protect her from physical harm, but would enable the two of them to keep in close communication from that day forward.

And so, from the spring of 1993, and for the next eight years, Senta received spiritual instruction via thought transmission from Mahatma Damodar on a regular basis. I, of course, was aware of the unique nature of her studies throughout this period, but both of us were sworn to secrecy about Damodar's role in all of this. After her death in August, I occasionally wondered if there would be any significant consequence of those studies with Damodar for her in the afterlife, and now everything seemed to fall into place.

Things were starting to move rapidly, now that the ostensible impediments to the publishing of the series of articles by Damodar had been overcome. But other less obvious impediments lay just around the corner.

Chapter 9

T he Religion & Family Section of the *Washington Tribune* normally appeared in the Friday edition of the paper, so Wednesday morning, when Chet asked me if it would be possible to get an article from Damodar by Thursday, I told him I was pretty sure that would be possible. Where Damodar was concerned, *anything* was possible.

I sent an e-mail to Senta, bringing her up-to-date on what had transpired here at the newspaper. I told her about the anticipated arrival of the first article by Damodar and then asked her some questions about things that I myself wanted to know more about—tons of questions.

"What did you remember about the last hours and moments before your death? Did you experience much physical pain? How would you describe the physical and spiritual transition from life to death? Did you recall reviewing your past-life experiences at the moment of death? How and when did you first become aware that you had entered *kama loka*? How would you describe it? Could you see and communicate with others in that realm, including predeceased members of your family and possibly others, including well known persons who had died before you did? Are you aware of other non-human entities in *kama loka*, and if so, what are they like?Has your theosophical background and learning been helpful during and since the transition to the afterlife?"

I basically wanted to know everything that happened to her and only hoped she could tell me any of it at all. Senta's reply, which came a few minutes later, was replete with information.

"Darling, I will try to answer your questions as best I can. As to my physical pain, no, the morphine took care of that, but I can clearly remember the feeling of slipping away from physical life in those last few moments, and I knew you were near me, holding my hand. There was no sense of regret or fear. Beyond that, I cannot recall any specific thoughts, except my undying love for you.

"Once my stomach cancer was diagnosed, I sensed my appointed time on earth in this lifetime was fast coming to an end, and I had no desire to engage in heroic efforts to prolong it. That's why I purposely refused radiation or any other life-prolonging measures, only taking morphine to ease the pain, which it did. I hope you haven't been too burdened by the paperwork and physical running around necessitated by my death."

As I read these words I was relieved to know that she had no pain at the moment of death. The price we'd paid for that was her inability to speak coherently for any length of time those last few days because morphine clouded her mind. But at least I had been able to hold her hand and be with her when she died, and I'm glad she was aware of that. I continued reading.

"Yes, I clearly remember the extensive life review. It was like looking at a videotape of my life running backwards very fast. I could see in full detail all my acts, words and thoughts over my entire lifetime, even some passing thoughts and conversations I had when I was still a child. And I must tell you, I was not altogether proud of what I saw.

"There were many things I know I have to correct in my next lifetime. I'm glad that you saw to it that my body remained undisturbed for several hours after my life ended, so that my brain could process all those flashbacks and give my soul a chance to evaluate them."

Senta always was honest in her self-criticism, so these last words were not too surprising. And as for the quiet time she referred to, I had made sure that no one was allowed to disturb her body for nearly ten hours after she died, neither the hospice people nor anyone else. H.P.B. had written about the importance of that on various occasions, and it was nice to see Senta confirming the importance of quiet in those hours immediately after death.

"And when that review was over, I guess I simply went to sleep. When I awoke, and I don't know how much time had elapsed, I became aware that I no longer had a physical body and no longer felt any pain. The transition from life to death was merely a separation of my physical body from my consciousness, somewhat like the way people have described their near-death or out-of-body experiences. I was fully conscious, but on a different plane of existence, and because of my theosophical training, I knew it had to be *kama loka*."

Lucky girl! Her theosophical training had paved the way for her understanding not only what had happened, but also where she was. Would that everyone had such insights after passing out of earth life. No fear whatsoever. I read on.

"From a physical standpoint, darling, you know that *kama loka* is merely a state of consciousness, so unless and until I create a thought form of the specific locale I want to be in, such as a beautiful landscape or ocean scene, or in a concert hall, I am simply in a void, neither pleasant nor unpleasant, just a colorless void. When I communicate with you, I visualize how you might look in your apartment, for example, and that's what I see in my mind's eye. The magnetic thread that binds me to you in the astral makes the process so much easier.

"As to my ability to see other individuals who have predeceased me, unless they are still here in *kama loka*, I would have no way of seeing or contacting them. Since arriving here, I have been able to see the transparent faces—but not the bodies—of others I've known who have predeceased me, people like Jon, my sister Santra, my brothers Artie and Hank, Isabelle, Mr. Perzeoli, Mildred Jackendorf, and Margaret James. As to those who are still in this state of consciousness, all I have to do is visualize them in my mind's eye and there they are, their astrals, that is. Although I know intuitively that I can communicate with any of them telepathically, so far I haven't been inclined to contact anyone in particular, at least not yet. It just doesn't seem as pressing a need or desire as I had assumed it might be. I sense them here—and that is satisfying in itself."

"On the other hand, famous writers, politicians, musicians, scientists and entertainers who have been dead a long time, people like H.P.B. or Judge, for example, or

Eli P. Bernzweig

Louisa May Alcott, Chopin, Albert Einstein, Franklin D. Roosevelt, Rudolph Valentino or Isadora Duncan are not within my ken.

"I have no way of knowing specifically what others in *kama loka* are doing, but I assume they are working out their particular spiritual destinies just as I will be doing when this experiment is over. Suicides, both young and old—and there appear to be lots of them here—are simply in an in-between waiting state until their natural life spans are reached. You can tell they are unhappy, angry and intensely frustrated after they realize that, even though they've lost their physical bodies, they're alive in all other respects and still have their earthly passions and desires. They all seem terribly distressed.

"The astrals of accident victims also are everywhere, but they seem to be more dazed than angry or frustrated, like the suicides just mentioned. Still, they, too, must remain here in *kama loka* until their natural life spans have been reached. As you know, according to the teachings, the Dhyân Chohans protect the egos of innocent victims of violent forms of death in a special mysterious way during their sojourns in *kama loka*.

"I know from the theosophical teaching that those here in *kama loka* who have died normal deaths are involved in attempting to rid their souls of their earthly passions and desires before shedding their astral bodies once and for all and moving on to *devachan*. I have to undergo that process myself, but as you know, all that has been put on hold for me while our project is underway, so I really don't know how long I will remain here in *kama loka*, perhaps a few weeks or months. I really don't know.

"As I mentioned before, since there is such a strong, magnetic bond between you and me in the astral, I am aware of what you are doing and how you are feeling practically all of the time, but I am not aware of other events on earth or what's happening to other people who are still living, nor do I particularly care. And no, I have no absolute sense of time here, not unless either you or Damodar brings it to my attention."

68

A Death Interrupted

I recall various writers on the subject saying that the spirits of deceased persons in the world beyond are more like centers of energy rather than human forms, so here was Senta's confirmation of those non-physical states.

The reference to Mr. Perzeoli was interesting. He had been the chicken farmer who brought his farm fresh eggs to Senta each week and always enjoyed spending time talking with her about life in general. I recall her once saying to me, "Mr. Perzeoli is a simple chicken farmer who can hardly speak English, but he has more true spirituality and understands more what life is all about than most members of the clergy. He's a pure delight to talk to, and I look forward to his arrival each week." I was pleased to learn that she has already seen Mr. Perzeoli's astral in *kama loka*.

I was curious as to why Senta hadn't yet tried to contact either her late husband or her sister, Santra, but assumed she had her reasons. The message continued:

> "I sense a multitude of other non-human entities or spiritual forms about me, but I'm not sure who or what they are. I suspect that many are the elementals that H.P.B. and Mr. Judge occasionally spoke about. They have a whole variety of shapes, as you would expect, and seem to be more like vibrational centers of energy. That's all that I can say about them, darling, except that some have lovely bright translucent appearances, while others appear dark and hideous."

This was fascinating information because Senta and I had talked about the elementals from time to time, and neither of us was entirely sure what role they played in the activities of living persons, as well as those who have died, although we both knew they were extremely important. H.P.B. had said that they were creatures evolved in the four kingdoms or elements—earth, air, fire, and water—called gnomes, sylphs, salamanders and undines by the Kabbalists and the Eastern mystics. And she said that these forces, among other things, were the servile agents of Adepts and occultists as well as of black magicians, but only infrequently elaborated on the specific roles of these entities.

> "You also asked whether my theosophical background has been of help during my transition from physical life to the afterlife, and the answer to that is a resounding 'yes.' I've known for years what to expect in

the afterlife, so from my perspective everything that is happening here is proper and orderly. No surprises, none at all. And it is this knowledge—that we have had many bodies and have died and been reborn many times—that sustains me now. You know, of course, it is this sort of information that Damodar wants your readers to know, too. I think that answers most of your questions, darling.

"I am very happy that your editor agreed to publish Damodar's articles. The articles should do much to show readers that death is not something to be feared. And now, my dearest, how are you holding up? I am so proud of you for dealing with your editor so firmly and steadfastly."

I replied that I was managing all right so far, but that I worried about having to drag our personal lives into the limelight. "We've both been pretty private persons, dearest, and I had no idea that our personal lives would become so public. Are you sure you don't mind?"

"Not when I think about the relative good that it will do for so many people who are desperate for knowledge about their deceased loved ones, where they are, how they are faring, and so forth. Besides, I'm already dead and beyond the point of being embarrassed. Our love survived thirty-three wonderful years, and there's nothing we have to be ashamed of. In any event, you can decide what items of a personal nature you might want to withhold from the public."

She was right, of course, and I told her so before signing off and getting started on my latest editorial assignment. Although it was not his custom, Chet Walker attended our regular ten o'clock staff meeting to explain to the eight editorial staff members what led up to the series of articles that would be forthcoming from Damodar.

He started with my receipt of Senta's first e-mail, followed by the fact that Damodar had demonstrated his occult powers, without giving any of the details. Nor did he mention Adrienne's personal contact with Damodar or what she had learned about her son, Eric, through Damodar's intervention.

But he was definitely upbeat and did his best to explain who Damodar was and how I would receive the articles in e-mails sent to me on my computer. "This is a sort of experiment," he said, "one that the boss-lady herself has authorized with full knowledge of the likely consequences. So, let's keep open minds and see how things work out. Ray Tuohy will handle the editing."

He turned to me and said, "I'm going to have Lou Garza handle the cover story, Dave, so you can expect to hear from him shortly." Then he asked Sol Berman, the editorial board's administrative aide, to keep tabs on incoming calls, letters and e-mails from readers, and keep him informed daily. "Otherwise, let's just go about our normal activities. We're still the top newspaper in the nation's capitol and one of the best in the nation, so news is, and always will be, our principal focus."

With that, he left, and as he did so a hushed silence came over the room. The air was charged with electricity as my fellow writers tried to digest the incredible news. Eyes began darting back and forth and a few whispers were exchanged, soon followed by a deluge of questions from my colleagues, none of whom previously knew anything about my e-mails from Senta or my long-time interest in Theosophy. To put it mildly, they were flabbergasted. They asked me: How did I react when the first e-mail arrived? How did I know for sure that it was Senta? How did she describe the afterlife? Their questions came faster and faster, with increasing excitement in their voices and I barely had time to answer one question before another was posed.

Sol Berman, the only other Jewish person on the editorial staff, and a friend of many years, seemed more perplexed than the others after Chet explained what was about to happen, and he began asking some probing questions. "I knew you did a lot of theosophical research for your first book, David, but you never said you were personally involved in Theosophy. How long has this been going on?"

"Ever since I met Senta, Sol, over thirty years now."

From the look on his face, I could see that my stocky, bespectacled friend was surprised. He and I often lunched together over the years and this was the first time I had ever mentioned my long interest in Theosophy. His neck and face reddened and he looked genuinely hurt as he spoke. "How come you never said anything to me about it before? Are you saying that you've abandoned your Jewish faith and heritage?"

This is where it got sticky, so I measured my words carefully. "No Sol, Theosophy isn't so much a religion as it is a philosophy, a very spiritual way of looking at life . . . and death, too. I guess you could say that

I'm a Jewish Theosophist. There's no need for me to abandon Judaism, and certainly not my Jewish cultural heritage. It's just that there are aspects of the religion that I long ago refused to accept."

"Like what?" he asked, in a challenging tone of voice.

"Like the concept of a personal God, Sol. I can't accept the idea of an anthropomorphic deity one prays to for forgiveness or for achieving one's particularly personal desires. That's probably the biggest hang-up I have with Judaism—holding out God as someone with human attributes who is passionate and vengeful and dispenses justice arbitrarily."

My Jewish colleague—born and raised in New York in a Jewish home just like I had been—looked thoroughly confused, and began shaking his head. "So, you're saying that you don't believe in God anymore . . . that is, if you ever did?"

By now, the editorial staff was an absorbed captive audience to the spontaneous give-and-take of our impromptu theological discussion. They listened in rapt attention as the two of us set forth our respective views. "I'm merely saying that I don't believe in an anthropomorphic God, some omniscient entity endowed with human qualities to whom one prays and who sits in judgment on each of us, rewarding us or penalizing us for our good or bad deeds.

"Sure, I believe in God, Sol, but not some almighty supernormal being. To me, God is an impersonal Principle—life itself in all its manifested forms. In other words, God is in you, in me, in nature, the sky, the stars, and in every animal, plant and stone. The divine spark of God is the innermost self of every one of us. And Theosophy makes it absolutely clear that the only rewards and punishments we get during our lives are those coming to us under the inexorable law of karma."

A pained look drifted across his face as my obviously disturbed friend asked, "So you're saying you don't believe in religion at all?"

I gave a half-smile while shaking my head and replied, "No, I didn't say that, Sol. Religion is fine so long as it doesn't get all screwed up with dogma and ritual and the sanctimonious pretense that some external entity is going to look out for us and solve our problems. I believe that religions can and should teach morals, ethics and respect for our fellow man, but after that, the rest is up to each individual. You can't go through life relying on a theological crutch. We have to take some responsibility for ourselves."

Sol's face reflected his obvious dismay, and while several others nodded in agreement with my comment, most remained silent listeners.

Either because of the pressures of time or the awkwardness of the situation, Sol threw his hands up in the air and decided to end the discussion. He was still shaking his head, and as I looked at my obviously hurt friend, I felt both disappointed and saddened by his response. On the other hand, I realized that for the first time I had confronted one of my biggest shortcomings head on—my reluctance to talking openly about my views on Theosophy. And I felt good about it, very good.

When Sol was finished, the others were relieved to change the subject. They wanted to know a lot more about Senta, so I filled them in on the details as best I could. They treated me like a celebrity, which made me feel a little self-conscious, but their curiosity was understandable.

Ten minutes later, when I was back at my desk, one of the paper's more experienced local-news reporters, Lou Garza, came in to interview me for the background story that was to appear in the Friday morning edition. Lou was a hulk of a man, balding and in his early fifties, probably a good thirty pounds over his glory days of college football. His ill-fitting clothes and generally unkempt appearance belied his underlying intelligence. For a man of his intimidating size, he had an ingratiating way about him. I always liked Lou and respected his writing talents and his no non-nonsense approach to journalism.

Taking down notes in a steno's spiral pad, his preliminary questions were pretty straightforward, and I gave him all the relevant details about my personal relationship with Senta, including how, when and where we met, along with her physical appearance, her background in dance, and similar information. I also informed him that it was she who introduced me to Theosophy many years ago.

Then, I gave him a copy of her initial e-mail and the long e-mail I had just received containing her responses to my specific questions about the afterlife in *kama loka*, telling him, "This information should give you a pretty good picture of how Senta made the transition from life to the world beyond."

Lou quietly read the e-mails and then commented, "Yeah, this is fascinating stuff. But we'll need more, David. Our readers will be clamoring for all kinds of information about this special lady, so I'd like to give them something more personal, you know, the human interest angle."

That's just what I was afraid of, more personal information about Senta and our private lives. But I could see Lou's point, and Senta had already given me the green light, so I asked him to fire away.

"Let's start with her education first. What type of schooling did Senta have?"

"Other than the schooling she received at the orphanage, which would be the equivalent of a high school education, she had just one year of secretarial training, and that was it."

"Tell us more about her life at the orphanage."

"Well, it was an orphanage—which she always referred to as the 'Home'—just outside of New York City run by the Lutheran Church. Her father placed her there, along with two of her brothers and her older sister, after their mother died giving birth to her youngest brother. During the eight years she was there, Senta said she learned from the Lutheran nuns and pastors all about moral and ethical behavior, about truth telling, and reverence for all sentient beings. She said the orphanage played an extremely important role in teaching her how to judge human character and how to act ethically."

"How did she feel about being sent to the orphanage? And how did she get along with the members of her family—her father, sister and brothers—before the children were sent to the orphanage and after they came out?"

Senta had never expressed her personal feelings to me about being sent to the Home except to say that she, her sister and brothers all were confused and terrified at first, but eventually adapted to the new environment. Lou's question made me wonder why Senta rarely mentioned such matters. I responded to the question as well as I could.

"Senta always spoke about her sister and brothers in affectionate terms, at least when they were at the Home. As to their relationship afterwards, I'm not sure. I know she had problems with her sister Santra much later in life, primarily due to differences in their value systems. Senta saw life through a moral prism that few people could measure up to. I'm not sure how much contact she had with her brothers after they left the Home."

"What about her father? How did she get along with him after leaving the orphanage?"

I was stumped again. Senta seldom spoke about her father. She did tell me that he was a master plumber who had parlayed his plumbing profits into real estate—apartment buildings and the like—but eventually lost everything during the Depression. I answered the question honestly, "I'm not sure, Lou. Senta rarely talked about her father or her relationship with him after she left the Home."

I made a mental note to ask Senta about some of these matters in a future e-mail.

Lou nodded and then continued his questioning. "Since she started out as a Lutheran, how did she get involved with Theosophy?"

"That happened in 1960, right here in Washington, when she chanced to meet a woman by the name of Margaret James, who had been a practicing theosophist for many years. From their initial conversation, Margaret could see that Senta was spiritually quite advanced. She gave her a lot of theosophical literature, which Senta read voraciously, and she took her to several meetings of the local United Lodge of Theosophists. After Margaret died, Senta continued her theosophical studies and decided that she had found what she was looking for in the spiritual sense. When we met in 1968, she introduced me to Theosophy and I'll be eternally grateful to her for having done so."

Lou again nodded but I could see he wanted considerably more intimate personal information. His probing continued. "How would you describe Senta's personality, David? I mean, what were her likes and dislikes. How did she spend her time? How did she get along with people? Give us a more rounded picture of your lady friend."

I thought for a moment before responding to the balding giant. "Well, Lou, she was good at just about everything she undertook. Her modern dance technique, for example, was noticed by Martha Graham early on, which is why she invited Senta to be in her special five o'clock class for professional dancers. And Martha's colleague, the great dance educator and composer, Louis Horst, also admired Senta's dance technique—enough to warrant his making a special trip to Washington to watch her perform for him personally."

That's good. That's the kind of stuff I'm looking for," said the savvy reporter, with considerably more enthusiasm than he showed a few moments earlier. "What else? What can you tell me about Senta from the social or behavioral standpoint?"

"Well, let's see. From the dietary standpoint, she used salt and butter to excess and was flat out addicted to coffee—had to have her three or four cups of black coffee every day or else she would begin to experience withdrawal symptoms.

"On the other hand, despite those few idiosyncracies she was one of the early health food addicts and a devout follower of the early nutrition pioneers like Adele Davis and Carlton Fredericks, as well as Dr. Linus Pauling. She was forever trying new combinations of health food supplements to improve her health."

"How about her weight? Did she have a problem there, too?"

"No, Senta had a marvelous figure and never had to worry about her weight. As a modern dancer, she worked out daily in her studio, so weight was never a problem."

Lou tried a different tack. "How did Senta get along with people? Did she have any unusual social or behavioral characteristics?"

I could see where Lou was going with this, but there really wasn't anything to conceal. "No, most people who met her liked Senta immediately. She had a spontaneous smile and people warmed up to her quickly. But she was a stern judge of people's character and was the strongest-willed person I ever met. She could get angry with someone who lied or was a hypocrite or was discourteous or whose moral character was deficient. And she rebuked them right on the spot, with no pulling of punches.

I smiled slightly before telling him a few of her foibles. "She wouldn't allow anyone to see her without makeup and, without exaggeration, she was a motor moron—couldn't master anything mechanical, like electric can openers, TV remotes, ATM machines, and so on. By the way, even though she loved music, she couldn't hum or sing a note, not even 'Happy Birthday.'

Lou changed the subject. "What were her aesthetic interests? You've already mentioned music and dancing. Anything else you can tell us?"

"That's an easy one. Senta was an aesthete through and through. She designed and sewed her own clothes, made her own drapes and throw pillows, and had a heightened sensitivity to all aspects of beauty. That included such things as home decoration, clothing style and fashion, jewelry and perfumes, and flower arranging—and what a varied, expensive collection of artificial flowers she had! But, as I said, music and modern dance were her major aesthetic outlets. She listened to classical music whenever she was at home."

"Well, that gives me a little more to go on," Lou said, "and now I'd better start working on the story. I've got a short deadline." He asked if he could borrow the framed photo of Senta and me that sat on the credenza behind my desk. As I handed it to him, I told him that it was taken while we were on vacation in Bermuda in 1998.

A Death Interrupted

Garza then left to draft the bizarre news story of the *Washington Tribune* editorial writer who was contacted directly by his lost love from the world beyond. There would be no turning back now.

Chapter 10

S enta realized that David had raised several questions in his last communication that she found hard to deal with. The one that troubled her most was his question about her relationship with her father before she went to the Home and what it was like afterward.

There wasn't much good she could say about her father. After her mother died in childbirth, her father—who at the time was well off financially—showed little interest in raising his five little ones, and farmed them out to various relatives in the Brooklyn area, begrudgingly paying miserly amounts to help with their support.

But the biggest hurt of all came in the summer of 1939, when he told Senta, Santra and the two oldest boys that he was taking them in the car to spend a vacation week at their great-aunt's country home in Westchester County.

"Pack some clothes and dress nicely for the trip to Tante Sophie's," he had said, and they all looked forward with joy to the change of scene to Westchester County, especially during that particularly hot Brooklyn summer.

But they never went to Tante Sophie's. He took them instead to the Lutheran orphanage, where they were to remain for periods ranging from four to ten years, varying with their ages. The initial shock eventually wore off, once the children realized they had been hoodwinked into the institutionalization, but eight-year-old Senta could never forgive her father for the deceitful manner in which he tricked her and her siblings into entering the orphanage.

And her feelings about him after she left the orphanage didn't change. By then, he had lost his apartment houses in bankruptcy, had turned to drink and had become a womanizer, seldom spending much time with his children. Once they left the Home, most of them, including Senta, eventually found jobs of their own and didn't have to depend upon their father for any sort of financial support.

Mulling over these events rekindled Senta's feelings of betrayal and abandonment by her father and this was why she had said nothing to

David about him when he asked in the e-mail. She simply had no desire to contact and communicate with her father in *kama loka*. His callous abandonment of her and her siblings was something she could not forgive—not yet, at least. Then, her husband Jon's premature death from leukemia only nine years after they were married left a gaping hole in Senta's life, one which she interpreted as another, even if involuntary, form of abandonment. First her mother and then the two most important men in her life were no longer around to give her love, guidance or financial support.

The more she thought about it, the more she began to appreciate that she had built a psychological wall around herself, especially when it came to her relationships with men. She had to admit that her reluctance to marry David, although ostensibly for valid reasons, was in large part due to her fear of abandonment by yet another important man in her life. She made a mental note of this introspective observation and determined to explore its ramifications further while in *kama loka*.

Her sister Alexandra—who preferred, and in fact insisted on, being called Santra—was an entirely different story. Senta got along reasonably well with her older sister as they were growing up, with one major exception: Santra didn't share Senta's moralistic views on life, and they quarreled about this from time to time. Four years before Senta's death, she and her sister had had a major falling out, which occurred while Santra was visiting Senta in her Washington home.

The argument related to Santra's thirty-year-old son, Alan, a bachelor living at home with his mother whose effete, narcissistic behavior and excessive preoccupation with material things irritated Senta enormously. From time to time, she had chastised Alan directly about these matters, but on this particular occasion, she lectured her sister: "Why do you let him carry on like that, Santra? Most men his age, unless they're openly gay—which I know he isn't—either are already married or at least show some interest in dating women. And if not that, they seem more interested in sports or other masculine pursuits. But not your precious Alan. From what I can see, he spends all his free time in antique stores, poking around for furniture, paintings and objets d'art and you've encouraged him in this direction over the years, when you should have been pointing out to him that he's materialistic, prissy mama's boy."

"I don't see what business it is of yours to criticize Alan's marital status or his interest in acquiring nice things," Santra replied, plainly displaying her deep resentment. "Besides, he's my son, not yours, and if I want any advice from you, I'll ask for it."

Senta threw her hands up into the air in disgust. "Well, if I can't tell my own sister how she's ruining her son's life, then I think our relationship is meaningless."

As a result of this conversation, Santra cut short her visit and left Washington in a huff. The two stopped speaking to each other and had had no other contact for the next three years, right up to the time of Santra's death in 1999.

As she reflected on this, Senta realized that maybe she had been too hard on her older sister, and she mentally determined to communicate with her in *kama loka* and see if she could make up with her. She also determined to contact Jon, to explain her irrational feelings of abandonment upon his death, and to ask for his understanding and forgiveness, as well.

The more she thought about it, Senta resolved to contact a number of her predeceased relatives, provided they were still in *kama loka*, to ask forgiveness for hurtful statements she made to them or hostile or angry attitudes she exhibited while they were alive. These were among the various incidents that disturbed her when viewing the scenes of her past life at the moment of her death.

But, her father presented another problem entirely. She wasn't quite sure whether she was ready to forgive his callous behavior towards her and her siblings when they were young children. She'd have to think about that a little more before deciding whether to contact him.

Chapter 11

Thursday was Thanksgiving Day and, while still at my apartment in the morning, I received a phone call from my eighty-seven-year-old mother, who I hadn't spoken to in over a month. When Senta was alive, my mother invariably invited the two of us for Thanksgiving dinner at my parents' Riverside Drive apartment, but we both knew that my mother's invitation to Senta was more pro forma than sincere, which is why Senta always declined the invitation. So, our usual routine was to drive to Manhattan, where Senta would spend the Thanksgiving weekend at her sister Santra's apartment on West 86th Street, while I would spend the Thanksgiving holiday with my parents.

As a first-generation American brought up by immigrant orthodox Jewish parents, my mother, Rivka Eliashar—the family name I changed to Elliott after I graduated from Columbia—resented my interest in Theosophy from the moment I first mentioned it to her. She resented Senta even more, not merely because she was a *shiksa*, but because she got me involved with Theosophy.

"Theosophy, Shmeosophy," she taunted, when I first mentioned the subject to her. "You're a Jew, Duvid, and always will be. Why do you waste your time on this Theosophy nonsense?"

Mom insisted on calling me Duvid, the Yiddish pronunciation of my name, or Duvidel, little David, especially when lecturing me. And it was this limited, parochial point of view—which, to a lesser extent, also represented the view of my father—that had created a rift between us over the intervening years, a rift that was palpable and hurtful. At the beginning, I made a stab at explaining some theosophical doctrines and philosophy to Mom and Pop, but to no avail. Their orthodox Jewish upbringing simply wouldn't countenance any other points of view, so after the initial unproductive attempts, I simply gave up trying.

Today was different, however. Because I knew that Friday's *Tribune* would carry the story about my receipt of Senta's e-mail message and Damodar's first article on the afterlife, I felt compelled to tell her what she should expect before she and Pop read about it in *The New York Times* the following day, or first heard it on the nightly news.

"Why do you get involved with such foolish nonsense, Duvid? Why should anyone care about what happens after they die?"

"But Mom," I asked, respectfully, "aren't you even a *little* bit interested in that subject. "Don't you ever wonder what happens to people after they die?"

"Not in the least," she retorted, condescendingly. "Jewish people— that is *smart* Jewish people—don't waste their time thinking about what happens after we die. That's left in God's hands. The rabbi and mourners recite the Kaddish at the cemetery and that's it. Into the ground you go. When it's over, it's over. And that goes for you, for me and for everyone else. Why can't you understand that?"

I did my best not to voice my contempt for her narrow, sectarian view of death and the possibility of an afterlife. As if the Kaddish—the Hebrew prayer for the dead—was the final word on the subject! I knew for a fact that within the ranks of Judaism some of the smartest rabbis wrote about and debated what happens after we die, admittedly a subject on which there is a wide divergence of opinion. Instead of arguing the point, however, I simply told her that everything she would read in the newspaper or hear on television was true—that I had indeed heard from Senta via e-mail even though she is dead—and that I fully intended to continue proving to the world that our communications were real.

With a tone of resignation in her voice, she finally decided to change the subject, asking me how I was feeling physically, what else was occupying my time and other minor issues. I asked about my father, Milton Eliashar, who had retired from his private accounting practice a few years ago, but now suffered from osteoarthritis of both knees and a weak heart. Once I left home, we didn't have much to talk about and hardly ever spoke. After giving me a quick, "Miltie's okay, and he sends his love, too," Mom said she had to go and our conversation ended. But the damage was done, and afterward my heart was heavy. I felt both sad and frustrated, as I had so many times after similar conversations over the years.

I decided to "change the elementals," as Senta used to say, by going down to the office and working on my latest editorial assignment until time to get ready to go to dinner. Even though it was Thanksgiving, I wasn't alone when I got there. The job of getting out a major metropolitan newspaper seven days a week never stops and a number of other reporters also were at work. While I was still mentally reviewing my rotten relationship with my parents, the e-mail containing Damodar's first article arrived on my computer. I was pleasantly surprised to see how lucidly he presented the subject, beginning with a series of questions that any intelligent reader might have wondered about.

"Individuals have been asking questions about death for centuries. What is it like? When we die, do we simply lose consciousness forever and are annihilated, or do we enter a new dimension of existence? If there is some continuity to life after death, what is it like and how is it manifested? Is there a Heaven and a Hell? Can those who have left their physical bodies communicate or otherwise interact with the living? How does the afterlife pertain to the Soul, to various states of postmortem consciousness, and to the concept of reincarnation?

"There are answers to all of these questions, and many more, which will be set forth in this and future articles being submitted to this newspaper by the writer, based on the ancient Eastern esoteric philosophy on these issues. These articles are being sent via electronic messages directed to David Elliott, an editorial writer for the newspaper whose interest in this subject matter provided the spark for this series.

"One thing should be made clear at the outset. Although there are many things about death and dying that must remain incomprehensible to us at our current stage of mental development, one thing is sure and easy to grasp. There is no more to fear death and the immediate period after death than there is to tremble at the thought of being born. Death is simply a transition before being born into another life on earth. Everyone in the human race is proceeding along a succession of objective lives and subjective deaths with a definite purpose to a definite conclusion.

"But there is a clear causal connection between the type of life a person spends on earth and the nature and intensity of his joy in the postmortem state, the afterlife. In short, our activities and preoccupations in our present existence most decidedly color our experiences after we leave our physical bodies, as well as those of our next incarnate life.

"To understand the nature of the postmortem states, however, we must first discuss what manner of being man is. Only then can we talk intelligently about what it

Eli P. Bernzweig

is that dies, and what it is that lives on, for without question, the real, inner man does live on after physical life
on earth comes to an end. Parenthetically, I should state
that, although the words 'man' or 'he' will be used
throughout this brief series of articles simply for ease of
presentation, they are intended to signify all members of
the human family, both male and female."

The article then set forth man's seven-fold constitution—which Damodar referred to as principles—as a necessary preliminary to describing
what happens to these principles when we die.

"Man is more than simply a body and a soul; he is a
seven-fold entity comprised of an upper triad and a
lower quaternary. The upper triad is called in Sanskrit
atma (spirit), *buddhi* (spiritual soul), and *manas* (mind).
These are the aspects of our existence that continue on
after physical death. They constitute the inner, invisible
entity, the Spiritual Ego, or Soul, that retains all the spiritual experiences of the life just ended. Sometimes
referred to as the immortal *individuality*, it is this immortal individuality or Soul that reincarnates into another
body after an interval that varies from person to person,
bringing with it the talents, character traits, tendencies,
abilities and the like garnered during its previous incarnations.

"Our four lower principles, the ones that play a major
role in our personal, everyday functioning lives, include
(1) the physical body itself (called in Sanskrit the *rupa*),
(2) the life energy or vital principle (called the *prana-jiva*),
(3) the astral body (called the *linga-sharira),* which is the
etheric double and design body for the physical body,
and finally, (4) the seat of man's animal passions, the
body of emotions and desires (called the *kama-rupa.)*
These four lower principles are the mortal constituents
that comprise what is called the *personality*, the temporal aspect of man that does not survive death for any
appreciable length of time.

"In life, of course, man's upper and lower principles
operate interdependently, but after death they separate,
and it is the temporal *personality*—the lower quaternary—
that begins to separate and disintegrate at death. A
good analogy to better understand this differentiation is

that of an actor who assumes different roles in several different theatrical productions. The role performed in any particular production is merely the actor's temporary persona, while the real man—the actor himself—is the immortal, indestructible entity that is his reincarnating Ego or Soul.

"Even though we acquire an entirely new body (*rupa*), a new brain (which is merely the instrument of *manas*) and a new personality in each successive lifetime, our immortal Souls are eternal. Our life-to-life personalities are merely the beads strung on a thread, while the thread itself represents the permanent Ego or Soul that keeps evolving in each incarnation, striving toward greater spiritual perfection.

"At the moment of death, the immortal part of man leaves the physical body and immediately reviews the life just lived down to the smallest detail, and he or she sees it in a way not seen during life. By that I mean the whole field of the life just lived is illuminated, and the meaning and spiritual significance of all the experiences gone through are shown. And when this review is completed, consciousness withdraws entirely and the entity passes into a second state of existence or dimension known as *kama loka*. There it falls into a sleep the nature and length of which will vary from person to person, depending on the baseness or relative goodness of the life just concluded.

"The good and the pure have a quiet, blissful sleep, full of happy visions of earth life, and their stay in *kama loka* is relatively short. The indifferent individuals sleep a dreamless, albeit quiet sleep, while the wicked ones will, in proportion to their degrees of grossness, suffer the pangs of a nightmare lasting years. Hence, the more spiritual the life, the shorter the time spent in *kama loka*."

Damodar next explained that my beloved Senta was in *kama loka* and that he contacted her in that state of consciousness in order to initiate the current series of articles "as a demonstration of the principles and concepts involved." He added that eventually she would be moving to a higher state of existence known as *devachan,* roughly equivalent to the Christian Heaven or Jewish Gan Eden, which he would describe in a future article, after first detailing the nature of the *kama lokic* experience.

The first article by Damodar ended with the following:

> "Fear of death of the physical body is unwarranted when one understands that 'we' are not our bodies; that 'we' are simply Souls that temporarily inhabit physical bodies, and that at the moment of death 'we' don't die, only our physical bodies die. To think that death amounts to total annihilation and the finality of one's existence would make a mockery out of life. That which follows death is simply life on another dimension of existence, and such life can be made more truly meaningful once we understand the ultimate goal of all evolution which, for human beings, is a conscious return to our spiritual origin and the achievement of individual conscious divinity."

After I finished reading it, I immediately forwarded Damodar's e-mail to Ray Tuohy for review and editing, with a copy to Chet Walker, since I knew that both were in the office today. I had no idea how Ray would handle the editing of Damodar's first article, but it wasn't long before I saw how decidedly negative he felt about the whole subject. I had assumed he would make the usual editorial marks and changes, but Ray gutted it, eliminating many of the basic references to the Eastern esoteric philosophy, all Sanskrit words, and leaving in only the most prosaic observations and comments.

To my surprise and relief, Chet himself came to the rescue. He restored the essential guts of the article, and had it sent to production essentially as submitted by Damodar, with copies to Ray and me.

In accordance with Adrienne's advice, Chet drafted a brief comment to readers introducing the forthcoming series of articles. The executive editor may have been an impatient, ill-tempered curmudgeon, and decidedly lacking in refinement, but he was a damn good writer.

He began his introduction by noting, "Although the subject matter of the following series of articles is unusual for a newspaper of the caliber of the *Washington Tribune*, we believe it is of sufficient general interest to warrant addressing the issue in a serious, thoughtful manner. This series on what happens after death will be written by an extraordinarily gifted proponent of what is called the Eastern esoteric philosophy, a man who styles himself a Mahatma or Master of Wisdom and prefers to be called simply Damodar. I and three others at the *Tribune* have seen ample evidence of his incredible occult powers and his obvious knowledge of matters pertaining to the afterlife."

Chet remarked that even though he was impressed with the credentials of the contributing writer, he could not vouch for the accuracy or authenticity of the information the latter would present in the forthcoming series.

"Nothing in life is more certain than death," he continued, "yet most of us are generally uncomfortable thinking about death and dying because it brings us face to face with our own mortality. We especially fear the dying process, always hoping we will achieve the elusive ideal of death with dignity. Thoughtful persons have long pondered what happens after we die. Is there something in us that lives on, and if so, how is that new dimension of life manifested? We intend to explore this and related issues in the forthcoming series of articles.

"We are publishing these articles for one more very special reason: David Elliott, a member of our editorial staff claims to have received a direct communication via e-mail from the woman he loved for some thirty-three years. This love of his died several months ago and in her e-mail she avers that she is in a dimension or state of existence where all who die must pass some time before moving on to other realms in the afterlife.

"We have investigated our writer's claim that e-mails have been received from, and sent to, his loved one and it passed the test of credibility, which is why we have agreed to make the relevant portions of their e-mail messages public. We shall respect their fundamental right of privacy, of course, but to the extent possible we will keep our readers informed of their correspondence through this unique method of communication. [See related news story in the main section]"

I went home that evening with mixed feelings, but on the whole good ones. Just knowing that I was still able to communicate with my beloved Senta gave me added courage to face whatever challenges might come my way. We were still a team, one discarnate and one alive, but still a team.

Chapter 12

B y the time I arrived at the newspaper on Friday morning, an air of excitement pervaded the newsroom with reporters buzzing among themselves about the story of Senta's e-mails and Damodar's first article. Since the switchboard operator had not been given any particular instructions as to where to direct calls about Damodar's article, she routed most of them to Ray Tuohy, since he was the Religion & Family Section editor. Ray made a point of telling the callers he had nothing to do with the article and declined to comment on it. He suggested that they call the executive editor or me instead.

Chet Walker had received a barrage of calls also, mostly from editors of other newspapers who found it hard to believe that a paper as responsible as the *Tribune* would print an article by a hitherto unknown contributing writer on a subject that was so controversial. All wanted to know more about the mysterious person he had described as 'an extraordinarily gifted proponent of the Eastern esoteric philosophy.' He parried the callers as best he could with promises of more detailed information in future articles.

There were fewer reactions to the key philosophical points outlined in the short article by Damodar than there were to the news story about my personal e-mail contact with Senta. I had over twenty-five telephone messages waiting for me on my voice mail when I got to my desk, and because there were so many, I just took them in chronological order.

One woman wanted to confirm the fact of my actual receipt of messages from Senta. She asked, "Is this a genuine story, or just something the paper has cooked up to stimulate sales?" When I assured her it was one hundred percent true she told me how lucky I was to be in touch with my loved one and immediately begged me to make contact with her deceased husband. "Can you intervene with this Damodar person to help me try to reach my Benny? He was such a wonderful husband, and all I do is think about him and wonder if he is all right, and if he misses me as much as I miss him."

I politely declined, but advised her and all the other callers with similar requests to read the entire series of articles before jumping to any conclusions about their ability—or inability—to communicate with their deceased loved ones.

Meanwhile, I passed along the initial statistics on phone calls to Sol Berman, as Chet had directed. From the sound of his voice, Sol appeared to have gotten over the feelings of religious betrayal that had surfaced during our staff meeting on Wednesday.

I e-mailed the boss myself, telling him about the huge number of voice-mail calls I had received and the fact that callers were asking me to intervene with their deceased relatives, and how this created an uncomfortable situation for me. "These are total strangers, and they're pleading with me to intercede like I was some high priest or miracle man."

The boss retorted caustically, "You started this business and now you're going to have to see it through. Suggest you handle things as best you can." His e-mail then informed me of the deluge of calls he had also received, primarily from editors all over the country, adding, "We're going to have to monitor this situation closely, so keep me informed what readers are saying or asking, or whatever."

Not all callers wanted to communicate with their deceased loved ones. One of the more irritating calls that came through after I finished my voice mails came from a Dr. Earl Beckley, who identified himself as a professor of parapsychology at the University of Michigan and vice-president of the Committee for Responsible Investigation of Alleged Paranormal Phenomena. In a haughty, belligerent tone of voice Beckley berated me mercilessly. "You've done a great disservice to people all over the world by raising their hopes that they could contact their deceased loved ones. There is absolutely no scientific evidence for life after death. You know as well as I do that there is no possibility of contact with the dead, and those who claim they have done so—including yourself—base their claims on such spurious means as contacts through mediums, out-of-body or near-death experiences, and a whole slew of grief-induced hallucinations. So why are you doing this?"

His air of superiority and defiant tone of voice pissed me off. I particularly resented his allegation that I was a dupe and that the *Tribune* was perpetrating some sort of fraud on our readers. I took a couple of deep breaths to calm my nerves and keep my blood pressure in check. When Beckley was done venting, I told him in as calm and courteous a voice as I could muster that everything in the news story was one hundred percent correct, that Senta had indeed communicated with me by e-mail, and that nothing he said was of any concern to me. "We'll see about that," was his curt response, in a smug tone of voice that implied a threat of some sort as he slammed the phone down. His comments irritated me but if anything, they made me even more determined to let the whole world know that my experience was a real one.

By mid-morning, the news about my communicating with Senta was making the wire services and other news outlets. Then, within minutes of each other, I received phone calls from program scheduling personnel at the local stations of the major television networks and CNN requesting my appearance on their respective interview programs. I denied all of these requests, at least for the time being. For those who asked, I also confirmed that the information they read about Senta's e-mails in the first *Tribune* article was accurate and that more details would be forthcoming in future articles.

A man who said he was a writer from the supermarket tabloid, *Bizarre Events*, offered me $10,000 in cash if I would give them an exclusive interview and provide personal photos showing me and Senta together in various locales. When I reminded him that I worked for a newspaper myself and was planning to tell the story exclusively to the readers of the *Washington Tribune*, he acted as though he hadn't heard a thing I said because the simpleton merely increased the offer to $15,000. I hung up on him and a moment later the phone rang again.

This call came from a George Applebee, who said he was engaged as a local researcher in what he called the After-Death Communication (ADC) Project, which he said had been started in 1988 by two people I had never heard of, Bill and Judy Guggenheim. "We track things like this from reports all over the world. And to be honest with you, your experience—receiving e-mails from your deceased Senta—is a first in that category, so far as I'm aware. What's really novel is not only the unique method of communication, but the fact that your communications were truly interactive."

Applebee asked me if I kept copies of our e-mail correspondence, and I told him that I did, which caused him to remark, "Frankly, this is the best evidence of an ADC I have ever heard of." When he asked me if I would provide him with further information about my communications with Senta, I told him that everything, except the most personal, intimate aspects of our discussions, would appear in future *Washington Tribune* articles. Although he didn't sound too enthusiastic when I told him that, he signed off with a cheery "Talk to you again soon," as if we had developed some enduring connection in this brief call.

A call I received from the high priest of the Washington, D.C. coven of Wiccans provided a decidedly different point of view. He complimented me on the breakthrough I had achieved in communicating with my deceased Senta via e-mail, adding that it helped their cause considerably because it showed that one could deal with the touchy subject of communicating with the dead in such a straightforward manner. "Keep up the good work," he said, approvingly. "We'll be following the articles in the *Tribune* with great interest."

When that call ended, all I could do was stare at the phone, chortle and shake my head.

The flood of e-mails, letters to the editor and phone calls continued over the weekend and by Monday, November 26th, the newspaper was virtually under a state of siege. By eight o'clock in the morning, a small crowd had begun to assemble outside the newspaper's office on 15th Street as well as in the downstairs lobby. With what amounted to superstitious awe, they hoped to get a glimpse of the man who has received e-mails from his deceased loved one or, better yet, get a chance to speak with me directly.

Following the terrorists' attacks of September 11th, the *Washington Tribune*, like all major metropolitan newspapers, instituted stepped-up security procedures to guard against possible acts of terrorism against the press. When the security guard for the building informed Chet Walker about the impromptu assemblage at the front door and in the lobby, Walker told him to be polite but firm. "Don't let anyone in without the appropriate credentials or who has advance permission to come upon the premises. Better keep a close eye on things, however, and if the crowd gets too large, or unruly in any way, don't hesitate to call the D.C. police."

Ray Tuohy undoubtedly was gloating as he sent me an e-mail saying, "I've received over a dozen calls from priests, ministers, rabbis and other clergymen who are shocked that the *Trib* is covering this story as a serious exposition of factual information. They've asked me to intervene with the executive editor to halt publication of any further articles. Several have pointed out that what the newspaper is doing amounts to the encouragement of necromancy, which is considered an abomination by nearly all religions. I know what Chet promised you, but I think this whole thing is getting out of hand and I believe we have to nip it in the bud."

I concluded he probably had solicited at least half a dozen of those complaints from clergymen whom he had called when the first article appeared. I knew that the theosophists also considered communicating with the dead an abomination and traditionally have deprecated the practice; but I also knew that the series was given the blessings of the Mahâ Chohan, so I wasn't overly concerned about the necromancy issue.

Although I never had ulcers, my stomach was becoming painful and I could feel tension invading my body once again. Nevertheless, I decided we had to proceed. More than that, I *wanted* to proceed.

In my e-mail reply to Ray, I told him he could take any action he deemed advisable, but that I was not going to vacillate. He replied that he would pass the negative information along to Chet Walker immediately. As if I'd expected differently!

A short while later, I called Chet to see if he had heard from Ray and, if so, what was Chet's reaction? To my surprise and relief, he said he had told Ray that he was not going to interfere with publication of the series in any manner. He had reminded Ray that the boss-lady had enthusiastically authorized the series, and further told Ray he was convinced that there would be a lot of valuable information in the articles and that he wanted the *Tribune's* readers to judge for themselves whether the information was useful or not.

But, because of the early morning crowd in the lobby, and because he knew that taking the time to respond to all the calls and e-mails was making it difficult for me to handle my regular writing assignments, Chet suggested that I work out of my apartment for the next several weeks "or at least until this thing simmers down." I liked the idea immediately, and so informed my colleagues in the editorial department and a few others in the newsroom whom I thought should know. We could all still communicate with each other by e-mail, but only two or three had my unlisted home phone number.

Before leaving the office, I received a new e-mail from Senta. She was aware of the flurry of activity resulting from the first of Damodar's articles, since he had already brought it to her attention via thought transference and she was pleased. Based on the calls I had received so far, I knew that our personal lives now were essentially public property, and I called this to her attention. She replied reassuringly:

> "Never mind, darling. It's more important to get the proper information out to those who are willing to learn. As I told you earlier, you can tell your readers whatever you want about our relationship, using good taste and judgment, of course. There's nothing we have to hide."

I had to admit she was right, and told her so. Then, I asked her if she had finally communicated with her sister, Santra who had died in 1999. Santra had been a widow who, coincidentally, also had lost her husband to illness early in her marriage. Senta replied that she had, indeed, spoken telepathically with her sister.

> "Santra apologized for having been so indifferent to many of the theosophical concepts and spiritual issues I had brought to her attention over the years. And I, in turn, apologized for having been so rigid when dealing with her on matters of her personal character as well as Alan's. All in all, it was a satisfying interchange and I'm glad we've had the chance to understand each other better. I expect we'll be communicating again soon via thought transmission. By the way, I've also spoken with my brothers Artie and Hank, and the three of us had a wonderful time sharing reminiscences when we were youngsters."

I then asked her, "What about your father? You didn't mention anything about him in your last e-mail. Do you plan to contact him, too?"

> "I haven't tried to contact him, yet, David, because I've been reluctant to dredge up old wounds. The reason I rarely mentioned my father to you was because of things he did to me and my brothers and sister after my mother died. For one thing, even though he was financially well off, he rarely gave us toys and refused to pay for our support, so we were sent to live with one relative after another. And finally, he tricked us into entering the Home after telling us he was taking us to Tante Sophie's place.

"He seldom visited us at the Home, and by the time we left there, he had lost all his properties and had turned to drinking and running after women. For years he rarely looked in on us. In effect, he abandoned us, and that's why I held him in such low regard."

This at last explained Senta's reluctance to talk about her father over the years. More importantly, she had never referred to him in terms of having abandoned her and her siblings in any of our prior conversations, which indicated that she must have been terribly hurt by his unfatherly behavior. I couldn't help but feel her hurt, even though she had theoretically left all her earthly woes behind and no longer had to confront the pain of her father's contemptible behavior. I wrote:

"I'm so sorry, *herzele*, I never knew you felt that strongly about your father."

She replied:

"Of course not, darling. I was too ashamed to tell you. But now that I'm here, I'm thinking seriously about contacting not only my father, but others with whom I've had poor relationships, to see if I can't set things straight. I see now how important this is to my spiritual growth, and I definitely don't want to make the same mistakes the next time around."

I agreed with her and then changed the subject. I told her about my working out of my apartment for the next several weeks at Chet Walker's suggestion.

"I'll be in touch with the editorial staff and will participate in the daily staff meeting by telephone conference call, so that shouldn't be a problem. And I won't have to run the gauntlet of people in the lobby hoping to make contact with their deceased loved ones through me. But I'll be able to communicate with you and Damodar from my computer at home."

With that, we ended our brief conversation.

A Death Interrupted

As I was driving home that evening, my thoughts reverted to Ray Tuohy's comment about necromancy, and it troubled me that I didn't have a quick answer. When I got home, I turned on my computer and sent an e-mail to Damodar asking for information and advice on this issue. His response came only a few minutes later, and was revealing.

> "My dear Mr. Elliott, in occultism, it is the motive, and the motive alone, that makes any exercise of occult power either white magic (beneficent) or black magic (malevolent). When someone uses his occult powers to control another person's actions—as in stage hypnotism, for example—or to cause physical or mental harm, or for other evil purposes, that is out-and-out sorcery or black magic.

> "When the Adept uses his knowledge with no other thought than to benefit nature and man, the result is white magic. By way of example, on three separate occasions during her lifetime, when H.P.B. was dying of serious illnesses, white magic was employed to keep her alive. In each instance, her Master, who was a high Initiate, undertook to reorder the atoms of her body to restore her physical health.

> "When the Mahâ Chohan gave me permission to convey your Senta's thoughts to you by occult means, he did so because he concluded that the end result would be beneficial to a receptive humanity. This particular form of communication with one who has entered the state of *kama loka* is not intended to, and is not likely to, have any harmful effects on the living. On the contrary, the intent is to help explain what really happens following the cessation of physical life, and how that should be seen as a spiritually enlightening and perfectly natural experience. Moreover, it does not involve consulting the dead for divining the future, which is the primary thrust of necromancy."

I thanked Damodar for this information and felt much better about the charges of necromancy that Ray Tuohy had brought to my attention earlier. But I knew Ray wouldn't give up easily, and still worried about his intentions with respect to the forthcoming articles.

Chapter 13

R ay didn't at all like the way things were going since he first told Chet what David was up to. First, there was that disturbing demonstration by Damodar, which had taken all the wind out of Ray's sails, even though he had to admit the fire-destroyed photograph of his family that was produced out of thin air was a baffling and amazing occurrence.

And then, there were the harsh words Chet used when Ray again tried to caution the executive editor about publishing the articles on the afterlife. In the short run, Ray had lost every battle and it was beginning to appear that he had also lost control of his own section of the paper. He seethed with anger and his body trembled as he felt the rage building up inside, but he had both immediate and long-range plans that he was sure would win the ultimate war. Getting David fired would be such sweet revenge!

After the first article was published, his plan of action was to call several friendly clergymen in the Metropolitan D.C. area and explain his own views on the entire situation. He would encourage them to write letters of complaint to the editor and to make phone calls to Chet Walker urging him to stop further publication of Damodar's articles, for obvious religious reasons. He also would suggest that they consider forming a committee and request an opportunity to meet with Chet personally. They liked that suggestion and he finally began feeling better about the whole situation, especially when Chet agreed to an early meeting with the ad hoc group of six clergymen.

The more he thought about it, the more he liked it. Part of Ray nodded in satisfaction at the vision of the committee praising him, of Chet calling David into the exec's office to give him the ax, and of David packing his office possessions into boxes and vacating the *Trib* for good. Yet, another part of Ray wanted more than just a firing. David's haughty air twisted in Ray's gut whenever they talked. And Ray never forgot his daddy's periodic tirades against Jews, calling them 'the offspring of Satan,' when he was a youngster. No, a firing was not a personal enough form of revenge, Ray thought. Something much more personal was required, and he knew just what it was.

A Death Interrupted

Around lunchtime on Monday he drove up to 13th and Euclid, a predominantly black neighborhood, where he knew the United Christian Fellowship Church maintained a soup kitchen. As he arrived near the intersection, he spotted a lanky African-American man with bushy black hair standing alone on the corner. He looked to be in his early fifties and was wearing a dark, frayed and tattered trench coat. From the man's demeanor, and the toothpick in his mouth, it appeared he had just exited the basement soup kitchen, which was used by many homeless people in that part of the District of Columbia.

After parking the car, Ray sauntered over toward the man and as he got closer he could smell the aroma of cheap wine on his clothes. The man's matted, bushy hair and the stubble on his face poorly concealed a four inch razor scar running from his right ear to his lower right chin. Ray engaged the man in casual, innocuous conversation and in talking to him Ray could tell that he was reasonably intelligent. He learned that the man's name was Archie Taylor and that he had only recently been released on parole from Lorton Prison where he was serving time for assault and armed robbery and was currently unemployed. With that background information, Ray felt he had the right party.

"How would you like to make an easy twenty bucks?" he asked the wine-smelling man, as he slowly removed the bill from his wallet.

The sight of the money caused the unemployed drifter to raise his eyebrows and ask furtively, "What do you have in mind?"

"I want you to send a letter to someone, that's all." Ray then took a blank piece of paper and wrote out the exact words he wanted to be used in the letter to be sent to David. He also gave David's address at the office, telling the now-enthused accomplice, "Send this letter in your own handwriting to this man at this address. Use any kind of scrap paper you like, but don't forget the stamp. I'll check back with you next week. Maybe I'll have you send a few more letters at that time . . . or maybe I'll have another job for you. By the way, how can I get in touch with you?"

"I got a room over on Florida Avenue; more like a closet, but I ain't got no phone. Anyhow, until I get a job, you can always find me here at the soup kitchen around meal times. Thanks for the dough. Don't worry, I'll take care of the letter." He never asked his benefactor's name but quickly pocketed the much-needed twenty.

Ray made a note of Archie Taylor's name and then returned to the office. He was feeling a lot better now.

Soon, he mused, this whole thing will go away, and if I'm lucky, that kike Elliott will be out on his ass.

Chapter 14

I continued working out of my Kalorama Road apartment and found the escape from phones, e-mails and faxes a welcome relief, even though by Wednesday I was beginning to miss the daily camaraderie of my fellow editorial writers. As the week progressed, I learned that the paper had received more and more phone calls, faxes and letters to the editor about the initial after-death article by Damodar, some decrying the publication of articles on such a subject, but apparently more were curious about the nature of my personal contact with Senta. On Thursday, I provided Lou Garza with a few additional comments I had received from Senta for his use in a follow-up article scheduled for the Religion & Family Section of Friday's edition of the *Tribune*.

One item that the paper's courier delivered to me along with my other mail was disturbing. Inside a dirty envelope addressed to me was a piece of cardboard, apparently ripped from a cereal box, with the words, 'You Devil worshiper shall die' scrawled in black ink. My spine shivered at the words. This was the first time anyone had ever threatened me and the sensation was like receiving an electric shock; I had a sense of exposure that made my skin cold. I personally delivered the threat—along with the smudged envelope—to the desk sergeant at the Third Precinct on V Street. His initial reaction was one of complacent indifference—after all, he informed me, people threaten people all the time—but when I identified myself as the *Washington Tribune* writer who had received e-mails from his dead lady friend, he showed considerably more interest. "Oh, you're that guy the newspaper story was all about. I remember now. Here, leave your name, address and a number where we can get in touch with you. I'll pass this stuff on to the chief of detectives right away."

On Wednesday, when Damodar e-mailed the second of the articles on the after-death states, I was again impressed with the lucidity of his presentation. This one dealt with the *kama loka* experience:

"The first article in this series noted the seven-fold nature of man, and I remind you that throughout these articles 'man' is a gender-neutral term meant to include both males and females. I pointed out that man is essentially dual in nature, that he is both a *personality* and an *individuality*. During life, these two function together, but at death they separate. The individuality—also called man's Spiritual Ego or Soul—is the immortal aspect of each of us, the Eternal Pilgrim that never dies, and the aspect of us that reincarnates many times.

"It is the temporary personality alone that is dispersed once physical life has ended, and the realm in which that change takes place is called in Sanskrit *kama loka*, which literally means the place or realm of desire. The term '*Kama loka*' is the origin of the Christian purgatory, the place where the Soul undergoes purification from its evil deeds and frees itself of its *kamic* clothing before moving on to the higher and considerably more blissful state of rest called *devachan*, which is roughly equivalent to the Christian Heaven or the Jewish Gan Eden. However, *kama loka* should not be thought of as a physical place. It is more a state of consciousness or plane of existence whose locale is the astral region that is in, on, and surrounding the earth.

"By the time a person enters *kama loka*, his physical body and energy have been cast off. As the physical body dies, two other parts of a person—the astral body (the etheric double of the physical) and the desire body (all desires and passions)—coalesce and merge into a new entity, called the *kama-rupa*, This newly-formed entity, which contains the mass of passions, desires and aversions of the life just concluded, will slowly disintegrate, as did the physical. In the meantime, it is by separating from the *kama-rupa* that the person's Spiritual Ego is able to purify and rid itself of all character weaknesses acquired during earth life. This includes all purely sensual passions and desires, all evil tendencies, all envy, and all feelings of hate, vengeance or lack of compassion.

"The Spiritual Ego or Soul assimilates only the most spiritual aspects of the recently-deceased person: his feelings of universal love; his genuinely altruistic nature; his feelings of brotherhood and compassion for all sentient beings; his qualities of sacrifice, patience and steadfastness; and his desire to live the purest and most unselfish life in accordance with the dictates of his conscience.

"This process of separating the bad from the good impulses is sometimes referred to as the 'death struggle' because it is the final phase of separation between the Spiritual Ego and the lower psychic elements of the personality. How well the *kama-rupa* of the deceased sorts out and rids itself of the negative *kamic* qualities mentioned above is the test of the death struggle. And since no two persons are identical, and their relative degrees of spirituality and non-spirituality necessarily differ, the length of time spent by each in *kama loka* will also differ. Eventually, the conjoined *kama-rupa* and astral body disintegrates, not unlike the way the physical body disintegrates.

"It should be noted that our after-death states—both in *kama loka* and in *devachan*—are literally in our own hands. In order to live a conscious life in the world on the other side of the grave, the individual must have acquired a belief in that world while alive. Not only that, but he must live a life seeking the noblest of his human dreams and aspirations.

"When the Spiritual Ego or Soul, acting through the astral body, has finally separated itself from the temporal passions and desires and absorbed all the noble qualities that were active during the individual's earth life, the death struggle ends, and this event is called the Second Death. At this point, the being falls into a condition of heavy sleep, which precedes his Spiritual Ego's passage from *kama loka* into the blissful state of *devachan*.

"One may wonder, once the process of separation is completed, what happens to all the discarded passions and desires, the lust, anger, pride, hate and selfishness sloughed off in *kama loka*? The answer is, after the separation is completed, the lower principles remain an astral entity in *kama loka* as a *kama-rupic* 'shell' until that shell eventually disintegrates after exhaustion of the effects that created it. It is this shell, now devoid of its guiding higher principles, that unfortunately becomes the being that is attracted to seances. I will have more to say about the nefarious influence of the *kama-rupa* shells—also called 'astral spooks'—in a future article."

The remainder of Damodar's article covered other aspects of the *kama loka* experience, including the following brief exposition of what happens to those who commit suicide and those whose lives are cut short due to accidents, murders, or court-decreed executions.

"Some distinctions need to be made between those who die natural deaths—about which we have just been talking—and those whose deaths are caused prematurely by suicide, murder, court-ordered execution or pure accident. And there are distinctions to be made even between these categories. Tragically, one who commits suicide to avoid the physical or mental pain of continued life finds himself in a worse condition than that from which escape was sought. To be sure, he has destroyed the physical instrument—but he is not truly dead, only partially dead.

"As occultists know, the law of cohesion operates among all of man's seven principles, so that before the end of one's normal life span, those principles cannot separate. The premature death of one by purely mechanical means, by suicide or accident, for example, can only bring about the death of three of the four temporary aspects of personality: the physical body, the life force and the astral or etheric double. What remains is the *kama-rupa* or desire nature, which will remain until the individual's naturally predetermined time of death. Hence, a suicide, or someone killed by accidental or homicidal means, as well as one murdered by means of court-decreed execution, must remain in *kama loka* until his natural life term is reached, whether it be six months, six years, or sixty years. That is occult law.

"How these shells live in *kama loka* differs considerably. The suicide lives in an unhappy state, continually reviewing the thoughts leading up to the desperate final act he hoped would relieve his physical or mental pain. He continues to be informed and inflamed by his passions and desires, but is unable to act upon them. It is truly a tragic state of affairs, one that most decidedly is a state to be avoided at all costs.

"As to victims of accidental and homicidal death, they too must remain in *kama loka* until what would have been the natural duration of their lives, but because they were not responsible for their deaths, they sleep a dreamless profound sleep until the hour of normal death has arrived. Moreover, the Dhyân Chohans, who are the planetary spiritual guardians and who ordinarily have no hand in the guidance of living human Souls, use special powers in watching over and protecting the hapless victims of accidental or homicidal death who are violently thrown out of their element into a new one (*kama loka*) before their normal time.

"And finally, there is the matter of court-decreed execution—capital punishment—a greatly misunderstood concept, fraught with highly undesirable consequences. Just as in the case of suicides and accident victims, the executed criminal is only half dead, with his astral body now inflamed by pent-up feelings of rage and revenge, constantly seeking sensitive individuals (whether conscious mediums or unwitting mediums) whom they can affect in the most vicious ways. Especially at seances, these half-dead, executed criminals seek to repeat in the astral light the scenes of blood and violence that led to their eventual capture and execution, often suggesting like behavior on the part of their sensitive audiences. Many heinous crimes have been caused by individuals whose only explanation to the police was that 'some irresistible impulse made me do it,' or 'a voice inside of me incessantly kept pushing and leading me on.'"

I forwarded Damodar's second article on to Ray Tuohy by e-mail for editing, wondering how he would carve it up this time. I also told him about the disturbing threat I had received in the mail. Along with the copy of Damodar's article that I forwarded to Chet, I also mentioned the death threat letter and the fact that I had turned it over to the Third Precinct police.

When they heard about it, my colleagues at the paper were disturbed by the news of the anonymous threat letter, and also disturbed by the growing crowd of people they encountered as they entered the building each morning, which had grown to approximately one hundred. The police finally had to be called to disperse them. One of my editorial associates reported seeing a few placards accusing me of being an evil henchman of the devil, a practitioner of voodoo, and several other unflattering epithets. It gave me the creeps to think of the lengths some people would go to show their displeasure with my communicating with Senta via e-mail.

As I was thinking about this a short while later, I was jarred back to reality by a call from Miriam Green. "Do you remember what Damodar said about my heart?" she asked, in an excited voice.

"Sure. Why do you ask?"

"Because he was right, David. Oh boy was he right! I didn't tell the doctor anything about Damodar's diagnosis, but my doctor didn't like my heart symptoms and ordered an angiogram, which they did on Tuesday over at GW. The diagnosis was total occlusion of the left anterior descending artery. Isn't that something? I mean, the *exact* diagnosis that Damodar made, only he did it *without* an angiogram! I'm scheduled to have an angioplasty done in a couple of weeks."

"It certainly is amazing, Miriam, but understandable. A true occultist like Damodar can see into an individual's magnetic aura, and also has clairvoyant powers, which is what he utilized in your case. Did you tell anyone else about this?"

"Yeah, I told Ray, and all he did was raise his eyebrows and say 'hmphh.' He's beginning to get on my nerves. And I'm sure yours, too. You know he's rounding up articles from a bunch of the local clergymen to counter the stuff being submitted by Damodar."

"No, I didn't know, Miriam, but it figures. He's determined to make a fool of me."

"Well, I just thought you should know. Gotta run now. Hang in there, pal."

I appreciated Miriam's candor, and particularly the information she provided about Ray's planned strategy. Five minutes later, Ray called.

"I received the second article by Damodar," he began, "and, in light of what happened last week, I haven't edited it at all. But I thought I should tell you that in Friday's paper I plan to include several articles by some pretty learned clergymen setting forth views that are directly opposed to those contained in Damodar's articles. His smug tone of voice was almost unbearable, but I held my fire.

"That's perfectly all right with me, Ray." I responded calmly. "The paper is obligated to provide balance on all subjects of a controversial nature, so I have no objection."

"I wasn't asking your permission," he replied snidely. "I was merely informing you out of courtesy." And with that he slammed the phone down. So much for courtesy!

Ray was becoming a first class pain in the ass. As I hung up the phone, I could feel the pressure intensifying, knowing that he was hell-bent on embarrassing me or causing me grief of one kind or another. In a way, however, I was relieved to learn that opposing points of view would appear in the paper because that would make Damodar's points so much more vivid by contrast. It should also counter any pressure on the paper for having run such a controversial series.

As I left the apartment to get an early dinner at a nearby Chinese restaurant, I walked to the carport behind the apartment house to put some papers in my car, and that was when I noticed the black spray-painted words "Devil Worshiper," "Satan," and "Voodoo Priest" covering the front hood, doors and rear deck of my silver Lexus.

I was furious, and quickly looked up and down the block, hoping I might see the culprit in flight, but I could see no one. Then, a shiver ran up my spine as I thought about the death threat in the letter I had received earlier and turned over to the police. I wondered if the writer really meant it and was capable of doing it. This is the District of Columbia, after all, and as a reporter here for many years I knew that stranger things have been known to happen in this cauldron of urban crime.

It made me mad to think someone was really trying to inject fear into my life for merely reporting about the e-mails from Senta. *What 'n hell is the world coming to?*

More disgusted than alarmed, I threw the papers into the car and walked the block and a half to the Shanghai Palace.

Chapter 15

Thursday began badly. After showering, dressing, and getting a bite to eat, I called the Third Precinct to report the damage to my car, and ten minutes later a squad car with two policemen showed up. They saw the spray-painted markings on the Lexus, took a few pictures, and asked me the usual questions. When I told them that I was the person in the news who had been contacted by his deceased love, and that that might have something to do with the damage caused, they chose to label it an act of vandalism rather than a "hate crime," because, so they informed me, I would have a better chance of getting my insurance company to cover the damages.

That turned out to be the case, as I learned in my second call of the morning to my insurance carrier. They told me to get an appraisal of the damage and the cost to re-paint the car at a specified garage on nearby Columbia Road, but reminded me that I had a $100 deductible on my comprehensive coverage. That didn't bother me as much as the time I would waste in getting the appraisal done and the car repainted, along with the paperwork involved. Then, the nagging fear that it could all just as easily happen again preyed on my mind.

It was a little while after the regular ten o'clock editorial staff conference, with me participating via speakerphone, that I received a call from Chet Walker.

"I'm afraid we've got a little problem, Dave, and I'd like you to come on down here for a meeting I've scheduled for eleven."

"What's going on, Chet? What kind of meeting?" It didn't take much to figure out it had something to do with the new series by Damodar, but the sinking feeling in the pit of my stomach told me this must be something pretty serious or he wouldn't have made the call himself.

He dismissed my question. "Later. You'll see when you get here." The weary tone of his voice amply reflected the burdens of newspaper management.

There was no reason to hang around the apartment any longer than necessary, so I hopped into my spray-painted car and headed downtown.

Traffic was light and there was a chill in the air, presaging an early winter storm, possibly even some snow. I arrived at the parking garage on 15th Street around ten forty-five.

Once at my desk, I knew I was in for trouble when I saw the overly enthusiastic way Ray Tuohy greeted half a dozen clergymen in the newsroom lobby before cheerfully ushering them into the main conference room. It didn't take a rocket scientist to figure out that he had engineered the whole thing. So, this was the "problem" that Chet referred to over the phone and without a doubt I was the one designated to take the heat.

The delegation of six religious leaders, all men, represented several of the major denominations in the Washington Metropolitan area. It was obvious they were not a bunch of happy campers by the looks on their faces and the manner in which they spoke in whispered voices to each other and to Ray before the *Tribune's* executive editor called the meeting to order.

To my surprise, Adrienne Thayer also showed up for the conclave, which was quite unusual for her, and although I felt her presence lent an air of dignity and authority to the occasion, it simple made me more nervous. I noticed that Chet's trademark cigar was nowhere in sight. He was obviously in a serious mood. After considerably overdone introductions of the six clerics by the fawning Ray Tuohy, Chet began the meeting.

"I've invited all of you here this morning to discuss and, if possible, resolve some apparently bothersome issues arising out of the articles we've just begun publishing regarding the afterlife. Now, since I've already received letters, e-mails or phone calls from most of you, I think I'm pretty much aware of how you feel about the matter, but it's only fair to hear what you have to say since you've come down here to speak to me in person, so why don't we begin with you, Father Dougherty."

The pudgy, florid-faced priest coughed twice nervously before speaking. "Yes, thank you, Mr. Walker. I believe what I have to say reflects the views of just about everyone here, but speaking for the Catholic Church, not only in this diocese but everywhere, what you are doing with this proposed series on the afterlife is not only facilitating, but actually fostering, the evil practice of necromancy—communicating with spirits of the dead, which has been condemned by the Church for centuries.

"To make matters worse, the information being disseminated comes from an entity who is not even a live human being but some sort of supernatural, invisible purveyor of occult knowledge who calls himself a

'Mahatma' or 'Master of Wisdom.' It's beyond comprehension how you justify presenting to the public the word of such an imaginary non-entity, and I use the term advisedly, on a subject as arcane and unknowable as the nature of the postmortem states."

Upon hearing the term 'non-entity,' Chet smiled wryly and glanced at David with a raised eyebrow, but otherwise showed no reaction to Father Dougherty's complaint. Adrienne was equally unmoved. I shifted uneasily in my chair during the accusatory tirade, knowing that eventually the task would fall to me to explain the paper's position. Chet turned and nodded to Rabbi Joseph Pekarski as the next speaker. The bespectacled spiritual leader of Washington's conservative B'nai Sholom Congregation, wearing a tiny, black knitted yarmulke, seconded Father Dougherty's comments in a calm and deliberate voice, but added a few words of his own to illuminate the Jewish position on the subject. "Moses warned that attempting to seek truths from the dead was abhorred by God, who made it punishable by death. But when King Saul, who was then at war with the Philistines, was fearful about the outcome of an imminent battle with the enemy, he sought out a woman at Endor who was a medium and asked her to call forth the soul of Samuel, the deceased prophet whom King Saul respected so highly. Once Samuel's ghost was evoked, he prognosticated Saul's defeat and his death the following day. And that is exactly what happened," said the Rabbi. "The willful disregard of the prohibition against necromancy was the direct cause of King Saul's death."

After a brief pause, he continued, "According to Jewish tradition, it is an abomination for the living to try to communicate with the dead, and doing so violates one of the 613 commandments of the Torah. As I see it, these newspaper articles can do nothing but harm, giving people the false hope that they can communicate with their loved ones when we know that that's impossible, and will only compound their feelings of grief and disappointment over the losses they have already suffered."

"Your points are duly noted, Rabbi," said Chet dryly, as he glanced at me and then at Adrienne before nodding to Reverend Elijah Johnson that it was his turn to speak. The slightly built black minister, wearing a clerical collar and sporting a neatly-trimmed gray stubble beard, was the spiritual leader of the Second Baptist Church, located in nearby Brentwood, Maryland, just outside the District line. For a man of his relatively small stature, Reverend Johnson spoke in a deep, resonant voice that commanded considerable attention.

"I, too, find the proposed articles, emanating from a newspaper of the stature of the *Washington Tribune* troubling in that they appear to be presented with the imprimatur of credibility on a subject we all know is too arcane and too esoteric to warrant any assurance of credibility. I, for one, would like to know how you determined that the supposed e-mails received by Mr. Elliott are in fact genuine and not hoaxes. Also, how, and why, you would take the word of an invisible being—if he is, in fact, a being, rather than a product of someone's imagination—on such a highly-disputed subject as the afterlife, and finally, what do you hope to accomplish with this series? Perhaps, if we got adequate answers to questions like these, we might feel a little better about what is happening, or at least understand your motives for proceeding."

Murmurs and nods from the others indicated their approval of the minister's points, and everyone turned their eyes to Chet Walker for his response. By the look on his face, I knew that Chet had heard enough and fully expected him to pass the buck to me, and in nervous anticipation I started to perspire. But, to my surprise, he responded himself, in a quiet, measured tone of voice that I had seldom heard him use.

"Thank you for your comments, gentlemen, and rather than drag this out unnecessarily, I will assume the remainder of you feel essentially the same way as those who have already spoken." He paused only briefly for assenting nods. "That being the case, then let me begin by saying, first of all, that I respect your opinions on this delicate subject, knowing only too well how organized religions must regard our involvement in a matter so far afield from our normal journalistic endeavors. But this is an unusual situation we find ourselves in, so let me explain.

"Mr. Elliott is one of our more experienced editorial writers, a man not inclined to participate in hoaxes of any kind. That said, he brought to my attention just before Thanksgiving a few e-mails allegedly from the recently deceased Senta Trondson, a woman with whom he had a significant personal relationship for many years. I'm going to let Mr. Elliott speak for himself about the hoax issue in a few minutes, but before I do that, I want to address the question of why we would allow a so-called 'non-entity' to present his views to our readers on a matter of such importance.

"To begin with—and I don't know where you got the idea, gentlemen— nothing in the *Washington Tribune* article said anything about Mahatma Damodar being a non-entity. Let me assure you, Damodar is not a figment of someone's imagination or a non-entity, as has been alleged or implied, but a real, live person who has demonstrated his knowledge of the occult and his ability to control elemental forces of nature—including electrons—that few of us can comprehend, but whose efficacy, I assure you, is undeniable."

I looked over at Ray and by the sheepish look on his face realized that he was the one who planted the idea in the minds of the clergymen about Damodar being a non-entity. And they, in turn, also looked chagrined at being caught in this verbal faux pas.

Chet continued his comments. "Mr. Tuohy has witnessed and participated in one such demonstration that showed without any doubt that Mahatma Damodar is a real person, even though he can produce effects that defy normal scientific explanation. Isn't that right, Ray?"

Caught offguard, the embarrassed religious editor replied softly, "Yes, that's true."

"Wait a minute!" Father Dougherty exclaimed, pointing at the executive editor, "Are you saying that you've met this man personally and are prepared to vouch for his knowledge on these highly-disputed matters?"

"No, I have not met him in person," Walker replied, carefully choosing his words, "because he has chosen to remain temporarily not visible to our eyes for reasons he explained and which make perfectly good sense to me, but I can assure you he's real and has given ample proof of his existence and powers, not only to me and to Mr. Tuohy, but to Miriam Green, our Travel Section editor, and to Mrs. Thayer, as well."

The baffled looks on the faces of the clergymen were a sight to behold, and the obvious question on all of their minds was posed by Rabbi Pekarski: "Would you mind amplifying on that statement, Mr. Walker? What type of proof are you talking about?"

Chet proceeded to recount in detail the demonstration that took place in this very same conference room a week earlier, pausing only for effect as he related the three specific tests that Damodar had successfully completed. When he was done, Reverend William Chambers, pastor of the Westminster Presbyterian Church, immediately challenged Walker. "Have you ever considered the possibility that this Damodar is not actually a so-called Mahatma or Master of Wisdom but merely a discarnate entity who has come to you through some sort of channeler or medium with an evil bent who hopes to foment unrest and disturbance of the very sort we are here discussing?"

"Okay, let's assume you're correct, Reverend. If Damodar's comments and articles are the product of a channeler or medium, who is that person and by what means does he manage to get them onto Dave's computer? And, although the information presented admittedly sets forth an Eastern philosophic point of view, I fail to see how that, by itself, can be characterized as fomenting unrest or disturbance of any kind." Before Reverend Chambers could reply, an obviously annoyed Adrienne Thayer seized the opportunity to join the discussion.

"Gentlemen, I want you to know that we've considered the various possibilities of fraud, hoax or chicanery and I, for one, was the most adamant of all that this series *not* go forward until I received personal proof of the de facto existence and bona fides of the person called Damodar. But, I can assure you, he *does exist*, and more than that, he seems capable of doing exactly what he says, whether it's making e-mails appear on computer monitors, making photographs appear out of thin air or, in my case, making it possible for me to receive a very personal message from my long-deceased son, Eric."

There was a moment of stunned silence, before Rabbi Pekarski asked in a soft voice, "May I ask how you received that message, Mrs. Thayer?"

"In an e-mail on my own computer upstairs. And it was no hoax, I assure you. I received a message from Eric in response to a question I had asked of this Damodar, and the reply from Eric—in his own words and not through some medium or channeler—contained information no one else in the world could possibly have known but my son. No, gentlemen, I admit we're dealing with something strange and extraordinary here, but it's real and we can't pretend it isn't."

"Then, you're telling us that not only Mr. Elliott, but you, too, have communicated directly with someone who is no longer alive?" Father Dougherty asked, his incredulity now taxed to the limit.

"That's absolutely correct," Adrienne firmly replied, only too happy to inform the clergymen what Chet and I had learned earlier—and the real cause of her sudden change of heart about authorizing the series. She concluded with a penetrating question, looking directly at Father Dougherty: "And while we're on the subject, why is it that our Christian religions entreat us all to pray for life everlasting but then vilify anyone who claims to communicate with a deceased loved one in that realm as though he or she was a demon incarnate?"

No one responded and the collective frustration of the clergymen was evident on their faces. Their momentary silence gave Chet the opportunity he was waiting for to drag me into the fray. Looking squarely at me, he said, "Why don't you tell them about the e-mails, Dave?"

"Okay, but before doing so," I began, "I would like to respond briefly to the charge of necromancy that was raised earlier. In the world of the occult, motive is everything. The communications I have received from my recently deceased friend have in no way involved the subject of divination of the future, witchcraft, fortune telling or anything of that nature. Mahatma Damodar, the Master of Wisdom who has made all this possible, has merely used this unique method of communication to show to the world that death of our physical bodies does not terminate the soul's journey from birth to death to rebirth over and over again until it reaches the stage of spiritual perfection."

I then described how I had received the first and subsequent e-mails from Senta, including the test I had devised to rule out my being the subject of a hoax. When I finished my narrative, I passed out copies of the e-mails to everyone at the table, which they devoured with the intensity of lions attacking the remains of a fresh kill.

After a few moments, an apparently distraught Ray Tuohy broke the awkward silence with a statement he obviously had pent up within him since the start of the meeting. "Despite the demonstration that has been referred to, nothing has convinced me that the e-mails Mr. Elliott has received are, in fact, from someone who is deceased, despite the contrary beliefs expressed by others in this room. And, because of that, I agree with our guests and think it is not in the best interests of the *Tribune* or its readers to proceed with the series of articles on an arcane issue that has been the subject of controversy since time immemorial."

Adrienne, clearly irritated by Tuohy's comment, addressed him directly. "Well, Ray, apart from the fact you're ignoring what you saw with your own eyes, as well as the message communicated to me by my son Eric, the mere fact that a subject is controversial hasn't stopped the *Washington Tribune* from printing a story in the past. And, as to whether or not it's in the best interest of the paper to proceed with this series, that's a decision that I've already made. We may, in the long run, regret it by being shown we've been duped or hoaxed, or whatever, but it isn't as though we haven't tried to anticipate that and taken pains to avoid that result."

"Yeah, Ray," Walker concurred, with a noticeably hard edge to his voice, "this may be a different kind of story than we usually cover, but mere novelty or controversy surrounding a subject hasn't deterred us up to now. If what Damodar has to say flies in the face of what others have to say about the afterlife, so be it. We'll be happy to print the pros and cons in the paper and let the readers judge for themselves what points of view make the most sense. I believe some of you have already submitted articles on the subject that will appear in tomorrow's paper."

Ray was clearly shaken by the forceful, public rebukes by his immediate superiors, who obviously opposed the course of action he was suggesting. The assembled clergymen likewise noted the thrust and tenor of the comments directed to Tuohy, and I could see that they felt they had been rebuked as well. Reverend Johnson seemed particularly upset, heaving a sigh and wistfully remarking, "Well, I can see we're getting nowhere here, so we may as well consider this meeting concluded."

Chet's ire was aroused by Johnson's comment. "What did you expect to accomplish, Reverend Johnson? Were you hoping to squelch a point of view just because it conflicts with sectarian religious doctrine? That won't fly in this day and age. Even if we're wrong—and I admit that's always a possibility—that's no reason for us to refuse coverage of a story that appears to be of widespread interest to our readers, which it definitely is, judging by the flood of e-mails, phone calls and letters we've already received."

"Well, so be it," responded the obviously disappointed cleric as he stood to leave. Father Dougherty genuflected and uttered half-aloud, "May God forgive you for your actions," and several others uttered similar remarks or gave upturned gazes to heaven as they rose and exited the conference room, some without so much as a 'goodbye' out of ordinary courtesy.

My relief at the way things turned out was almost palpable, though I did my best to conceal my true feelings. Before leaving the room, Adrienne thanked me for having produced copies of the series of e-mails between Senta and me, which, she observed, made it hard for the clergymen to challenge my assertion of de facto two-way communication with my deceased love. Chet gave me a reassuring smile and an unaccustomed pat on the shoulder as he turned to leave the room.

For the first time in days, I felt the knot in my stomach slowly beginning to unwind. After the meeting ended, I gathered some materials from my desk and headed home, stopping briefly at a grocery store on Rhode Island Avenue to get some groceries for the weekend.

Chapter 16

Early Friday morning I headed for a nearby luncheonette, mainly because I wanted to see a copy of Friday's *Tribune*, since I don't get the paper at home. As I munched on a doughnut and nursed my first cup of coffee, I read not only Damodar's second article but all the Religion & Family Section articles, including one from a high-ranking Catholic priest from the Washington Diocese. He excoriated me for intimating I had actually communicated with a dead person. Another article was from a Lutheran minister along the same lines, a third from an Episcopal Bishop who berated the paper for being so irresponsible as to report seriously the receipt of e-mails "supposedly from a dead person."

Nothing new there. These were the articles Ray had warned me about, and I assumed that he had done his best to brief the writers on the results of the conference held at the beginning of the week. Damodar's article was given preferential placement, as was Senta's e-mail explaining what *kama loka* was like, followed by Lou Garza's interview of me describing Senta's personal traits. It read well, and I was pleased. After paying the check I ambled back to my apartment. To my surprise and delight, I saw that Senta had sent me another e-mail:

> "Darling *herzele*. Both Damodar and I are pleased with the way things are going. I know how difficult it must be for you, but you seem to be holding up all right. Yes, I can see —or perhaps 'feel' is the better word —what you are going through.
>
> "Damodar has brought to my attention a troubling circumstance: he sees in the astral an array of evil forces focused against you and specifically aimed at interrupting the series of articles he has begun. He says he has picked up some negative vibrations and wants you to be on your guard at all times. In fact, darling, he said your life might be in danger. He told me to tell you to keep your silver talisman with you at all times.

"He also told me to tell you that the next article, dealing with *devachan*, will be ready soon. Keep up the good
work, my love. I'm proud of you, but please be careful."

I replied immediately, acknowledging the warning sent by Damodar, and her words of praise. And I promised I would continue to wear the talisman on a chain around my neck, as I have been doing since she gave it to me two months before she died. After finishing my e-mail, I reflected on the fact that evil forces already were at work, as evidenced by the threatening letter I had received and the black painted epithets sprayed on my car. I resolved to be even more vigilant about my personal safety.

At ten o'clock sharp, I joined my editorial page colleagues in the morning staff meeting via telephone conference call. One of the writers brought up the subject of the increasingly noisy crowds in the building lobby each morning and asked whether the way the public was responding to the series was worthy of an editorial. I said I didn't think so. "Editorials are used to express a newspaper's policy or position on an issue, and I don't think that either Adrienne or Chet has gotten to that point yet. I think it's too early for the *Tribune* to editorialize on that subject."

The majority agreed with me, although I sensed a growing uneasiness about the situation. I started work on my new assignment when the conference call ended, and continued working until mid-afternoon, when the phone rang. It was Chet.

"I'm afraid I've got some bad news, Dave. Just as circulation has started to soar, the boss-lady has received a letter from the Right Reverend William Hollinger. He's the Bishop of the Episcopal Diocese of Washington. Hollinger castigated her personally—since she's an Episcopalian—for allowing the after-death series to continue, and advised her that letters have gone out to all parishioners in the diocese advising them to cancel their subscriptions to the *Trib*. We don't have statistics on our readers' religious affiliations, but if they take the advice, you can be sure we'll lose a hell of a lot of subscribers, and that ain't good." He paused, as though waiting for my reaction.

"What do you want to do?" I asked, genuinely concerned.

"Don't know. It's a real dilemma; that's for sure. I'm gonna talk to Adrienne about it in a few minutes, but thought I'd call you first, to see if you had any thoughts."

"I'm afraid I don't Chet . . . except that, if you stop the series now and the word got out that it was because of a boycott by the Episcopalians, wouldn't you be setting a bad precedent for the handling of future stories that might upset other religious groups? I think you should at least take that into consideration."

"Yeah, I've thought about that. Well, we'll see how the boss-lady feels about it. I'll let you know, one way or another." And with that he hung up.

The threat of a newspaper boycott clearly didn't fall into the category of an event of the sort Damodar had warned about. But it was a troubling circumstance, nevertheless, and I wondered how Adrienne and Chet would handle it. I got my answer half an hour later, when Chet called to say that Adrienne approved the continuation of the series regardless of any threatened Episcopal boycott. "She agreed the precedent would be a bad one, and also thought the attempt at a boycott would probably attract more readers than ever. Tough lady. I sure admire her guts. Incidentally, I want to talk to you about some different strategies for placement of the series, so would you mind coming in on Monday for thirty to forty-five minutes, say, about ten?"

"I'll be there," I said. "Who else is coming?"

"Just you, Ray, Lou Garza and Solly Berman," he replied. "Don't be late."

The hue and cry generated by Damodar's second article, as well as the related articles and my interview about Senta, was turning into a battle between polarized forces: those who believed and those who didn't. The believers wanted more information on how they might replicate my experience with Senta, while the religionist advocates were strongly opposed to any discussion of the world beyond. Sol Berman was keeping a close eye on the statistics and it was clear that the believers group far exceeded the non-believers. He informed Chet that he had compiled a list of questions readers had for me and/or Senta, which Chet sent on to me for my reaction and handling.

The questions all reflected a serious desire to learn more about the afterlife, with little concern about the issue of necromancy. Some I knew were related to topics that Damodar hadn't yet covered, but I decided nevertheless to pass them along to Damodar and Senta for their responses.

On Saturday morning, after receiving the insurance company's okay, I took my Lexus to the Columbia Road garage to have it repainted. As the week ended, I mentally reviewed the series of events that had occurred, and by and large I was pleased with the way things were turning out. Being able to communicate with my beloved Senta was the pièce de résistance, without a doubt. But the damage to my car, the threat received in the mail, and Damodar's cautionary warning for my safety was giving me genuine pause for reflection. Although Chet's request for a strategy meeting on Monday was a positive sign, somehow or other I felt uneasy even about that.

Chapter 17

Ray didn't like the sound of it when Chet told him to be available for a ten o'clock meeting on Monday morning. Chet would only say that the purpose of the meeting was to develop a new strategy for publishing the Damodar articles, but Ray knew that whatever Chet had in mind was going to affect him considerably. After hanging up, he could feel the anger and the tension invading his body. *All because of David! That damn Jew will cost me my job yet.* The only thing that mattered now: how could he get even with David?

That ridiculous story about David's receipt of e-mails from Senta Trondson had caught on with the public, not only in the nation's capitol but all over America, and Ray suspected that Chet wanted to re-position future articles by Damodar and all related stories to the main section of the paper. At this rate, there would be no need for a Religion & Family Section editor at all. In fact, Chet hinted as much in a half-joking manner following the meeting with the clergymen.

When Chet mentioned that the only other staff people invited to the Monday meeting were David, Lou Garza and Sol Berman, Ray got the first glimmer of an idea. Maybe, just maybe, he could eliminate the problem once and for all.

Around twelve-thirty on Sunday morning, Ray drove into the District after telling his wife he had to pick up some papers at the office. This wasn't at all unusual behavior on a Sunday since, after abandoning the ministry, he had stopped attending church services on any regular basis. He simply didn't like the direction the church was taking, especially its ultra-liberal stance on ministers presiding at wedding-style ceremonies for gay couples.

A chill penetrated the air as he approached 13th and Euclid. The icy street stood empty; no people or cars in sight. After parking on a side street, he walked a block and a half to the United Christian Fellowship Church. By the time he got there, the morning's services had let out and the congregants gone, but the church's principal outreach program would be in full swing. Ray cautiously maneuvered down the ice-glazed side steps to the basement.

As he entered the basement, he was amazed at the sheer number of poor people, mostly blacks, stuffed into the large all-purpose room. Some were trying to sleep on army cots lined up near one end of the room. Others sat and talked in small groups, holding paper plates with food. What appeared to be lay volunteers were serving hot food in the kitchen area at the far end of the room.

A surprisingly large number of young mothers with children either waited in line or were already seated at long tables. At least the room was warm, and the aroma of the cooked Sunday meal—chicken with mashed potatoes and green beans, with a dollop of Jell-o for dessert—was quite pleasant.

Ray, dressed in jeans and wearing a khaki, fleece-lined sport jacket, went virtually unnoticed by the motley assortment of humanity who frequented this haven of comfort almost daily during the harsh winter months in D.C. After a quick scan of the room, he spotted Archie Taylor sitting near the end of one of the long tables, and Archie spotted him at the same moment. They exchanged nods and Ray motioned with his head for Archie to come his way. After giving his fellow diners some plausible excuse for leaving, Archie rose from the table and walked slowly in Ray's direction.

As Archie approached, Ray quickly turned and exited the basement. Archie followed him and a few moments later the lanky black man, whose unshaved stubble only partially masked the scar on his right cheek, met his benefactor on the same corner where they had first met. Tuohy gave Archie a weak smile and nod by way of greeting, but Archie forcefully grabbed Ray's hand and pumped it vigorously, which made the newspaperman extremely uncomfortable, given the drifter's questionable degree of cleanliness.

"How 'ya doin'?" Archie asked, enthusiastically.

"I'm okay," Ray replied with a serious look on his face. "Let's go to my car. I have something important I want to talk about, but not out here in public."

The two of them walked silently to Tuohy's dark blue Oldsmobile Sedan, and after Ray had warmed the car for a couple of minutes, he turned to his now-eager companion—who, mercifully, no longer smelled of wine—and began with praise for his letter writing effort. "You did very well with that letter, my friend. It had the very effect I intended. But now I've got something a lot more important for you to do, only it's a lot riskier job." He paused before continuing, "How would you like to make some *real* money this time?"

A Death Interrupted

"I'm all ears," said the black man, thoughtfully stroking the stubble on his chin as he contemplated the prospect of making more money.

Ray coughed nervously and then spoke in soft, measured words. "Here's the deal. I want you to shoot someone . . . not to kill him, just to scare hell out of him. But, I do want you to hurt him bad enough so he'll be out of commission for a long, long time." Ray paused to see Archie's initial reaction, but getting none, continued. "I know you're familiar with guns, but it's got to be done right. You've got to hit him in the arm or leg, not the head. And it's got to be done at ten o'clock in the morning—tomorrow morning, to be exact, which means it'll be in broad daylight. Do you think you're up to it?"

Archie frowned a little and cupped his cheek before answering. "Like I said, I'm all ears. What are you offering?"

"There's $3,000 in it for you—half now and half when the job is done."

"Three thousand!" the Lorton parolee shouted excitedly. He watched with fascination as Ray withdrew an envelope from his jacket pocket and opened it slightly; just enough to show Archie that it contained a wad of fifty-dollar bills.

"That's a nice piece of change, and I could sure use it," Archie said as he stroked his chin, weighing the ramifications of getting caught and winding up in the hellhole of Lorton again against the wad of greenbacks still held enticingly close.

Ray could smell the man's mixture of fear and excitement, like an animal salivating for a crumb but fearing a swift kick for his efforts. Ray snapped the envelope closed, saw Archie's eyes flicker and his fingers twitch. "I thought you could use it," Ray said. "But are you up to it? I mean, do you think you can pull it off? Are you a good enough shot? You've got to understand, I don't want you to kill the man."

With an air of bravado, Archie laughingly replied, "Are you kidding? I've owned guns for years. Got a 9-millimeter Beretta in my room right now and I can bag a squirrel at fifty yards. But who's the target? Is it the same guy?"

"Yes, it's the same man you sent the letter to. He works with me at the *Washington Tribune* . . . over on 15th Street near K. He'll be there at the front entrance tomorrow morning a few minutes before ten. I've got a picture of him here." He produced the picture of David that appeared in Friday's newspaper story accompanying the Lou Garza interview. Archie

119

fingered it a couple of seconds in silence as Ray continued, "You can have it. Now, obviously, you've got to make a clean getaway. Do you have a bike by any chance?"

Archie shook his head no, "But don't worry about that. I can get one," he said with his crooked-teeth smile and a knowing wink.

"Then you'll do it?"

"You bet I will," Archie replied, enthusiastically.

"Then it's settled," Ray said, with a genuine sense of relief in his voice. Worried that Archie might make a mistake about the address, Ray decided to give him his business card, which contained the *Tribune's* address. Archie took it, studied it a moment, then suddenly his eyes narrowed. "Ah, how do I . . . I mean, you say you'll pay me the rest on Tuesday, but . . ." Ray saw in Archie's wary look how suspicion about the balance of his reward being paid had clearly replaced any fear of detection. As if this scum had any right to question Ray Tuohy! The journalist snapped the card from Archie's hands and wrote on the back, '$1,500 Tuesday. 12/4/01, R. Tuohy.' "For heaven's sake, don't say a word about this or show this card to anyone. And be sure you're there at least ten minutes before ten o'clock tomorrow morning. I'm counting on you to do it right. You hear?"

Ray handed the drifter the card and the envelope containing the money at the same time. After giving a quick look outside, Archie started counting the fifties, and when he got to one thousand, he stopped, put all the bills back into the envelope and shoved everything into an inside pocket of his grimy trench coat. "Looks like it's all there," he said happily. "Don't worry. I'll take care of everything just the way you want it."

"That's what I was hoping you'd say. Good luck, and I sure your aim is as good as you say it is. If everything goes as planned, I'll pay you the rest at noon on Tuesday, right here. Not at the church. I don't want anyone to see us. I'll be here at twelve o'clock sharp. Got that?"

"You bet. I'll be here." And then, scratching his head as he studied Tuohy's business card, he observed softly, "So, you work at the paper, too?"

Ray recognized the veiled threat of exposure or retaliation if the final payment wasn't made as promised or if something else went wrong. But, he concluded, it was too late to worry about that now. Besides, that's the price one had to pay for setting up something as risky as this. "Yeah, I do," he answered. "But you just do your job, and I'll be here with the other fifteen hundred at noon on Tuesday."

"Don't you worry. I'll be here," Archie repeated with even more emphasis as he exited Ray's car. Ray watched the tall man walk away briskly until he disappeared around the corner.

As Ray drove through the quiet streets of the District on his way back to Fairfax, tinges of excitement mixed with guilt. At first he couldn't quite believe the audaciousness of his plan, but once the die had been cast he began to savor the likely consequences. At the very least, David would be physically disabled, certainly for an extended period of time, but possibly for life. Sometimes it amazed him how much hatred he had for David. Ray's heart rate quickened as he thought, *That will put an end to all that Jew's blasphemous e-mail nonsense once and for all.* Thinking about it, he recalled his father's constant denunciation of Jews as evil, and he felt the same way.

Then, too, he would not only get even with his long-time personal enemy but the adverse publicity surrounding the incident undoubtedly would reflect negatively on Chet's and Adrienne's decision to continue publication of the articles by Damodar in the first place. Ray's spirits were lifted by the thought that they just might come around to his way of thinking. *They'll see that I was right all along. A first-class newspaper like the Trib shouldn't be encouraging communicating with the dead.*

His momentary concern that what he was doing was evil and morally wrong barely entered into the picture. If the end was justifiable—and about that he had no doubt—then so was the deed. The only issue was, could Archie pull it off successfully? Would the man stay sober? Was he really as good a shot as he said? Could he make his getaway without getting caught? These were the imponderables that worried Ray. The thought that the whole thing might backfire never entered his mind.

No doubt about it; tomorrow would be a big day.

Chapter 18

Monday, December 3rd started out as a cold, crisp day in the Nation's Capitol, and I was glad to hear on morning television that no precipitation was anticipated. Before heading downtown for the ten o'clock meeting, I sent an e-mail to Senta telling her about the meeting and brought her up-to-date on how the series was beginning to make a real impact, not only in Washington but nationwide. She was pleased. She reminded me that the thirty-third anniversary of our first meeting—December 18th—was not far off, and we exchanged nostalgic thoughts of those early days.

Since my Lexus wasn't available, going downtown required alternate transportation. So, at nine-thirty I called for a taxicab and waited in the front hallway of my apartment house until it arrived about ten minutes later. I spent my time in the taxi re-reading the draft of my latest editorial dealing with Medicare benefits for Alzheimer's patients. The ride took roughly fifteen minutes. As I exited the vehicle at the front entrance to the *Tribune* on 15th Street, I checked my watch. It was 9:55 a.m.—just in time for the scheduled meeting.

As the taxi pulled away, I casually noticed a shabbily dressed black man leaning over and checking the tire pressure on a shiny red bicycle resting against the building. The momentary thought that crossed my mind was the incongruity of such a seedy-looking person owning such an expensive sports bike, but I really didn't pay too much attention to the man—that is, not until I reached for the door handle at the main entrance. After glancing in the man's direction once again, I noticed that he had gotten up and was now moving toward me and, to my horror, I saw he was holding a handgun pointed directly at me. Before I could open the door or move out of the way, two shots rang out. I heard the first one but not the second as I felt intense searing pains in my chest and right shoulder, followed by a sudden wooziness, and then everything went dark as I lost consciousness.

The scene on the street became instant chaos. As the shooter jumped on his bicycle and began pedaling away, an elderly woman screamed, while a younger woman who also had been standing nearby ran into the building to summon help. The *Tribune's* security guard raced outside and bent over my body to see where I was wounded. He told a passerby to put her shopping bag or something else to prop up my head, and then used his portable cell phone to call for an ambulance and the police.

Then, something totally unexpected happened: All of a sudden I could see that I was no longer a part of my physical body. I felt weightless and was drifting above the scene on the street below, where I could observe everything that was happening to me completely without emotion, as though I were watching it happening to some stranger in a movie. Of immediate interest was the crowd forming on the sidewalk. I could hear a male passerby calling 911 on his cell phone, and a few minutes later I could see the simultaneous arrival of an ambulance and two Metropolitan D.C. Police cruisers.

I watched with fascination as the two EMT technicians tried to resuscitate me, and heard one of them shouting to the other, "I can't get a pulse. He's in total arrest." Several policemen arrived and were busy interviewing witnesses and cordoning off the street. After a few minutes, reporters from the *Tribune* came downstairs and I could see that a fairly large crowd had begun to form around my body on the street. Eventually, I saw the EMT men put my body on a stretcher and transport me by ambulance to George Washington University Medical Center with sirens blaring. I could see that during the ride one paramedic kept pumping my chest to try to restore a heartbeat. The fascinating part of all of this was that I was so calm, so entirely pain-free and so seemingly disconnected from what was happening to my physical body.

Then, in what seemed like just a few seconds, I was no longer hovering above my body and watching the scene below, but suddenly I was in a calm, quiet atmosphere where, once I got my bearings, I saw standing before me the ethereal form of my darling Senta standing in her living room at home. And to my delight and amazement, she looked exactly the way she did when we first met thirty-three years ago, not the way she appeared as a seventy-year-old woman dying of stomach cancer. To top it off, she was wearing a dress that I loved, a black fitted sheath with a gold choker and matching bracelets, and I swear I even detected a trace of Ondine, her favorite perfume. In short, she looked and smelled absolutely wonderful.

It was at that moment I realized that, as a result of the shooting, I must have been transported in my astral body to *kama loka*, although I was not sure whether I was dead or still alive. But, one way or another, there was my beloved Senta. At that moment, I couldn't think of anything in the world I wanted to do more than to hug and kiss her. How I loved kissing her, touching her, feeling her warmth and softness against my body! The emotional effect of our embrace—two semi-ethereal bodies coming together like two dynamic forces of energy—overwhelmed me. I never thought I would ever see Senta again, let alone hold in my arms the healthy, stunning beauty I knew when we first met. What a heavenly surprise! Pun fully intended.

After our lingering embrace, I heard her soft and sweet voice, but it was in my head! Senta, I thought, I can hear you inside! She laughed that lyrical laugh I loved, and I realized that in the astral, telepathy was the only way we could talk without physical bodies. "Have I died?" I asked her. "The last thing I recall is some man aiming a gun at me. I remember hearing a shot, and then everything went black."

"No, you're not dead, darling, just wounded. Damodar told me that the talisman saved your life. You are here in your astral body, having an out-of-body experience, while the doctors are working to bring your physical body back to consciousness, which won't be too long, now."

As we talked, I noted with humor the complete reversal of our age differences, she now thirty-seven and me older by twenty-five years. "Since *kama loka* is a world of thought forms," she explained, "I thought you'd like to see me as I looked when we first met, and right here in my living room, so that's the thought form I created."

"Oh, precious, you couldn't have made a better choice. Seeing you like this brings back memories of how we met and fell in love, the thrill of our first kiss, the first time we made love and all the wonderful times we spent together over the years."

"I'll never forget those moments, either, darling. Ours certainly was a charmed life." I noticed a rueful look suddenly appear on her face as she continued, "But now that it's over, David, my only regret is that we never married. I believe that that would have made it all perfect."

Her remark took me by surprise. "But you always gave me good reasons, like your desire to be independent, your dancing, and your study of Theosophy. I understood."

"Yes, *herzele*, but I had a secret I never told you: I had a fear—a real one, even though it was unreasonable—that you, like my father and Jon, the two other important men in my life, would also abandon me, and I was terribly afraid of having that happen to me again. But now that I look back on my life—on *our* life, really—I see how much better it could have been if only I hadn't feared the abandonment. It was not only foolish of me, but selfish, since you never gave me any reason to doubt the sincerity of your love."

Senta's personal anguish in telling me this made me very sad, since I, too, would have preferred marriage to the arrangement we had worked out over the years. I saw her often, but not as often as I would have liked. And even though she told me several times that she didn't want a child, who knows what might have been if we were married?

I reached out and held her face in my hands, brushing her cheeks tenderly. "I'm so sorry that you felt that way, darling. I never would have abandoned you. It's not in my nature." I kissed her lightly on the lips and wiped a glistening ethereal tear from her cheek. Then, I hugged her close to my chest and we stood nestled together silently for nearly a minute.

When we separated, Senta smiled softly and changed the subject. She told me that she was aware of what had just happened to me out on the street, and that the attempt on my life was the occurrence that Damodar had warned me about. He had informed her, however, that I was not mortally wounded, because my silver talisman had deflected the second bullet away from my heart. Also, he said I would return to my physical body shortly and would recover fully in due time.

"Since you're here in your astral body, *herzele*," she said, "I know that you can't feel any pain from the gunshots, but if you weren't wearing the talisman, you might have been killed. I'm delighted to see you, but you still have a lot of work to do, and I'm sure that your time to leave your physical body permanently is still a long way off."

"I know, dearest. But what a joy it is to be together again! The day of your death you were so weak and so heavily dosed with morphine you could hardly speak. I barely had time to say a proper goodbye before you slipped away. Seeing you now, the way you looked when we first met, makes up for that heart-breaking final moment. And, by the way, before I return to my body, is there anything special I can do for you?"

Senta furrowed her brow and pondered the question only briefly before replying, "Now that you ask, there is one special favor you could do for me."

"Certainly, what is it?"

"As you know, I left everything to you in my will, but now that I think about it, I would like my niece, Francine, to have the Serapi rug, you know, the one I had in the study, with the small tear in it. Fran always admired that rug and on second thought I'd like her to have it, if you don't mind. I'm sure you can retrieve it from the auction house and arrange to have it sent to her in New York. Would you do that for me, darling?"

"Consider it done. I'll take care of it as soon as I get out of the hospital. I think it's a very thoughtful gesture on your part."

"Oh, good. I'm so glad you'll take care of that," she said, as she gave me one of her dazzling smiles that were always such a delight to behold.

I changed the subject. "And how have you been spending most of your time here?"

"Well, now that the afterlife series of articles is underway, I've been contacting my friends and relatives—so far, Jon, Santra, my brothers Artie and Hank, Isabelle, Mr. Perzeoli, and Margaret James. All of them seemed delighted to talk with me once again—and don't forget, these conversations are one hundred percent truthful; there's no possibility of lying here in *kama loka*. By the way, I'm planning to contact my father, and possibly Martha Graham in the near future."

"And when you're not conversing telepathically with your family or friends, how do you spend your time?"

"Mostly listening to music from the dances I used to dance to and imagining that I am still dancing. I've been exploring some new modern dance choreographic ideas that I was just beginning to develop when I stopped dancing."

"I'm glad to see that you've adapted to *kama loka* so beautifully."

We talked for another several minutes about various personal matters before I was treated to another unexpected surprise. Mahatma Damodar suddenly appeared in our midst. He was tall, swarthy and clean-shaven, looking quite handsome in a white tunic with matching white leggings and wearing a royal blue turban. He appeared to be younger than I am, more like fifty to fifty-five years old, not the one hundred and forty years he had to be chronologically.

After greeting us with palms joined and uttering *namasté*, he began talking to me, confirming that the shooting was the negative event he had foreseen in the astral which he did his best to warn me about. "Have no fear, however, you will be returning to your body soon. The talisman saved your life. But I have something important to tell you.

"When you return to your body, there is something you should tell the police authorities. The man who shot at you is a convicted criminal whose last name is Taylor. He lives in a small apartment at the rear of

2230 Florida Avenue in the northwest section of your city." Damodar
paused to let me assimilate the name and address, before hitting Senta
and me with a bombshell. "This man was hired to seriously injure you—
but not to kill you—at the behest of the man you know as Raymond
Tuohy. The connection between them, unfortunately, will have to be discovered by the authorities, but the key to the connection will be
something found in Taylor's apartment."

I was horrified, of course, and all I could think of saying was, "What'll
I tell the police about the source of this information? After all, I was the
man who was shot. How could I possibly know all this?"

"I am aware that that is a problem," Damodar answered, frowning as
he spoke, "but you will have to deal with it in whatever way you see fit,
my friend. I would have no objection to your telling them you learned it
from me when you were here in *kama loka* while out of your physical
body."

"That's not going to be easy to do, I'm afraid. You, Senta and I understand how that can occur, but the police are not likely to give it any
credence. Besides, no one has ever seen you, and a great many people
have already concluded that you're a figment of my imagination—a fictitious entity created by me out of whole cloth."

Damodar paused a second before responding, "Yes, I see your dilemma, but you will just have to make the best case you can. Perhaps if
you tell the police that the bicycle was stolen earlier this morning, that
may help them find the culprit."

"Yes, it might," I replied, glumly. "Well, I'll do the best I can."

Damodar then explained that the doctors would be reviving my body
soon, but told me that he and Senta would like to keep in touch with me
by e-mail while I was hospitalized, and suggested that I request a portable computer as soon as possible. With that he said goodbye and for a
brief moment his majestic mien stood in the center of a halo of brilliant
light, and then he vanished as suddenly as he had arrived. I knew then
that it was time for me to say goodbye to my beloved Senta. I hugged and
kissed her tenderly once more—knowing full well that this would be the
very last time I would ever hold her in my arms—and promised to keep
in touch with her via e-mail.

A few moments later, she, too, disappeared from my sight, and I suddenly felt a force like a giant magnet drawing me back into my body in
the emergency room at GW. An electric shock suddenly jolted my consciousness, blindingly brilliant, hot, searing. Then I felt the defibrillating

paddles pressed tight to my chest by the ER doctor to restore normal rhythm to my chaotically beating heart. After two unsuccessful tries, the doctor hollered, "Everyone stand clear," and pressed the paddles to my chest once more. This time, the electric jolt—like a sledge hammer whacking me on the chest—caused my body to jump nearly a foot off the examining table. At that point, I heard a female nurse shout, "We've got sinus rhythm and his vitals are coming back."

I knew I had regained consciousness because I could feel the searing pains in my chest and shoulder where the bullets had entered. The next thing I heard was the male doctor's voice barking orders, one after the other, "Start him on 100 milligrams lidocaine, rapid IV, and 1 milligram epinephrine, IV. Got to get him stabilized before we can do anything about those slugs. Swab and cover both entry wounds and start him on cephazolin 2 grams, IV."

The activity in the ER in response to the doctor's orders was at a high tempo but orderly. One nurse immediately began administration of the ordered IVs, while another swabbed my skin with an antiseptic solution around the bullet entry wounds and placed temporary bandages on my chest and shoulder. A third nurse kept a close eye on the cardiac monitor and my other vital signs, and after three more minutes had elapsed, she announced that my condition had stabilized.

The young ER resident in charge picked up the talisman and let out a soft whistle as he examined it. "Jesus, if this strange metallic object hadn't deflected the bullet, it would have killed him for sure. You can see where it's bent concave right in the middle. Make sure it stays with his belongings." Then he quickly issued more orders to the nurses: "When you're finished with the IVs, take him to X-ray for chest pictures, front and side, and then get him upstairs to the surgical ICU . . . and be sure he's hooked up to telemetry. We can retrieve the slugs tomorrow or Wednesday, provided he's still stabilized. And because of the arrest, there's undoubtedly been some damage to his heart, so let's get a cardiology consult with Doctor Ellis first thing tomorrow."

After thirty minutes or so in the ER, I was taken by gurney to the second floor medical-surgical intensive care unit. As I was being rolled along the hallway with an IV stuck in my arm, I could see reporters and television cameras everywhere and I suddenly realized what it meant to be a celebrity. I found out afterwards that once the word got out about the shooting—particularly, who the victim was— reporters and television crews from all over the city converged on GW University Medical Center, waiting for news of my condition. The scene was media bedlam, with television and press reporters camped out in the parking lot, near the ER and in the front lobby.

Of course, no one was allowed into my private room except the unit resident in charge and a nurse. Well, that's not entirely accurate. Once I was hooked up to the telemetry electrodes and a fancy monitor that checked my pulse, blood pressure and temperature, a tall man wearing dark pants, a black shirt with a nondescript tie and a hounds-tooth check jacket with suede elbows approached my bed. He looked to be in his mid-forties and was good-looking in a rough-hewn sort of way. His features and demeanor reminded me a little of Clint Eastwood. After introducing himself as Detective Anthony Fiori of the Metropolitan Police Department, he took out a small spiral notepad and then asked me how I was feeling.

"As well as can be expected, I guess. The drugs are taking care of the pain."

He began his questioning. "According to a couple of eyewitnesses, a tall African-American man with bushy hair and wearing a dark trench coat shot you twice at pretty close range and then hightailed it up 15th Street on his bicycle. The doctor says you took two bullets, one in your right shoulder and the other in your chest, and the last one would have killed you if it wasn't deflected away from your heart by some metallic object you were wearing. By the way, what was that thing?"

"That's my good luck talisman. It was given to me by my friend, Senta Trondson, shortly before she died."

"Well it sure worked." He paused a second before pointedly asking, "Do you know why anyone would want to shoot you?"

"I'm not sure *why*, but I can tell you *who* did it and where you can find him. Look, I'm pretty weak right now, so I'd like to tell this story only once. Do you think you could bring in a stenographer or someone who can tape record what I have to say?"

Fiori's eyes lit up. "You bet I could," he said, and he raced out of the room to report what was happening to his superiors at police headquarters and to try to locate an available police stenographer. The reporters in the hallway sensed something was up by Fiori's long, determined strides as he exited my room and began shouting at him, "What's going on?" to no avail, of course.

While Fiori was out of the room, I decided it was urgent to speak to Chet Walker in private, so I asked the Unit nurse if she could locate

Walker among the crowd of reporters outside. When Chet Walker heard what happened, he too had raced over to the hospital. The nurse found him almost immediately and, with the okay from the hospital security guard seated outside my door, he was allowed to come in. A few of the out-of-town reporters began to complain, but most of the locals recognized Chet Walker and understood why he was allowed in. His trademark cigar was dutifully stowed out of sight.

"How're you doing, Dave?" he began. "My god, I thought we were going to lose you for a while there." Before I could say a word, he asked the same question Fiori had asked. "Why would anyone want to shoot you?"

I knew that Fiori would be back soon, so I raised my left arm to signal I wanted to speak. "Chet, I've got something important to tell you. *Very* important. So please let me tell it all to you while I still have the strength and before the detective gets back. He only left to get a stenographer."

The gangly editor pulled a chair up alongside the bed. "Sure, Dave, go right ahead."

"After the demonstration at the office, you're probably one of the few persons in the world who would even understand what I'm about to tell you. So, here goes. I was shot by an African-American man I saw fixing his bicycle near the front entrance to the building. Afterwards, I lost consciousness and shortly after that I had one of those near-death experiences—you know, all of a sudden you're outside of your body and can see what's going on below, what people are doing and saying about you while you're lying there."

From the look on Walker's face, I could see he wasn't a believer in near-death experiences any more than he believed in the astral light, but I had to proceed. "As I was watching what was going on, I suddenly felt myself being drawn elsewhere, to a different, quiet environment, no long tunnel with a dazzling white light at the end, or anything like that, but all of a sudden, there was my beautiful Senta standing in her living room. I'm not kidding, Chet. Not only was she there, but she looked just like she did the day we first met, when she was thirty-seven years old. We even joked about the fact that I was now the older one."

"Now, hold on a minute, Dave. Don't you think you might have been hallucinating or something? You *did* lose consciousness, after all."

"Chet, believe me. I not only saw her, I hugged and kissed her and we spoke."

"You actually *spoke* to her?"

"Yep, we spoke telepathically; that's the only way you can when you're out of your body. She said she knew all about the shooting and told me that I would be all right and that I would be returned to my physical body soon. Damodar had given her that assurance."

"Holy shit," was all Walker could say, as he shook his head in disbelief.

"You haven't heard the half of it," I said, my voice starting to weaken because of the medication I was receiving intravenously. "Damodar himself appeared a few minutes later."

"You mean you saw him in person?" Chet's face showed his disbelief.

"As big as life, wearing an impressive dark blue turban and a white tunic outfit like they wear in India. Quite a handsome guy, by the way. Well, what he told me, Chet, is not going to make you happy, but here it is. First, he gave me not only the name, but also the street address and apartment number of the guy who shot me. His name is Taylor, and Damodar said he was a common criminal and—are you ready for this?—he shot me at the behest of Ray Tuohy. Those were Damodar's exact words, 'at the behest of Ray Tuohy.' He said the plan was only to injure me severely, not kill me." I stopped to see Chet's reaction, His face had turned ashen and he was momentarily speechless. Gradually, he pulled himself together, but I could see he was upset.

"Now, wait a minute, Dave, how'n hell would Damodar know all that?"

"C'mon, Chet," I chided. "Damodar explained the astral light to you. You know he's an Adept and can see all kinds of things in the astral that you and I can't see. But he was definite about Tuohy. Said the police would find evidence of his role in the shooting in this guy Taylor's apartment, somewhere over on Florida Avenue. I wanted you to know before the police found out, for obvious reasons."

Walker stroked his chin while thinking what to do, then said in a quiet, deliberate tone of voice, "Dave, tell 'em what you want about the guy who shot you, but don't mention Tuohy's involvement— if there is any—not yet at least. I know Damodar has some highly unusual talents when it comes to occult matters, but he just may be wrong on this one. I've known Ray Tuohy for ten years, and I just can't believe he would do a thing like this. Not premeditated violent injury or murder."

"Why not?" I asked. "Ray has been smarting ever since the tongue lashing you and Adrienne gave him in front of me and the group of clergymen, and he's never liked me personally, as you well know."

"Yeah, I know, but we're talking about a dislike of an entirely different order. Try to understand, if Ray *is* involved and it were to be proved in court, he could go to jail for a hell of a long time. And sure, it's not particularly good PR for a paper like the *Trib* to have internecine warfare erupt among two of its top staff members. So, if you don't mind, hold off on the Tuohy angle for the time being, okay? Let nature take its course. If the police make a connection themselves, so be it. I'd rather not have it come from you. And, you can be sure I'll keep it to myself as well."

I took the latter remark to mean he wasn't planning to tell the boss-lady.

"Okay, out of deference to you and my loyalty to the paper, I'll keep quiet about Ray's involvement for now. But the man *did* try to have me disabled, possibly for life. I can't forget that. If Damodar is right—and I feel certain he is—the evidence linking this Taylor character with Ray Tuohy will be found by the police in Taylor's apartment in any event, so let's wait and see what happens on that score."

I had no sooner said that than Detective Fiori returned, along with a pretty, young police stenographer with horn-rimmed eyeglasses and a braided ponytail lugging a portable steno machine. Walker nodded at them, stood up and said to me, "Hang in there, pal. Don't worry about a thing. I'll be in touch by phone," as he started to leave the room.

I suddenly remembered what Damodar had said about keeping in touch by e-mail and I hollered, "Wait a minute, Chet. Do you think you could have a laptop sent to me here at the hospital, so I can keep in touch with you and others at the office via e-mail?"

"Good idea. I'll have Solly bring one down to you later today or early tomorrow." And with that he left.

Detective Fiori introduced the petite, bespectacled stenographer as Sally Marshall, gave her time to set up her portable steno machine and administer the oath to me, and then he began the official interview. "This sworn statement is being given by Mr. David Elliott. It is taking place in Room 2104 of George Washington University Medical Center; the day is Monday, December third, two thousand and one, and the time is eleven-thirty a.m. Present are Mr. Elliott, police stenographer Sally Marshall, and myself, Detective Anthony Fiori, working out of D.C. Homicide." Fiori started the questioning:

"Mr. Elliott, someone shot you twice around ten o'clock this morning in front of the offices of the *Washington Tribune*, then fled on a bicycle, according to several witnesses. What can you tell us about the incident?"

A Death Interrupted

I raised the head of my bed and began by relating what I remembered before I became unconscious. I then added what happened to me during my out-of-body experience, including my meeting Senta in *kama loka*, how we embraced and what we spoke about. By his frequent furtive glances at the stenographer, I knew that Fiori was increasingly disillusioned by the direction the interview was taking, but nevertheless he kept asking, resignedly, "What happened then?" What I told him next, finally made him perk up.

"Then Mahatma Damodar appeared," I replied. "He's the Master of Wisdom who has been furnishing articles to the *Washington Tribune* on what happens after we die." I paused a second before asking Fiori, "Perhaps you've read or heard about that series of articles?"

"Yeah, I've read some of them," he replied, to my surprise. "That's why we have such a crowd of reporters and TV cameras outside. They all want to know about you. So, continue with your story. What did you or this Damodar say?"

"Well, this is what will interest you the most: Damodar told me that the person who shot at me was a man with a criminal record whose last name is Taylor, and that he's got a small apartment at the rear of 2230 Florida Avenue, NW. Damodar said that if you check this man's apartment carefully, you'd find evidence there that someone else put him up to it. Also, he told me that the bicycle this man used to get away from the scene of the shooting was stolen by him earlier this morning. Now, at least you have something to go on, and you can arrest this Taylor guy without having to do a lot of investigative work."

"I'm afraid it's not that easy, Mr. Elliott. We couldn't possibly arrest someone—even if he *was* the perpetrator—without some probable cause, and the word of some person you spoke to while having a so-called 'out-of-body experience' just wouldn't fly if the arrest were challenged in a court of law. We've got to have some independent corroborating evidence before we'd have enough probable cause to arrest him. You get the picture?"

I could see the logic of his position, so I simply shrugged my shoulders. "Well, maybe between the eyewitnesses and the bicycle thing you'll be able to get your probable cause evidence."

Fiori ignored my comment and repeated his earlier question. "Can you think of anyone who might want to kill you, Mr. Elliott, possibly someone who disagrees with what you have been or claim to have been doing—this communicating with your deceased lady friend by e-mail?"

"Well . . . I did receive an envelope containing a handwritten death threat in the mail last week, and I turned it over to the desk sergeant at the Third Precinct."

Fiori perked up. "Oh? When was that?"

"About Tuesday or Wednesday, I believe."

He wrote it down. "Can you think of anyone else who might want you dead?"

"Not at the moment," I lied, already regretting the promise I made to Chet not to mention Tuohy's name to the police.

In his official voice, Fiori said to the stenotypist, "Well, if that's all, then this sworn interview of David Elliott is terminated at eleven-fifty a.m." He thanked me for my trouble and wished me a speedy recovery as he and the stenographer prepared to leave.

"We'll be in touch," were his final words, and then, suddenly, I felt like all my energy had been drained, so I closed my eyes to get some needed rest.

Chapter 19

When Anthony Fiori got back to police headquarters on Indiana Avenue, NW, he found it a little difficult to explain what he learned in the interview, but he told his boss, Superintendent of Detectives Wilton Roberts, everything David had said, buttressing it with the stenographic notes. Roberts knew as well as Fiori that the word of an invisible entity like Damodar would not meet the standard for probable cause for an arrest either in the District of Columbia or anywhere else in the United States, but something inside told him that there might be more to the story than the simple hallucinatory impressions of a man while unconscious.

"Check out this Taylor guy, Tony," Captain Roberts directed. "Just for the hell of it, see if someone by that name really does live at the Florida Avenue address, and on the outside chance it's true, see if he has any kind of a record. Who knows? There may be more to this story than appears at the moment. I just hope it won't turn out to be another one of those wild goose chases caused by a lousy tip from a headline-seeking psychic."

By police radio, Fiori immediately had a squad car check the Florida Avenue address, and when the report came back positive in less than ten minutes, he gave orders for the two patrolmen in the squad car to try to learn Taylor's first name, "but not by knocking on his door. Just check the mailbox, the trashcan, stuff like that."

"His name is Archibald Taylor," came the radio response a few minutes later from patrolman Ivan Kedjierski. Fiori told Kedjierski and his partner, Joe Lassiter, to remain in the general area and await further instructions. Then he remembered the bicycle. "Did you fellows by any chance see a bicycle near this Taylor's apartment? If you do, see if there are any tags or ID on it, because the guy who shot this Elliott character earlier today was seen riding away on a bicycle."

The report came back over the police radio five minutes later: "There's an expensive red Raleigh bike behind the apartment and it has a number engraved on it, number 866934 dash Hal."

Fiori ordered the patrolmen to stay in the general area, but not be too visible. He told them, "I'll check the bike out right away."

Indeed, a Harold Kirstein had reported his Raleigh bike with #866934-Hal engraved on it was stolen from his apartment house on Beekman Place at nine that morning, and had filed a stolen bicycle report with the Third Precinct around nine-thirty. "Bingo," shouted Fiori triumphantly, as he smelled he was getting closer to pay dirt. And while he was contemplating his next move, a report from Statistics and Records showed that an Archibald Taylor of 2230 Florida Avenue was out on parole, having only recently been released from Lorton after serving five years of an eight-year sentence for armed robbery and felonious assault in 1996.

With this information, Fiori knew he had all the probable cause he needed and, with Captain Roberts' okay, radioed the officers in the squad car to arrest Archibald Taylor on suspicion of aggravated assault and attempted murder of David Elliott, as well as suspicion of grand theft of a Raleigh bicycle and possible other charges yet to be determined. He also directed the patrolmen to search Taylor's premises for any other evidence that might link him to criminal activity. Minutes later, the two police officers entered Taylor's ramshackle apartment and arrested him on the charges Fiori had set forth. As he was being handcuffed, Taylor was given his Miranda rights but began talking in a rapid and excited voice, knowing all too well that the aggravated assault charge—involving the use of a deadly weapon—could keep him behind bars for at least another twenty to twenty-five years.

"I only did it because I was paid to hurt that guy, not kill 'em. Here, I can show you who put me up to it, he's a guy who works right there at the newspaper. Look in my right pocket." The police officer retrieved from Taylor's pocket Ray Tuohy's business card with the notation, '$1,500, Tues., 12/4/01, R. Tuohy.' written on the back in blue ink. Moments later, the police officers found a brown paper bag with $1,500 in large bills in a drawer in Taylor's grungy bedroom. While one officer was talking to Taylor, the other one continued searching the apartment and eventually came up with a 9mm Beretta and a box of bullets. Putting on rubber gloves, he smelled the gun's barrel and then gingerly placed the gun in a large manila envelope which he marked with the word 'evidence,' preparatory to taking it downtown.

The policemen radioed Detective Fiori and told him what they had retrieved from the premises, including the fact that the handgun had recently been fired. He was elated. "Good work, guys. I think we've got our man. Before you bring that stuff downtown, wait there until the Third Precinct picks up the stolen bike and have them bring it down here so we can have it dusted for prints. And also, they're holding an envelope at the Third with a death threat to this David Elliott, he's the man who was shot this morning. Bring that downtown, too. Be sure to handle it carefully. It's evidence."

Fiori shook his head in disbelief. *No one in the DA's office is going to believe me when I tell them how we got this guy.*

Chapter 20

Cardiologist Robert Ellis visited me late Monday afternoon and told me that my damaged heart had developed an abnormally slow beat as a result of the injuries and subsequent cardiac arrest. "It looks like you're a prime candidate for a pacemaker," he said, "but we can do that later, after you've recovered sufficiently from your wounds."

My mother and father visited me briefly at the hospital on Tuesday morning after hearing the news about my near-assassination on the Monday evening TV news programs. To my surprise and relief, there was no talk about the likely cause of my wounds, merely parental concern for my welfare. Mom brought me a homemade kugel, a noodle pudding which she knew was a long-time favorite of mine. They weren't allowed to stay long because the doctors wanted me to conserve my energy for the follow-up surgery to recover the two slugs from my body, scheduled for later in the day.

The phone kept ringing constantly on Tuesday, with calls from Miriam Green and other co-workers at the *Trib*, as well as from others who knew me and Senta both. I noted that Ray Tuohy was not one of the callers, a fact I pointedly mentioned to Chet Walker when he called around eleven.

"Well, Dave, they apparently found the man Damodar had fingered and, so far as I know, Ray's name hasn't come up. Maybe there was no connection after all."

I knew better, but held my fire for the moment. Apparently, the police had done a good job of concealing Ray Tuohy's possible connection to the shooting, merely reporting that Archibald Taylor, a parolee with a long record of armed robberies and other felonies, did the dastardly deed. But I knew he wasn't alone in this, and also knew that it would just be a matter of time before Tuohy was implicated. How Ray met this morally depraved character was beyond me, but he must have met him somewhere and given him the assignment, and that's all that counted. I let Chet's comment go unanswered; reminding him instead of the laptop he promised to get for me.

"You'll have it this afternoon," he said, "I've already told Solly." And then he rang off after saying he would keep in touch. I think he really felt he got away with his plan to keep Tuohy's role in all of this a deep, dark secret. The fact that the newspaper's reputation was deemed more important to him than the fact he had a would-be murderer as an employee was terribly disappointing. What a twisted sense of priorities, I thought.

At two, I was taken to the OR and had the two slugs removed from my chest and shoulder in a short procedure that lasted only forty-five minutes. The slugs were given to a police official who was present during the surgery, and Fiori told me in a later phone call that the slugs came from the same type of weapon found at Taylor's apartment. He also said that the envelope containing the death threat had been sent for preliminary DNA testing to a lab in suburban Maryland, to see if the saliva on the envelope matched with Taylor's DNA.

"His saliva would be enough for DNA purposes," Fiori said. "But I'm sorry to inform you, sir, that when we arrested Taylor, he told us that someone else was the instigator of the attempt on your life . . . a colleague of yours by the name of Raymond Tuohy."

I feigned surprise at learning this, but then asked Fiori for more details. He told me that Ray's business card was found in Taylor's pocket when he was arrested, containing the words, '$1,500, Tues., 12/4/01, R. Tuohy,' but he was quick to add, "It still won't be easy to establish Mr. Tuohy's connection with the shooting. All we have is Taylor's word—the word of a common criminal—and that business card. If there was some way to get a sample of Tuohy's handwriting for comparison purposes without raising anyone's suspicions, that would help our handwriting analysis enormously."

I thought of Miriam immediately. "I may be able to help you in that regard, detective. Let me see what I can do."

"Well, any help will be appreciated," Fiori replied, sounding practically cheerful compared to the way he sounded when he first interviewed me.

As soon as he hung up, I called Miriam. After some brief chit-chat about my medical condition, I said, "Miriam, you're one of the few persons I'd really like to see. Do you think you might be able to pay me a visit tomorrow?" When she responded with pleasure in the affirmative, I added, "And, Miriam, before I forget, there's a short note from Ray in my top right desk drawer. He wanted me to know how unhappy he was about the after-death series and was urging me to call it off. Would you mind bringing that, too? I'd like to look at it again."

"You shall have it," she said, cheerfully. See you tomorrow morning."

In the late afternoon, Sol Berman stopped by with the laptop I had asked for. He told me how relieved everyone was that I survived the shooting, and told me that the story was page one news, not only at the *Trib*, but also elsewhere in the country. "And the mail keeps pouring in. You really started something, David."

I smiled and said, "You mean *Senta* really started something. It was all her doing . . . and Damodar's." I decided to change the subject. "Are you still pissed with me about the way I spoke about my feelings toward God and Judaism?"

"No, I can understand why you feel that way. Others have said the same thing, but I just couldn't understand why you wouldn't talk to me about it all these years. *That's* what pissed me." In a softer tone of voice, he added, "Still does."

"You're right, Sol. I should have, and I'm truly sorry."

"Aw, that's okay," he said, scrunching his nose by way of acknowledging my apology. "By the way, Chanukah begins on Sunday night and we light the first candle. You think you'll be out of here by then? If you are, then I'll take you to Hofberg's and we can fill up on some really good Chanukah latkes."

"I doubt it, Sol. They want to run some more cardiology tests before they give me the green light to go home. Thanks for the invite anyhow, and Happy Chanukah to you."

As he got up to leave, I thanked him again for the computer and for the news about how the media were handling my near-murder, but I couldn't wait for him to leave so that I could log on and contact Senta and Damodar. With the help of a hospital technician, I was provided with an Internet connection and as soon as I was able to get online, I sent my first hospital-based e-mail:

> "Mahatma Damodar and dear Senta, as you probably already know, the man who shot me was arrested yesterday and the police say they have all the evidence they need to have him convicted of maiming and attempted murder. But, my boss begged me not to tell the police about Ray Tuohy's connection to the crime, and like a fool, I relented and said nothing to them. Now I feel terrible. It was a cowardly thing to do."

A moment later, Damodar responded.

"Do not castigate yourself so severely, dear friend. You reacted as any normal person would have reacted under the same circumstances. But fear not, the role played by your colleague at the newspaper will be revealed to the police soon enough. And now, if I may, I should like to send you the third article in our series, this one dealing with *devachan*."

In the next ten minutes he sent the entire article, which I saved on the flash drive that Sol Berman had left with me. Then, I asked to speak with Senta via e-mail.

"Seeing you in *kama loka*," I began, "was an experience I will never forget. You looked more beautiful than ever, and the fact that I was able to hold you in my arms and kiss you was almost too good to be true. It was undoubtedly a first in world history, but who cares, just so long as we were able to get together one more time. How I love you!

"Your admission about not wanting to marry me because of your subconscious fear I might abandon you came as a shock and caused me to feel an overwhelming sadness, but I can understand how you might have felt that way. Irrational fears can dominate our lives, but it sure must have been heavy baggage for you to carry all those years. Never mind, we'll make up for it in our next lifetime.

"Incidentally, I will take care of the rug thing as soon as I get out of the hospital, which I imagine will be in another week or so, if not sooner. I think Chet's in for a rude awakening when the word about Ray Tuohy's instigation of my intentional maiming and possible murder is made public. And you can be sure it will come out. I'm having Miriam Green bring me a note Ray sent me a couple of weeks ago at the office, so the police can compare it with the handwriting on Ray's business card that Taylor had in his possession when he was arrested. Damodar said that the police would make the connection, and he was right. Naturally, I won't say anything to Miriam about who was behind the plot to kill or severely injure me."I'm feeling better now that the bullets have been removed from my body and pretty soon I should be able to eat some regular food. I can't wait to get back on my feet again and get out of this place, though I must say that the doctors and nurses all have been very nice to me. Incidentally, it looks like I'm going to need a pacemaker, but the cardiologist said he wants me to be in a better physical condition before he puts it in."

She acknowledged my remarks and after a few more words to each other our communication ended. Shortly afterward, I called Sol Berman to tell him I had received Damodar's third article. He said he'd pick it up a little later, and at that I decided to take a nap. The whole train of events had finally caught up with me. My muscles ached and my eyes could barely stay open, so as exhaustion overcame me I welcomed the chance to sleep.

Damodar's third article dealt with *devachan* which, he pointed out, like *kama loka* is not a place but a state of consciousness, a dream state that is purely personal and subjective. After noting that the Sanskrit term *devachan* means "place or dwelling of the gods," he detailed its characteristics and what happens there.

"The act that sends us into *devachan* is our letting go of the *kama rupa*, which is the body of desires, our whole desire nature. It may be a little difficult to comprehend, but we ourselves create our own *devachan*. That feeling which is strongest in us at the moment of death, when we see the entire events of our life down to the minutest detail marshaled and reviewed in a few seconds, that feeling will become the fashioner of our *devachanic* bliss. And since the nature of each individual's feelings about their existence is as infinite and varied as there are Egos in the world, it follows that each resultant *devachan* is just as infinitely varied.

"The Spiritual Ego or Soul is reborn into *devachan* to experience the happy continuity of the good and the noble within each of us. For the time being, the karma of any evil generated during the life just ended remains dormant until it is time for the individual's next reincarnation, but the karma of good follows him into the bliss of *devachan*. While earth-life is the place where karma has its operation, the Spiritual Ego must have some rest; otherwise it would succumb to the strain of working through earth-life after earth-life, continuing to create new karma, without a break in between. The place of rest provided by Nature is *devachan*.

"*Devachan* is purely a world of effects, an idealized and subjective continuation of earth-life. It is, in point of fact, a state of intense selfishness during which the Spiritual Ego of each person reaps the reward of his unselfishness on earth. He is completely engrossed in the bliss of all his personal earthly affections, preferences and thoughts. No pain, no grief, just unalloyed happiness.

"Note that the Ego is unable to see or be aware of any evils, sorrows or woes to which those it loved on earth may be undergoing. That would hardly be a state of bliss. On the other hand, in *devachan* the Soul lives in a sweet, dream-like state of its own creation, surrounded by all the people and things it loves and longs for, whether those loved ones have already passed over or are still remaining on earth. It has them near itself as happy, as blissful and as innocent as the disembodied dreamer himself.

"What about direct contact or communication from *devachan* with those we have left behind? Since the Soul has no objective consciousness, it cannot have direct communication with other entities in *devachan* or on earth. To have it otherwise would be to negate the whole concept of *devachan*, where the Soul is rewarded for the spiritual aspirations and development of its life just ended. On the other hand, since the *devachanee* creates his own world, he is with all those he ever loved, not in bodily form and companionship, but in a world that is to him real, close and blissful. And because spiritual holy love is immortal, under karmic law all those who loved each other with true spiritual affection during their earth-lives are destined to incarnate once more in the same family group.

"Returning to the nature and quality of our stays in *devachan*, much depends on how one has prepared for the experience while still alive. Those who do not believe in a life after death, have no life after death. That is occult law. Your belief affects you in a very direct manner. Life after death is produced by your aspirations and spiritual development while alive. According to the growth of each, so is his life after death. Those with spiritual longings, desires for a higher life, and aspirations for noble things, will see them come to flower in *devachan*. Those who have no such aspirations or higher longings, and no belief in any life after death—in short, those who are rank materialists—will have no place in *devachan*, and in many cases will reincarnate almost immediately. In an entirely new body and personality, they will have to face the hardships and vicissitudes of life once again, generating new karma in the process.

"The situation in *kama loka*, discussed in my previous article, is decidedly different. Some people there are aware that they left the earth, while others are unaware of it. Some are able to see those they left behind, others not. Inhabitants of *kama loka* cannot routinely communicate with their loved ones on earth, as Senta Trondson—the principal subject of this series of articles—has been permitted to do. For the moment, she is aware of matters occurring both on earth and in *kama loka* and through me has been able to communicate to the man she has loved so deeply for many years. Soon she will be leaving her *kama lokic* state and will enter into *devachan*, where her Reincarnating Spiritual Ego—her Soul—will remain until the time for its incarnation into a new body. But in exceptional circumstances, those in *kama loka* can and do offer protection against harm or divine guidance to their surviving loved ones.

"In a future article I will explain how some individuals may be able to contact their loved ones who are in the *kama lokic* state. As previously noted, mediumship clearly is not the answer."

Around five in the afternoon, Sol picked up the flash drive containing Damodar's third article, saying he'd talked to Chet and was taking it right to him. At this point, I guessed that Chet wouldn't let Ray mess with it, which I appreciated.

The meeting I was scheduled to attend on Monday morning, before I was shot, was intended to review strategies for revised placement of the after-life series. Sol told me that the meeting had taken place later that day, and the decision had been made to move Damodar's third article up to Thursday's edition and to place it in the Metro section of the paper, instead of the Religion & Family Section, along with the story about the attempt on my life. Sol gave me a sly wink as he mentioned this to me, knowing my feelings about Ray, and I smiled inwardly as I thought of the frustration that move must have brought to Ray when Chet announced it.

Chapter 21

M iriam brought Ray's handwritten note to me on Wednesday morning, just as she promised. As I half-reclined in my yellow paisley hospital gown, she gave me a big kiss on the forehead, set a beautiful bouquet of flowers that she had brought on the window ledge, and handed me a slew of cards from colleagues at the office. She also showed genuine warmth and concern for my health. Seeing Miriam's concern, hearing her sensuous voice, and watching her voluptuous figure as she moved about the room arranging the flowers, stirred up romantic feelings that I thought had long disappeared from my body.

Under other circumstances, I would have said something to Miriam about the religion editor's role in my planned demise, but after my prior experience with her I was wary about trusting her to keep the information about Tuohy to herself. So, we chatted about a variety of little things before she said she had to get back to the office. She kissed me again on the forehead and I smiled and blew her a kiss as she left. The faint whiff of perfume that lingered in the air after she departed was decidedly pleasing.

As soon as she left, I phoned Fiori and he said he'd have a subordinate retrieve the note within the hour. He said it would probably take a day or two before the comparative handwriting analysis could be made and the results known, and he thanked me profusely for all my help, adding, "In all my twenty years of police work, I've never had a case where we were able to get reliable and accurate information about the crime from such a weird source. But the accuracy of this Damodar's information was just amazing; not like the bits of information we usually get from so-called psychics that usually prove to be of little or no help. And, if things keep up like this, we're just liable to have enough evidence to arrest Mr. Tuohy. I'll let you know, but please don't say anything to anyone else." Once again I promised I would keep silent.

A Death Interrupted

Damodar's third article appeared on page three of the Metro section of the paper on Thursday, December 6th, accompanied by the story of the failed attempt on my life, including a long article about Archibald Taylor's arrest and background, and related stories. As I read them from my hospital bed, I wondered how Chet would react when the news about Ray Tuohy's instigation of the scheme to injure or kill me became public. Something told me that Adrienne wouldn't approve of his decision pretending not to know and failing to inform the police, not where matters of such moral significance were concerned.

Using my new laptop, I communicated with Senta several times over the weekend, filling her in on details of my medical condition as well as events taking place at the paper. After I reminisced about some of the happier moments we had spent together over the years, she volunteered some additional information about her long yearning to dance.

> "You know how much I wanted to be a modern dancer, but had to put all that aside for a variety of reasons. Well, I'm looking forward to resuming my interest in modern dance when I enter *devachan*, and I have some fairly good ideas how I would like to progress in that realm. You may recall that the direction I was taking while still in my physical body was moving toward a more mystical type of dance movement, as Louis Horst noted, and I think I now know how best to implement that concept. We'll see if I'm right when I get there."

Senta added that Mahatma Damodar detected evil forces at work planning to interfere with the continued publication of his articles, but she said he was not overly concerned because he knew exactly how they planned to accomplish this and was confident that he could deal with it. When I asked her if Ray Tuohy was involved in this activity, she answered,

> "No, not this time. But Damodar said he will have to consult with the Mahâ Chohan in order to decide the proper and most effective response to this new threat."

With that enigmatic reply, Senta signed off and I took another needed nap.

Chapter 22

A s he sat at his desk on Monday, December 10th, Chet agonized over what to do about Ray Tuohy's involvement in the plot to severely injure David. Despite the strange source of the information, he had seen the demonstration of Damodar's occult powers firsthand and knew enough about his abilities to believe that the revelation concerning Ray's role in the plot more than likely was true. But what to do about it? That was the question.

So far, it looked like the police hadn't made any connection between Ray and the shooting outside the *Tribune's* offices, but how long would that last? The more he thought about it, the more he realized that Ray had become a serious liability and had to go, to save Chet's own ass if nothing else. But, there was also the reputation of the paper to consider. After mulling over the pros and cons of the matter a few minutes, Chet decided to take decisive action before anything further surfaced in the matter. He clicked the intercom to his secretary, "Get Touhy in here right away."

When Ray got the call to report immediately to the executive editor's office, he knew something serious was up, but since he didn't know what it was, he had no way to prepare for it. By the time he reached Chet's door and was waved on in, his hands were trembling and his face was ashen. The tension in the room was palpable.

"Sit down, Ray," Walker said, grimly motioning to a chair while chewing on his Honduran cheroot. He began speaking in a strong, clear voice, his eyes unflinching. "I'm afraid I've got some bad news. Don't ask me how, but I've learned that you were the person who instigated the shooting of Dave Elliott by the man the police arrested." Ray gasped involuntarily, as though he had received an electric shock, but showed no facial emotion. It was all the confirmation that Chet needed, and it reinforced his already-negative feelings about the former clergyman. He continued. "I knew you two weren't friends, but planning to severely injure and possibly kill him is, in my opinion, nothing short of revolting. I haven't told what I know to anyone, not here at the paper or elsewhere, but that's no guarantee it won't come out sooner or later. And if it did, that would be bad news not only for you, but for me and the *Trib* as well.

"So, I'm afraid we've come to the end of the line, my friend, and I'm giving you notice that I'm terminating your contract with the *Trib* for cause, on grounds of moral turpitude. You'll be put on administrative leave for the next two weeks and then you're on your own. I think you would be well-advised to utilize the time to search for other employment." He stared at Ray for a brief moment, waiting for some sort of response, but got none. The Religion & Family Section editor sat speechless. His face turned scarlet and his eyes were a strange mixture of anger and sadness, but otherwise he just stared at Chet and made no attempt to deny or explain.

That surprised Chet. He had expected at the very least Ray would say he was sorry, or that he had made a terrible error of judgment, or offer some other rationale for what he did, but all he got was silence. Chet was more than a little disappointed, having known Ray professionally for so many years, but, getting no response, he pressed on. "If you choose to challenge this action legally . . . well, that's your prerogative; but I'll have no alternative but to bring your putative role in this whole matter to the attention of the authorities, and when that leaks to the press, I doubt that you'll ever be able to get another job in the newspaper business."

Ray sucked in his breath and looked like he finally wanted to say something, but then checked himself and continued to remain silent. Chet took Ray's silence as a clear-cut admission of guilt by one who had no plausible defense for his actions. Chet wanted nothing more to do with Ray, so he signaled the meeting was over by waving his arm toward the door, swiveling his chair around and starting to type something on the computer behind his desk. No handshakes; no goodbyes.

As Ray got up from his chair and walked slowly to the door, Chet glanced at the former minister for one fleeting moment with a tinge of compassion, all the more pronounced as he noted Ray's drooped shoulders and unsteady gait, which made him look almost like a condemned man walking to his execution.

Ten minutes later, Chet's phone rang. It was Doctor Earl Beckley, the University of Michigan parapsychology professor, one of the people who had called David after the first of Damodar's articles was published.

"Mr. Walker," he began, in his usual overbearing manner, "my colleagues here at the Committee for Responsible Investigation of Alleged Paranormal Phenomena—CRIAPP, for short—have authorized me to speak to you in my official role as Vice President of the organization. To get right to the point, we are incensed at the effrontery of the *Tribune* in choosing to publish articles by an unseen entity on a subject so disputed and so sacrosanct as what happens to people after they die. We are so convinced . . ."

The impatient executive editor broke in, "Yes, yes, doctor, I hear what you're saying, but incensed or otherwise you have the right to submit articles or letters to the editor in opposition. And you wouldn't be the first if you did."

"That's not the way we operate, Mr. Walker. Our organization investigates spurious paranormal claims and then we publish our findings in our own magazine, *The Paranormal Skeptic*."

"That's fine with me, doctor, then why the call?"

"I'm calling to make a proposition to you in my official capacity."

Chet's mind immediately reverted to David's use of nearly identical words, and his reaction was the same. "Proposition? What kind of proposition are you talking about?"

"Well, if you'll give me a minute," the pompous Beckley whined, "I'll explain. Our Board is so convinced that you are barking up the wrong tree on this afterlife stuff that we're willing to bet one million dollars that you've been taken in by this character called Damodar."

Chet snorted a laugh and couldn't get over the fact that the series had gotten so many people worked up. "A million dollars? Now that's big money, Doctor. Tell me what you're getting at. I don't have all day."

Beckley coughed nervously before proceeding. "Well, our organization is so certain that you are being duped by this scandalous character that we are prepared to put him to the test once and for all."

Chet rolled his eyes hearing those words and thought to himself, *Not another test*. "Be specific, doctor, what are you referring to?"

"Here's our proposition, Mr.Walker. Our paranormal investigators have come up with three challenges, and if your so-called 'Master of Wisdom' can pass all of them successfully, we will donate one million dollars to the charity or charities of your choice within fifteen days of the challenge. But if he fails to pass all three tests—which we believe is more than likely—then the *Tribune* must agree to cease publication of all future articles by this Damodar on the subject of postmortem consciousness, and issue a public apology to your readers on page one of the paper. That's it."

Chet was thoughtful as he chewed on his cigar, and then responded. "Well, doctor, one million dollars is a hell of a lot of money, so you must feel pretty confident that Damodar won't pass the tests. So what are they?"

"Well, it's a three-part challenge. The first part would see if this entity you call Damodar can get a score of ninety percent or better in providing accurate, verifiable information about five deceased persons who are relatives of members of CRIAPP. Prior to the test, comprehensive information about the decedents will be provided by the CRIAPP survivors, which will be placed in coded envelopes. The second part will challenge Damodar's clairvoyant ability to see if he can predict the closing figures on the Dow, the S&P 500 and the NASDAQ on the day of the challenge."

Beckley paused at that point, undoubtedly expecting some reaction from Chet, but he got none. Instead, Chet quietly asked, "What's the third part?"

"We have learned from a minister who attended a meeting at your office a little over a week ago that you said this Damodar is so proficient an Adept that he can control the forces of nature—those were the exact words you used, so this party told me. So, the third and final challenge is for your Damodar to make it rain here in the District at a specific time during the day of the test and make it stop precisely five minutes later."

Walker shook his head trying to assimilate what the professor had said but gave no verbal hint to Beckley as to his belief in Damodar's ability to meet the three tests. After a brief pause, he said to the avowed skeptic of paranormal phenomena, "From the way you speak, you sound pretty confident you can't lose on this challenge."

"You're absolutely right. So, what do you say to my proposition?"

"Hmnn. I'll need some time to reflect on all of this. How about if I get back to you tomorrow?"

Beckley was elated that the executive editor of the *Tribune* was willing to consider his offer, and politely replied, "By all means. Think it over." Whereupon he gave Chet his phone number at the University of Michigan, where he was on the faculty of the Psychology Department.

In all his years as a journalist, Chet Walker had never been presented with such a tempting proposition and he virtually shouted as he hung up the phone, "Damn, if that doesn't take the cake! A million dollars!" All he could think of was the publicity this could garner for the paper and the likelihood of increased readership. He called Adrienne immediately and told her he had a couple of important matters to discuss with her. Since she wasn't otherwise occupied, she told him to come right up.

With a serious look on his face, Chet told Adrienne about his firing of Ray Tuohy fifteen minutes earlier. "I had no choice in the matter, Adrienne, once I learned that he was the one who put that derelict up to shooting Dave Elliott."

"How and when did you learn *that*?" she asked, in a state of near shock.

"Damodar told Dave that's what happened the day of the shooting. He said that Ray hired that man to shoot Dave, but not to kill him. But that wasn't the way it worked out, because he sure came close to killing him."

Her face showing how seriously disturbed she was, Adrienne asked, "And who else knows this, that is, besides Damodar and David? Do the police know?"

"Not so far as I know," he fibbed, "unless they found out some other way."

"So, how long have you known this, Chester?" She was clearly irritated.

Hesitating, Chet replied, "I learned about it from Dave at the hospital; but I wasn't really sure, so I didn't want to say anything to you, or anyone else."

"Not even to the police?" She scolded him, "You had a moral as well as a legal obligation to tell them what you knew. I'm surprised at you. Whatever possessed you to do such a thing?"

"I was only trying to protect the paper, Adrienne," Chet meekly replied.

"Well, you should have known that sooner or later it would come out. Why are you telling me about it now? Has something happened? Have the police made the connection by themselves?"

"Not that I know of. But, I think they may pretty soon."

"Why do you think that?"

"Because Damodar predicted they would, so Dave told me, and I decided I better believe Damodar. He's never been wrong in the past."

"No, and I, too, believe he's right when it comes to things like this. How he does it, I don't know, but he sure has his finger on everything."

"You're right, of course. I should have discussed it with you earlier and I apologize, but somehow or other I wanted to give Ray the benefit of the doubt before taking any further steps. He's worked for us nearly ten years."

"Yes, I know. I was responsible for bringing him on board. Well, what's done is done. How'd he take it? The firing, I mean. What did he have to say?"

"Not a damn thing. He just looked and stared at me as I told him what I was doing and the reason for doing it. If ever there was an indication of his guilt, that was it. He just walked out of the office without saying a word. I gave him two weeks on administrative leave, and then he's through."

Adrienne nodded, then got up from her desk and in a more relaxed tone of voice asked, "What do you plan to tell the staff, and when?"

He thought a moment before replying, "I think I'll tell them he requested an extended sick leave . . . that he was not feeling well and needed some time off to rest. How does that sound? You know, he hasn't been looking well at all lately."

"That sounds all right. And only David knows the real reason, and I'm sure he won't spill the beans."

"I told him not to, and I'm sure he'll keep his word."

Adrienne's voice softened as she shifted gears. "What was the other important matter you wanted to discuss with me?"

"Well, this you're going to find hard to believe, but then again maybe not, since it involves Damodar again."

Chet then repeated what Beckley had proposed, leaving out none of the details. Her initial reaction was not exactly the same as his. "Well, Chester, I'm not so sure this is such a great thing. First of all, can Damodar really *do* those things, and secondly, would he *agree* to do them even if we approved of the idea? What really worries me, however, is what happens if he tries and doesn't succeed? At that point, from what you tell me, we're supposed to stop all publication of the articles and—heaven forbid!—apologize to the public. We've never done that before. Forget about the million dollars for the moment. Stopping publication and apologizing could lose us a tremendous number of subscribers, to say nothing of the ridicule and adverse publicity we'd receive."

Chet listened thoughtfully before responding. "You're right, of course. I have no way of knowing if Damodar can do those things, or whether he would *want* to do them. On the other hand, this CRIAPP organization is pretty influential and if we throw in the towel now, they'll probably send out a press release saying we turned down their offer because we knew that Damodar couldn't cut the mustard. So there's the possibility of negative publicity either way. The only imponderables are: can he do it, and is he willing to try?"

Adrienne steepled her fingers and brought them to her lips before asking, "Tell me more about this organization Chester. Who are they?

What kind of reputation do they have? Do they have that kind of money, and can they be trusted to live up to their agreement, in case we decide to accept their offer?"

"They're legit, so far as I can tell. Been around for quite a while. They spend their time and money investigating paranormal and fringe-science claims, but I gather their real purpose is debunking those claims and reporting the results in their quarterly magazine, which they call *The Paranormal Skeptic*. I can have Jim Rafferty do a Dunn & Bradstreet on them if you'd like, but my guess is that they probably have the money. We can insist that they put the money in escrow before we agree, but I doubt that they'd risk being publicly humiliated—or sued—if they didn't come across with the million if they lost. I can check with our lawyers on that issue."

"I'm not so sure about their financial viability. Before we make any decision on the matter, have Jim do the D and B, and then I guess you'd better talk this thing over with David Elliott. If he thinks Damodar can do it, and is *willing* to do it, then we might just come out of this with the biggest publicity coup in years. I'm certainly impressed with Damodar's abilities, but he may not be willing to undertake this sort of challenge. See what Elliott thinks, and keep me informed."

Chet said he'd get going on it right away, and returned to his office.

Chapter 23

M iriam picked me up when I was discharged from GW on Monday, December 10th, but not before I retrieved my severely bent talisman from the ER. She drove me to my Kalorama Road apartment house just before noon. I was feeling much better and the only outward sign of my injuries was the arm sling to reduce the pressure on my right shoulder and collarbone, where one of the bullets had entered.

Once we got to the apartment, Miriam was very solicitous and really fussed over me, wanting to make sure I had enough food in the apartment and that everything was in order before she left. After thanking her for her kindness, I gave her a warm hug and a quick peck on the cheek before insisting that she return to the office, which she did a few minutes later. It was a nice feeling being home again, and I relished the quiet and privacy.

The first thing I did after Miriam left was to call Wexler's Auctioneers. I told them to remove Senta's Serapi rug from con-signment and send it via truck to Senta's niece, Francine, at her Manhattan apartment, which they readily agreed to do. So, mission number one was accomplished successfully. Mission number two was to retrieve my car from the auto repair shop on Columbia Road. The new paint job did the trick and the car actually looked like new. I managed to drive it the short distance back to my apartment house by removing my arm from the sling and driving very slowly and carefully, but my right shoulder and collarbone hurt badly enough to make me want to forego any more driving for a while.

Around three in the afternoon, I received a phone call from Chet. He had two items of interest for me. The first item was a shocker. "I've fired Ray, Dave. After thinking things over, I realize his actions with regard to you—his hiring that man to shoot you—went way beyond the pale and are morally unacceptable. He'll get two weeks' pay on administrative leave, and then he's through. I thought you should be the first to know. Incidentally, I'll be putting out a memo to the staff tomorrow morning, but I'm going to tell them simply that Ray requested extended sick leave. Nothing more than that."

The news stunned me, but not unhappily. I knew that it would just be a matter of time before the police would make the connection between Ray and Archie Taylor, and once that happened, Ray's writing career would be over. I wondered what made Chet change his mind. Was it his moral sense of the right thing to do, or was it simply his fear of getting caught in an unpleasant public relations mess? I also wondered if Adrienne had anything to do with it. As these thoughts crossed my mind, Chet reported the second item of news.

"A guy by the name of Beckley called me this morning. Said he's a parapsychologist and an officer in some organization called the Committee for Responsible Investigation of Alleged Paranormal Phenomena, or CRIAPP—isn't that a stupid acronym?—and he tossed us a challenge."

"Yeah, I know who he is," I replied. "He chewed me out royally right after Damodar's first article appeared. Left me with the impression that he was going to get even with us."

"Well, he's making good on that threat. Listen to this: he said that their organization claims that Damodar is no Master of Wisdom but simply a bogus medium, and they're willing to bet one million bucks to prove it. If Damodar wins, we can designate the charity or charities of our choice. And if he loses, then we have to agree to stop further publication of the articles and publicly apologize to their organization and to our readers on the front page of the paper."

"One million bucks!" I exclaimed. "What for? I mean, what kind of challenge does he have in mind?"

"Well, it's a three-part challenge. First part would see if Damodar can get a score of ninety percent or better in providing accurate information about several deceased persons, with the verification information being provided by this CRIAPP organization in coded envelopes. Second, Damodar is supposed to prove his clairvoyant ability by predicting the closing figures on the Dow, the S&P 500 and the NASDAQ on the day of the challenge. I can see where Damodar *might* be able to pull those two off, but the third one is a doozy."

"What is it?"

"They want to challenge Damodar's contention that he's an Adept who can control the forces of nature, as he has on occasion informed us, so the challenge is for Damodar to make it rain here in the District at a precise time on the day in question and make it stop exactly five minutes later. Now *that's* one hell of a challenge, I'm sure you'll agree."

"Well, maybe not as hard a challenge as you think, Chet." I thought about it a moment before explaining, "You see, the Dhyân Chohans—the planetary spiritual guardians—are able to affect the weather on the planet through their control of the Maruts, the storm gods."

Chet interrupted with, "What'n hell are you talking about—Maruts and storm gods?"

I could see that I had a lot more explaining to do, but simply said, "It gets kind of involved to explain, Chet, but the bottom line is, yeah, I do think it's possible."

"Well I'll be damned!" Walker exclaimed, excitedly. "You mean you think he could actually pull it off?"

"I wouldn't be surprised," I replied, "if he's given permission to do so. A Mahatma like Damodar would be fully initiated into *Gupta Vidyâ*, which is the secret science of all things pertaining to man and nature, and goes well beyond our ordinary conceptions of magic and the supernatural. I've never seen anything like that done, but I've read about it and I'm pretty sure he could do it if he was put to the test. The question is, would he want to? In the past, the Masters have avoided and even condemned that kind of phenomenal activity."

"I told the boss-lady that it was a long shot, and she of course told me to check with you first, but the publicity alone from a stunt like this could increase our circulation by the thousands. Would you send Damodar an e-mail and ask him if he's willing to help us out."

I said I would, but I knew that the chances were slim. A hundred years earlier the Adepts had declined all challenges to their supernormal abilities—not unlike H.P.B. herself, after she saw that it didn't seem to make a difference in the spiritual lives of those making the requests. But I also knew that highly undesirable adverse publicity to the paper, and my own ability to communicate with Senta, hung in the balance, so I sat down and sent an e-mail to Damodar right away.

To my surprise, his response was in the affirmative.

"Mr. Elliott. I have been aware of Dr. Beckley's challenge for some time now, having seen his thoughts in the astral, but I didn't want to discuss it with you until it was made formally. You were absolutely correct in telling your boss that our Himalayan Brotherhood does not look favorably on demonstrations of our occult powers. And we will never display such powers merely to titillate the profane. However, the present circumstances are unusual in that the articles I have submitted are already bringing about an increased awareness of what happens after we die, and to bring that modest degree of success to a premature end at this time would impede our objective of explaining the true nature of the postmortem states of consciousness.

"I have spoken with the Mahâ Chohan about this matter and he has given me permission to accept the challenge that has been presented to the editor of your newspaper. Since their thoughts on the subject have been visible to us in the astral, we see no difficulty in my meeting any of the challenges. The final challenge, relating to making it rain at a precise time, is not something we would normally undertake, but it is well within our capabilities. So, feel free to pass this information on to Mr. Walker."

Those words buoyed my spirits and I called Chet immediately. And he, in turn, happily reported the news to the boss-lady.

Adrienne gave her full blessings to the challenge, subject to approval of the specific terms and conditions of the challenge by the *Tribune's* lawyers, as well as proof that CRIAPP could make good on its offer of one million dollars in case it lost the challenge.

Over the next several days, legal documents flew back and forth between the lawyers representing the paper and those representing CRIAPP, and eventually an agreement satisfactory to both sides was signed. It was decided and agreed that CRIAPP could name three neutral judges for the event, while the *Tribune* could do likewise.

Chet asked me to contact Damodar for detailed instructions about handling the challenge. "Ask him how he will make his presence known, and how he intends to provide the answers to the three challenges?"

I said I'd get on it right away. In a brief e-mail, Damodar explained how I should be prepared. His reply was simple:

"All that will be necessary is for you to have your computer set up to project its images onto a large screen in the front of the room. I will respond to the test questions and other matters by means of your computer. For the second challenge related to the stock market indices, it will be sufficient to place an empty envelope on a table in full view of everyone. And for the third challenge, it would be helpful if several television cameras could be positioned at key places on your National Mall, the cameras linked, of course, to the room where the challenge is to take place. Otherwise, just watch and be prepared for a surprise or two."

I passed this information on to Chet, who later informed me that Tuesday, December 18th had been set as the date, and the National Press Club on 14th Street had been chosen as the site, of the unusual paranormal challenge, since that venue had all the technical facilities for handling a media event of this magnitude.

I thought it was quite fitting that the anniversary of my meeting Senta was the date chosen for this historic event, and I told her so in a short e-mail after hearing from Damodar. Soon, people all over the world would see firsthand what an initiate in *Gupta Vidyâ* could accomplish.

Chapter 24

The fateful day of Damodar's challenge, December 18th, opened with a clear, sunny sky above the nation's capitol. At nine o'clock, the temperature was hovering around forty degrees and it was forecasted to rise to close to sixty. It was also the thirty-third anniversary of the day Senta and I first met, a day that we traditionally celebrated together. However, I knew that today was going to be a far more significant one.

When word got out about the CRIAPP challenge, the news media all over the world gobbled it up. It was the biggest story since the terrorist events of September eleventh. Every network wanted to be in on this extraordinary story dealing with paranormal faculties and the controversial subject of postmortem survival of consciousness.

Television crews and print media journalists from all the major European networks as well as the United States packed the thirteenth floor ballroom of the National Press Club well before the program began. The large, ornate room was a good choice for the telecast because it had superb acoustics and all the facilities for radio and television transmissions. When I arrived with my laptop around nine-thirty, Chet and Adrienne were already there, sitting together near the front, and both acknowledged me and wished me well, with Chet giving me a thumbs-up sign. I quickly hooked up my laptop, positioning it on a table near the front of the room and established an Internet connection. The day before, I had arranged with Press Club personnel to set up a large screen to receive the images that would be projected by my computer, and a second screen alongside it to receive images from a standard multimedia projector.

I had also alerted network television personnel the day before to Damodar's request to have several television cameras located on the National Mall—located roughly half a mile south of the Press Club—with microwave links to the National Press Club, and they assured me this would be done. When I arrived, technical personnel from the networks told me that all the TV arrangements had been made, with six cameras along the Mall already having been linked by microwave to monitors and network feeds in the Press Club.

A Death Interrupted

After setting up my laptop, I introduced myself to Anthony Riordan, the person designated to be in charge of the program, and explained to him the items Damodar had requested, including the television cameras on the Mall. I made it clear to him that my only involvement during the challenge would be to receive messages from Damodar on my computer and project them onto the large screen.

Precisely at ten o'clock, Mr. Riordan, took his place at the lectern and addressed the assembled audience as the television cameras began to roll. "Good morning, ladies and gentlemen, and to our viewers everywhere. My name is Anthony Riordan. I'm President of the American Society of Newspaper Editors and I will be announcing events as they occur today in this unusual program. We are here this morning to witness a challenge presented by the Committee for Responsible Investigation of Alleged Paranormal Phenomena to the *Washington Tribune*, arising out of the *Tribune's* current series of articles on alleged postmortem survival of consciousness.

Reading from a document in his hand, Riordan began, "Briefly, here are the contentions of the parties: the *Tribune* maintains that its series of articles have been authored by a person called Mahatma Damodar, who is a living Master of Wisdom in the Eastern occult philosophy and whose normal abode is in the Himalayan Mountain ranges of Western Tibet. Damodar, according to the *Tribune's* statement, is not only highly spiritually evolved, but also has acquired extraordinary occult powers, including the ability to be present here today—although not visible to our eyes—and, among other things, to effectively control the forces of nature. It is claimed that this person has made it possible for Mr. David Elliott, an editorial writer for the *Tribune*, to communicate by e-mail with the woman he loved for over thirty years, and who died a little over three months ago. Mr. Elliott is here with us today"—pointing to me—"and any responses from Damodar will be directed to Mr. Elliott's computer and from there directly projected onto the screen in front of the room as they are received. Other than that, Mr. Elliott will play no role in the events taking place here today."

I was happy to hear him repeat what I had said earlier, because I wanted the demonstration to speak for itself.

Riordan continued, "For its part, CRIAPP—which is the acronym that I will use from this point on—contends that there is no such person as Damodar, and that the articles on the afterlife as printed in the *Tribune* are merely, and I quote, 'the pretentious claptrap of a bogus medium, and any alleged messages from persons who have died are in reality being directed to Mr. Elliott's computer through some electro-mechanical energy source that they believe could be replicated, given the necessary time to analyze it and do some reverse engineering.' End of quote. They also vigorously challenge the claim that anyone can control the forces of nature. I think that about sets forth the respective positions clearly enough.

"Each side has been allowed to select three judges for this challenge. CRIAPP has selected the president of the American Psychological Association, the president of the American Federation of Scientists, and the president of the American Society of Magicians. The *Tribune* has selected the president of the American Bar Association, the president of the American Psychiatric Association, and the Chairman of the National Research Council." He paused to nod at the panel of judges who sat at a table to the left.

"As has been made quite clear in the press and on television, if Damodar—and thereby, the *Tribune*—wins this challenge, CRIAPP will donate one million dollars to the charity or charities of the newspaper's choice, while if the challenge cannot be met, the *Tribune* has agreed to publicly apologize to CRIAPP on page one and has agreed to cease all future publication of articles on the afterlife submitted by the individual known as Damodar."

Riordan paused, looked over at Chet, Adrienne and Dr. Beckley, who were sitting to the right, and then looked at the panel of judges to see if anyone had any corrections or additions to make to his introductory remarks, and seeing no objection, he continued, "I am now going to spell out the three tests that CRIAPP has prepared. First, to test Damodar's professed ability to make contact with persons who have died, and his professed ability to establish meaningful communication between the living and the dead, five sealed envelopes out of a total group of twenty-five, shall be selected at random. These envelopes are all marked only with code numbers that have been placed in a separate envelope, each code number identifying a specific deceased person.

"Now, the challenge is this: each of these envelopes contains information of a highly personal nature about a particular deceased relative of a CRIAPP member who is here today to verify or refute whatever information is presented by Damodar. Neither CRIAPP nor any of the members in question will know in advance whose deceased relative has been selected.

A Death Interrupted

"Once an envelope is selected, Damodar—if he can—will undertake to produce specific personal information about the deceased person, which will be transmitted through Mr. Elliott's computer to the screen in front," (pointing to the large screen.) "That information will be compared with information contained in the coded envelope, which will be displayed on the other screen in the front of the room," (pointing to the second screen in the front of the room.) All eyes followed his gesture and the entire audience remained silently attentive—more intent than I'd seen any group of journalists at other press conferences. I thought, well, at least they are open to the possibilities so far.

"In addition," Riordan continued, "the CRIAPP member whose relative is the subject of the test will be available to verify or dispute any information revealed by Damodar about the decedent. Each correct bit of information, as decided by our panel of judges, will be labeled a 'hit,' and all hits will be recorded as such.

"When all five envelopes have been reviewed in this manner, if a combined total score of ninety percent hits or better is achieved, the test will be deemed a success for Damodar and the *Tribune*. If not, it will be considered a failure. I hope I made that clear enough, but if anyone on the panel needs further clarification, please indicate by raising your hand."

No one seemed to need clarification, so Riordan continued speaking as a mild buzzing of excitement began throughout the crowded room. "All twenty-five envelopes have been placed on the table here in front and now I'm going to ask Dan Abernethy of ABC News to shuffle them and select at random the five that are to be the subject of this challenge."

Abernethy came forward and selected five envelopes, which were left on the table, while the remaining twenty were removed and discarded. Riordan then picked up the first envelope, code marked with the number 218, and, with a nervous glance at the audience of hard-nosed newsmen and women, announced in a self-conscious manner, "Damodar, if you can hear me and are in a position to give us any of the details about the deceased person whose envelope is numbered 218, please do so now."

Despite a couple of snickers and a few shaking heads, a general hush came over the crowd and my adrenaline pumped wildly as I—and everyone in the room—stared intently at the blank screen and wondered what would happen next. We didn't have long to wait. Words began to fly across my computer monitor and simultaneously were projected onto the large screen.

"Good morning to you all. I have been made aware of the three challenges that will be presented to me today, but before I begin, I should like to make the point that the Great White Lodge of Adepts to which I belong does not look favorably on tricks of magic or the gratuitous production of occult phenomena either to prove that we really exist or the validity of the Eastern occult philosophy that we espouse. We have long maintained that the philosophy should stand or fall on its own merits, but because we have, in this isolated instance, gone out of our way to prove our ability to communicate with deceased persons who are on other planes of existence—the validity of which is here and now being challenged—this test will proceed.

"Envelope number 218 contains information about a person known during his earth life as Horace Daniels. He left his physical body on June 29, 1996, at age forty-three, from complications of the condition your doctors call chronic obstructive pulmonary disease. He was a carpenter by trade and worked in a milling factory in Everett in the State of Washington. Mr. Daniels left a wife, Nancy, who was his childhood sweetheart, and four children, two of whom have already gone on to college, while two remain at home with their mother. Nancy was at one time a schoolteacher, but now stays at home to take care of the children.

"While alive, Mr. Daniels tells me he enjoyed the sport of bowling and was one of the top bowlers on his local bowling team. He was also a crack marksman and a member of the local rifle club. At his funeral, the minister spoke highly of him as a free thinker and man of great courage, citing his exploits in the Vietnam War, for which he was awarded a Bronze Star for bravery.

"I have to add, with a certain degree of sadness, that Mr. Daniels also had certain fixed prejudices which he did not overcome in his lifetime; he disliked persons of color, Hispanics and persons of the Jewish faith. He also believed that owning handguns was not only his constitutional right, but a duty owed by every loyal citizen, to protect his family, and he was a member of local organizations that held similar views. Much of his time in *kama loka* has been spent considering the spiritual consequences of these biases and leanings, and cleansing his higher Ego of them prior to moving on to the state called *devachan*."

The message ended at that point, and the voices of the spectators rose in a crescendo as they reflected on the enormous specificity of Damodar's comments. Riordan asked for the code list and was informed it was indeed Mr. Horace Daniels of Everett, Washington whose brief bio was outlined. When the panel was shown the biography in full—projected onto the second screen— they saw to their amazement that everything in the biography was reflected in the information Damodar had provided, matching nearly word for word, confirming a score of one hundred percent of 'hits' on the decedent.

Damodar's comments on Mr. Daniels' prejudices and the organizations he belonged to, had not been contained in the biographical material, so Riordan asked, "Would the CRIAPP member who prepared the bio on Daniels, please come forward."

A tall, well-dressed man about forty-five years old ambled to the front of the room, scratching his head and glancing furtively at Dr. Beckley as he came forward. He told Riordan that his name was Charles Hansen, that he was the nephew of Horace Daniels and that he had prepared the biographical material on his uncle. Riordan asked Hansen, "What can you tell us about the items Damodar mentioned that weren't in the biographical on your uncle? How accurate were they?"

With an uncomfortable, sheepish look on his face, Hansen replied, "Everything he said was absolutely true. Of course, Uncle Horace's organizational memberships and attitude towards handgun ownership were well known in the community, but that other stuff is amazing. Uncle Horace was a loving husband and father, but he held all the prejudices that were mentioned, causing my aunt and the rest of the family much concern and embarrassment, which everyone did their best to conceal. I just can't imagine how this Damodar could have known about all of Uncle Horace's racial and ethnic prejudices."

Riordan thanked Hansen for his comments, and the look on Riordan's face showed his awareness that something extremely unusual was happening as Hansen returned to his seat. A few "Wow"s and other expressions of amazement were uttered by the journalists in attendance who by now realized they were witnessing history in the making. And just as they were digesting the significance of Charles Hansen's remarks, something unexpected occurred: on David's computer screen there began to appear slowly, pixel by pixel, a photograph of the deceased subject. It showed Mr. Daniels about a year before his death operating a lathe at the mill where he worked. "That's him! That's Uncle Horace!" Hansen shouted from the audience, causing goose bumps to form on my body, and I can only guess how it made others feel. I knew immediately that this was the surprise Damodar had told me to look out for. After roughly thirty seconds, the picture on the screen faded away and the room again became quiet . . . or at least quieter.

The second envelope, numbered 766, was placed on the table and Riordan, in a far less self-conscious voice, asked Damodar to give his analysis of that one. The Mahatma did so, again without delay, with his comments appearing for all to see on the large screen.

> "Envelope number 766 contains information about the person known during her lifetime as Louise Trent. Louise was only seventeen years of age when she left her physical body on January 14th, 1999, as the result of a terrible crime committed against her. She was sexually assaulted and then strangled in a wooded area of her hometown of Meriden in the State of Connecticut.

> "Louise was a talented musician, an accomplished pianist who hoped to pursue her musical studies at the Julliard School of Music in New York City, where she had already been accepted as a first-year student. Louise tells me that her secret wish was to have her parents one day see her perform in a recital at Carnegie Hall, and that her father learned of this by a note he found in her diary after she left her physical body.

> "Her passing caused her parents and siblings untold pain and anguish, and led to a great deal of local publicity about the problem of sexual predators. She is aware that her mother has become an active member of the organization known as the Polly Klass Foundation.

> "Because of her exceptional spiritual and artistic qualities, Louise will remain in *kama loka* under the special protection of the Dhyân Chohans in a quiescent, dream-like state until her normal life span has been reached. I can also tell you that her next incarnation will give her ample opportunity to demonstrate her proficiency as a concert pianist."

The presentation ended at that point, and the usual buzzing commenced among the assembled reporters, but before Riordan could even compare Damodar's comments with the material in envelope number 766, something else intervened. On the screen came a follow-up by Damodar to his comments about Louise Trent.

> "I see that the police were not able to ascertain the name of Louise's murderer, but she tells me that she knew the man who assaulted and killed her. He was a former part-time gardener and handyman at her parents' home, a man by the name of Townsend—Harold Townsend. A search of the home where he now lives, in the nearby city of Waterbury, will reveal his connection to this long-unsolved crime, specifically, an item of clothing that Louise was wearing at the time of the assault and which was missing when her body was found."

Cold shivers ran up and down my spine as Damodar made this revelation, and it caused an uproar among the reporters, several of whom immediately ran out into the hallway to call their papers. I knew that Damodar's ability to see into the astral made his comment about Louise's murderer a matter of fact, and I had little doubt that prompt police activity would ensue.

Riordan quieted the crowd and then compared Damodar's first comments with the biographical material in envelope number 766, and once again they matched nearly word for word. The comments on Louise's protection in the afterlife paralleled points Damodar had made previously in his newspaper articles, which I assumed most of the seasoned journalists in attendance would have read by way of preparation for today's event. When Riordan called upon the CRIAPP member who had prepared the information in Louise's envelope, the member—Louise's godfather—confirmed that all the facts as outlined by Damodar, including the diary information, known personally to him, were entirely correct. He acknowledged that the information about Townsend was totally new information, but said he was glad that it would be turned over to the Connecticut police.

After Damodar's references to Louise's murderer, everyone looked eagerly at the screen, and sure enough, a few moments later there appeared a photograph of Louise taken during a recital she had given some six months before she was murdered.

The whispered voices of reporters and cameramen unable to contain themselves could be heard throughout the room as the level of excitement grew dramatically. All realized that they were participating in an event of monumental significance. Only the hardcore skeptic CRIAPP members who were present remained silent. But I could see that they, too, were astounded by the baffling ability of Damodar—a being whose very existence they disputed—to reproduce not just the gist, but virtually the exact words in the envelopes presented. I knew that this was a double blind test of their own design which they were certain would prove that Damodar, whoever he was, was no better than someone doing "cold readings." That's the way charlatans offer banal, generic comments supposedly made by deceased loved ones—a sham procedure that many CRIAPP members have claimed they are able to replicate.

The third envelope, marked number 822, was selected next and Damodar was given a moment before presenting his information via my laptop computer.

"Envelope number 822 contains information about the person known as Edward LaMotte, who left his physical body on April 10th, 1975, as a result of a stroke, at the age of eighty-three. He resided in Lincoln, Nebraska at the time. Mr. LaMotte was a scientist with many patents to his credit. He tells me that his greatest achievement was in the field of acoustics, when he invented a special device to reduce the signal-to-noise ratio in sound systems to virtually zero. For that, he was awarded a special medal by the Society of Audio Engineers in 1974.

"He tells me he was an agnostic when it came to religion, although he was raised as a Baptist by his church-going parents when a youngster. Mr. LaMotte left a wife, Loretta, with whom he was very much in love. He told me that on the day of his funeral his wife placed in his casket a special cameo brooch containing a miniature picture of herself, which she never mentioned to anyone. He is aware that she grieved for him almost constantly following his death, and secretly wished to join him in the world beyond. She died two years after he did, and I can tell you that they have since communicated with each other telepathically on their current plane of existence, and in fact, have renewed their marriage vows, eliminating 'until death do us part' and substituting the words 'for all eternity.'

"Mr. LaMotte's scientific bent and interests made it difficult for him to accept anything about the occult or paranormal that was not strictly provable by scientific investigation. Nevertheless, once he passed over to the next world, he realized his mistake and admitted that his narrow-mindedness prevented him from appreciating the true nature of occult or paranormal events. He specifically mentioned his nephew, Richard Zumwalt, as someone who has taken the same narrow-minded direction in his work as a nuclear engineer and as a member of the organization that has sponsored the present challenge."

As it happened, Richard Zumwalt, sitting in the third row, was the very person who prepared the envelope for his uncle, Edward LaMotte, and, from the look on his face seemed astounded to see the comments that referred to him. When asked by Anthony Riordan, Zumwalt did not dispute the essence of the presentation, however, and the panel chalked it up as another success for Damodar. Again, thirty seconds later, Mr. LaMotte's photograph slowly appeared on the screen, showing him together with the very same Richard Zumwalt in a rowboat on a lake near Lincoln, Nebraska a year before he died. Again, loud murmurs could be heard all over the room, along with a few poorly-concealed whistles, but the photo caused Zumwalt to gasp and mutter something to himself, which Riordan and several others noticed. As he did his best to hush the audience, Riordan asked Zumwalt, "Is something wrong, Mr. Zumwalt? Is that not a picture of your uncle?"

"It certainly is, and that's me right alongside of him," Zumwalt answered, in a voice cracking with emotion. I remember the day very clearly, but you see we were out in the middle of the lake all by ourselves, a good mile from shore. There was absolutely no one nearby and we had no camera, so there was no way *anyone* could have taken that picture! I can't figure out how he did it!"

As the noise level in the room increased substantially, I of course knew how Damodar did it: he simply looked into the astral, that Great Recorder of all human actions, thoughts and emotions.

As the photograph on the screen slowly faded away, Zumwalt took his seat and I could see the fear of failure on Dr. Beckley's face and the faces of his CRIAPP colleagues. It was patently obvious to one and all that Damodar was winning the day handily. Riordan signaled for the fourth envelope to be selected for review, but this time the response from Damodar was immediate and angry:

> "This envelope is a sham and is highly insulting to me. It does not contain information about someone who has died, but is a deception intended to trick me into giving information about an invented personage who does not exist. That will not happen, because all such efforts are clearly seen in the astral and I can assure you that the pretended decedent, a make-believe person given the name of Helen Moore, does not exist and the information about her is pure fiction, a figment of someone's imagination. Since it is all contrived, I will not waste my time commenting on it."

Near-bedlam broke out as Riordan turned to the prim, white-haired Dr. Beckley and asked, "Is this true, Doctor Beckley? Did you include bogus information for the express purpose of tricking Damodar?"

Beckley sheepishly nodded 'yes' as he weakly explained, "We've seen many alleged mediums produce a wealth of information about individuals who have 'crossed over,' to use their terminology, even though we knew that no such persons even existed. While I apologize for employing that stratagem in this test, we thought it would be worth exploring—just another type of test—given our previous experiences with other so-called mediums."

"But doctor," Riordan asked, "how could you be sure that this hypothetical Helen Moore's information would be one of the five envelopes randomly selected? You saw Mr. Abernethy shuffle the envelopes when we started, and discard twenty of them."

Beckley reluctantly confessed, "Well, to be honest, because we couldn't be sure, we placed information about non-existent persons in five of the twenty-five envelopes. Statistically, we knew that there was a good chance at least one of the fictitious envelopes would be included in the final five selected . . . as indeed it was."

The assembled reporters and television crews smiled and nodded in their amazement at Damodar's ability to discern immediately the attempted trick by Beckley and his colleagues. Chet Walker shook his head, then turned to Adrienne and whispered gleefully, "You see, they openly admit that they violated the terms of the agreement. We can claim the one million right now if we want to. What do you say?"

"No, Chester, not yet. They've made perfect fools of themselves front of the whole world and it serves them right, but let's see what happens next before we end the experiment. I, for one, am thoroughly fascinated at the details about these deceased individuals Damodar has been able to come up with, aren't you?"

"Sure I am, but I just thought you might want to bring this thing to a resounding halt."

"Not yet . . . not yet. Signal Riordan to go on with the test."

Walker did just that, and the room fell quiet once more as everyone stared at the fifth envelope on the table, marked number 17. Damodar's comments came quickly.

> "The envelope marked number 17 contains information about Dr. Alvin Murdoch, a 60-year-old man who left his physical body on December 13th, 1988, after he suffered a ruptured aneurysm in his heart. Dr. Murdoch was the Director of the Anderson Clinic in Mobile, in the State of Alabama. He was an obstetrician-gynecologist of some repute. He is survived by his wife, Ruth and by his daughter, Evelyn, who is also a physician.
>
> "Dr. Murdoch is a gentle man of considerable intellect. As a practicing specialist in female problems, he was an ardent advocate of each pregnant woman's right to choose whether to proceed to term or to abort her fetus. He now tells me that he believes he was wrong in performing the number of abortions he did, and also wrong in failing to advise patients against having abortions if their lives were not thereby jeopardized.
>
> "Dr. Murdoch is a trained flautist and tells me he enjoyed playing the flute in a small orchestral group in Mobile, and he is now enjoying, as well as creating, flute music while in *devachan*. He is occasionally aware of what his wife and daughter are doing in their earth lives, but he cannot communicate with them directly. He asked me if I would send his love to them, and I said I would do that."

Riordan asked for the read-out of envelope number 17. The words in the envelope and those projected on the screen by Damodar were virtually exact duplicates. And although his added comments about the decedent's second thoughts regarding the performing of abortions were clearly gratuitous, they were certainly relevant. Once again, a photograph slowly appeared on the screen, this one showing Dr. Murdoch playing the flute in a small musical ensemble. By now, the vast majority of the audience had accepted the fact that Damodar could make photographs appear out of thin air, so seeing this photo didn't generate the same intensity of reactions that the earlier photos did. But suddenly, while the photo of Dr. Murdoch playing in the ensemble was still on the large screen, the mellifluous sound of a flute playing the familiar strains of the "Barcarolle" from Offenbach's *Tales of Hoffman,* could be heard throughout the room, creating the impression that Dr. Murdoch was playing it right then and there! No one could figure out where the sound was coming from, and once again, Damodar had surprised the journalists and technical personnel with his occult powers.

After the photograph and accompanying music faded away, Riordan turned to his panel of judges and asked, "Is there anyone here who could deny that the biographies given by Damodar were all substantially accurate?" All six heads shook 'no' in unison. "Well, then, I will state for the record that the first challenge was successfully met. So, we'll take a short ten-minute break before we proceed to the second and third parts of the challenge."

The looks of wonderment and surprise on the faces of seasoned reporters and radio and television personnel were evident throughout the room, and near-bedlam broke out as audience members began conversing excitedly with one another while television news reporters brought their respective viewing audiences up-to-date on what had happened thus far and then went to commercial breaks.

My own sense of relief mingled with worries about the tests yet to come. I had never had occasion to discuss his clairvoyant faculties with Damodar, and certainly not his ability to affect the weather, but before agreeing to accept the CRIAPP challenge he had assured me this would not be a problem, so I took him at his word. Still, there are always doubts when matters as momentous as these are put to the test, so I knew it wasn't going to be a slam-dunk situation.

I looked over and could see Chet Walker smiling as he talked to Adrienne Thayer while nursing his unlit cigar. It's funny, I thought to myself, how two individuals who, up to three weeks ago, knew absolutely nothing about the world of the occult, had now become such firm believers. I wondered what Ray Tuohy would be thinking if he were here. More than likely he would be seething inside, refusing to believe his own eyes. I was pretty certain that he was at home watching his television set just like millions of others worldwide. Still, I had to restrain myself from allowing my disgust for him get the better of me. The mere thought of Ray caused me unconsciously to roll my shoulder, and a deep tinge of pain rewarded my effort. I took a deep breath; I would heal in time, and, in the meantime, I knew that Ray's karma had already started to catch up with him.

The ten-minute break ended and the red lights came on as the TV cameras began to resume whirring away. Anthony Riordan called the room to order and announced, "Damodar's second challenge is to try to predict today's closing averages on the Dow Jones, the Standard & Poor's 500 and the NASDAQ, within a margin of error not to exceed one one-hundredths of a percent on each index." Riordan noted that it was now eleven-thirty, Eastern Standard Time, and that the stock market would close at four, a full four and one-half hours away. When I could see he was momentarily stumped with regard to how Damodar would make his answers known, I conveyed Damodar's previous suggestion to simply place an empty 9 by 12 envelope on the table and open it as soon as the market closed to see what, if anything, Damodar had predicted. That would mean postponing the result of the test for several hours, but no one seemed particularly concerned about that circumstance.

Riordan readily agreed to my suggestion and had an empty manila envelope, marked 'Stock Market Results' placed in full view of the audience (and the TV cameras) in the center of the table. But at this point, most everyone focused their attention on the third, and arguably the most difficult of all the tests: Could Damodar prove his control over the forces of nature by making it rain in Washington, D.C. at twelve noon and ending exactly five minutes later?

Chapter 25

T he dramatic paranormal event taking place at the National Press Club was being communicated around the world either through direct television feeds or intermittent news updates, and of course was being transmitted on all the wire services. When Riordan made his last remarks, the time was eleven-forty a.m., and while several television stations broke for local news and commercials, the major networks turned to their anchors to analyze the proceedings thus far and to provide background information on CRIAPP and—to the extent known—on Damodar. One or two mentioned my connection with the event, but they didn't dwell on it.

The unexpected paranormal twists demonstrated by Damodar in each of his biographical recitations were highlighted by all of the journalists, but the reference to Louise Trent's previously unknown murderer proved to be the pièce de résistance. I had little doubt that the authorities, after witnessing Damodar's performance so far, would make serious efforts to locate the man who Damodar had said was Louise's killer.

Since the third challenge involved Damodar's ability to change the weather in Washington in a very specific manner using his occult powers, a significant amount of time was taken up by network and local-station meteorologists discussing the current weather and the forecast for the noon hour—sunny, with an expected high of sixty degrees Fahrenheit— hardly a typically cold December day in Washington.

When the gathering reconvened at precisely eleven fifty-five, Riordan explained the third and final challenge and announced to the audience that, in accordance with Damodar's prior request, six television cameras had already been set up at various locations on the National Mall and all were linked by microwave to six television monitors and to the network feeds in the Press Club. He then noted for the record that the outside temperature was currently fifty-eight degrees and that the skies were sunny and clear over Washington, D.C.

As we waited anxiously for the allotted time, Chet Walker leaned over and said in a quiet voice, "This one really worries me, Dave. I've never heard of anyone making it rain at a precise moment, not even those highly-touted Navajo Indian rainmakers."

Adrienne added, "I'm worried, too. I certainly hope he can pull it off."

Although a little tremor of fear knifed through me, I felt more confident about Damodar's ability to control the forces of nature than most in the room. With less than a minute to go, the tension level increased significantly, with dozens of eyes shifting back and forth from the ticking hand on the Press Club wall clock to the six TV monitors positioned at strategic locations around the room. I couldn't help comparing the expectant atmosphere to that of the launch control room at Cape Kennedy immediately before a NASA shuttle launch. Just as the second hand struck twelve, someone shouted, "Look!" and all eyes fastened first on one television monitor and then on the others.

"But that's not rain . . . it's snow!" another voice called out over the hush of the crowd. To the wonderment of everyone—not only in Washington, but around the world—heavy flakes of snow were cascading down on the Mall, and *only* on the Mall, at such a rapid rate that in just a few minutes the ground was blanketed with nearly six inches of fluffy white snow. Visitors on the Mall at the various veterans' memorials and those waiting in lines at the Washington Monument and on the steps of the Lincoln Memorial couldn't believe their eyes. Young children started making snowballs and throwing them at each other, while their parents and other adults looked around and could see the sun shining while the snow was falling only on the Mall. The assembled journalists and technicians in the National Press Club ballroom let out spontaneous whoops and howls of laughter when they realized what was happening. I felt enormously relieved and so did Chet. Adrienne clasped her hands, shook her head and burst out laughing as she watched the television monitors. "Snow at fifty-eight degrees!" she chortled in a voice loud enough for all nearby to hear.

Damodar had surprised us all. Snow, not rain, fell for the prescribed five minutes, and just as suddenly as it started, it stopped. Riordan, with a broad smile on his face, turned to the panel of judges and asked, "I think we can all agree that Damodar has passed the third test with flying colors, can we not?" The heads of the judges all nodded affirmatively. "Then, I'm adjourning these proceedings now, so we can get lunch and take care of other matters. We'll reconvene precisely at three-fifty, before the stock market closes, to see how Damodar makes out on that final challenge."

With those words, the telecast ended and the hubbub of activity and reactions to the proceedings really began, with several reporters laughingly giving high-fives, and others simply shaking their heads in disbelief as they stood up to leave.

Chet and Adrienne decided to return to the *Tribune* offices, while I chose to remain downtown, grabbing a quick bite at a small luncheonette on E Street. As I sat munching a particularly tasty bacon, lettuce and tomato sandwich, I wondered if Damodar had any more surprises in store, not only for the reporters at the National Press Club, but for the world in general.

By the time the reporters reconvened in the ballroom of the National Press Club later that afternoon, the nation—and the world—was abuzz with the preliminary results of the CRIAPP challenge to Damodar and, judging by the huge number of phone calls and e-mails sent to the networks as the morning's events were completed, viewers could hardly wait for the resumption of the proceedings. Even more reporters showed up for the afternoon session, which made the room more jam-packed than it was earlier.

In a relaxed, buoyant mood, Anthony Riordan approached the lectern to reopen the proceedings. "It is now almost four p.m. Eastern Standard Time and we are waiting for the New York markets to close before we open the previously empty envelope marked 'Stock Market Results,' which has been left undisturbed on the table under the watchful eyes of Press Club security personnel. This is the third and final test of Damodar's paranormal abilities, and I remind all of you that in this final challenge he has to predict the closing index averages on the Dow Jones Industrials, the Standard & Poor 500 and the NASDAQ within a margin of error not to exceed point zero one on each index.

National Press Club personnel had tuned a television set in the front of the room to the *Financial News Network*, and thirty seconds after the final bell at the New York Stock Exchange the closing prices of the selected indexes were shown as follows: Dow, 9,998.30, up 106.40; the S&P 500, 1142.92, up 8.56; and the NASDAQ, 2004.76, up 17.31. Riordan recorded the numbers, casually remarking to the audience that it was clearly an up day for the market. Then, Riordan addressed the security guard, "Sir, will you please hand me the envelope, and can you attest to the fact that it has been untouched and in no way tampered with since I first placed it on the table at around eleven-thirty this morning?"

The security guard responded affirmatively and, as a hush again came over the crowd, everyone's eyes focused on Riordan as he opened the envelope and withdrew from it a large piece of white paper with handwriting on it—an amazing occurrence in itself, since the envelope was empty when first placed on the table.

Riordan took a few seconds to compare the recorded closing numbers with those Damodar had predicted, and then, with a half laugh while shaking his head in total amazement, he announced that Damodar had predicted the *identical* numbers for each of the indexes. Not even off by a hundredth of a point on any one of them! He handed the paper to the panel of judges and each of them, in turn, examined it with great interest, since its very existence and the manner of its appearance was so extraordinary.

Riordan then declared that the challenge proceedings were over and announced that Damodar—and the *Washington Tribune* as a consequence—had won the three-part challenge indisputably. He added, "Since the Committee for the Responsible Investigation of Alleged Paranormal Phenomena has lost the challenge, it will have to honor its commitment to send a check or checks totaling one million dollars to the charity or charities of the winner's selection. In accordance with the agreed rules of the contest, that transfer of funds shall take place no later than next Monday, December 24th, 2001."

Chet Walker stood up and courteously offered his hand to Dr. Beckley while doing his best to conceal his schadenfreude. Beckley looked crestfallen as he extended a limp hand to Walker, and was about to say something when, to everyone's surprise, the image of a tall, swarthy figure slowly began to appear on the large screen. In an instant I realized that it was Damodar himself! He was dressed exactly as I had seen him during my out-of-body experience: white tunic and matching white leggings, and wearing his royal blue turban. The audience watched spellbound and breathing virtually stopped as Damodar's clean-shaven face gradually came closer until it nearly filled the screen. All knew that they were witnessing something extraordinary.

Unlike all his previous communications, which were confined to words on the computer monitor, this time Damodar spoke directly to the audience. His words, spoken in a clear, mellifluous voice, and without any trace of an accent, filled the entire room.

"I have been challenged by a series of tests which, I think everyone will agree, I have passed indisputably. As I said earlier, this is not my customary behavior, nor that of any other member of our Himalayan Brotherhood. In fact, it is quite demeaning to have to prove in this manner either our de facto existence or our transcendence of the normal frontiers of scientific knowledge, including our ability to control the forces of nature. It was permitted in this isolated instance by the Mahâ Chohan, our revered leader, because of the unusual circumstance of my contacting Mr. David Elliott of the *Washington Tribune* and, through him, submitting articles to his newspaper on the nature of the postmortem states of consciousness according to the Eastern occult philosophy.

"Many attempts have been made to interfere with the publication of the articles in this series—including the infliction of severe injury on Mr. Elliott himself—but all have failed, including the present one. Invariably, when efforts are made to bring eternal truths to the minds of the public, dark forces are energized to prevent them. We have always been aware of that and were fully prepared to meet those maleficent efforts whenever they arose. The use of fraud and chicanery in today's test is merely another example of the extent to which the forces of darkness will go to achieve their evil goals.

"Occult phenomena have always been misunderstood and misrepresented by science and religion alike, both of which refuse to recognize the existence of the latent powers and possibilities in man. Let me assure you, not one of the phenomena demonstrated here today was paranormal or supernatural, and certainly not miraculous. All were produced by a power over perfectly natural, though largely unrecognized, forces. In the final analysis, however, the attainment of true wisdom isn't achieved by phenomena, but through spiritual development that begins within each individual, and that has been our objective all along.

"In a future article to the *Tribune*, I will present information never before presented to the Western world explaining how one may, in certain limited circumstances, contact the Souls of loved ones who have departed earth life. Although you are seeing me today in my natural body, this will be the only time you will see me in this manner. Henceforth, I will communicate only with Mr. Elliott in the way I have communicated with him heretofore, that is to say, by means of electronic messages directed to his computer. And now, I bid you farewell."

As he made a well-executed *namasté*, Damodar's image on the screen gradually faded and a moment later was gone. A media circus atmosphere ensued after Riordan announced that the proceedings were over and the network television feeds were terminated. Journalists and technical personnel in every part of the room began talking excitedly to each other, some shouting, some giving high-fives, but most simply smiling and shaking their heads in dumbfounded amazement.

In a matter of moments, TV cameramen and reporters with mikes in hand swarmed around me asking questions: "Who is this Damodar? How long have you known him? Are you still receiving e-mails from your lady friend? Where can we get more information about the Eastern occult philosophy?" There was no way I could give intelligent answers to all the questions in this kind of setting, so I raised both hands in a wait-a-minute gesture and, when it finally got quiet, said, "You're entitled to answers to all of these questions, but not now and not here."

"Why don't you go on one of the talk shows?" a female voice suggested, "like *Meet the Press* or *Face the Nation* . . . or one of the morning talk shows?"

"I may well do that," I replied, "because at least I'd be able to provide more detailed answers to your questions than I can here today." And, saying that, I turned away and continued collecting my personal belongings. As the reporters finally relented and dispersed, I walked over to where Chet and Adrienne had been sitting. Both gave me warm smiles and extended their hands in congratulation. Adrienne chuckled and was most effusive in her comments. "David, that was the best performance I've seen in years—maybe in my whole life! Damodar deserves a lot of credit for doing what he did, especially under those trying circumstances. I can't get over it; he actually made it snow at fifty-eight degrees, and only on the Mall! And, oh, the publicity!"

"It was amazing to me, too," I said. Well, we've made history today, that's for sure."

Chet also commented on Damodar's performance and then asked me "How're you feeling? Is the shoulder still bothering you?"

"Yeah, a little, but it's getting better. I tire a lot quicker than I did before I received the bullet wounds. In fact, I feel like I'd better head for home right now and get some needed rest."

"Do that," Chet said, as he gingerly pumped my hand once more and said goodbye.

I taxied home, ate a nondescript TV dinner and lay down on my bed to reflect on the extraordinary events of the past two weeks. Without question, my life had changed dramatically: Senta and I had become celebrities; Archibald Taylor nearly killed me; I had an out-of-body experience that gave me a chance to see my beautiful *herzele* one more time; Ray Tuohy had been fired and was no longer in a position to cause me any further aggravation; and today Damodar put on a scintillating display of his occult powers for all the world to see.

I had been reflecting on these events while staring at the ceiling when I felt a sudden urge to go to the computer. Sure enough, Senta had sent me another e-mail.

> "My darling David, Damodar's magnificent performance today should stimulate great interest in the Eastern philosophy. At the very least, it should whet the public's appetite for Damodar's remaining articles. He said that his next one would be sent to you shortly.
>
> "Damodar also told me he's pleased with the way things went today and with the way you've handled yourself throughout the past several weeks. He's got another surprise in store for you, but didn't tell me what it was. Get some rest, darling. I sense our time is running short."

With those enigmatic remarks, Senta signed off. Before going to bed, I decided to watch several of the late-evening news telecasts to see how they handled the dramatic paranormal challenge at the National Press Club. The TV footage of the snow falling on the Mall was aired endlessly, and TV journalists reported bizarre reactions everywhere. In Los Angeles, psychics and mediums interviewed on the situation were ecstatic about the proceedings, stressing the fact that Damodar's ability to contact the dead was proof positive of the ability to contact departed loved ones, something that they had maintained all along.

All the networks reported the arrest of Harold Townsend at his home in Waterbury, Connecticut, upon the direction of the District Attorney of New Haven County, with footage showing the former handyman-gardener claiming his innocence in the Louise Trent murder case and violently protesting his arrest based solely on information provided by 'some flaky invisible creep.'

It surprised and disturbed me to learn that in Chicago masses of people were reported flocking to churches in the belief that Damodar's appearance heralded the imminent forthcoming of the Messiah, while angry clerics, in exasperation, did their best to discredit the idea.

Also surprising—and considerably more disturbing—was a late-evening report on CNN in which economic experts predicted that the financial markets would take a beating at tomorrow's opening in light of fears of worldwide religious reactions to the appearance of the long-anticipated Messiah or possibly the Antichrist. Apparently, overseas markets already had begun collapsing, and sporadic outbreaks of violence by ultra-conservative religionists were reported in France, Germany, Greece and Italy.

All these reports were dismaying, to say the least, because they illustrated reactions that were the exact opposite of the objective that Damodar was hoping to achieve. He went out of his way to point out that the producing of occult phenomena was not the important issue; that what *was* important was the attainment of true wisdom through individual spiritual development. I wondered if anyone really listened—or understood—what he was saying. So, despite my best intentions, I suddenly felt a strong sense of guilt that I was instrumental in bringing about physical violence—possibly even some deaths—and potential financial ruin to millions of people around the world if the financial markets continued to collapse. That thought made me feel rotten.

I suppose that, as a newspaperman, I should have known that the media would exploit and pervert the Damodar challenge and make a mockery of the beautiful message he did his best to enunciate. On the other hand, Damodar himself had noted that, when eternal truths are brought forth to the minds of the public, dark forces are energized to counter them, and it was clear to me that that's exactly what was happening.

The late evening news further reported that in Washington, various Members of Congress saw the negative economic fallout as the most critical item to be addressed. One senator told CNN that he would be introducing legislation on Wednesday that would make it a federal crime for "psychics, clairvoyants, fortune-tellers, or any other person claiming paranormal powers, to make predictions on radio or television programs—including cable television—of stock market or commodity market prices or future events likely to trigger changes in stock or commodity prices."

A congressman from Pennsylvania vowed to hold oversight hearings on the genesis and conduct of the National Press Club event itself, characterizing it as "a perversion of the airwaves to conduct what amounted to nothing more than a televised gambling contest."

A wave of exhaustion, both emotional and physical, suddenly overwhelmed me, and I felt the need to withdraw, to block out all the horror, guilt and pain I was feeling. The day's events had taken their toll on my strength. As I finally sought the kind mercy of sleep, my mind turned momentarily to what Senta had said about Damodar's performance generating interest in the Eastern philosophy, and that thought gave me a small degree of solace for the way the challenge had turned out.

Chapter 26

The worldwide excitement caused by Damodar's phenomenal performance at the National Press challenge was a phenomenon in itself. Newspapers around the nation, and, indeed, around the world, pushed to the background stories about Al-Qaida and the hunt for Osama bin Laden in favor of headlines like "Mahatma Causes Snow to Fall on National Mall," "Historic Paranormal Event in Washington," "*Tribune* Wins Million Dollar Paranormal Challenge," and "Amazing Damodar Shows Incredible Psychic Powers."

The electronic media gobbled it up with nearly round-the-clock coverage, including endless television news replays of the now-famous snow scene on the Mall. For the most part, the American press reacted reasonably objectively, reporting the challenge much the same way they would describe a NASA shuttle launch, a medical breakthrough or a major scientific discovery, but with no particular emphasis on the underlying philosophy that made it all possible. The *Tribune* was a notable exception, offering a feature story on page one that gave due credit to Damodar and the source of his powers—the Eastern occult philosophy.

I continued to work out of my apartment, both because it gave me more time to recuperate from my injuries and because it shielded me from the continuing onslaught of telephone calls from those who wanted to know more about Damodar or about my e-mails from Senta.

I checked my voice mail messages several times on Wednesday morning. In a strange, though understandable, reaction from the scientific community, I received calls from meteorologists at the National Oceanic and Atmospheric Administration (NOAA) and several universities asking me if I could possibly arrange for Damodar to replicate the snow demonstration so they could take appropriate measurements and analyze the results. Of course, I told them that that would be impossible, and reminded them what Damodar had said about the demeaning nature of producing such phenomena. I even received several voice mail requests from ski resort owners in the New England area who said they were prepared to make offers of large sums of money if Damodar would make it snow in the off-season. I never even bothered to reply to those calls.

Another unexpected consequence of the Press Club challenge were some complaints I received from unhappy investors who claimed that Damodar's ability to pinpoint the exact closing prices of the major stock market indices proved beyond a shadow of doubt that the markets were 'fixed,' something they had charged was occurring all along, and several said they would file formal complaints with the SEC. I couldn't figure out who they felt was doing the 'fixing' or how they thought Damodar fit into their conspiracy theories, but found the reaction fascinating, nevertheless.

On a less amusing note, I became the lightning rod for some particularly vicious attacks by a few members of the foreign press who minced no words about calling me the Antichrist, Satan, the Devil, the Prince of Darkness and other contemptuous epithets. I didn't fare much better with the organized religions. *L'Osservatore Romano*, the Vatican weekly newspaper, carried a papal statement condemning me as well as Damodar for fostering the "unholy belief in the ability to communicate with the dead," but stopped short of labeling either of us the Antichrist. Nor did it mention any of the other challenges that Damodar met. Other major religious denominations issued some equally strong statements of condemnation, which were not unexpected after the meeting with the six clergymen that Ray Tuohy had engineered.

None of this caused me any particular concern, but that was not the case with a feature article in *Bizarre Events*, the widely-read American supermarket tabloid which featured stories about the occult, the weird and the bizarre. With Damodar's televised image on its cover, and a heading, "Has the Antichrist Arrived?" that publication went out of its way to suggest Damodar as being the Antichrist and cast me as an evil tool of the Devil for communicating with my dead loved one, and accused me of giving others false hope that they might do the same.

I had become familiar with the Washington editor of this New York-based publication some years earlier, a man named Bud Morrison, who had a reputation for concocting sleazy stories about celebrities and happenings, often with little regard for the facts. In this instance, using quotes from several of Damodar's articles out of context, Morrison accused me of facilitating blasphemies and false miracles while labeling me, among other things, 'the Devil's apprentice,' a 'wicked Jew,' the 'tool of the Antichrist' and flatly stating that the Eastern occult philosophy was an out-and-out hoax.

For me, the personal invectives were easier to take than the outrageous attempt to ridicule and belittle the Eastern occult philosophy, a philosophy that had been put forth by the neo-Platonist philosophers of Alexandria as far back as the first two centuries after Christ. I was upset, but the more I thought about it, Morrison's aspersions differed little from the disparaging sort of rhetoric H.P.B. had to put up with during her lifetime. I decided I wouldn't take any direct action against the tabloid at this time.

Several calls I received came from some of the same program scheduling personnel at local television stations who had called me after Damodar's first article appeared in the *Tribune*. Each pleaded with me to appear on their morning talk programs and I promised to get back to them promptly. I was mindful of my remarks at the Press Club and felt I had to appear on at least one such program or I'd be hounded endlessly for weeks, if not for months.

Later in the day, I got a call from Chet Walker congratulating me for my part in the Press Club proceedings and asking me if I had any ideas about the charities the *Trib* should designate as recipients of the challenge-winner's proceeds. He said, "I was thinking that, in light of Damodar's magnificent performance, perhaps we ought to make donations to the cause that he espouses—the Eastern occult philosophy, and the boss-lady agrees. What do you think?"

"I think it's a great idea, and the closest thing to that would be Theosophy, since it's based entirely on the Eastern occult philosophy. I'll get you the addresses of the major organizational divisions of Theosophy in the United States: the United Lodge of Theosophists, the Theosophical Society in Pasadena, and the Theosophical Society of Adyar, India, whose American headquarters are in Wheaton, Illinois."

"Yeah, do that, and give them to my secretary. We have until Monday to let the CRIAPP people know how much and where to send the checks. The boss-lady is as happy as I've ever seen her, and listen to this, our circulation has gone up by five thousand copies per day," he chuckled, adding, "notwithstanding the cancellations by quite a few disgruntled Episcopalians who followed the recommendation of Episcopal Bishop Hollinger."

"Wow, that's quite an increase in circulation," I said, "but it doesn't surprise me. What does surprise me is how that bunch of pseudo-scientists thought they could get away with their ridiculously brazen cheating. The funny thing is, CRIAPP's professional investigators invariably accuse persons who claim paranormal powers of one form of cheating or another when CRIAPP has undertaken so-called 'scientific' studies of paranormal phenomena. The challenge they lost yesterday to Damodar, despite their attempt to cheat, was a monumental blow to their vaunted objectivity and the reputation of the organization as a whole."

"It sure was," Walker agreed, "and what a hefty price to pay for their arrogance."

I told Chet about all the requests I had received to appear on local and national television shows and he said he had no objection to my appearing on one or two of them, adding, "My original fear that your going public with this whole e-mail business would turn you into a media freak and tarnish the reputation of the paper at the same time hasn't materialized. You can tell 'em what you want, Dave. And while you're at it, be sure to remind them that more articles by Damodar will be appearing in the *Trib*."

After he hung up, I called the producer of the *Wally Winston Show* and accepted his invitation to appear on their Friday morning program. He was delighted and offered to have a Town Car pick me up and return me home after the program, which I gladly accepted.

A while later, I received a call from Miriam. She asked how I was feeling and congratulated me on the outcome of Damodar's challenge at the Press Club. But she then turned to the subject of Ray's sudden, unexpected departure.

"I knew he was unhappy about the way things were going with the Damodar series, but to pack up and leave with no explanation or goodbyes, seems awfully fishy to me. Of course, no one believes the story that Chet put out about Ray asking for extended sick leave."

"Well, I can't say I'm unhappy that he's gone." I decided not to say anything further.

"No, I'll bet not," she said, with a chuckle. "Can't say it'll bother me, either."

I quickly changed the subject. "By the way, what's with your heart situation? When are you going in for your angioplasty?"

"In another week; right after Christmas." There was a slight pause before she added, in that delightful, husky voice of hers, "Please promise you'll come and visit me, David."

"Of course I will. Keep me informed, Miriam . . . and good luck." As I hung up, I recalled Damodar's comment about Miriam's heart and mused about how he had become so intertwined in the lives of so many people associated with me—including Miriam.

I wondered how Detective Fiori was making out in his attempt to connect Ray with Archie Taylor. I couldn't get over the nerve of that bastard Tuohy—paying someone to shoot me—and if it weren't for my lucky talisman, I might have been killed! I made a mental note to give Fiori a call tomorrow.

Chapter 27

W hen David called on Thursday morning, Detective Fiori told him
that he had just received a report from the District's ballistics laboratory clearly linking the two slugs retrieved from David's body with
Taylor's 9mm Beretta. But he was still waiting for a report from the suburban Maryland forensics laboratory that might confirm Taylor's DNA
on the envelope that contained the death threat.

"Unfortunately," he told David, "the two eyewitnesses to the shooting weren't able to positively identify Taylor as the man who shot you
when we put Taylor in a lineup," so, all we have at the moment is the ballistics evidence on the gun and, if we're lucky, the DNA evidence. I don't
think we'll have any problem proving our case against Taylor."

"I know," David said, "but I'm more interested in the case against
Tuohy, for obvious reasons."

"We're working on that, too," Fiori assured him. "I'll keep you informed."

Fiori was just as interested as David was in determining Ray Tuohy's
possible role in the murder attempt. The District's Questioned-
Documents Examiner had told Fiori that he had little difficulty in con-
cluding that Ray Tuohy's handwriting was on the business card found in
Taylor's possession when arrested. But, Fiori was still looking for evidence of a direct connection between Tuohy and Taylor. He wanted to
know how and where the two men met to hatch the plot and when and
where the financial arrangements were made.

As it turned out, Archibald Taylor's court-appointed lawyer, Arthur
Lane, provided the key to solving that problem. Earlier that morning,
Lane had had his client plead not guilty to attempted murder of David
Elliott at his arraignment in U.S. District Court, but when the experienced
defense attorney learned from his client that Ray Tuohy had instigated
the plot to maim David, he wasted little time in letting Detective Fiori
know that fact. Lane knew it could reduce Taylor's sentence considerably
if he were held to be a co-conspirator rather than the sole perpetrator of
the crime. Lane promptly arranged to have Taylor give a tape-recorded
confession to Fiori at police headquarters on Thursday afternoon.

On the basis of that sworn statement, which provided the missing information about Tuohy's role in the plot, Captain Roberts directed Fiori to arrest Raymond Tuohy for conspiracy to commit aggravated assault and the attempted murder of David Elliott.

As a matter of courtesy, Fiori called Chet Walker to give him the news. "I'm sorry to have to tell you this, Mr. Walker, but we've got a warrant to arrest one of your employees, Raymond Tuohy, in connection with the shooting of David Elliott. We could have him arrested in Virginia, where he lives, but that would necessitate extraditing him to the District of Columbia and we'd like to avoid the expense and delay in doing that, so we plan to arrest him at your offices. I know this will be temporarily disruptive to your business, but we don't have much choice. I promise you we'll make it quick and with as little disruption as possible," Fiori explained.

Chet at first feigned surprise at hearing Fiori's mention of Ray's involvement, but then replied, "He's not here, detective. He's on extended sick leave, which began a couple of weeks ago . . . oh, wait a minute. Come to think of it, he called my secretary this morning to say he'd be in around four this afternoon to pick up some of his things."

"Thanks for telling me. My associate and I will be there in plenty of time," Fiori replied, in a determined voice, "and it goes without saying that you shouldn't say anything to him about this, in case he gets there before we do. We'll be out of your way as quickly as possible."

When Detective Fiori and a fellow plainclothes detective showed up around three forty-five p.m. on Thursday, reporters all over the *Tribune's* newsroom speculated as to who they were and why Chet had them wait in the large conference room unattended. But they didn't have to speculate too long because, shortly after four, when Ray Tuohy showed up to retrieve some personal items from his office, Fiori intercepted him. After showing his badge and identifying himself, Fiori ushered Ray into the conference room. Once there, he confronted the long-time Religion & Family Section editor in a normal tone of voice, but one that the uncommonly quiet reporters in the newsroom could hear, "Raymond Tuohy, you're under arrest for conspiracy to commit aggravated assault and the attempted murder of David Elliott on December third, two thousand and one."

Tuohy's face turned beet red as Fiori uttered those words and then gave him his Miranda rights. While he was being patted down and handcuffed, Ray gave an embarrassed look around the newsroom to see who might be witnessing the arrest, but otherwise made no comment or asked any questions. Neither Chet Walker nor Adrienne Thayer was anywhere in sight as the two detectives led Tuohy away. The entire incident lasted less than three minutes.

At that point, the buzzing of the reporters in the newsroom increased substantially and they tried to figure out why Ray Tuohy would want to have David killed. But, Ray's sudden departure on so-called extended sick leave—which no one on the staff had taken seriously—at last made some sense.

Ray was taken to the District's jail facility at Indiana Avenue, where he made a call to attorney Robert Hannaford, a Virginia neighbor of his and an experienced defense attorney. After meeting with his new client, Hannaford contacted the U.S Attorney's office and asked to speak with someone about the evidence against his client. Assistant U.S. Attorney Nan Holmgren told him about Taylor's sworn statement, which clearly implicated Tuohy. That surprised Hannaford, but even so, he doubted that a jury would take the word of a common criminal—only recently released on parole and with a record of assault and armed robbery—over the word of a former Methodist clergyman and highly respected newspaperman.

Although attorney Lane felt he had accomplished a lot by having Taylor give a sworn confession implicating Ray Tuohy, he believed he had an even better card to play. When he learned from the U.S. Attorney's office how Detective Fiori obtained the information about Taylor's commission of the crime—information transmitted to the victim telepathically by a person known only as Damodar during a so-called 'out-of-body' experience—he saw the distinct possibility that the entire case against his client could be thrown out before it even started.

The Court had set January 14th as the date to hear all pre-trial motions and January 30th as the tentative trial date.

Chapter 28

I received a phone call from Detective Fiori early Friday morning telling me that I should be prepared to testify in court in Tuohy's case, if that became necessary. He said I would be hearing from the U.S. Attorney's office in the near future on that score. It was not pleasant news, but something I had known was always a distinct possibility.

Sol Berman called to say that Damodar's stellar performance at the National Press Club had stimulated considerable interest in the articles on the afterlife, and he asked me when we might expect Damodar's fourth article. When I broached that subject with Damodar a little while later, he responded:

> "You shall have the next article later today, my friend. But, the Mahâ Chohan has informed me of an urgent matter that will require my personal attention elsewhere for possibly a week or two, so I will be unable to provide any further articles during that period. Rest assured, however, that I shall be in touch as soon as I return. I hope your editor will understand, and I offer my apologies to him and to the readers for this unexpected interruption."

As promised, the fourth article arrived a little while later, this one dealing with the dangers of mediumship. I forwarded it by e-mail to Sol and I told him to pass it along to Chet for editing purposes now that Ray was out of the loop. I also told him to inform Chet about the expected delay in receiving the next article in the series from Damodar, and the reason Damodar had given, as well as his expression of apology.

Of more immediate concern was my appearance on the *Wally Winston Show* at ten o'clock. At just the thought of it my stomach knotted and my heart jumped a little. Writing for a major newspaper was one thing; appearing as a national celebrity on TV was something else again. I reviewed in my mind what I would say about the key events that occurred and made a concentrated effort to relax after that was done by closing my eyes and meditating quietly for several minutes.

After the Lincoln Town Car dropped me off at the studio on L Street, I was met by a solicitous young man who hustled me to a make-up room, where I had my face lightly powdered to mask any reflective highlights. Then a young female assistant ushered me down a labyrinth of hallways, past the wardrobe and prop departments, and eventually to the studio where the *Wally Winston Show* originated, a cavernous room with blackened walls and accessories. Despite the size of the studio itself, I was surprised by the relative compactness of the set and equally surprised to see the vast number of klieg lights, which made the air in the room feel exceedingly warm, almost hot. Four television cameras were positioned to cover all angles of the set, which had a large, comfortable upholstered guest chair facing a modern mahogany desk with an executive swivel chair for the host. I was amused to note that the background of the set was designed to appear like a large window overlooking the National Mall—the very place where Damodar had made it snow a few days earlier.

Advertising industry numbers showed that the *Wally Winston Show* consistently had the largest percentage of morning television viewers in the Washington Metropolitan area. Wally had been hosting the ten a.m. program on WTOC for more than twenty years and was considered one of the top television personalities in the nation's capitol.

Wally sat at a desk and momentarily interrupted his reading of some staff-prepared program notes when we were introduced, giving me a warm smile with his hello and handshake. He was over six feet tall, trim and fit. He had strong, confident face, and warm, brown eyes. Athletically built, he looked to be about forty-five years old, and was smartly dressed in a light gray suit, white shirt and a white-polka-dotted blue tie. His calm, easy manner helped settle some of the butterflies in my stomach and made me feel quite at ease before we went on the air. I could see why he had become a local TV favorite. Even my thumping heart had finally settled into a more-or-less steady rhythm and my stomach knots had gradually disappeared.

Still, when the sweep-second hand of a large clock just off-stage indicated the program was going to begin in fifteen seconds, I swallowed hard and my heart began thumping again. At the precise moment of ten, I could hear the familiar strains of the program's theme music and then an announcer's voice off-stage welcoming the unseen television audience to "the top morning show in the Nation's Capitol. And now, here's your host . . . Wally Winston." The red light on the television camera facing

Wally directly came on and the affable TV host started the hour-long program with a brief welcome to his viewing audience and then got right to the subject of the day.

"This past Tuesday, the nation and the world was treated to an extraordinary display of psychic and occult powers by a person called Damodar, who successfully met three of the most daunting paranormal challenges ever conceived—all devised by the Committee for Responsible Investigation of Alleged Paranormal Phenomena, an organization dedicated to exposing paranormal frauds, and the group that instigated the challenge. The highlight of the day's events was Damodar's ability to produce the now-famous cascade of snow on the Washington Mall for exactly five minutes at high noon. We'll be talking about the snowfall and other aspects of that unusual event with today's guest, the man who was the prime factor behind all of this activity—David Elliott. David is an editorial writer for the *Washington Tribune* and a long-time resident of Washington who claims to have received e-mail messages from his deceased lady friend, Senta Trondson, which started the series of events leading up to Tuesday's unusual demonstration by Damodar. Welcome to our program, David."

"Thank you, Wally. It's nice to be here," I said.

"Let's begin with your background, David, where you grew up, went to school . . . and anything that might shed light on why *you* were singled out to get e-mail messages from someone who has passed away."

Winston's non-confrontational opening put me further at ease and, after taking a deep breath, I quickly reviewed my upbringing in Manhattan, my schooling at Columbia, and my work on the small newspaper in upstate New York before coming to Washington. Then, I told about my job at the former Department of Health, Education and Welfare, and how this led to my meeting Senta there before I moved on to become a reporter and later an editorial writer for the *Washington Tribune*. Winston picked up on the reference to Senta.

"For those in our viewing audience who don't already know, Senta Trondson started sending our guest e-mail messages approximately three months after she died. Did I get the timing right on that, David?"

"Yes, that's correct."

"Tell us how it all came about. I know the essential facts were all laid out in the first couple of *Tribune* stories, but for the benefit of those who may not have read or heard about them, why don't you refresh our recollections a little."

I took another deep breath to calm my nerves before telling Wally the manner in which I received the first of Senta's e-mails, and how I had some doubts as to the legitimacy of the message. "The more I read, the stranger I felt, because I couldn't believe what I was reading. I mean, it made sense, but I knew that receiving e-mails from a dead person was impossible . . . so, obviously, something weird was happening, and I was beginning to think I was losing my mind!"

Winston interrupted, "What do you mean when you say it made sense?"

"Well, the message contained information that I knew was true or at least jibed with things that had happened which only Senta and I knew about."

"Could you be a little more explicit?" Winston asked.

"Sure. You see, Senta and I both have been students of Theosophy for many years, and in her e-mail she referred to the fact that I was planning to write a book about the after-death states from the theosophical point of view. That's when she brought Mahatma Damodar's name into the picture."

"How so?" Winston asked. "And I want to hear a lot more about Da-modar, too."

"She said that Damodar had contacted her shortly after she left her physical body and realized that she was in *kama loka*. That's the first plane or state of consciousness we all go to after dying. He told her—telepathically—that he wanted to conduct an experiment involving the two of us."

"And what was that?" the TV host asked, inching his elbows forward on the desk where he was sitting.

"He said he would temporarily interrupt her death process—literally put it on hold—and during this period he would make it possible for her to communicate with me via e-mail. He told her that all she had to do was think the sentence she wanted to say and he would convert her words into electronic signals that he would transmit directly to my computer. And he added that, during this period, he would provide valuable infor-mation to me in the same manner for my forthcoming book on the theosophical view of the afterlife."

"All this was in the first e-mail?"

"Yes, or at least that's what it said, if I could believe it."

"And did you?" the TV host inquired. "I mean, this message must have sounded awfully weird. Weren't you even a little bit skeptical?"

"You bet. I didn't know what to believe at first. So, I devised a test to see if the sender really was my deceased Senta."

"What kind of test?" Wally asked, as I noticed him glancing ever so briefly at his notes. I then realized he probably had no background info about my original test.

"I asked the sender to respond to five very detailed, specific questions about various people, dates and events that only Senta and I would have known. And in less than two minutes the answers were there on the screen—she answered everyone of them absolutely correctly."

"Wow!" Winston said, in amazement, as he stroked his forehead. "Would you mind telling us what some of the questions were?"

"Sure. One of them asked for the date and place where we first met, and the answer came back, 'December 18, 1968, at the Department of H.E.W.'s Christmas party,' which was right on the button."

"H.E.W. referring to the former Department of Health, Education & Welfare," Winston explained to his unseen audience. "Can you give us another example?" the popular TV personality asked, as he began warming up to the subject.

"Well, Senta spent eight years at an orphanage in Westchester County, New York, and another question was: What was the name of the teacher at the orphanage who gave you a special present at Christmas, and what was that present?"

"And the answer?"

"A pair of ice skates, and the teacher at the orphanage who gave them to her was Pastor Von Bussey, which was correct."

"And I assume that the answers to your other questions were also correct?"

"Yes," I said, " and no person alive today could have known the answers to those five questions. So, that was all the proof I needed."

After asking me a few more questions about Senta and our relationship, Winston began questioning me about Damodar. "Three days ago, viewers throughout the nation—and indeed throughout the world—were treated to a phenomenal display of paranormal powers by the person called Damodar. Now, he's someone we'd all like to know more about, David. Tell us who he is, how you came to know him, and anything that would enlighten us further about this extraordinary character."

"Mahatma Damodar is a very special person, Wally. By that I mean, he's an initiated Master of Wisdom in the Eastern occult philosophy, which is more commonly known as Theosophy, but has been around for ages under a variety of names. Damodar was a Hindu Brahman who, back in 1879 at the age of eighteen, joined with Helena P. Blavatsky to help her in the cause of Theosophy, which was just then getting underway in India, after having been begun in America four years earlier. Later, he became her spiritual pupil, or *chela*, and eventually was summoned to the home of the Himalayan Brotherhood in Tibet to study for his eventual initiation as a Master of Wisdom."

Winston blinked, shook his head with an amused half-smile, as if at an obvious error, and said, "Wait a minute, David. You say he was eighteen in 1879 . . . " He cocked his head a bit, to give me an opportunity to correct my figures.

"That's right, Wally."

He blinked again and leaned back. "But if my arithmetic is correct, that would make him one hundred and forty years old today! Yet, when he appeared on the screen at the National Press Club, he looked to me to be no older than forty-five or fifty!"

"Again, that's right, Wally. But you have to understand that once an individual has reached the degree of spiritual perfection of a Mahatma like Damodar, his body is no longer subject to the same vicissitudes or physical infirmities as those of ordinary beings. So, yes, Damodar is as old as you said, and I'm sure that there are other Mahatmas in the Brotherhood who are even older."

Winston shook his head in disbelief. "That's amazing! Sort of reminds me of James Hilton's *Lost Horizon*, where he describes the mythical city of Shangri-la, tucked away in the Himalayas, whose residents never show any signs of age." A motion from someone off-stage caught Wally's attention and he finished with, "Well, we'll talk more about Damodar right after this commercial break."

During the break, Wally asked me if I had any other revelations about Damodar, things that his viewers might find intriguing and not previously reported, since that was how he kept his audiences interested. I told him that I had nothing specific in mind but that just about everything I could tell about Damodar was new and intriguing. Following the commercials, Winston resumed his questioning. "David, Tell us how you met or came to know Damodar."

"I first learned about Damodar at the time Senta became the custodian of Morya Bennett, the twelve-year-old Indian spiritual prodigy who resided with her at her Washington home for a few months in late 1992 and early 1993. During the time he was there, young Morya told Senta that he was receiving spiritual instruction from Mahatma Damodar during his daily meditation periods, and as a theosophist, Senta of course already knew who Damodar was.

"Morya had to return to India in the spring of 1994, and shortly after Senta said goodbye to him at the departure gate at JFK airport, Damodar appeared alongside her—in the flesh—and he offered to become her mentor and guide on theosophical matters from that point on, using the same method of instruction as he had used with Morya."

"And what was that?" Winston asked.

"Thought transmission, and precipitation,"

Wally gave another half-smile. "I've got a pretty good idea what thought transmission is—like mental telepathy—but I've never heard of precipitation. What's that all about?"

"Well, it's a little complicated, Wally, but let's see if I can simplify it. Precipitation is the occult process of making words or pictures appear in print on paper or other substances. To understand it, you have to recognize what occultists have always known, namely, that all metals, pigments and chemical substances exist in suspension in the ether around us at all times. Knowing this, the trained Adept or occultist like Damodar first forms the mental images of words or pictures that he wishes to be laid down on a chosen surface. Once the mental image appears in the ether—or the astral, as it's called by occultists—the Adept uses his will power to draw from the ether the particular pigment or chemical that is needed and causes the mental words or images to be deposited on the paper or other surface in question.

"You may recall that I had suggested to Mr. Riordan during the second challenge to Damodar at the National Press Club telecast that he place an empty envelope on the table, which he did. And after the stock market closed, they found in the envelope a piece of paper with all the stock market indices written down, just as if someone had handwritten them. Well, that someone was Damodar, using his clairvoyant faculties first to 'see' the final numbers in the astral ahead of time and then, using his will power, to precipitate them onto a sheet of paper which he also fashioned out of the ether."

Winston let out a "Phew!" as he shook his head and then proceeded with the questioning. "So, how long was Senta in touch with Damodar before her death?"

"Eight years. And although I was aware of that contact, I personally never had any contact with Damodar and was sworn to secrecy about it until after Senta died . . . that is to say, when the e-mails began back in November."

"Well, I've got to say, Damodar's powers impressed me enormously," the television host asserted candidly. "His naming of the murderer of that Trent girl in Connecticut literally sent chills up my back. By the way, I understand that the police arrested the man that Damodar mentioned and the case has been re-opened."

"Yes, I heard that, too."

Winston asked several more questions about Damodar's ability to communicate with deceased persons before asking about the snow on the Mall. "Tell me, David, how was Damodar able to make it snow on a specific section of the city when the temperature was more than twenty-five degrees above freezing, and then turn it off like a light switch five minutes later?"

"I can't answer that question, Wally, because it gets into areas of the occult that I know nothing about, but I can assure you it was not a feat that an Adept like Damodar would normally agree to undertake. The leader of the Great White Lodge of initiates, the Brotherhood that Damodar belongs to, personally had to approve the weather demonstration that Damodar gave, which was simply another type of precipitation. It's all part of the secret science the Adepts call *Gupta Vidyâ*."

"We all know that you've been receiving e-mails from your Senta fairly regularly since this all began, but have you also been receiving informational materials from Damodar by this strange precipitation process you just outlined?"

"No, not as yet. We've been in touch on many matters and, of course, he has been forwarding all his articles on the postmortem states for publication in the *Washington Tribune* through e-mails he directs to my computer. By the way, he's told me that in the near future he'll be sending a couple more articles for the *Tribune* series."

"That's great. I'll be looking forward to them. Incidentally, I understand that, since the big telecast last Tuesday, other papers with syndication rights have begun printing Damodar's articles as well."

"That's my understanding, too."

After another commercial break, Winston devoted the balance of the program to brief questions about various aspects of Theosophy, including karma and reincarnation, more about H.P.B. and *The Secret Doctrine*, and spent the final few minutes talking about my continued contact with Senta.

"How long do you expect to be in contact with Senta through this e-mail process, David?"

"Not much longer, I'm afraid, Damodar's articles are nearly finished, and he's already told Senta that we're nearing the end of this unique interruption of her death process. So, I'd guess we've got only another week or two."

Winston paused slightly before asking in a soft, lower voice, "What happens then?"

"What happens then," I replied, wistfully, "is that my e-mail contact with Senta will end and from that point on all I'll have is my memories of her and our wonderful life together. I'll probably start a book on some aspect of Theosophy, or perhaps a book about everything that's happened to me since receiving that first e-mail."

"Well, I'm sure we'd all like to know more about this whole strange series of events, and I, for one, would welcome such a firsthand story. I hope you do it."

The program ended a minute later, and with a sense of relief, I shook Wally's hand and left the studio. I later learned that a huge number of television viewers worldwide had seen either the original program or repeated versions both in the United States and abroad. And even though I felt the interview had gone well, something inside me told me not to be too smug. I was well aware of the way the public misconstrued many things Damodar had done and said during the big Press Club telecast— thankfully without all the dire consequences that had been predicted—so I knew that the same sort of thing could happen as a result of my interview by Wally Winston.

Back at the office, Chet congratulated me on my television appearance and told me that he thought my idea about writing a personal memoir of everything that has happened was a good idea. A little later, Miriam also called to congratulate me.

Chapter 29

The story about Ray Tuohy's arrest was placed on page three of Friday's *Tribune*, although it made the first page of other major newspapers. In light of the great interest in the subject of the afterlife generated by Damodar's Tuesday performance at the National Press Club, Chet decided to feature Damodar's fourth article in the main section of Sunday's paper, where it would get considerably more attention than its usual placement in the Religion & Family Section. He had Lou Garza write a brief summary of the earlier articles, along with a short piece detailing the extraordinary proceedings at the Press Club. Chet himself wrote a small sidebar in which he explained that Damodar's fifth article would be delayed briefly "due to exigent personal circumstances" but, hopefully, not for long.

Damodar's fourth article included new information about the *kama-rupa* and the dangers of mediumship:

> "In an earlier article, I mentioned the postmortem existence of an entity called the *kama-rupa*, which is the repository of all the desires and aversions of a person whose life just concluded, and the entity from which the Spiritual Ego or Soul must separate itself before it can move on to *devachan*. You will recall that this process of separation was referred to earlier as the death struggle, and its completion was termed the Second Death.

> "What is left of the *kama-rupa* after the death struggle is over is an entity that will disintegrate in time, depending on the intensity of the desires, emotions and passions that made it up. If they are unusually strong, that is, if the desire-forms are those of wicked, hateful or evil people, the *kama-rupa* will last as an entity for a relatively long time on the astral plane.

> "*Kama-rupas* have no will or direction, yet—as coherent masses of unwholesome desire, envy and lust—they are a constant threat to those who are passive and those who dabble in psychic practices. If they are the

desire-forms of ordinary good men and women, the *kama-rupas* will float around aimlessly for a short while and soon disintegrate.

"Note, however, that since the *kama-rupa* is formed from and continues its existence in the astral plane, it retains essentially all the memories of the life just concluded, including the individual's habits of thought, speech and personal idiosyncrasies. These *kama-rupas*—which are nothing more than empty astral 'shells' devoid of will or direction—are what psychics and mediums often refer to as the 'departed souls' of loved ones.

"But the Spiritual Ego or true Soul is not there; it has separated from the entity and moved on to a state in which it cannot be contacted or disturbed. All that is evoked by mediums is the playing back of the words and thoughts of the 'dearly departed' prior to their deaths, not unlike playing back words recorded by someone on a tape recorder.

"In short, those entities contacted are merely temporary shells momentarily reawakened by the medium, but this reawakening of the memories of the past life is good neither for the medium, whose moral health is thereby placed in serious danger, nor the *kama-rupa*, since its normal rate of disintegration is thereby greatly hindered. Each contact reinforces that *kama-rupa*'s energy, prolonging its existence unnecessarily, and to no good end.

"You will recall in my earlier article on *kama loka*, that the Ego's stay on that plane of existence usually lasts a relatively short time, after which it moves on to the blissful plane of *devachan*, but this is not the case for those whose lives have been cut short by accident, homicide, suicide or by court-ordered executions. Until their normal life spans have been reached, these unfortunate beings are unable to experience the cleansing and healing process of the death struggle. Such individuals are not really dead; only their physical bodies are dead. They remain living persons in the astral realm of *kama loka* and, through mediums, occasionally do communicate with those left behind or, in some cases, with completely innocent persons whose psyches are unusually sensitive and receptive to such contacts. They remain in *kama loka* as unfulfilled earth-walkers, some of whom seek ways to communicate with and, if possible, influence the living.

"Although the innocent accident victim or victim of homicide who has a preponderant degree of goodness is watched over by the Dhyân Chohans until the time he would normally enter *devachan*, the situation is not the same with respect to suicides and executed criminals. It is precisely because they are devoid of will or direction that the *kama-rupas* of suicides and executed criminals tend to seek out and fasten upon mediums, and this is exactly why the practice of mediumship is so dangerous.

"The earth-walkers who were executed criminals are a particularly great problem. The elements of hate, anger and revenge predominate in such individuals and they constantly seek ways to avenge their legally-mandated deaths by injecting thoughts of hate and murder into the minds of sensitive persons, and are helped to do so through the harmful and degrading practice of mediumship.

"Mediums are passive and docile instruments in the hands of invisible powers that they little understand. Thus, attendance at seances and seeking to communicate with departed loved ones, or relying on the words channeled through New Age mediums, all present inherent dangers. The words and ideas presented could be from the empty and potentially evil *kama-rupa* shells or could be from the deceptive and often vengeful earth-walkers. In all cases, these experiences pose dangers to the medium as well as to the sitters and should be avoided at all costs by those of enlightened mind and purity of heart."

As I re-read Damodar's article, I knew how upset mediums all over the world would feel when they read it. Mediumship has become big business everywhere. It is a field rampant with deceptions and frauds perpetrated by would-be spiritualists and psychics. Channeling is another form of mediumship concerned with contacting dead people, but channelers seem less interested in conveying messages from departed loved ones than in dispensing New Age spiritual wisdom and guidance from ancient spirit guides. I was aware that hordes of people are devoted followers of specific channelers and are loyal buyers of their books, tapes and programs.

Damodar's article had explained where the messages from New Age mediums and channelers really came from, and I hoped it would at least deter some well-intentioned persons from paying exorbitant fees to psychic mediums for trivial and inconsequential information about their deceased loved ones. And the dangers of attending séances are real, as Damodar noted.

As I was reflecting on Damodar's article, I received a new e-mail from Senta.

> "Darling *herzele*, I'm taking advantage of Damodar's presence to get this off to you before he goes away. I have some very interesting news for you. Yesterday, I spoke with my father for the first time, here in *kama loka*, and it was a truly emotional experience—for both of us.
>
> "I'd been hesitant about communicating with him because of his atrocious behavior when I was a little girl. I thought of him as an insensitive coward who ran out on us children after Mom died. Still, I knew that I ought to at least talk to him, and I'm glad I did, because our conversation brought to light issues I had been entirely unaware of. We talked for quite a while, during which I learned about Pop's fears of inadequacy both as a husband and a father, fears that steered him to drink, gambling and womanizing shortly after Mom died.
>
> "He said to me, 'You don't know how bad it can get, Suzy, until it happens to you personally; the loneliness, the incredible responsibility to raise five kids; the need to pay off markers on huge gambling debts—all stuff you kids never knew anything about. Oh, sure, I told everyone that I lost the apartment houses because of the Depression, but that was only a partial truth. The real reason was paying off my tremendous gambling losses to loan sharks and mobsters. And I'm lucky I wasn't killed by those bastards.'
>
> "As he talked, tears welled in my eyes, especially when he called me Suzy, his pet name for me as a child. I suddenly realized how unfair it had been of me to judge him on the meager information we children had to go on. All we knew was that he ran out on us and never seemed

to care. Putting us in the Home was the final straw, something for which I could never forgive him. I told him that I had been bitter thinking about that experience my entire life, but now recognized that my condemnation of him only hurt me in the long run, and that I had to rise above that, spiritually.

"I felt so ashamed when he said to me, 'Don't hate me forever, Suzy. I still love you—all of you kids—and you mustn't carry grudges beyond the grave.' He was right, of course. I told him, 'I love you, too, Pop, and the hating stops right here and now.' With that, we embraced and I promised to keep in touch with him while we're both still in *kama loka*. His final words were those he used to say to me as a child: 'You're still my beautiful Suzy; always will be.'

"I'm happy to tell you all this because it not only makes me feel better emotionally, but it serves as a lesson for others who hold similar bitter feelings about deceased relatives and who never get the opportunity to make amends during their lifetimes."

As I read Senta's comments, I couldn't help feeling sorry for her that she missed out on having a closer and more loving relationship with her father while she was growing up. But then, when I thought about how her psychological feelings of abandonment by her father had stood in the way of her willingness to marry me, a lump formed in my throat and the overwhelming sadness of the situation brought tears to my eyes. *Damn it! Why do people have to die to learn these important things?*

I was about to congratulate her for seeing the wisdom of forgiveness and reconciliation, even after death, when I noticed that she had added something else:

"A final thought, darling: I love you dearly, and always will, but I worry about your emotional state now that you are alone and without someone to love and to love you in return. As we both came to appreciate, love can be a source of joy that is unobtainable in any other experience. You are entitled to that, *herzele*. Now that we are no longer physically part of each other's lives, don't let our undying love for each other stand in the way of a new-found love in your remaining years of earth life."

Reading those final words, I smiled ruefully as the tears continued rolling down my cheeks.

Chapter 30

Christmas came and went before I knew it, possibly because it fell smack in the middle of the week but more likely because the flurry of continued phone calls, voice mails, e-mails and frequent conversations with Chet blurred time for me. The weather turned cold and we had a few light snows, but nothing out of the ordinary—certainly no deluge of arctic-sized flakes of the sort Damodar produced.

I received no e-mails from Senta during this period because Damodar was unavailable to act as the intermediary for our communication. This was disheartening because Christmas was always special for us. It brought back memories of our first meeting at Christmastime in 1968 as well as memories of the holiday atmosphere that Senta loved to create. She always decorated her home with all sorts of Christmas finery: a splendid large wreath on her front door, mistletoe and garlands of other Christmas greenery, pine cones, bright red velvet streamers, and colored Christmas tree balls and ornaments placed in bowls throughout the house. I reminisced wistfully about the ways we had spent previous Christmas holidays—enjoying our traditional hot cocoa and Christmas pastries—knowing full well that time was running short for our continued communication by e-mail. And this time I knew our parting would be a lot longer than just three months.

Miriam entered GW Medical Center for her angioplasty the day after Christmas and I was one of her first visitors the following day. She said the doctor told her that the angioplasty was successful and she again mentioned the prescient advice given by Damodar about her worsening heart condition. This led to a discussion about the chain of events that had focused the attention of the world on Damodar, the *Tribune* and me. I also mentioned my increasingly-vigorous defense of Theosophy in various settings, brought about by the recent chain of events.

"It's becoming a part of you, David, this Theosophy stuff, and there's nothing wrong with that. Both you and Senta have been at it for a long time, and while it was in her nature to talk like a theosophist no matter who she was speaking to, it's just starting to rub off on you. I think that's fine."

She was right, of course. I had always been the student, while Senta was the teacher, but since her death I'd been forced to assume the role of teacher more and more. It wasn't as hard as I thought it would be, just a change of attitude and emphasis. In the past, mainly because of my Jewish background, I didn't feel comfortable talking to people about Theosophy or theosophical doctrines, but since the day I received the first e-mail from Senta, everything had changed. Of course, having Damodar in my corner certainly had made it a whole lot easier, along with Senta's constant encouragement. It was a strange feeling having people look up to me for advice and guidance in an area of life that is of such keen interest to them. Until all this happened, I never knew how many bereaved persons longed to contact their departed loved ones.

"I guess it is," I acknowledged. "It's a little frightening, but at this point it seems to be my karma—as well as my duty."

"You're a good man, David, and it's obvious you've been through a lot this past month, but so far as I can tell, you've held up pretty well. I wonder if things would have been different if I hadn't told Ray about our conversation in the restaurant."

"Oh, of course not, Miriam. If he hadn't spoken to Chet first, I might not have had the opportunity to make the points I did. And don't forget, it *did* lead to the demonstration of Damodar's powers and Chet's agreement to publish the series."

"Yes, but to think that Ray Tuohy would want to have you seriously injured or killed. It's simply beyond my comprehension." She shook her head and then changed the subject in that delightful, sensuous voice of hers, remarking, "So, first I visit you at the hospital and now you return the favor." She smiled and our eyes lingered for an extra second. I'd noticed before that Miriam was attractive, of course, but it never really affected me—until now—undoubtedly because over the years Senta was the one and only love of my life.

We chatted for another five minutes before a nurse's aide who had come to check on Miriam's IV connection interrupted us, so I took the occasion to make my departure. I stood, bent over, gave Miriam a kiss on her forehead, squeezed her hand and said goodbye.

A Death Interrupted

As I left the hospital, I got the warm feeling that something nice was happening and I reflected on Senta's earlier comment about being open to finding someone else to love and to love me. It dawned on me that she must have had Miriam in mind all along. She certainly wouldn't have disapproved.

With the CRIAPP challenge out of the way, I resumed working at my office at the *Tribune* three days after Christmas. I was happy to be back where I had all my files and where I could be in closer touch with my fellow editorial writers, and they were happy to have me back. The crowds had long since disappeared and security was no longer an issue. During the second week of the new year, Damodar returned from his special mission and I resumed my communications with Senta and Damodar by e-mail every day. When I told Senta about my visit to Miriam at the hospital, she surprised me with words I hadn't expected to hear:

> "I'm very glad to know that you visited her, *herzele*, because she's basically a good woman and someone who you *should* get to know better. As I've said before, you need a woman in your life at this time.
>
> "I know you could never love her—or anyone—the way we loved each other all these years, but there's no reason why you couldn't learn to love again. The most important thing to me is that you have a helpmate and companionship—yes, even sexual companionship—during your remaining years on earth. So, please give the possibility of becoming closer to Miriam serious thought. Will you do that for me, darling?"

Senta's frank comments were in line with what she had said earlier and I knew her well enough to understand why she said what she said. She was, and always will be, the broadest-gauged person I have ever met. It only made me love her that much more.

I replied, "Yes, darling. I'll give serious consideration to what you have suggested. Of course, it's not all up to me; Miriam certainly will have something to say about the matter."

> "You won't have to worry about that," she replied. "From what I could tell when we met at the *Tribune's*

Christmas party last year, she'll be more than happy to take up with you, darling. The important thing is that you should not be alone at this point in your life, and seeing her at the hospital was a good start."

I acknowledged her response and told her how much I appreciated her attitude and concern for my welfare. After exchanging a few more personal bits of information, I asked her to let me speak with Damodar.

"Master Damodar," I said, "ever since you began sending articles to me for this series, I have been getting dozens of requests from people of all backgrounds with regard to making it possible for them to communicate with their deceased loved ones. You have already made it clear that such communication with those who are in *devachan* is an impossibility but that in certain circumstances such communication has been possible with those Spiritual Egos that are still in *kama loka*, sometimes for the worse, but not always. Do you think you could respond to these concerns in a way that will give them guidance?"

His response was right to the point:

"Yes, dear friend, I intend to do so in the next article in this series, which will be my final one. In fact, I am contemplating the wording for that article at this very moment and anticipate transmitting it to you within the next day or so."

I thanked him for his response and buried myself in my latest editorial assignment. As I did so, I found my mind diverted more and more to my conversation with Miriam at the hospital and my dialogue with Senta *about* Miriam.

Chapter 31

T he legal maneuvering in the Archibald Taylor case attracted a fair amount of publicity. The pre-trial-motion hearing was held before Judge Wade DeForest in U.S. District Court on Monday, January 14th, and I decided to attend, even though I was told it was not necessary for me to be there.

Attorney Arthur Lane, not surprisingly, moved to have all charges against Taylor dropped and further moved to suppress all items of evidence obtained during Taylor's arrest on grounds that it violated the Fourth Amendment's prohibition against unreasonable searches and seizures except upon a finding of probable cause. Since both sides had filed the necessary affidavits with the court prior to the hearing, the issues raised were not a big surprise.

Lane gave three reasons in support of his motions: first, because there was no eyewitness evidence to support the arrest; second, because the arresting officers had no personal knowledge of facts that would give rise to a finding of probable cause; and third, the direction to make the arrest that was given to the officers by Detective Fiori was itself without probable cause. "Specifically," Lane told the Court in oral argument, "Detective Fiori ordered the arrest not on information obtained either from an eyewitness to the alleged crime or from a reliable informant, but solely on the basis of information relayed to him by the victim, which the latter allegedly received during some 'out-of-body' experience from an invisible being known simply as Damodar."

Assistant U.S. Attorney Nan Holmgren, on behalf of the prosecution, argued that the Supreme Court's ruling in the 1971 case of *Whitely* v. *Warden* governed. The ruling in *Whitely*, she contended, granted a policeman the right to make an arrest upon the strength of a direction from a superior officer, whether made by radio, Teletype, telephone, or other mode of communication. "Hence," she told the Court, "the direction from their superior officer to arrest Taylor was sufficient probable cause for the arresting officers to do so." She declined to comment on the source of the superior's information, but Judge DeForest noted and attacked that omission forcefully.

"The issue, Ms. Holmgren, is not whether the arresting officers were entitled to act on the direction of their superior, but whether the superior himself had probable cause. If probable cause was lacking at the source, the *Whitely* rule would be inapplicable. Mr. Lane has raised the issue, and I think properly so, that Detective Fiori's only basis for issuing the arrest order was the clearly hearsay information he received from the victim, information allegedly received by thought transmission from some phantom individual called Damodar, whose abode is said to be in Tibet. Are you contending that information from a source like that would meet the Fourth Amendment's requirement of probable cause?"

Holmgren asked for a moment to confer with her legal associate and with Detective Fiori, who was also sitting at the counsel table. When she resumed argument, she told the Court, "Your Honor, we maintain that the very fact that Detective Fiori's source had every detail correct, including not just the name, but the address of the alleged perpetrator, the fact that he was an adjudicated criminal, the fact that he had written proof of who put him up to the plot to shoot and maim, all constituted the type of wealth of detail that would entitle a reasonable police officer to conclude it was accurate and reliable. In short, Detective Fiori had ample reason to assume probable cause in this instance."

"I'm afraid I don't agree, counselor," DeForest countered, "You're looking at the situation *after* the fact, but this Court is concerned with finding probable cause for an arrest at or *before* the time the arrest was ordered. The information received in this instance may indeed have been reliable and accurate, but it was not made by an eyewitness or a known, reliable police informant. It was more in the nature of an anonymous tip. How did this information differ from the sort of information the police might have received from a psychic?"

"I can't say, your Honor. But you can't dismiss the fact that it *was* one hundred percent accurate."

"Well, to my knowledge, information from a source like that hasn't been recognized as the basis for a finding of probable cause in any American jurisdiction that I'm aware of, notwithstanding the ex post facto finding of the accuracy of the information proffered. Under the circumstances, I am ruling in favor of defendant's motion to have all charges dismissed, as well as his motion to suppress all evidence obtained by the police at the time of his arrest, in violation of his Fourth and Fourteenth Amendment rights. An order to that effect will be issued by the Court today, and upon its receipt, the defendant will be released from custody. There being no further issues before the Court, this hearing is concluded." We all stood as he rose to return to his chambers.

If Holmgren and Fiori were understandably crestfallen, I was in a state of near-shock. I couldn't help wondering: what's wrong with our crazy criminal justice system? The man who tried to inflict grievous bodily injury on me—and might have killed me, if it weren't for my talisman—was going to be set free even though he admitted in a sworn statement that he had committed the crime and even implicated the man who put him up to it! Talk about getting away with murder!

As we all prepared to leave, Fiori asked Attorney Holmgren, "What about Taylor's sworn statement implicating Raymond Tuohy? Can that at least be used in the case against Tuohy?"

"I'm afraid that's included in the suppression order, too," she answered, sullenly. "Once a ruling has been made that there was no probable cause for an arrest, all the poisonous fruits of the illegal arrest must be suppressed. I'm afraid that would include all the evidence found at Taylor's apartment as well as his later sworn statement implicating Tuohy, so it can't be used either in the case against Taylor or in any other case arising out of the same set of facts. Unfortunately, it looks like Mr. Tuohy may have lucked out on this one."

Fiori, obviously frustrated, kept plugging away. "Well, what about the bicycle Taylor stole? That wouldn't be considered one of the poisonous fruits of the arrest, would it?"

Holmgren paused to think for a moment before replying, "No, now that you mention it, I don't think it would. Only the evidence that was found in Taylor's apartment—the gun, the money, the business card with Tuohy's signature on it, and things like that—would be suppressed. If you can connect Taylor to the theft of the bicycle parked outside, and prove that it was more than $250 in value, you could re-arrest him and hold him for First Degree Theft under the D.C. Criminal Code."

"And if we can get a conviction on that," Fiori said, with excitement rising in his voice, "he will have violated the terms of his parole and in all likelihood will go back to Lorton to serve out his time and probably several more years. So, maybe he won't get away with murder after all."

"Well, that would be better than letting him go free entirely," I added, finally beginning to feel a little bit better. "Have you been able to connect him with the bike theft yet?"

"Well, we know his prints were all over the bike, and it was an expensive Raleigh—the owner valued it at over $700 when he reported it stolen—so I know it would qualify as a First Degree Theft. I'll get forensics to prepare the necessary slides, and we'll re-interview the two eyewitnesses right away. Meanwhile, we'll re-arrest him on suspicion of First Degree Theft and keep him incarcerated until the case comes up for trial."

I heaved a sigh of relief as we parted at the courthouse and I taxied back to the newspaper. Though I was disappointed at today's legal turn of events, at least half a loaf was better than none. Still, the thought that Ray Tuohy would escape punishment for his primary role in the plot to severely injure me was almost too much for me to handle. Intellectually, I knew that his karma eventually would catch up with him, but deep down I wanted the satisfaction of seeing him suffer *now*! And as I reflected on that realistic desire, I realized how far I still had to go before achieving spiritual perfection.

Chapter 32

T he print media and television news reporters had a field day with the odd turn of events in the Taylor case. As usual in cases of this nature, there were those who decried the seeming unfairness of the result, while the ACLU and others who believed in strict interpretations of the Constitution applauded it as consistent with prior court rulings in Fourth Amendment cases.

When I returned to the office, my disappointment about the outcome of the court hearing only deepened when I spied the flashing icon on my computer, "New Mail." Usually, I would rejoice at the thought of hearing from Senta, yet a knot swelled in my throat this time. I feared before I clicked it open that this might be her last message to me. Senta began her communication:

> "*Herzele*, darling, Damodar has informed me that this may be one of the last times we will be able to talk to each other via e-mail. That's sad, of course, but you and I both know that interrupting the normal process of my death could not be postponed indefinitely, and that I must move on. Moreover, you—along with the articles by Damodar—have achieved virtually all that we had hoped for in bringing to the attention of Western society the specific nature of the stages of consciousness our reincarnating Egos go through after we leave our physical bodies.
>
> "And please don't fret about Mr. Tuohy's apparent escape from punishment for instigating the shooting that might have cost you your life. As Theosophy explains, karma is unfailing as a law of moral compensation. Focus instead on getting on with your life, whether that be writing or doing other things. We were blessed to have had a beautiful, loving relationship for so many years and we should both be grateful for that. I know I am, and your love will sustain me until we meet again. My main concern now is for your physical well being, and

that's why I mentioned that you should be open to new relationships. You're a good man and deserve to love and be loved during the remaining years of your life."

I wrote in response:

"Dearest, I understand what you are saying, and realize that our time is running short. We've been granted a unique opportunity to communicate with each other by e-mail, one that surely will go down in the history books.

"Although I'm doing quite well by myself in most regards, my biggest problem is adjusting to life without your physical presence after so many years of nearly daily contact. I will keep in mind what you have said. I love your thoughtfulness and concern, dear heart. And now, I must get back to work."

Around three in the afternoon, I received Damodar's fifth and final article and I immediately noticed the difference in its tone and thrust:

"The series of writings submitted heretofore have dealt with the more-or-less mechanical, albeit metaphysical, aspects of the postmortem states of consciousness. But, if there is one idea that our Eastern occult philosophy continually emphasizes it is this: nothing is begun or ended, it is merely changed, and that which we call death is only a transformation. Death is a doorway into a wonderful world, and no one should be afraid of it. That which follows death is simply life on another plane of being. Each of us has lived on earth many times before and will live in a body similar to the one we now have over and over again. The evolutionary pilgrimage of the permanent Spiritual Ego, the Soul, requires a long series of incarnations before the stage of conscious divinity is reached.

"Why is this so? Because we need time to accumulate all the kinds of experience life has to offer; time to assimilate the meaning of those experiences; time to develop our capacity to apply our growing knowledge and to understand the ultimate goal of all evolution, which is a conscious return to our spiritual origin. That practical need for time is met by the process of reincarnation.

"What do I mean when I say that we will live on earth again? Surely I do not mean the same body or the personal aims and desires that we normally think of as ourselves will be reborn. Even within one lifetime those can change from minute to minute. Surely not our character, which becomes modified rather haphazardly as we grow in years and experience, and not always for the better. These elements are but the temporary clothing of the actor within who is the Eternal Perceiver, which I have most often referred to as the reincarnating Spiritual Ego, but which many commonly call the Soul. It is the latter which, in successive incarnations, gains knowledge and experience, utilizing the body of various personalities that appear on the stage of life, sometimes as a man, sometimes as a woman, sometimes in a brown or red body, sometimes in a black, yellow or white one.

"So, the first thing we must do is to stop thinking of ourselves as merely our bodies. When someone we love dies, we don't mourn the body, we mourn the Soul that was in that body. And that Soul or consciousness lives on, however many changes of body it may assume when it passes from one lifetime to the next. The momentary loss one feels when a loved one dies is merely the loss of day-to-day physical contact, but having met your loved one on the Soul level during this lifetime, rest assured you will meet him or her again on the Soul level in your next lifetime. That, too, is occult law.

"Once the knowledge that death is not total annihilation and that postmortem consciousness continues, albeit on different planes of existence, it will become evident why attempts to prolong the lives of the chronically ill with costly drugs and life-prolonging equipment are completely misguided. Death should not to be regarded as an implacable enemy that must be fought with all the technological, often demeaning, measures at one's disposal. This is especially true with respect to those elderly persons whose normal life spans are near at hand and whose astral bodies have already begun to lose their cohesiveness and disintegrate. For persons in that condition, hospice care is surely the most humane treatment.

"There is much talk about dying with dignity, but in the final analysis, the greatest dignity to be found in death is the dignity and nobility of the life just ended. It is not how we *die* that matters, it is how we have *lived*, and how well we have achieved our beliefs, hopes, ideals and aspirations for a better life, not only for ourselves, but for all mankind, for that is what true spirituality is all about."

I was impressed with Damodar's conclusion about living a meaningful life, but wondered if he was going to say anything about contacting deceased relatives. In the very next sentence he provided the answer.

"I am aware that many bereaved individuals who have been reading the newspaper accounts of Mr. David Elliott's e-mail communications with his beloved Senta Trondson—who left her physical body several months ago—wish that they too could contact their deceased loved ones. I can now tell you that there is a way, but it is not a simple or easy one.

"The whole purpose of evolution, that every person should eventually achieve individual conscious divinity, is the key to such efforts. Let me explain. The aspirant seeking personal communication with his deceased loved one must first develop a universal love, something that transcends merely personal love. He must live the purest and most unselfish life he possibly can. He must cultivate his mind and detach it as far as possible from worldly pleasures, worldly desires and worldly objects, and must set his heart as undividedly as his strength permits on doing good to all living things, including animals, and to preserving the fragile ecology of the planet on which we live.

"I urge you to demonstrate the qualities of love, gratitude, compassion, sacrifice and steadfastness, for these and like qualities have been valued as fundamentals of life throughout the ages. And finally, I urge you to develop feelings of true brotherhood with men of all races, ethnic and religious backgrounds, for that is the most important quality of all, and the key that will most surely prove magical.

"To those who dedicate themselves seriously to acquiring qualities of the sort just mentioned, doorways to the psychic world will open, including the doorway to communicating with deceased loved ones, provided they are still in *kama loka* and engaged in ridding their Spiritual Egos of the lower passions and desires of their *kama rupas*, as described in earlier articles.

"And now, I can tell you that those who reach the stage of spiritual development just described will indeed be able to contact their loved ones. In the world of the occult, there is a force known as *kriyasakti*, which is the mysterious power of thought that enables it to bring about phenomenal results by its own inherent energy. The ancients held that any idea will manifest itself externally if one's attention is sufficiently concentrated on it.

"Hence, if the desired result is to contact a deceased loved one, it can be obtained by concentrated effort and meditation on one or all of the following special days of occult significance: February 19th, March 7th, August 11th, and November 17th. On those specific days, meditate on the Sanskrit word OM, the sacred mystic syllable of the *Vedas* and the syllable that the gods themselves use when addressing the Supreme Spirit. It is a sound of mystical quality that acts as the awakener of vivifying power throughout the universe. While uttering this sound, some of you may experience sentient signs, such as a feeling of the departed one's presence, and in some cases visual or auditory contacts. Others may receive olfactory or tactile impressions, and a few—a special few—may receive messages transmitted electronically to their computers, just as happened with Mr. Elliott.

"Do not be discouraged if the hoped-for contact is not made on the first attempt. But remember: living the spiritual life and loving your fellow man—true Brotherhood—is the key to making any contact at all. The religion of humanity is, and should be, love.

"I bid you success in your endeavors, and with these final words, I have now completed this series of articles on the afterlife and you will not hear from me again. In addition, Mr. Elliott's communication with his loved one in *kama loka* soon will come to an end, as he has already been informed. I bid you farewell and conclude my comments with the motto of the Theosophical Society, 'There is no religion higher than truth."

I passed Damodar's final article on to Sol Berman for Chet's review prior to publication in Thursday's edition. Meanwhile, Fiori filed the necessary affidavit to have Taylor re-arrested for the theft of the bicycle on the day I was shot. At least that matter was moving along with dispatch, even though there wasn't much that could be done about Ray Tuohy.

Chapter 33

Ray Tuohy had been lying on his jail cell bunk trying to make sense out of his tormented life when he heard voices and footsteps coming in his direction. At first, he thought the jail guards might be coming to move him to a larger holding cell—a request he had made repeatedly since he was first incarcerated—but his hopes were dashed when he recognized one of the voices as that of his lawyer, Robert Hannaford.

When Hannaford learned about Judge DeForest's ruling in the Taylor case, he understood that the entire case against Tuohy relied on the evidence obtained from Taylor—evidence the judge had now suppressed. Knowing that Tuohy was no longer subject to prosecution, Hannaford had hurried over to the District's main jail to give his client the good news.

"You're off the hook, Ray," he announced in a loud, cheerful voice, as he entered the surprised journalist's cell and, when Ray stood up to greet him, began pumping the accused man's hand vigorously.

"Why . . . what's happened?" Tuohy asked, genuinely perplexed as he received the news and extended his limp hand to the ebullient lawyer.

"The evidence against Taylor was thrown out by Judge DeForest on grounds of lack of probable cause for his arrest. And, under the Fourteenth Amendment, his taped confession and all the evidence the police found, including the card with your handwriting on it, was ruled inadmissible in court—not only against him, but against you, as well. You're a free man, Ray . . . or rather, you will be, shortly."

Tuohy felt stunned, but after digesting the lawyer's information, recovered sufficiently to force a thin smile, but not much more.

"What's the matter, Ray?" Hannaford asked. "You don't look as happy as I'd thought you'd be. Is something wrong? Have they been mistreating you here?"

Still in a half daze, Tuohy replied, "No, no. I'm okay. I guess I just never thought it would be over so soon. I . . . I can't thank you enough, Bob. " And then, with growing enthusiasm in his voice, he asked, "Tell me, how soon can I expect to get out of this miserable hell hole?"

"Probably within forty-eight hours; as soon as I can prepare the necessary motion papers and file them with the court. But, you don't have to worry, it's a done deal!"

The former Religion & Family Section editor for the *Tribune* nodded his understanding and patted Hannaford on the shoulder as the lawyer left the cell with a cheery, "You'll be hearing from me in a day or so."

After Hannaford's departure, Ray tried to come to grips with his wildly conflicting emotions, emotions that he had been desperately trying to cope with since his incarceration and barely managed to conceal from his attorney. Yes, he was relieved to know that he wouldn't have to stand trial for his part in the plot to gravely injure David. But his days of solitude in the D.C. jail since his December 20th arrest had given him time to reflect more fully on what he had done, and he knew intuitively that there still would be a price to pay.

Ray tried to confront his demons head on: his lifelong hatred of Jews and blacks; his failure as a Methodist minister; his failure as a husband; his inadequacies as a writer and editor, and most of all, his growing spiritual depravity, as evidenced by his willingness to commit an unforgivable criminal act. His soul was tortured by what he saw in himself: a bigot and a gutless pretender who lied and cajoled his way through life, always trying to please the persons who could make his life easier — people like his father, his seminary instructors, the Methodist Church hierarchy, as well as Chet Walker and Adrienne Thayer — and seldom with success. He saw himself as a complete failure, and the black mood that had overcome him while incarcerated was only momentarily pushed to the background when his lawyer gave him the unexpected good news about his forthcoming release.

Ray knew he had to resolve these negative feelings and make important changes in his life to palliate his tormented soul . . . and soon.

As his lawyer had predicted, Ray was released from jail Wednesday afternoon. After retrieving his car from the lot where the police had impounded it following his arrest, he returned immediately to his Fairfax, Virginia, home. His next-door neighbor, who had been sweeping her porch when his car pulled into the driveway, scurried inside to avoid saying hello or speaking with the man who reportedly hired a Lorton parolee to shoot a newspaper colleague. Ray could hardly avoid seeing the sudden retreat made by the lady he and his wife had known socially for over ten years. Her actions confirmed his worst fears about the stigma associated with his arrest.

He greeted his wife, Carole, affectionately enough, but she could see that he was sullen and depressed. Their talk at the dinner table was about trivial, inconsequential matters—a neighbor's cat killed by a teenager speeding in his graduation-gift Toyota; an increase in local utility rates; and miscellaneous unimportant telephone calls—with Ray giving perfunctory responses to every subject brought up. At bedtime, he said to Carole, "You go on up, dear. I'll be up shortly. I've got some papers to look over, first."

She dutifully complied, but as her form retreated from his sight at the top of the stairs, he heaved a sigh of sadness as he took one last look at the woman who had stood by him through thick and thin throughout the twenty years of their marriage. After removing his hand from the smooth banister he had been clutching, he walked with slow, heavy steps to the chair behind his desk in the library. Ray had given a lot of thought to what he would do after he was released from his jail cell. His life had become a chaotic mess, and he felt he was no longer in control. Among other things, because of the adverse publicity associated with his arrest, he knew that his job prospects in the Washington Metropolitan area were essentially nil.

After dallying nearly fifteen minutes in a semi-dream-like state while wearily rubbing his eyes with his cold fingertips, he took several pieces of stationery from a portfolio on his desk, and began writing three notes. The first was to his wife, telling her how much he loved her, but explaining that his humiliation was too much to bear to continue living. In a second note, directed to Chet and Adrienne jointly, he apologized for all the trouble he had caused the *Tribune* as a result of his recent immoral behavior. He addressed the third handwritten note to David. In it, he asked David's forgiveness for paying Taylor to shoot him. His hand stopped, ready to sign the note, yet he hesitated. There was more . . . much more . . . and his eyes welled as, without planning it, he added his deep remorse for all the hatred he held for Jews throughout his life, which he attributed largely to the influence of his bigoted father, but which he knew in his heart to be morally wrong.

He finished with a rueful comment to David: "How ironic that my life should come to an end because of my fruitless attempts to thwart the series on the afterlife. Well, at least now I shall learn firsthand whether Damodar was right in what he said about the fate of suicides in *kama loka* — if, indeed, there really is such a place."

After completing the notes, he slowly retrieved the Smith & Wesson revolver he kept in the credenza behind his desk, loaded it with a single bullet, placed the gun against his right temple, took one final deep breath, and pulled the trigger. His body slumped forward on the blood-splattered desk, with his head dropping not six inches from the framed photograph of the Tuohy family that Damodar had materialized in the conference room a month earlier — a mute witness to the journalist's tragic end.

Chapter 34

A somber air of sadness permeated the offices of the *Tribune* on Thursday as word of Ray Tuohy's suicide got around. Adrienne sent an e-mail to the entire staff extolling his qualities as a writer and conveying her deep regrets and condolences to the Tuohy family. She deftly avoided any reference to his arrest or related issues. I couldn't help recalling Senta's comment yesterday about karma being an unfailing law of moral compensation and her advice that I should forget about Ray's apparent escape from punishment. Thinking about the immediacy of the karmic cause and effect sent shivers down my spine.

For me, the sadness throughout the building was compounded a short while later when I received the following message from Senta:

> "The news of Ray Tuohy's suicide was sorrowful, both to me and to Damodar, as I'm sure it was to you, too. Damodar said that Ray's note—which he could see in the astral—was a positive sign of a change of heart that bodes well for Ray's future spiritual development.
>
> "And now, darling, I regretfully must tell you that this will be my final e-mail communication. It's time for my Soul to move on. I hope you will continue with your writing. It's your obligation to your fellow man in a crazy world where violence and strife seem to be the order of the day. Ideas have always ruled the world, and sharing noble thoughts and ideas should be your main objective from this point on in your life.
>
> "We've loved each other dearly for many beautiful years, and we both know that spiritual, holy love is immortal, so there is no need to fear that our physical parting will have any effect on the continuance of our love throughout eternity.
>
> "As I say farewell for the last time, dearest, I send you one final loving kiss. I shall be with you spiritually throughout the rest of your natural life and shall look forward to our happy reunion when it's time for you to join me in the world beyond."

A lump formed in my throat as I read those final words from my sweetheart. I squeezed my eyes against the tears of pain before my emotions would let me respond.

> "My dearest love, I understand the situation perfectly, and I, too, want your Soul to move on to its ultimate destination in *devachan*. The two of us, along with Damodar, have made world history by communicating with each other the way we have this past month or so. I'm proud of you, too, darling, and I will carefully consider your advice about my personal welfare. You have my undying love, *herzele*. Farewell until we meet again."

With those words, I signed off and stared at the screen. I couldn't stop the overwhelming sadness I felt as it finally hit me that I would never again be in touch with my beloved Senta in this lifetime. Emotions that were suppressed for months finally engulfed me. Tears flooded my eyes and ran freely down my face as I began to sob uncontrollably. The realization of utter loss clutched my heart and I sat at my desk depleted and unashamed to show my pain openly. How ironic, I thought, that I should experience Senta's death all over again—bereaved *twice* in less than five months!

Seeing me sobbing and staring at my computer screen, my editorial colleagues quickly concluded what must have happened and came over to comfort me. Sol Berman's eyes also filled with tears as he patted me on the shoulder and offered words of comfort.

Once my crying jag subsided, I knew I couldn't do anything more at the office, so I threw a few papers into my briefcase and prepared to go home. On the way out, I dropped by Chet's office to tell him where I would be, along with telling him about Senta's final message. Chet nodded in understanding and told me to take a week off, an offer I gratefully accepted. It was clear I needed time to get my life together.

I got a sudden urge to visit Senta's grave early on Friday morning so, after grabbing a quick cheese Danish and a cup of coffee, I drove over to Oak Hill Cemetery in Georgetown. After parking on a side street near Montrose Park, I carefully maneuvered my way down the rain-washed, gravel drive that led to Senta's grave. I stood there for five or ten minutes looking at the simple marker bounded by two small evergreen plants, then began talking to Senta mentally. First, I told her she was the one and only true love of my life, and thanked her for making this lifetime such a beautiful and rewarding experience for me. Then I told her I thought she was a far more spiritually-advanced person than I had originally thought, and that her support and encouragement during the past two months is what kept me going. Finally, I wished her well in her desire to achieve mastery over her dancing skills and artistry in *devachan* and finished by saying I eagerly looked forward to our meeting again.

As I walked back to the car, parked near the entrance to Montrose Park, I noticed a tall, dark-complexioned man coming in my direction, dressed in a western-style business suit, but wearing a white turban. Moments later, Mahatma Damodar stood in front of me. He gave me a broad, friendly smile, and I was again conscious of his youthful appearance, but his lively gait and the piercing nature of his dark, sunken eyes also impressed me.

Seeing the Master of Wisdom in his physical—as opposed to his astral—body surprised me and my amazement must have shown on my face because, after greeting me with his customary *namasté*, he remarked, in his strong, baritone voice, "Do not be so surprised, my friend. I am here in the flesh because I have some important things to tell you in person, which is why I mentally suggested that you come here this morning. I shall return to the Himalayas as soon as we are finished." He motioned for me to sit with him on a nearby park bench.

"You have served the cause of our occult Brotherhood well in the manner you have dealt with the various problems and impediments arising out of the newspaper articles, and we will not forget it. As you are aware, ingratitude is not one of our failings. But there is still more to do, and in that connection I am here to make you an offer."

I was obviously curious, but remained mute while Damodar continued.

"I have already established a psychic link with you through the work we have just completed, and I am aware that you plan to continue your writing on theosophical subjects in the future. We think that is admirable and wish to help you in any way we can. So, here is my offer: I will respond to any and all inquiries you make to me concerning our philosophy that might assist you in your writings. You can make such inquiries by thought transference during prescribed periods of meditation, as your Senta did for many years, I will respond either directly or will precipitate my replies on paper, so that you can use them as you see fit."

"But I don't know how to transmit my thoughts in that manner," I objected.

"In fact, you do," he replied. "Throughout our many contacts during the past two months I have established a clear magnetic link with you, so that will not be a problem. And there is one more connection that I will discuss in a moment. What is important is your desire to proceed in this manner."

"Oh, I certainly do, Mahatma Damodar. Your offer is an honor I would not refuse."

"Good, then so be it. My work along these lines with your beloved Senta proceeded in this manner for eight years—eight productive years, I might add, because her Ego was so well prepared to absorb the information proffered. As an aside, I can tell you that she is well on her way to becoming a *bodhisattva*, which is why the Mahâ Chohan chose her for the experiment that has just concluded."

I knew that the term *bodhisattva* denoted a highly evolved person close to achieving true spiritual enlightenment—and I was extremely impressed. "I kind of figured that something like that might have been the reason. And I am so glad that I was able to communicate with her again after she left her physical body."

"Yes, my friend. And now, I have one more little surprise for you. Please show me the talisman that saved your life."

I reached into my left pocket for the severely bent medallion and handed it to Damodar. He clasped it between his palms and softly recited a few words in a tongue I did not understand. When he opened his palms, the talisman had been restored to its original perfect shape, with no sign that it had ever been struck by a bullet. "Here is your charmed talisman. Keep it with you at all times, as it will not only protect you from harm but will provide an additional magnetic link between the two of us. And now, I must return to my normal abode in the Himalayas. I have enjoyed working with you, dear friend, and I look forward to our contacts hereafter telepathically."

With that, he stood, said 'Satyât Nâsti Paro Dharmah,' and vanished into thin air a moment later. If contemplating my future was what I needed time for, what had just happened made it all fall into place. I was thrilled to know that I would become a student of such a spiritually developed being as Damodar. And this time it would be a book or a series of books, not a series of e-mails.

Chapter 35

On Friday, February 1st, Chet met with Adrienne in her top-floor suite to review events of the past two weeks, but primarily to apprise her of the *Tribune's* improving financial picture. He was happy to report that everything was up—readership, subscriptions and advertising—and that the paper's reputation had been enhanced by Damodar's articles on the afterlife and his incredible performance during the National Press Club telecast.

Handing her an interim profit-and-loss statement prepared by the *Tribune's* accounting department, he gleefully explained, "Our financial picture is outstanding, Adrienne, the best one we've had in five years. And it's all due to Damodar."

She smiled, but it was a controlled smile. "Well, not entirely, Chester. It really all began with David Elliott. He's the one who brought it all about, and don't forget, he had to do it over your initial protests and poor Ray's constant backbiting."

"Yeah, I guess you're right. Dave's the one who got the whole thing rolling. Have you been keeping up with the fallout from the telecast?"

"I'm aware of a number of things, like the restoration of sanity in the world financial markets and the quieting down of all that talk about Damodar being the Antichrist. Is that the sort of fallout you're referring to?" she asked, while casually brushing a lock of hair away from her forehead.

"No, but I was happy to hear that things have begun simmering down, too. We've got enough trouble just trying to deal with Osama bin Laden and his Al-Qaida terrorists. What I'm referring to is what our competition has been saying about us editorially."

Taking a sheaf of half-folded newspapers from his weather-beaten leather portfolio, Chet arranged them haphazardly on her desk and then picked one up and began reading. "This is from the *St. Louis Post-Dispatch*: 'We applaud the *Washington Tribune* for its pure guts in agreeing to publish articles on the afterlife that most papers would have avoided like the plague. After reviewing the now-famous Damodar-Challenge telecast, we confess to being impressed enough to warrant reprinting of the entire series of Damodar articles under our syndication rights with the *Tribune*."

"You see that? They're gonna republish the whole series! And they're not the only ones. I'm telling you, Adrienne, we've started at groundswell with the Damodar articles."

"That's marvelous, Chester. I did read the editorial in the *Atlanta Constitution* the other day, the one that said they were going to support scientific and religious efforts to confirm or repudiate the points made about the afterlife. And, you know something, I'm delighted that they're taking that position."

"Why do you feel so strongly about *that*?" the executive editor asked, curious as to Adrienne's focus on that subject.

Adrienne took a deep breath before replying, "Because, frankly, Chester, I am quite impressed with the aims and thrust of the Eastern philosophy, and I think it's high time people started focusing more on the spiritual side of life, just as Damodar pointed out in his final article. I'll tell you a little secret: last Sunday, I decided to attend the local theosophical lodge meeting over in Bethesda, and what I heard was not only interesting, but really stimulating."

"Is that right? What were they talking about?" Walker asked, with eyebrows raised.

"Some young doctor from the National Institute of Mental Health was lecturing on current research on near-death experiences—all from the theosophical point of view. I was fascinated to learn from him about H.P.B.'s intimate knowledge of near-death-experiences, as reflected in her *Key to Theosophy* and her article, *Memory in the Dying*, which she wrote as far back as 1889. But what really amazed me was how much current scientific work is being done in this field, according to the young doctor."

Chet was genuinely impressed and nodded approvingly. "Well, well, Adrienne. So, you're starting to get interested in Theosophy. Are you planning to go to more of their meetings?"

"I might, but first I'm going to get a little more background from the basic theosophical literature. I've already ordered some of their fundamental works—H.P.B.'s *Secret Doctrine* and *The Ocean of Theosophy* by William Q. Judge. And the lodge people gave me a number of interesting pamphlets to take home, which I've been reading avidly all week."

"I think that's great, Adrienne. And all this because of Damodar's articles?"

"That, plus the fact that I was able to hear from my dear Eric with Damodar's help. Once I told the ladies in our luncheon club about that, they nearly went wild asking me how it happened and wondering if they could make similar contact with their deceased loved ones."

Chet chortled, "And what did you tell them?"

"I suggested that we take Damodar's advice and begin meditating on the four days he mentioned. One of the ladies even suggested we form our own local OM group—and, by golly, that's just what we're going to do!"

"That's great, Adrienne. I can see that Damodar—and David, too, of course—has stimulated some real changes in your life. I'm happy for you."

"Yes, things will never be the same, now that Damodar has entered our lives." And then, the socialite-publisher of the *Tribune*, glancing at the pile of papers Chet had laid out on the desk, asked Chet, "What else have you brought to show me?"

"Well, here's an item in yesterday's *Detroit News* about our famous Dr. Beckley. Quote: 'The Board of Regents of the University of Michigan today announced the formal termination of the contract of employment of Dr. Earl Beckley, longtime Professor of Parapsychology, in the Department of Psychology. The grounds for dismissal were based on Dr. Beckley's public admission of his preparation of sham biographies during the now-famous paranormal challenge to the occult being known as Damodar at the National Press Club in Washington on December eighteenth. The challenge was telecast to millions of people worldwide. Doctor Beckley's appeal of his dismissal to the University's Grievance Review Board was denied yesterday and was confirmed by the Senate Advisory Committee on University Affairs.' Unquote."

"Well, isn't that something!" Adrienne chortled. "I wonder how his CRIAPP organization is faring."

"Haven't heard, but I'll bet they'll lose a lot of members this year. Incidentally, four or five bills have been introduced in the House and Senate that would make it a crime to offer financial rewards on television programs based on the predictions of psychics, mediums or clairvoyants—the gambling aspect is what they're mainly bothered about. But, from what I hear and read, the whole bunch of them—psychics, clairvoyants and mediums—are having a field day. And, if you can believe this, I see where a number of major police departments around the country are actively recruiting psychics to assist them in their crime-solving efforts!"

"Oh, sure, I can believe it," Adrienne answered. "Do you remember that young Indian psychic who single-handedly solved the Kevin Monell murder case over in Virginia about ten years ago using his psychic powers? . . . Say, come to think of it, wasn't that the same boy who David wrote about in his book last year? I forget its title."

"It's called *Psychic Witness*. Yeah, that's the book Ray trashed when he reviewed it for the paper. Dave told me the other day that the book has been selling like hotcakes ever since the telecast. In fact, the publisher has a massive reprint rolling on it. And now that you mention it, I think I'll have Lou Garza review the files and maybe we can get an interesting story linking that young spiritual prodigy to Senta and Damodar."

Adrienne nodded and then, in a more serious tone, asked, "By the way, how is David doing, Chester? I know you gave him some time off, but he must be pretty depressed now that he's no longer receiving e-mails from Senta."

"Yeah, he's still feeling the letdown of the whole situation. On the positive side, he told me that several publishers have approached him offering huge advances to write his personal memoir about the e-mails and everything that's happened, but he said he doesn't have the heart to do it so soon. Can't say as I blame him. And, of course, he's still being hounded to appear on more TV shows, but he's turned them all down."

"Then, he'll be staying with the *Trib* for the time being?"

"Yes, I think so. Don't forget he's been with us a long time and he's got a lot of friends here. By the way, I couldn't help noticing he seems to be spending more time with Miriam Greene these days. Maybe something's brewing there."

"Well, come to think of it, they'd make a nice couple. How are you making out with a replacement for Ray? Find anyone yet?"

"Got a professional search organization working on that one, but it shouldn't be too long because they tell me they've already screened four or five potential candidates."

She chuckled, "I sure made a mistake recommending Ray. I guess that'll teach me not to interfere with the hiring of staff people."

She looked at Chet for a reaction, but he judiciously looked away, saying, "That's all right. None of us knew what he was really like when he first came on board. Well, at least the Damodar series has focused a lot more attention on the Religion & Family Section of the paper. I'll make sure the next religion editor is familiar with all types of religious beliefs and movements, not just the traditional ones."

With that comment, Chet stood up and Adrienne gave him a pleasant wave goodbye before she returned to the planning of her forthcoming charity event at the Omni Shoreham Hotel—and the formation of the new local OM group.

Chapter 36

J ust as everything finally seemed to be quieting down, my mother called
  me at five o'clock in the afternoon on February 7th to tell me that my
father had suffered a fatal heart attack two hours earlier while walking in
Manhattan's Riverside Park. She told me that the paramedics had taken
him to Roosevelt Hospital but the emergency room doctors there were
unable to resuscitate him. In between sobs, she told me that she had been
in touch with Rabbi Horowitz from their orthodox congregation and that
funeral services would be held at noontime the following day at the Riverside Memorial Chapel on Amsterdam Avenue.

"You'll be there, of course," she said, making it a statement rather
than a question.

"Oh, Mom, of course I'll be there," I replied. "And I'm so sorry. I'll
take the shuttle tonight. How are you doing? Is anyone with you?"

"Yes, my next-door neighbor, Mrs. Wiesner, is here. She's been very
helpful. I think I told you that her husband passed away a year ago, so
she knows all the ropes. I don't know what I'd do without her help. She's
staying with me tonight."

"Good, Mom. I'm glad she's with you. I'm going to pack a few things
and I'll be there as soon as I can, probably between eight and nine o'clock,
depending on the city traffic."

I left a voice mail message with Chet's secretary about my absence to
attend the funeral. Then, I quickly threw a dark suit, a white shirt, and
assorted personal items into a duffel bag before cabbing to Reagan Washington National Airport for the shuttle flight to New York.

After the plane reached flying altitude on the short flight to La
Guardia airport, I leaned back and reminisced about my father and his
role in my life as I was growing up. He wasn't the most outgoing or de-
monstrative of fathers, but he was a kind man and a good teacher. As an
accountant, he taught me the importance of precision in thinking and
writing, and he always emphasized the importance of 'being your own
man.' More than likely he said that because he hadn't achieved that goal
in his own life. Mom was the *baleboosteh* in our house, the woman who

not only managed the household efficiently, but really made most of the key family decisions. Not that they didn't love and respect each other; my mother loved my father very much. He deserved to be loved. He was a very warm and considerate person. But it seems like Pop always demurred to Mom on the really critical issues. To his credit, he never bore the animosity to Senta that Mom did. In fact, he once confided in me, after Senta and I had paid a quick visit to New York in 1972, that Senta was "the prettiest and smartest *shiksa* I ever met." I appreciated his honesty. It pleased me that he always called me David or Davy, even though Mom insisted on calling me by my Yiddish name.

The memorial service and funeral went as well as could be expected. Mom sniffled and blew her nose on a couple of occasions as Rabbi Horowitz did his best to eulogize a man he barely knew, based on information provided to him a few hours earlier. A small crowd attended the services at the Riverside Memorial Chapel, probably thirty-five people who knew Pop and Mom for many years, but fewer came to the burial at Baron Hirsch Cemetery on Staten Island, where more Hebrew prayers were said and then the Rabbi recited the final Kaddish. As he did so, I couldn't help thinking back to Mom's comment some years earlier that life ends with the Kaddish. What an absurdity!

Right after returning from the cemetery, the *shiva* began—the seven-day period of mourning observed by members of the immediate family in accordance with orthodox Jewish tradition. Also, in accordance with tradition, all mirrors in the apartment were covered and a seven-day memorial candle was lit. Mrs. Wiesner took charge of the post-funeral reception and arranged to have a sumptuous array of foodstuffs brought in from Zabar's gourmet supermarket and delicatessen on Broadway.

As the only child, and out of respect for my mother's orthodoxy, I agreed to observe the *shiva* mourning period and remain in the apartment for the requisite seven days. During that period, non-mourners of all religious and ethnic backgrounds came to pay their respects and extend their condolences. In addition, every night during the week a minyan of the required minimum of ten Jewish men came to the apartment to recite the evening prayer services. I was surprised to see how many friends and business associates my father had. It was apparent he had touched a lot of people's lives. All praised him as an honest, diligent professional, but several of his Jewish colleagues went further, calling him "a real *mensch*," a Yiddish term used to denote high praise and just about the finest thing one could say about a person. I was duly impressed and I knew it would make Pop's passage through *kama loka* and eventually into *devachan* that much easier.

During the week, I called Chet and told him that I would be returning to Washington at the end of the mourning period. I also called and had a lengthy conversation with Miriam. In it, I told her that I was seriously contemplating leaving the paper in order to write my memoir about the historic events of the last two months. She agreed that the timing was right and was happy for me.

Near the end of the *shiva* period, when fewer people came to pay their respects and things had quieted down considerably, Mom pulled me aside in the kitchen to talk privately. "Duvid, darling, I've got a question. What really happens when we die? I was brought up to believe that after we die we go out of existence, we're asked to leave the *Olam Haba* in God's hands. But deep down I wish it were otherwise. With all this Theosophy stuff you've been studying all these years, I know that you don't believe we go out of existence, so tell me, Duvidel, what really happens? Where is my dear Miltie now? Where is his *neshamah?*"

Mom's question nearly floored me. She actually had brought up the subject of Pop's soul (his *neshamah*) and the afterlife. After ridiculing my interest in Theosophy for so many years, suddenly she wanted to hear what Theosophy has to say about death and the afterlife—a subject she had said was a waste of time and definitely 'not for smart Jewish people.' I faced her and took her hands in mine, looking squarely into her sad eyes as I spoke to her softly. "Mom, the afterlife—or *Olam Haba*, as you call it—is the same for everyone, whether Jew or Gentile. And Pop's *neshamah* is eternal, just like everyone else's. Death only changes our physical bodies, but it doesn't affect the *neshamah*. Even the Talmud says that the righteous continue to live and will be reunited with their loved ones after they die."

"It does? I didn't know that. So, you're saying that my darling Miltie is still alive and able to enjoy his chess games, his opera music and crossword puzzles where he is now?"

"Well, not quite, Mom. His soul first has to throw off the passions and desires of his lower nature, but when he finishes doing that, his *neshamah* will move on to Gan-Eden, or *devachan* as it is called by the theosophists. And there he will live in a world of his own mental making, whether that's listening to opera music, doing crossword puzzles, playing chess or even eating his favorite hot pastrami sandwiches."

"You're not kidding? He'll have all of that?"

"More than that, Mom. He'll have you in his heart and mind, just like when he was alive, just like you have him in your heart and mind right now. And I guarantee you that when it's your turn to enter the *Olam Haba,* the two of you will be reunited, just like I will be with my darling Senta."

She started crying and began wiping tears from her eyes with her handkerchief. "Oh, Duvid, what a wonderful thought! No rabbi ever said that to me, or to anyone I know who lost a husband or wife. And you got all of that from Theosophy?"

"Yes, Mom." After years of disagreements over our respective beliefs, I felt a sadness that it took Pop's death to bring us to where we could even talk like this. Hesitantly, I added, "And if you're really interested in learning more about the subject, I'll be happy to send you copies of the articles Damodar wrote for the paper."

Slowly, she wiped a tear from her cheek, her eyes glancing about as if following the thought of new ideas, or maybe the thought of past memories. Then she nodded 'yes' before adding, "I'm sorry I was mad at you all these years because of this Theosophy business." Her reddened eyes pleaded with me, "Can you forgive me, Duvidel?" She seemed to have found solace in the thought of our reuniting as a loving mother and son.

"Of course I forgive you, Mom. As Senta said in one of her e-mails, forgiveness is always in order, but it's much better when the person you're forgiving is still alive."

She wiped a last tear away. "Then you have to forgive me again, Duvidel. I now see that your Senta was not only a beautiful woman, but an intelligent, remarkable lady, and I'm sorry that I showed my dislike for her in your presence. That was unkind of me and if she were still alive, I would apologize to her. And I know that your father would feel the same way."

I leaned over, put my arms around my mother, kissed her lovingly on the cheek and hugged her with a fervor I hadn't shown in many years.

Chapter 37

I called Miriam from New York on February 14th—Valentine's Day—and invited her to spend the weekend with me at the Marriott on Hilton Head Island, and she jumped at the opportunity. Because of her connections with the travel industry, she volunteered to take care of the airline and hotel reservations, which was fine with me.

As we departed Washington's Reagan National Airport seated in first-class on our Delta jet, I took her hand in mine and we just sat there silently enjoying each other's company for the first thirty minutes of the flight, occasionally turning to smile at one another and squeezing hands. I had the strangely delicious feeling of falling in love as though it was the first time, even though it wasn't the first time for either of us. Still, we both savored the feeling. I had a lot to tell her, including what had happened between my mother and me last night, and I'm sure she had a lot to tell me, but all that could wait. For now, all I wanted to think about was a relaxing weekend in a sumptuous hotel environment with my attractive traveling companion. The future had already begun.

Both Miriam and I returned from the weekend at Hilton Head reinvigorated. We got to know a lot about each other during our brief sojourn, and we found we had many things in common. We talked about living together, but decided to take our time and think about it before making any final decision.

Something strange awakened me around six o'clock in the morning on Tuesday, February 19th—I heard the melodious tinkling of bells throughout my apartment. They sounded like the bells at a monastery where monks who have taken a vow of silence are called to Early Morning Prayer. When I got up to investigate the source of the bell ringing, I suddenly was overwhelmed by a waft of the most beautiful perfume throughout the whole apartment. I recognized it at once—Senta's favorite floral scent, Ondine—and then it dawned on me: today was the first of the four special days that Damodar had said some lucky individuals would receive signs from their deceased loved ones when meditating on the word OM.

I stood there in my pajamas, arms outstretched, listening to the bells and inhaling the wonderful fragrance deeply. In that beautiful moment, I knew my Senta had sent me a signal, one that I couldn't possibly misinterpret. I never did figure out where the bells came from, but that didn't matter. My heart jumped with joy just knowing that my *herzele* was still in *kama loka* and was still thinking of me.

As was inevitable, later I discovered that newspaper pundits soon labeled those four days "Big Om Days," both because Damodar had said that on those days "occult magic" could be produced by trained occultists and also because he suggsted to those seeking to contact their departed loved ones that they should meditate on the word "OM."

I moved in with Miriam in late February and began my daily period of instruction from Damodar shortly thereafter. He dutifully responded to my requests for information on specific theosophical subjects as he had promised, both through mental telepathy and through reams of handwritten notes that he precipitated onto my study desk. The hullabaloo about my e-mail contacts with Senta finally died down and I was able to resume my normal writing schedule in the editorial department without interference, at least for the moment. Miriam continued with her Travel Section editorial duties, as well.

But, as time passed, I continued to be pressured by several publishing houses to accept their offers of huge advances to write my memoir about Senta and Damodar while the subject was still hot so, in early April, I accepted the offer of publishing giant HarperCollins for an advance of $2 million—one million up front and the balance upon completion of the manuscript— and gave two-weeks' notice to Chet that I would be leaving the *Tribune* after having worked there for nearly thirty years.

At the farewell luncheon held a week later at the Mayflower Hotel, I choked up while recounting some of my experiences with various *Tribune* reporters and editors over the years, but the tears really started rolling when Sol Berman praised me as "my dearest friend and one of the finest editorial writers this paper ever had," before coming up to give me a big hug.

Both Adrienne Thayer and Chet Walker said very complimentary things about me, and Chet even did me the honor of referring to me as David, rather than Dave. But Adrienne really surprised me when she remarked, "I can honestly say that David single-handedly brought new life to this paper by sticking to his guns when everyone was telling him to keep quiet when he insisted he had received e-mails from his deceased lady friend, Senta Trondson. His persistence in the face of considerable opposition deserves the highest praise, and I salute you, David, for your tenacity and courage. We need more of that on this paper." Her heartfelt comments brought a lump to my throat.

Leaving the *Trib* after nearly thirty years was another form of death, but at sixty-two I knew that my days at the paper were already numbered. The pain of leaving was softened considerably by the receipt of the royalty-advance check for $1 million, and it forced me to start outlining my memoir as soon as possible. By far, the hardest part of leaving was saying goodbye to Sol Berman. We had one final lunch together at *The Newsroom*, during which we promised to keep in touch and we hugged each other one more time.

Chapter 38

By late spring, I was making good progress on my memoir and my relationship with Miriam was developing nicely. Working out of her apartment in MacLean Gardens, I was able to keep up with the local, national and worldwide news on my computer frequently. On the local newsfront, I learned that early in March, Archie Taylor was found guilty of stealing the expensive Raleigh bicycle and was sent back to Lorton to serve out his original term, plus an additional three years.

By the end of May, it was obvious that the Damodar series had created a groundswell of interest not only in the afterlife, but in all aspects of the occult and especially in Theosophy. I learned that the local branch of the United Lodge of Theosophists—located in nearby Bethesda, Maryland—was inundated with requests for information on Theosophy and theosophical teachings, as well as on H.P.B. and her *Secret Doctrine*. Overflow crowds were attending their regular Sunday morning meetings. And the same was true of theosophical organizations in other parts of the country and around the world.

One disturbing aftereffect of Damodar's articles was a plethora of articles in the trendy New Age magazines criticizing Damodar's negative comments on mediumship and channeling. But, since more than half of their advertising came from those sources, their criticisms were clearly biased. Mainline Christian publications—the Vatican weekly newspaper among them—continued their persistent onslaught of articles and letters to the editor in their religious magazines ridiculing the concept and method for contacting deceased loved ones that Damodar had outlined.

On the other hand, an unexpected offshoot of the series was the establishment of nationwide branches of the newly-formed OM Society by tens of thousands of bereaved relatives around the nation and around the world who were determined to make contact with their departed loved ones on the four days mentioned by Damodar in his final article. With the help of the Internet, they were able to increase their numbers dramatically.

Thus, it came to pass that on every nineteenth of February, seventh of March, eleventh of August and seventeenth of November, bereaved individuals all over the world sat at their computers and typed e-mail messages addressed to their loved ones @ kamaloka.com, each hoping to receive a personal reply, as I had.

Although none were successful at first, eventually—so we later learned—a few highly spiritual individuals were successful, but the rest never gave up hope, and all found comfort in the process. I was delighted when I learned about these efforts, knowing that between Damodar, Senta and myself, we had set forces in motion that had the potential to make a real difference in the lives of many individuals, and possibly for all humankind.

At least it was a step in the right direction.